NIrV

Adventure BIBLE

Book of Devotions for Early Readers

Revised Edition

Written by:

Marnie Wooding

ZONDERKIDZ

Adventure Bible Book of Devotions for Early Readers, NIrV

Requests for information should be addressed to:
Zonderkidz, *3900 Sparks Dr. SE, Grand Rapids, Michigan 49546*

This edition: ISBN 978-0-310-74617-1

Library of Congress Cataloging-in-Publication Data

Wooding, Marnie.
The NIrV adventure Bible : book of devotions for early readers / by Marnie Wooding.
p. cm.
Includes bibliographical references and index.
ISBN 978-0-310-71448-4 (softcover : alk. paper)
1. Children—Prayers and devotions. 2. Devotional calendars—Juvenile literature. I. Title.
BV4571.3.W66 2008
242'.62—dc22 2008026353

Art direction: Sarah Molegraaf
Interior composition: Carlos Eluterio Estrada
Interior design: Matthew Van Zomeren

Printed in the United States of America

14 15 16 17 18 19 20 /DCI/ 30 29 28 27 26 25 24 23 22 21 20 19 18 17 16 15 14 13 12 11 10 9 8 7 6 5 4 3 2 1

Contents

January

February

March

April

May

June

July

August

September

October

November

December

Angelic

Principal O'Neil stared at the pile of snow and ice blocking the school's front door. He looked around at the students responsible for this prank. "So whose idea was this?"

Angelica fidgeted. It had seemed like a funny idea last night, but now it wasn't so funny. She stepped forward. "It was me. It was my idea to block the door with snow."

Mr. O'Neil raised his eyebrow. "Angelica? Not very angelic of you was it? You and your partners in crime can spend the morning chipping away at this blockade of ice and snow so we can use the front doors." Angelica nodded and sighed. This was not the way to start the new year. She'd try to do better.

If Angelica is no angel, what is a real angel? We do know from the Bible that angels are spiritual heavenly beings, but it isn't very clear what they look like. Angels are cool, but we're not to worship them. Angels are God's messengers, helpers, and worshipers in heaven. Angels help us understand that God loves us. So, what does it mean to be angelic? If you are helpful and protective of others and you worship God, you may be called an angel.

Words to Treasure

Praise the Lord, you angels of his. Praise him, you mighty ones who carry out his orders and obey his word.

Psalm 103:2

Did You Know?

Did you know that two angels are mentioned by name in the Bible? One is Michael, who appears like a warrior angel. The other is Gabriel, who acts as God's messenger.

January 2

One Step at a Time

Morgan felt her muscles burn as she counted. "One thousand and one, one thousand and rest." She sat down on a step. Her uncle Ed pulled out the guidebook while trying to breathe. "The Eiffel Tower has 1,665 steps. Six hundred or so to go. We can do that." He sat beside her, wiping sweat from his face.

Words to Treasure

How you made me is amazing and wonderful. I praise you for that.

Psalm 139:14

Morgan inhaled, stood up, and began to climb again. "Just think how much easier it will be to walk back down."

Uncle Ed gulped more air. "Walk down! What about the elevator? Isn't going up enough?" Morgan smiled as she continued counting steps. Walking all the way to the top of the Eiffel Tower was a real endurance challenge, but Morgan was ready for it. Every day after school, she climbed up and down the hill behind her house.

Planning challenges is a good thing. Why? Because when we succeed in even small goals it helps build up our confidence to take on other things. God created us to be confident in the abilities he gave us. So go out and see what you can do. And pray about what challenges God has for you. God is cheering you on—so go for it.

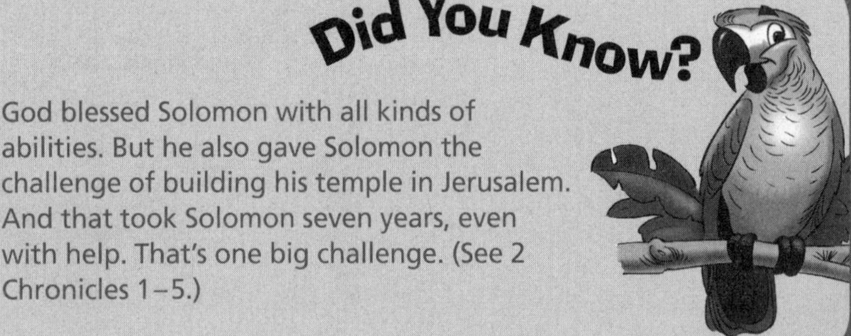

Did You Know?

God blessed Solomon with all kinds of abilities. But he also gave Solomon the challenge of building his temple in Jerusalem. And that took Solomon seven years, even with help. That's one big challenge. (See 2 Chronicles 1–5.)

January 3

Less Talk

Peter's grandfather leaned forward as he talked. "So, here I was, this rookie newspaper boy on my bicycle speeding down a cliff toward a highway. No brakes! My bike chain had snapped and fallen off. Nothing to stop me."

Words to Treasure

Pay attention and listen to the sayings of wise people.

Proverbs 22:17

Peter leaned forward as well. "What did you do?"

His grandfather's face crinkled, "I crashed into a hedge. Broke my arm." Peter looked at the scar on his grandfather's arm. "I learned something that day. Take good care of your bike, and it will take good care of you. I want you to remember that."

Peter nodded and picked up his video game controller but then put it down again. "Grandpa, do you want to help me check my bike?"

"Sure, Peter. I'd like that a lot."

Talking is good but listening to other people is important. Not only will you learn possibly life-saving advice, but you'll also get to know that person better. And you'll make them feel special and needed. Everybody likes that. Learning to listen to others just might be one of the most important things you'll ever learn. Jesus often said, "Whoever has ears should listen." Now that's something to hear.

Who has itchy ears? Well, the apostle Paul says it's someone who wants people to say only the things they want to hear. Do your ears itch? (See 2 Timothy 4:3.)

January 4

The Path

David and Noel walked along the worn dirt path along the river. Not just any river—the Nile River in Egypt, one of the oldest and most famous rivers in the world! Noel looked back at the ancient ruins they had just explored. "David, how many people do you think have walked along this path?" Noel looked around. "This trail could be thousands of years old."

Words to Treasure

She placed the child in the basket. Then she put it in the tall grass that grew along the bank of the Nile River. The child's sister wasn't very far away.

Exodus 2:3-4

David shrugged and said, "Thousands of people." The boys watched a felucca sail by, a type of sailboat used since the time of the pharaohs.

Noel climbed up on a rock. "Maybe Moses or Joseph sat right here. We could have followed their footsteps on the trail."

"Footprints would be long gone by now."

True! But the important thing to remember is that Joseph and Moses were real guys who lived in a real place called Egypt. And when we read about them in the Bible, we're learning important stuff such as how they learned to have faith in God in every situation, good and bad. Just because what they did happened a long time ago, doesn't mean it isn't important today. They may be dead guys, but they're still an example for us to follow. Cool, huh?

Discovering Archaeology

Did you know that when Joseph first arrived in Egypt, the great pyramids of Egypt were already hundreds of years old? Joseph could have been another pyramid tourist.

Lip-Syncing

The entire church was singing loudly, but Halley leaned over and listened to Jen sing. It was the strangest thing. Jen's mouth was moving but she wasn't actually making any sounds. Halley whispered, "Jen, why aren't you singing?"

Words to Treasure

My lips will shout with joy when I sing praise to you.

Psalm 71:23

Jen whispered back, "I sing like a frog. Nobody wants to hear me sing. So I fake it."

Halley whispered back, "Don't be silly. God loves the way you sing."

Jen thought about that for a moment. "Because he created frogs?"

Halley pointed to the lyrics on the screen up front, "No, because he loves you."

When you sing a song at church, it isn't supposed to be for some talent search on a television show. It's supposed to be about letting God know how you feel about him. We write and sing songs to help us express our love for God. That's called worship. God loves you, and he loves to hear your voice singing just to him in a very personal way. There's nothing to worry about or be embarrassed about. Sing with an I'm-singing-right-to-God-and-I-don't-care-who-hears-me kind of attitude. No lip-syncing with God.

People in Bible Times

In ancient Israel, people sang songs together at the temple. In fact, King David took time out from all his battles to help organize the temple choir and musicians. He loved to sing and play the lyre harp. He was a singing warrior king.

January 6

Friendship

Judy sat on the street curb waiting for her friend to arrive. She watched for her car to turn down the lane. She was watching so hard she had to remind herself to blink. Catherine was sleeping over, and Judy had everything planned. She had bought snacks and a movie they had both promised only to watch together. Her mom was making their favorite dinner. But what Judy was most looking forward to was talking with Catherine late into the night. They would sit on the bed and talk about everything—important things and stupid things. It didn't really matter what they talked about because they just liked being together. They were friends.

Words to Treasure

The Lord would speak to Moses face to face like one would speak to a friend.

Exodus 33:11

God is also someone you can talk to about anything. Important things, small things—just anything. You can share your deepest thoughts with God. Would it surprise you to know that the Creator of the entire universe, from planets to peanuts, wants your friendship? The Bible tells us that when Moses talked to God, they talked together like human buddies. Does that sound like a God who just sits around his universe not caring about you? Nope. God is excited and waiting to spend some time with just you. So what are you waiting for? Go talk to God—he really is the best friend you could have.

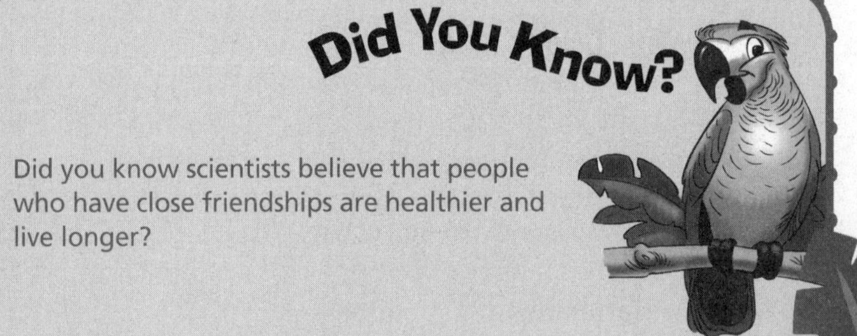

Did you know scientists believe that people who have close friendships are healthier and live longer?

January 7

First Time

This time when the drooling glob monster from Andromeda comes into the space station, Andy won't open the escape hatch door, because he and the glob monster will both get sucked out to certain outer-space death. How does he know this? Because last time that's what happened. Andy learned from his computer-world mistake the first time around.

But is that always true in real life? Do we always learn from our mistakes the first time? Sadly not. Although the consequences in real life may not be death by space exposure, that's not the point. Sometimes we do the same wrong thing over and over again. We make the same bad choices, such as not doing our homework, skipping our chores, not phoning home, or worse. So much so that sometimes teachers, parents, friends, and coaches may question our intelligence. Learning from our mistakes the first time saves us future problems and is part of that important thing called wisdom. It's okay to make mistakes—that's life. But making the same mistake over and over makes you just about as smart as a glob monster. And God made you smarter than that. Learn the first time, just like you do in a computer game.

Words to Treasure

Older people aren't the only ones who are wise. They aren't the only ones who understand what is right.

Job 32:9

Did You Know?

Did you know the world's most complex computers would become overloaded if they had to deal with the amount of information your eyes, nose, ears, taste, and sense of touch send your brain every minute? You are an amazing creation.

January 8

What's in a Name?

Laurie tried not to listen to the older kids on the bus, but they were very loud. She had heard swear words like that on television, in movies, and at school. Sometimes even famous people used Jesus' name like a swear word. That made her sad. But why?

Words to Treasure

Do not misuse the name of the Lord your God. The Lord will find guilty anyone who misuses his name.

Exodus 20:7

First off, some words are very rude and wrong. When people use them, they aren't showing respect or care for the people around them. And it doesn't look good on them either.

Other words hurt God deeply and are a sin. When people use the name of God or Jesus as a swear word, they are disrespecting God and Jesus in the worst possible way. Think of it this way—Jesus would never do or say anything to insult, hurt, or disrespect you. When he talks about you or says *your* name, it is always with kindness, love, and friendship. Shouldn't we be that way too? God's name is holy!

But remember, you can't police what strangers say. You can only be careful about what *you* say.

Do you think God knows your name? There are lots of cases in the Bible where God called people by their first names. God called to Moses from the burning bush. When the prophet Samuel was a little boy, God called his name over and over again. God doesn't need name tags; he knows who you are.

January 9

Raging

Adam was ready to explode. His model plane was smashed on the ground. His little brother had been in his room again. And now everything was wrecked! Adam had spent hours building that plane! Adam wanted to do something like lock his little brother in a closet for a zillion years. His anger was making him want to do something terrible.

Words to Treasure

Foolish people let their anger run wild. But wise people keep themselves under control.

Proverbs 29:11

Rage is a scary, scary feeling because it is so out of control. We see a lot of rage on television, such as wrestlers pounding each other with furniture or good guys going ballistic on bad guys. But that's all make-believe anger. Nobody really is upset, and nobody really gets hurt. Hurting someone for real isn't the same thing. You can be upset with someone, but hurting him is never okay—ever. Even when you know you're in the right, that doesn't give you the right to hurt someone.

God is often described as "slow to anger." This means it takes a whole lot to get God upset with us. It tells us that God is very, very patient. Are we slow to anger with other people just like God? When you feel really, really angry, it's time to walk away or talk to someone who can take charge of the situation, such as a parent or teacher. Give yourself some time to calm down (see Numbers 14:18).

January 10

The Better Way

Stacy and her mom were driving along a busy boulevard when suddenly a little dog ran out in front of their car. With brakes screeching, they stopped just in time. The dog ran back onto the sidewalk, but he was very confused and frightened. Left alone, he was going to get hurt for sure. Stacy's mom pulled over, got out, and called to the little dog. The dog looked uncertain but allowed her to wrap him in a car blanket. Stacy held the exhausted, trembling dog on her lap while her mom phoned the number on his dog tag.

Words to Treasure

When Jesus came ashore, he saw a large crowd. He felt deep concern for them. He healed their sick people.

Matthew 14:14

Stacy and her mom have something very important, and it's called "compassion." Having compassion means seeing someone else's problem or suffering and then doing something to help. It isn't just enough to see a problem and feel bad about it. Compassion is an *action* word.

Jesus told a story about an injured man on the side of the road who was ignored by his own people and neighbors. But a stranger from Samaria stopped, had pity for the injured man, and took care of him. Jesus asked who was this man's true friend, or neighbor. The answer? The very cool and compassionate guy from Samaria. And we can be just like him.

Beauty

Molly walked beside her new friend Udo as they herded goats toward the river. Molly loved being in Africa but hated to leave her new friend to go back home. Time went so fast. The girls sat down on the bank and watched the goats drink.

Udo turned to Molly, "You have light skin, and I have dark skin. Your eyes are blue, and mine are brown. Your hair is long and straight, and mine is curly." Udo laughed, "We are both very pretty but very different. We are different on the outside, but inside I think we are like sisters we are the same. I am very glad we are friends."

Words to Treasure

Instead, your beauty comes from inside you. It is the beauty of a gentle and quiet spirit. Beauty like this doesn't fade away. God places great value on it.

1 Peter 3:4

Did you know God's kind of beauty is about the person you are inside? It is about how you make people feel when they are with you. A huge, gigantic part of being beautiful is liking how God created you inside and out—and liking how God created other people too. Being happy about being you shows on the outside, and that is *beautiful*. And that's how God designed it to work. Being a good friend is God's kind of beautiful.

Did You Know?

Did you know there are between 15,000–20,000 different types of butterflies? They're all uniquely different and uniquely beautiful. Just goes to show you God wanted his world to be beautiful in so many different ways. Just like us.

January 12

Service with a Smile

Fynn put the entire galaxy-sized onion ring in his mouth. Half of his friends were impressed, and the other half were kind of disgusted. Then the sound of shattering glasses made the group jump. Their waitress had dropped an entire tray of plates and glasses. Fynn jumped up and started to help her clean up. The tired waitress looked surprised. "You don't have to help me; you're my customer. I'm supposed to be serving you."

Words to Treasure

"Be like the Son of Man. He did not come to be served. Instead, he came to serve others."

Matthew 20:28

Fynn smiled. "Well, that's okay. Next time I need help maybe somebody will help me even though they don't have to."

Jesus said, "It is more blessed to give than to receive." That means what you do for others is more important than what others do for you. So, when you see a way to help someone, even in little everyday things, go do it! Can you imagine a world where everybody is helping everybody else? Our planet could be completely changed by an army of people caring about each other. Imagine that.

Jesus wanted to show his friends how much he cared for them. So he decided to wash their feet. But this was something a slave usually did, and his friend Simon Peter didn't feel it was right for Jesus (the Son of God) to act like a servant. But Jesus explained that it is important that we follow his example by caring and serving each other.

January 13

Enjoy

Jason patted the surface of the water and waited. The bat ray swam just below the surface of the pool with strong flaps of its wing-like fins. The strange sea creature surfaced right in front of Jason and stared up at him with big eyes. The bat ray allowed Jason to stroke its leathery back just like a dog wanting a scratch behind the ears. Jason couldn't believe he was actually touching this amazing animal. He would remember this forever because it was crazy incredible!

Words to Treasure

You made human beings rule over everything your hands created.

Psalm 8:6

Ever wonder why God created the world? The answer may surprise you. God created the entire universe as a gift to us. This remarkable planet was designed for us to explore and enjoy. But sadly, we often take this incredible gift for granted. Sometimes we just forget to be amazed.

But, how can you not be amazed every day of your life? Just once a day, take time out of your busy schedule to look around at the world you live in. From the bugs crawling at your feet to the Milky Way galaxy above your head at night. The more you explore your world, the more you'll truly understand what a surprising and generous heavenly Father you have.

Not only was King Solomon wise, but he was really into nature. He loved to study plants and animals. Thousands of years later, this king's love of nature would inspire many scientists.

January 14

Money Troubles

Like a secret agent, Fred scoped out the landscape before he crossed the street to the corner store. For weeks now, he had been avoiding one of his best friends, Steven, because he still owed Steven the money he had borrowed for popcorn and cold drinks when they went to the movies together several weekends ago. Fred swung open the store door. Oh no, busted! Standing there by the cash register was Steven.

Words to Treasure

Love for money causes all kinds of evil.

1 Timothy 6:10

Steven walked over, munching on some sunflower seeds. "Hey, Fred, are you still my friend or what? I haven't seen you in weeks."

Fred hung his head ashamed. He confessed, "I've been avoiding you because I still owe you money!"

"Freddie, Freddie," Steven put his arm around Fred's shoulder. "It's just money. I really missed you!"

"You mean you're not mad?"

Steven offered some sunflower seeds to Fred. "You'll pay me back someday. Just don't avoid me anymore. Come on, let's go to the park."

People do a lot of stupid things over money. They let money destroy friendships. Money can get in the middle of so many good things. Friendship or money—which one is more important to God? Money is a useful thing, but it isn't the most important thing.

Discovering Archaeology

Before money was invented, people used to just trade stuff with each other. If you wanted somebody's cooking pot and they wanted one of your chickens, you just made a deal with them.

Useless or Useful?

Timothy looked out the window of his classroom and dreamed of snowboarding, mountain biking, and other great adventures. School was hard and boring. He wondered why he was learning this stuff in the first place. Would he really ever need to know math or where stuff is on a map? What was the point of school anyway?

Words to Treasure

Start children off on the right path. And even when they are old, they will not turn away from it.

Proverbs 22:6

Timothy isn't the first kid to have those thoughts. But stuff happens, and we never know what God is training us for in the future. Take King David. He probably wondered why he was sitting around day after day guarding his father's sheep. What was the point?

The point is that David learned to use his shepherd's sling, chasing off wolves, lions, and bears with the rocks he threw. Actually, God was preparing David for a showdown with a giant warrior named Goliath. The future of the entire kingdom would depend on David and his sling! Could he defeat Goliath?

He won the war and saved everybody with one throw of a rock. All that down time as a shepherd was important! Who knew? What's God training you for in the future? Hard to say, but what you learn today just might be very important in the future. You never know.

Discovering Archaeology

What David used was a shepherd's sling, which is basically two cords with a little pouch in the middle to hold a stone. Swing it around and release one side to send the sling stone flying. It's one of the world's oldest weapons.

January 16

Say It. Do It.

Nick had walked several blocks away from home when he realized every house on the street had garbage cans neatly lined up ready for pickup. He sighed and groaned, "Perfect." Today was garbage day, and he had forgotten to take old Mrs. Myers's garbage to the curb. He had promised to do it every week. Now, he'd have to walk back just to take out her garbage and then walk all the way back to school. He looked at his watch—he still had time but...

Words to Treasure

They keep their promises even when it hurts. They do not change their mind.

Psalm 15:4

Time to make an important choice. He could tell Mrs. Myers he forgot *or* go back and do it. Nick gave a heavy sigh and turned around. Garbage it is.

Everybody has moments when they have to make the choice to do what they promised or not. It could be big promises or little. But does the size really matter? The question is: can people trust you to live up to what you promised? God wants you to be someone people can count on all the time.

People in Bible Times

One night Jesus was very sad, and he asked his friends to stay awake with him. Three times Jesus asked them to stay awake while he went close by to pray. Each time he came back, he found them asleep. He was very disappointed. Jesus always does what he promises and never lets us down. And we should be the same way. So if you say you'll do something, do it.

Moment by Moment

Wendy wiped a tear from her face. Last week her kitten had gotten very sick, and it hadn't gotten better. It had died. She loved her kitten and already missed him so much it made her body hurt. She wondered what she could have done to stop him from getting sick. Or was God punishing her for something bad she had done? This was the worst day of her life.

Words to Treasure

My sadness has worn me out. Give me strength as you have promised.

Psalm 119:28

Sometimes sad things happen for no reason. The truth is, Wendy took good care of her kitten, but he just got sick. It wasn't her fault, and it wasn't because God was punishing her. God loves her—just as he loves us all very much. We can't avoid hard or sad times, but we can face them knowing that Jesus is walking beside us every step of the way. When you are having a hard time, pray and ask Jesus for the strength and courage to get through it. He cares.

Wise King Solomon knew life is full of all kinds of moments. Moments when you cry, and moments when you laugh. Times when you work hard, and times when you rest. Being sad sometimes is part of living the life God has given you. You may be having a hard day today, but there are lots of happy moments waiting for you too.

January 18

Get Out!

Ted walked quickly, passing the other kids on the way home from school. He couldn't wait to get home. Every day he and Troy got together after school and played. Ted knew everything there was to know about Troy because they went on a lot of adventures together. There was just one problem. Troy wasn't actually a real guy. He was a character on a computer, game. Not to say that didn't make him a nice guy, but he was the only guy Ted hung out with. And that's a global-sized problem.

Words to Treasure

The Lord God said, "It is not good for the man to be alone."

Genesis 2:18

If your closest friend is electronically generated, that might mean it's time to get out and talk to real people in the real world. Sure, real friends can't ride dragons with you, but they can go swimming and eat pizza with you. Making human friends isn't easy, but it's important to go out and try to meet new people and do new things in the ordinary world. So turn off the game and get involved in some activities at school, church, or a recreation center. You'll never know what kind of new friend you'll meet and what you'll have in common. Maybe there's another human kid out there looking for a new human friend too and some real life adventures.

Discovering Archaeology

People in Bible times played some of the same games we play today: checkers, dice, hopscotch, mancala, marbles and, many believe, a type of ancient chess.

Just a Little Hole

The shopping mall suddenly got very quiet. The only sound was Angela's own heart pounding loudly. She wondered if anybody else could hear. Her aunt winked. "I'll sign the form if you want to get another little earring in your ear. My treat."

Angela really wanted a cute little sparkly stud on the top part of her ear. But she also knew her mom and dad felt that having one piercing in each ear was enough. But her aunt *was* an adult, and if she said it was okay—then wasn't it? Angela stood in the doorway of the shop torn between what she wanted and what she knew her parents wanted for her.

Words to Treasure

Children, obey your parents as believers in the Lord. Obey them because it's the right thing to do.

Ephesians 6:1

Sometimes we make up a good reason to do something we know isn't what we should do. Like doing something we know our parents absolutely would disapprove of. And just because another adult will let you, doesn't mean it's a good idea. Remember, your parents trust you to act the same way with other people as you would when they're with you. The Bible teaches to honor your parents. And *honor* means to respect. Doing stuff behind their back doesn't sound like a whole lot of honoring going on. Respect is best.

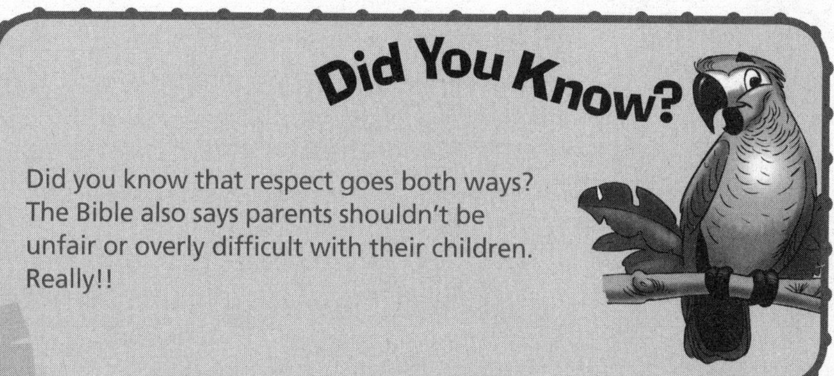

Did you know that respect goes both ways? The Bible also says parents shouldn't be unfair or overly difficult with their children. Really!!

January 20

S.O.S.

Jerry looked at his hands; they were wrinkled and old-looking. He held the duck while Uncle Drew washed it with soap. The smell of oil was everywhere. All day long people had been bringing in birds and other wildlife found along the shoreline, all covered in black oil. There had been a terrible oil spill.

Words to Treasure

hold on to you tightly. Your powerful right hand takes good care of me.

Psalm 63:8

There were too many animals and not enough people to get them clean, dry, and safe. So Jerry and his uncle came to help. Jerry was completely exhausted as he gently put a little duck in a warm holding cage with other cleaned birds. He caught up another oily bird and brought it over to the washing area.

"Hello, everybody!" The rescuers turned to see a team of firemen entering the warehouse door. One big fireman took off his coat and rolled up his sleeves. "How can we help?" The entire room cheered.

Things don't always go as we plan. But just maybe this out-of-control situation is very much in God's control, and he's got the entire situation covered.

Noah and his family stayed on the Ark helping the animals for 377 days. Now that's pet sitting of the extreme kind.

Mercy Calling

Claire leaned against the wall, not lifting a finger to help. The entire class was searching the museum for Brent's lost notebook. As if she was going to help! Brent was mean to everybody. It served him right to have lost his notebook. Why, even yesterday he purposely hit her in the head playing dodgeball. She had pretended to laugh, but it had hurt. In fact, knowing Brent was going to get in trouble was just a perfect ending to a fun day at the museum. She wished everybody would stop looking so they could go have lunch.

Words to Treasure

"Suppose you come across your enemy's ox or donkey wandering away. Then be sure to return it."

Exodus 23:4

Is that the kind of attitude Claire should have? What does the Bible say? Actually it teaches that if you find something that belongs to your enemy, go return it. Or if the guy who is mean to you is having a problem day, go help him anyway. We don't get to pick and choose the person we help. God wants us to help people no matter how they've treated us. That's called mercy, or kindness, and that's something we must do. God is kind, and we should be too.

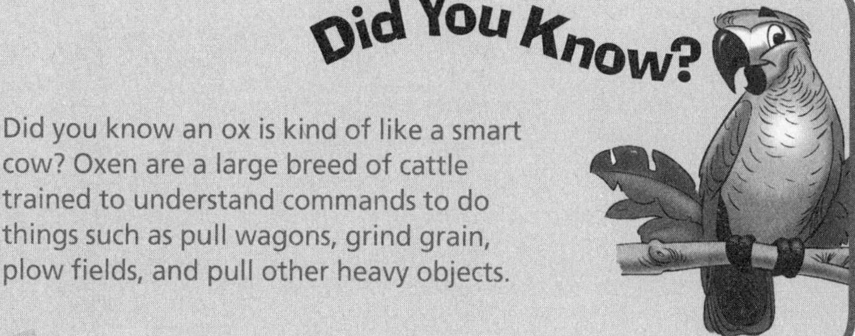

Did You Know?
Did you know an ox is kind of like a smart cow? Oxen are a large breed of cattle trained to understand commands to do things such as pull wagons, grind grain, plow fields, and pull other heavy objects.

January 22

Moves to Success

The crowd was silent as the chess pieces moved across the boards. Fran looked at her chess pieces and frowned. She was in big trouble. *So soon?* The Chess Master returned to her board and smiled kindly. He was actually playing ten players at once. He moved in for the kill. "Checkmate!" He reached over, shook her hand, and gave her a warm smile, "Very good game, young lady." She nodded, still studying the board and searching for the exact move where she had gone wrong. She found it and made a mental note not to ever do that again. Fran had a dream that one day she would be awarded the title of Chess Life Master. But that was a long way off.

Words to Treasure

All of us get tripped up in many ways.

James 3:2

There were still lots of games to win and plenty more to lose. But each game, whether she won or lost, was building her knowledge and moving her toward her goal.

Funny thing, sometimes we have to fail to win in the end. Being afraid of failing is a sure way of stopping you from succeeding. Nobody wins all the time, and sometimes what you learn when you don't win is the most important lesson of all.

Did You Know?

A reporter once asked the inventor Thomas Edison how it felt to fail seven hundred times on his experiments with inventing electric light. Edison replied, "I have not failed seven hundred times. I have not failed once. I have succeeded in proving that those seven hundred ways will not work."

January 23

Did You Hear?

Jackson felt the air flow past him before he hit the pool water. The world seemed far away as he swam back up to the surface. But Jackson knew already that he hadn't done his best dive. He climbed out of the water and saw the unhappy look on his coach's face.

Coach placed a towel around his shoulders. "What kind of a dive would you call that?"

Jackson pulled away. "Why do you care? You're leaving to coach in Florida anyway."

Coach looked puzzled, "I'm leaving?"

"Bobby said Pete heard that from Linda who heard Ms. Wong talk about it on the office phone."

Coach gave him a disappointed look. "If I were leaving, don't you think you'd be the first to know? I thought you were smarter than to listen to gossip."

Rumors should be ignored. Most rumors aren't true, and many rumors are spread just to be hurtful. And some rumors worry people for no reason at all—just like Jackson. So don't listen to buzz, and don't spread it either.

Words to Treasure

"Do not spread reports that are false."

Exodus 23:1

Simple rule: If you don't know for sure something you heard is the truth ... don't repeat it. That's an easy rule to follow.

January 24

Flattery

Cindy read the clue again. She was really good at mysteries, and now her treasure-hunting team was in third place out of twenty teams. A toy store had hidden a secret treasure somewhere around town. Marc walked over to Cindy. "I've been watching you, and you're really, really smart. You've got to be the smartest kid in this treasure hunt. I was wondering …"

Words to Treasure

With smooth talk and with words they don't mean they fool people who don't know any better.

Romans 16:18

Cindy smiled as she figured out the riddle and checked her map. She looked up at Marc, "Don't try to flatter me. I'm not going to change teams in mid-race and dump my friends."

Marc looked insulted. "How'd you know I was going to ask you that?"

"I'm smart, remember." Cindy jumped on her bike, and her teammates followed.

Sometimes people say nice things for all the wrong reasons. You can't stop them, but you can be careful. You don't need constant praise to feel good about yourself. Be confident in who you are and how God made you. Don't listen to flattery or smooth talk, and never say nice things you don't mean to get your own way or get what you want. Just be you, and be honest all the time.

Samson was the strongest guy in the Bible, but he was weak in the knees when it came to the flattery of a Philistine spy named Delilah. In the end, Samson told her the secret of how to defeat his God-given strength.

Don't Draw a Blank

The wall was big, blank, and freshly painted white. Carson stood with his friends in the dark, uncertain what to do. Daniel had just pulled some cans of spray paint from his backpack. He then pulled out a notepad with a sketch on it. It was a really good drawing of a kid surfing a wave, but the wave looked like a street.

Daniel showed the sketch to his friends. "This is *the* perfect wall for it. I figure the four of us can paint it in a couple of hours."

Carson knew the owner of the store—he was a nice guy. This wasn't right. Carson had never done this before, and he just decided he wasn't going to do it now.

Going past the store the next day, Carson saw the owner out painting his wall again—covering up Daniel's graffiti. Carson put down his backpack and picked up a paint roller. "Need some help?" Now, that's making an impression of the good kind.

Words to Treasure

"Do not follow the crowd when they do what is wrong."

Exodus 23:2

Discovering Archaeology

People have been displaying their art on walls for thousands of years. Long ago, people painted images on cave walls. Later, people painted on constructed walls, like those found inside tombs or on the walls of their homes. Kind of like ancient wallpaper.

January 26

Time Out

Abel opened his eyes and stared at the pattern on the side of the bowl on the table beside him. It was his chicken curry dinner. He had actually fallen asleep at the dinner table. This was crazy. Between hockey, soccer, church activities, school, homework, music lessons, and his paper route, there didn't seem to be enough time in the day. Abel was exhausted. Was he actually enjoying it all, or was he just surviving?

Words to Treasure

God rested from his work. Those who enjoy God's rest also rest from their work. So let us make every effort to enjoy that rest.

Hebrews 4:10–11

Good question. God really enjoyed creating the universe, but afterward did he rush out and do something else? Absolutely not. God took time out to relax, rest, and enjoy his creation. In fact, he told us that at least one day out of seven we should stop everything and take a break from work. God knows the importance of just hanging out.

In our busy, busy world we forget to stop. And that isn't good. If we don't leave any time for rest, we make our minds, body, and spirit tired. We can even make ourselves sick! That's called burnout. If you can't stay awake to eat dinner, maybe it's time to rethink and reorganize for some downtime. It's important!

Did You Know?

Did you know a big part of downtime is sleep time? If we don't get enough of it, we get sick. Have you ever stayed up really late and felt kind of grumpy in the morning? That's your brain telling you, "Hey! I need more downtime." Sleep, got to have it.

Creative Creatures

Hiro liked the feel of the clay through his fingers, the earthy smell, and the sound of the pottery wheel as it turned. He loved working in his grandmother's pottery studio in Japan. Already he could make simple pots, plates, and vases. He was even earning some money selling his clay work in his grandmother's shop. She said that with more experience and stronger hands he could become a master potter.

Words to Treasure

I have given ability to all the skilled workers. They can make everything I have commanded you to make.

Exodus 31:6

God made us to be creative creatures. He designed us to want to create or make things. Makes sense because God himself loves to create stuff—you know, like absolutely everything in the universe.

Some people design mathematical formulas while others cook great meals. God put special creative gifts in each of us. What is your creative talent? Sometimes we have to explore the world a little before we discover what we like to do. Don't be surprised if God has given you a number of abilities, because he wasn't stingy when he made you. You are amazing!!

In Bible times, it was a world without plastics. Look around your house and see how much of what you use is made of plastic. Back then, *clay* was one of the most useful materials around. Artists or potters could shape it into all kinds of things such as lamps, jars, bottles, and pitchers to store oils, water, food, and perfumes. Clay was the plastic of the ancient world.

January 28

Feeling Sad? Not Me!

Trish sat on the grassy hill overlooking the horses grazing in the pasture below. Every day she came out to this spot to watch them. She was working hard to save up to buy a horse of her own. She was doing odd jobs and helping her sister babysit, but saving money was taking a long time. It felt like she was never going to have enough.

Words to Treasure

"I will make a helper who is just right for him."

Genesis 2:18

Trish looked up to see her grandfather smiling down at her. "Tell you what. You save for the horse, and I'll buy the saddle and all the gear. What do you think?"

"Really?" Trish hugged him tightly.

God puts people in our lives to help and encourage us when we need it. Just like Trish's grandfather knew she needed something special to pick up her spirits. There are people in your life who want to give you a helping hand or an encouraging word. Your family, friends, pastors, coaches, and teachers are there when you need them. Just wait and see.

God could see that Adam was feeling a little lonely, so he made Adam a friend named Eve. Adam and Eve loved each other and spent the rest of their lives together.

Red Card

Trevor knew that he went after the ball too hard and had accidentally pushed an opposing player to the ground. Even though Trevor had a breakaway, he passed the soccer ball to one of his teammates, stopped, and offered his hand to the player. "Sorry."

The other player looked surprised. "Really?"

Trevor gave him a big smile. "Sure." He helped the other player up, and they shook hands. They both continued to play a great game of soccer. No hard feelings. After the game, the other player thanked Trevor for his sportsmanship. Then they talked and found out they lived in the same neighborhood. This could be the start of a beautiful friendship—even if they did play on opposing teams.

Jesus' younger brother James wrote, "Those who make peace plant it like a seed. They will harvest a crop of right living" (James 3:18). Peace or making friends should always be your first and best answer.

Words to Treasure

The Lord makes secure the footsteps of the person who delights in him. Even if that person trips, he won't fall. The Lord's hand takes good care of him.

Psalm 37:23-24

Daniel, Shadrach, Meshach, and Abednego were four famous friends who had an amazing adventure in a land far from home. Check out their story in the Book of Daniel in your Bible.

January 30

Waiting Room

Alita placed the newspaper by the door. It was early in the morning, and her friend Carla was helping her with her paper route

Words to Treasure

Let everything she has done bring praise to her at the city gate.

Proverbs 31:31

Carla kicked at a rock as they walked to the next house. "How come you're delivering newspapers? I thought you wanted to be an actor. You're taking acting classes and going to all those auditions."

"I do want to be an actor, and I still take acting classes," Alita shrugged, "but waiting to be an actor can't be my whole life. While I'm waiting, I do other things too, like delivering newspapers, playing soccer, and volunteering at the animal shelter. That's so much fun." She placed a folded newspaper by the next door.

Alita's right. Waiting for something doesn't mean you stop living until that special thing happens. Keeping busy while you're working toward your dream will make you a happier and more positive person. Having a dream is good, but not if it takes over everything else in your life. Things will happen in God's timing—so have fun while you wait.

Joseph knew that God had a bright future for him, but sometimes his life seemed to be going in the opposite direction. He was sold into slavery and later thrown into prison. But no matter how bad things got, Joseph always worked hard and did his best while waiting for his big break.

Wrong Address

He didn't know how it happened, but when he looked at the computer screen he knew he was at the wrong internet site. This was not the type of site he should be looking at. David's finger tapped the keyboard. He should exit. But maybe he could take just a quick look around. He was tempted. Who would know? *He would know*. David exited the site.

Temptation is wanting to have something or do something that you know you should avoid. Temptation can sneak up on you when you least expect it. And when it does, it is up to you to decide what's right. Other people aren't always going to be around to tell you what to do. It is a struggle, but a struggle you can handle by wanting to do what is right. When you get that funny feeling inside that tells you not to do something, that's the Holy Spirit giving you a little alert that it's time to walk away from a wrong situation.

Words to Treasure

My son, do not let wisdom and understanding out of your sight. Hold on to good sense and the understanding of what is right. They will be life for you.

Proverbs 3:21–22

Discovering Archaeology

In ancient times you couldn't just send an email to a buddy in a second. If you wanted to communicate long distances, you had to write it down and then send someone to deliver it. The Romans, using their good roads and horse teams, could send a message 500 miles in a single day.

February 1

Doesn't Look Good on You

Suna was a good snowboarder, and she knew it. People would often point at her as she sped down the slope. She looked good—real good. One day, Suna saw some kids resting on the side of the slope. She decided to cruise past, do some moves, and get their attention. They'd get to see she was good—really good. Suna pushed off but didn't see the patch of dirt in front of her. All of a sudden she was out of control and heading straight for a beginners' class. She didn't actually hit any of them when she crashed, but they sure freaked out and their instructor was unimpressed. Suna looked like the biggest show-off on the slope. Pride truly does come before a fall.

Words to Treasure

When pride comes, shame follows. But wisdom comes to those who are not proud.
Proverbs 11:2

Pride can mean having an overly high opinion of yourself and then showing off because of it. Pride doesn't look good on you. Pride isn't high on God's to-do list. In fact, it isn't even on his list. Show-off kind of pride is something to completely avoid. Or it just might trip you up.

People in Bible Times

Jesus told a story of a show-off who wanted to get attention by seating himself at the head table at a party. But the host of the party brought a humble friend from the back table to join the most important guests at the front table. This meant the host asked the show-off to move to the back of the room. And everybody was watching! How embarrassing!

February 2

Garden Walk

Sometimes Anthony just needed to get away from the noise of the house and go outside. He liked going to the garden because it was so quiet there, and it was easy to think. Anthony needed time alone to think about stuff. Sometimes he came out here to talk with God. Not out-loud talking but in-his-head talking with God.

It was a peaceful feeling being with God, because he knew his heavenly Father wanted to spend time in the garden with him too. It made Anthony feel as if he wasn't ever alone. No matter how crazy his life seemed to get, this garden time alone with God always helped him sort things out. God is a good listener.

Words to Treasure

"I will be with you, just as I was with Moses. I will never leave you. I will never desert you."

Joshua 1:5

Time with God is important because, believe it or not, he wants to spend time with you. Not to talk about the mysteries of the universe or to solve world-sized problems but just to spend time together—just like when you want to spend time with a friend. Never forget, God is your BFF.

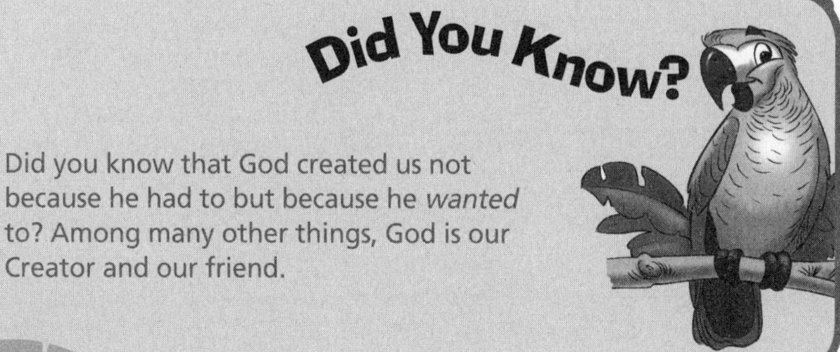

Did you know that God created us not because he had to but because he *wanted* to? Among many other things, God is our Creator and our friend.

February 3

Get Out There!

Brady cracked his fingers loudly as he paced. He sat down and stood up. And sat down. And stood up. Then he paced the hall some more. Finally he leaned against the wall and played air-piano, moving his fingers along an imaginary keyboard. He was next, and the results of this piano competition could change his future. But was he ready? Had he practiced hard enough? Questions ping-ponged around in his head. Could he really go out and play his best in front of all those people? Or would he mess up? Should he even try? "STOP!" his brain screamed. Brady calmed down.

Words to Treasure

That's because the LORD was with Joseph. He gave Joseph success in everything he did.

Genesis 39:23

Not try? Of course he had to try! If you don't take big risks, you won't ever learn how to face the big challenges God has for you. And that's disappointing for everybody. God knows exactly what you can do and what challenges you're ready to face. So get ready for a wild ride called *your life*. Play on!

Jesus told the story of a servant given money to use to make more money. But the servant was very afraid of losing the money he had. So instead of using it, he buried it in the ground. Later, when the master asked to see how much money the servant had made for him, the servant could only give back exactly what he had been given and no more. The master was very unhappy. God has given you some special talents, so don't be afraid and don't hide them. Go out and use them, just like Joseph.

What Do You Want to Do?

Anisa sat on the rock overlooking the ocean and ate her sandwich slowly. The longer it took her to chew, the longer it would be before she had to answer the question. Her grandfather watched her carefully and waited. What did she want to be when she grew up? Her grandfather was a doctor, and her dad was a doctor, and her aunt was a doctor too. Practically everybody in her entire family was a doctor. There were so many doctors in her family that they could start their own hospital. But Anisa had been around them enough to know that she didn't want to be a doctor. In fact, the sight of blood made her feel sick. She wanted to do something with art or designing things. Her grandfather was waiting, but she didn't want to answer the question, because she didn't want to disappoint him. She knew he wanted her to be a doctor too.

Words to Treasure

God gives wisdom, knowledge and happiness to the person who pleases him.
Ecclesiastes 2:26

What's right for one person may not be right for you. God created you in a very special way and to enjoy certain things. You can't work at something that isn't right for you just because somebody else wants it for you. God's got a plan just for the person you are, and he wants you to be the person he created you to be.

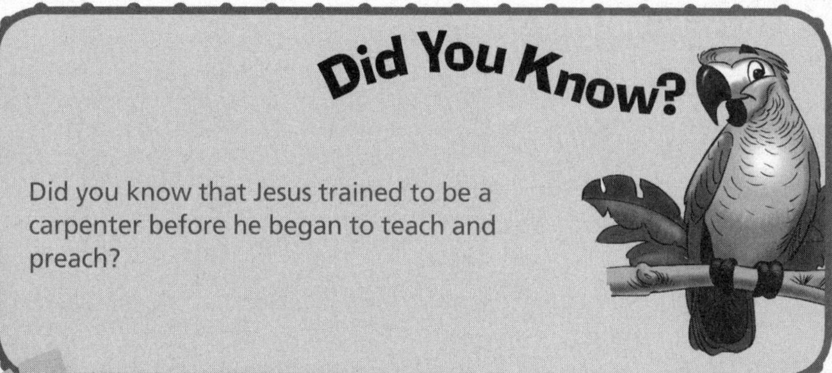

Did you know that Jesus trained to be a carpenter before he began to teach and preach?

Fair Play

After a short break, D.W. was ready to play more basketball. He was having a great game. But all of a sudden, Henry came rushing in, pulling off his tracksuit as he ran. He had almost missed the entire game—*again*. D.W. was just stepping back onto the court, when his coach stopped him. Instead Coach pointed to Henry and sent him on. "*What?!*" D.W. could hardly believe it. "Why?"

> **Words to Treasure**
>
> I have made myself calm and content like a young child in its mother's arms.
>
> Psalm 131:2

His coach looked at D.W. "Didn't you already get your fair share of play?" D.W. had to nod … he had. Coach passed him a water bottle. "Now it's Henry's turn. So what's your problem?"

"No problem, coach." D.W. said and then sipped his water.

Sometimes life can seem unfair from our point of view, but is it really? Or do we just think so because we're comparing ourselves to others? Well, stop it. Stop comparing. Just focus on what you get and be content with that. Sometimes *fair* isn't easy to judge. You don't always see the big picture.

People in Bible Times

A man hired some workers for his vineyard and promised to pay them a set amount for the day. Later he hired more men and promised to pay them the same amount. "Wait a minute," complained the first group of workers. "How come they work fewer hours but get paid the same?" The owner replied, "Aren't I paying you what I promised? That's fair." God treats us all with generosity and fairness no matter when we come to him—first or last.

Family History

Megan looked through the family photo album and listened to the stories her grandmother told her. Her great-grandfather had once saved a family from freezing to death in a great snowstorm.

Megan was visiting all her older relatives to look at their photographs and listen to family stories. She brought a recorder so she could write the stories down later on her computer. Her mom and dad were helping her research her family tree, and they had discovered that their family had lived in this same little cove for hundreds of years. Her family had actually owned a tiny island off the coast for many, many years: George Island named after her great, great, great grandpa George.

Words to Treasure

"May the Lord our God be with us, just as he was with our people who lived long ago."

1 Kings 8:57

Megan studied an old photograph of her great-great-grandmother and saw that they shared the same crooked smile. They could have been sisters.

Megan was saving family history and stories before they got lost forever. Family histories are full of amazing people and stories that can inspire us today. Talk to the elders in your family, and save those long-ago stories for the future.

Knowing your ancestral line was important in Bible times. It told people a lot about you, such as where you came from, what tribe your people were, and to whom you were related. Write the names of your parents, and then add grandparents, great-grandparents, and great-great-grandparents. See how many generations back you can go.

February 7

Growing Faith

The doctor carefully took the bandages off Reid's hand. Reid didn't remember much of the snowmobile accident or going into surgery. When he woke up, he was in a hospital bed and he had this big bandage on his arm. The doctors weren't sure how well his hand would work after that.

Words to Treasure

If you have faith as small as a mustard seed, it is enough. You can say to this mountain, "Move from here to there." And it will move. Nothing will be impossible for you.

Matthew 17:20–21

Now, after weeks of recovery they'd find out. Reid did a silent prayer to God. But did he have enough faith to believe that God would take care of him no matter what the results? The doctor gently touched Reid's hand. "Can you wiggle your fingers for me, Reid?"

The moment seemed to last a lifetime as his entire family watched and prayed. One by one, his fingers moved slightly. The doctor's smile was almost as enormous as Reid's.

What exactly is faith? It means believing and trusting in God's power to help us. How much faith do we need? What's the right size? Jesus said that even if we had faith the size of a tiny mustard seed that's enough to believe amazing things can happen. And, like a mustard seed, our faith can grow.

In ancient times, mustard was used to spice up or pickle food. It was often used as a medicine to heal all kinds of things from rashes, toothaches, colds, indigestion, headaches, sprains, and, some believed, scorpion stings and snake bites. The Greeks thought the little mustard seed was a gift to mankind.

February 8

Watcher

The wind-tossed branches scratched against the window, and the bathroom tap went drip, drip, drip in the sink. The room was dark except for a thin ray of light coming from underneath the closet doorway. That's when the red-eyed monster began to creep across the bedroom floor toward her. Emily was rooted to the spot. She couldn't move or run. She screamed and screamed.

Words to Treasure

Be on your guard.

1 Corinthians 16:13

The bedroom door flew open, and her mother flipped on the overhead light. Emily covered her eyes against the brightness. She still felt the dream with her, and she was still afraid. Her mother brushed her hair from her face.

"You okay?" her mom asked.

Emily nodded, realizing now that it had only been a bad dream.

Her mother looked her in the eyes. "At the sleepover, what kind of movie did you watch?"

"Scary," Emily answered.

Movies are fun, but you have to be careful about what kind of movies you watch. How do some movies make you feel after you watch them? Do they make you happy, scared, or angry? Just as too much junk food can make you feel sick, junk movies can also make you feel sick inside by giving you bad dreams or making you behave badly. So don't watch just anything. Before you watch something, check with your mom and dad first. Good movies make you feel good inside.

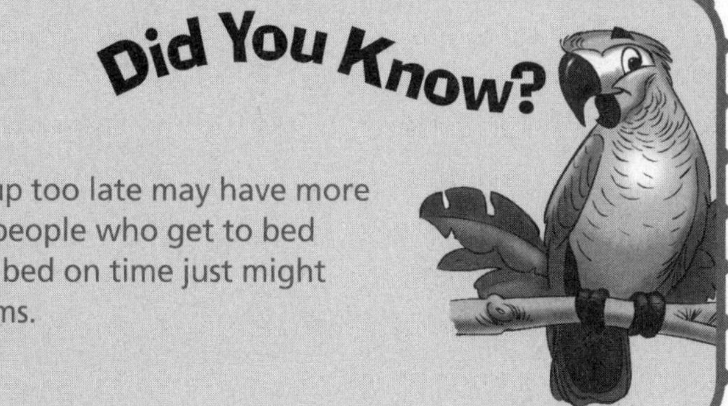

People who stay up too late may have more nightmares than people who get to bed early. So going to bed on time just might mean sweet dreams.

February 9

In Front

Justin pushed the buttons, making his bright yellow sports car accelerate across the bridge. His goal was to avoid an epic smashup. But then, with one slight turn of the wheel, his computer dream car was hurtling through the air and crashing upside down. It exploded with spectacular special effects. The race was over. He was destroyed. Sighing, Justin pushed a button to select a new type of dream car for the next race. Just then for some reason, he happened to glance over at his bedside table, where he saw his Bible, peeking out from under toys and other books. Clearly, his Bible was not as well-used as his computer.

Words to Treasure

I have lived the way the Lord wanted me to. I'm not guilty of turning away from my God. I keep all his laws in mind. I haven't turned away from his commands.

2 Samuel 22:22-23

God warned us not to make other things more important than him. It's okay to enjoy your games, but make sure you leave plenty of time for God too. Hey, even try putting your computer to use for God; check out fun websites that help you learn about the Bible. Activities that help you understand God are a must do.

Are there some areas in your life that kind of take over spending time with your heavenly Father? Maybe you need to power down so you can power up in him.

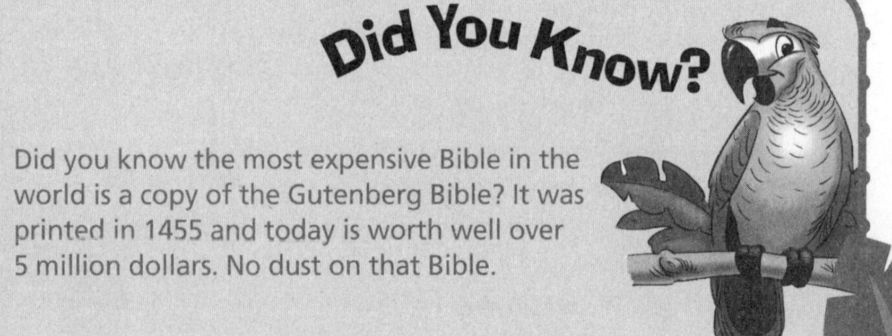

Did you know the most expensive Bible in the world is a copy of the Gutenberg Bible? It was printed in 1455 and today is worth well over 5 million dollars. No dust on that Bible.

Help Is Near

The teacher nodded, "Sally, tell the class why you believe in God." The entire class turned and stared at her. She didn't know what to say. She was nervous that the other kids would make fun of her.

But suddenly she wasn't nervous anymore. She talked about Jesus being her best friend and how that friendship made her feel good inside. Talking about Jesus didn't seem awkward; it just seemed normal. The class listened intently and then asked questions. Nobody made fun of her.

Words to Treasure

The Friend is the Holy Spirit. He will teach you all things. He will remind you of everything I have said to you.
John 14:26

Why wasn't Sally nervous anymore? That was the Holy Spirit helping her. Jesus promised that God would send us a helper who would never leave us: the Holy Spirit. That helper is the third person of the Holy Trinity, which includes God, Jesus, and the Holy Spirit. The Holy Spirit lives within us and acts as a teacher, helper, and friend. Like God, the Holy Spirit is always with you, loves you, and is right there ready to help when you need it.

People in Bible Times

The apostle Paul and his friend Barnabas went to talk to the governor of a place called Paphos. But something wasn't right with the governor's attendant. He was in fact an evil magician acting against Paul. But the Holy Spirit gave Paul the heads-up, and they sent the evil guy packing. Holy Spirit to the rescue! (See Acts 13:6–12.)

February 11

When to Follow

The sailboat was leaning way into the wind and going very fast. Brandon was following Scott's orders, but he wasn't happy about it. He scowled as he pulled the lines quickly, moving the white sails to the other side of the sailboat. The boat cut through the waves, making the ocean water spray Brandon in the face. Their sailing instructor had made Scott captain for this race. It wasn't fair! Brandon had wanted to be captain. So now he had to follow Scott's orders—but he didn't have to be happy about it.

Words to Treasure

Trust in your leaders. Put yourselves under their authority.

Hebrews 13:17

There are times in your life when God may want you to be the leader or the person in charge. And there are other times when you won't be in charge, because somebody else is. Whether taking orders or giving them, have a good attitude about it. Believe it or not, being a good follower helps you become an even better leader when the time comes.

A Roman commander asked Jesus to come heal his servant. Jesus agreed to go to the man's home, but the commander insisted Jesus stay right where he was. This soldier believed and had faith that if Jesus just gave the command, his servant would be healed back home. The commander was a man who knew both how to lead and how to follow. Jesus was amazed by this level of faith.

February 12

Did We?

Wendy twirled her spaghetti noodles onto her fork, but then she stopped. She looked at her parents with a puzzled expression on her face. "Did we say grace?"

Her mother laughed, "Yes, don't you remember?"

Wendy thought about it. "I don't remember doing it."

Her father slurped his noodles and made her giggle. "Maybe you should say it again."

Words to Treasure

I will pray with my spirit. But I will also pray with my understanding.

1 Corinthians 14:15

Sometimes we do things automatically. We say our prayers before we eat without thinking very much about it. We don't really remember what we said to God because it was like a recording that we turned on and off.

It's like someone phoning you with the same recorded message over and over again—a little rude and a little boring. God's not big on mindless chatter and doing stuff without really thinking about it. So next time you talk to God, don't be pushing any prerecorded message. Instead, really talk to him.

Did you know Jesus said you don't need a lot of fancy words to pray? Not at all. Why? Because your Father in heaven already knows what's in your heart. So just talk to God. It's nothing more complicated than that. (See Matthew 6:7.)

February 13

Putting Yourself Out

Clara hated the hospital smell, but as she walked down the hall, the nurses waved at her. Clara waved back.

> **Words to Treasure**
>
> But always be kind to me, just as the Lord is. Be kind to me as long as I live.
>
> 1 Samuel 20:14

Every day after school, her mom dropped her off at the hospital to visit her best friend, Becky. Becky had been very sick for weeks and weeks. But every day Clara came to cheer her up with get-well notes and other things from school. Clara had even dropped out of swimming so she could visit every day.

She made sure she had a smile on before she entered the room. "Becky! You wouldn't believe what happened today at lunch—a food fight!" Becky sat up in bed waiting for the news. Becky's mom gave Clara a smile as she left to give the girls some friend time.

Sometimes being a good friend means being there for that person when things are hard. Friendship isn't a someday thing; it is an everyday thing—no matter what. To have good friends you also have to be a good friend.

Prince Jonathan was best friends with David. You could say their friendship was legendary. Jonathan's father King Saul became *extremely* jealous of David and tried to kill him. But Jonathan managed to love both his dad and his friend and keep them apart. Cool friend, cool story—check it out in 1 Samuel 19–20.

February 14

Crushing

Jo sat with her friends, cheering for Jason. Even their names both started with a *J*. It was fate they should fall in love. Problem One—he was in ninth grade and she was in seventh grade. Problem Two—he didn't know she was alive. But tonight she would talk to him.

She approached him at the end of the game, "You play really, really well."

"Sure, thanks." He picked up his sports bag and caught up with his buddies. He was gone. Three months of getting up the courage to talk to him and that was it.

Words to Treasure

But I am like a healthy olive tree. My roots are deep in the house of God. I trust in your faithful love forever and ever.

Psalm 52:8

Having a crush happens to everybody. A *crush* is when you like somebody a lot. Sometimes we like somebody that really isn't right for us. There are a hundred reasons why liking somebody may not be the right thing for now. Just remember, God has the perfect person for you to like at exactly the right time, when you're ready. Having a crush can be a little bit crushing. But that won't always be the case.

If you need somebody to talk to about the person you like, your mom and dad or other adults in your family know all about it. They've had a few crushes of their own. They can help you figure out some of those feelings that come with love.

February 15

Up Front

Alke watched as the famous writer chatted with people at the book conference. She had read every one of her books. Alke wanted to be an author someday too. She wrote every day and had letters and poetry published at school already. She wanted to go talk to her, but why would someone so famous talk to her? It was a stupid idea to come here. The author caught her staring and motioned for her to come over.

Words to Treasure

He went ahead of you on your journey. He was in the fire at night and in the cloud during the day.

Deuteronomy 1:33

"Hello," smiled the woman. "What's your name?"

Alke's throat went dry. "Alke Smith."

The author's smile widened. "From St. Peter's Academy?" Alke nodded. "Your teacher, Mrs. Morrison, sent me some of your work and told me you'd be here today. You're a very good writer." Alke blinked in surprise.

God has a funny way of going ahead of us and getting everything ready and sorted out beforehand. Next time you're a little nervous about doing something, don't be surprised if God's already planning how to help you be a success.

When God plans something, he loves to take care of the details. When the Israelites traveled out of Egypt, God gave them a type of food to eat called manna. After the morning dew was gone, thin flakes were left on the ground. It was kind of like bread. The Israelites could eat as much as they liked. That was God planning ahead again. (See Exodus 16.)

What about War?

Ted felt funny talking to the computer screen, and it was strange because his dad's responses were delayed and sometimes sounded funny. His movements were all jerky. But this was the only way they could talk on Father's Day. His dad was a soldier and was away in a far-off country. Ted brushed a tear away. He wanted his dad home. But that wasn't going to happen today. His dad was going to be away for months. Ted wasn't sure how he felt about war. It was the thing everybody talked about and the thing that kept his dad away. Sometimes he wished his dad wasn't a soldier so he would stay home, and sometimes he was really proud of him. He felt all mixed-up inside.

Words to Treasure

Don't let evil overcome you. Overcome evil by doing good.
Romans 12:21

Sometimes a soldier's job is to protect people and keep the peace. That's not an easy thing to do. When a soldier believes in God, he or she can pray that God will help with all the situations that come up. Reading the Bible can remind a soldier about being kind and generous even in a bad situation. Talking to God about all your feelings helps you and helps your family. But also pray for everybody involved in a war and pray for peace.

Some soldiers asked John the Baptist how they should behave. John told them not to use their power as soldiers to do wrong things.

February 17

When in Trouble

They were finally here. Amelia and her family were at the biggest amusement park ever. Rides everywhere, buildings everywhere, and people everywhere. Amelia didn't know if she wanted to go on Mountain Madness or Explorer River first. She and her brother started to run down one of the pathways.

Words to Treasure

"He was lost. And now he is found." So they began to celebrate.

Luke 15:24

"Wait!" Her dad ordered them back with a wave. "See that mountain ride over there?" They nodded. "If you get lost, go straight to the information booth right next to it. If you can't find us, talk to a park employee, then wait for us. They will help you until we find you. Keep these two maps with you. I circled where you should go. Okay?" Amelia and her brother nodded again and tucked the maps in their back pocket. "Okay, let's go ride rides until we're sick!"

Do you know who to go to when you need help or get lost? Talk with your parents about the people and the plan you should use if you ever face trouble. Safety first.

People in Bible Times

There was a young man that got himself soooo lost. How lost? Well, he left home and partied until he was so broke he was living with pigs ... no seriously, in a pig sty. But, he knew exactly where to get found and helped. He went home to a loving father. Getting found is the best feeling in the world. Check out this riches to rags to riches story in Luke 15.

February 18

Houston, We Have a Problem

All the bad feelings spilled out of James. "I didn't get my class project done because it's boring, the class is lame, and my teacher doesn't understand me."

His dad drove without looking at him for a long time. "I don't think you're bored, and Mrs. Graham is a great teacher. What's up?"

James had held in his secret for so long that he didn't know what to do. "Dad, sometimes I don't understand how to put things down on paper. It gets all confused. I'm dumb or something." The terrible secret was out.

His dad turned into a drive-through fast-food restaurant. "Want a milkshake?"

James wasn't expecting that! "What?"

His dad ordered two milkshakes. "You might have a learning problem. We can find out what kind and see how we can get you back on track. Son, this isn't the end of the world. You're a really smart kid. When I was a kid I had the same kind of problems."

"You did?" James felt better already.

Keeping problems a secret only makes them worse. For every problem there is a solution, if you're willing to talk about it.

Words to Treasure

Ask, and it will be given to you. Search, and you will find.

Matthew 7:7

Live It!

If you're having problems learning, hearing your teachers, seeing the blackboard, or just reading your books, talk to your parents or teacher. Don't pretend nothing's wrong, and don't avoid the real things that worry you. Talk about them! You'll become worry-free when you do, and you'll find out that your problems are smaller than you thought.

February 19

God's Way

Tina marched right up to Brenda and stopped. "You are invited to my birthday party." She shoved the invitation at Brenda.

> **Words to Treasure**
>
> When the way you live pleases the Lord, he makes even your enemies live at peace with you.
>
> Proverbs 16:7

Brenda's mouth hung open. "I didn't think we were friends anymore."

Tina thought about it. "We had a misunderstanding. I said some mean things, and you said some mean things. But that doesn't mean we have to avoid each other forever. Come to my birthday party." Brenda took the invitation, but she was still kind of puzzled. "Thanks!"

Did you know that one of Jesus' friends pretended like he didn't even know Jesus? Peter felt really badly about it after. Do you know what Jesus did? He forgave Peter and reassured him they were still really good friends. Why? Because that's what friends do.

People in Bible Times

Paul needed some friends, big time. It seemed that everybody wanted to kill him. The Jews were angry because he had changed and didn't want to hurt Christians anymore. But Christians didn't want him because they were still upset that he *had* hurt Christians. But a guy named Barnabas stood up for Paul. Because the Christians trusted Barnabas, they were willing to give Paul a second chance. That's a friend! (See Acts 9:26–30.)

February 20

I Wish

Beth sat on the edge of her bed and prayed very hard for a very long time. Her birthday was coming up, and she really wanted that new bike. It was the most beautiful retro cruiser bicycle she had ever seen. It was deep red with white Hawaiian flowers. She imagined cruising down the street with a new puppy riding in the big wicker basket she was planning to get for the front. It would be the perfect birthday with the perfect gift.

Words to Treasure

Find your delight in the Lord. Then he will give you everything your heart really wants.

Psalm 37:4

Hold that thought. God isn't your personal shopper, processing your heavenly order forms. God is *not* the genie in the magic lamp. If when you talk to God it's a whole lot about your needs and wants, then it's probably time to backpedal. That isn't the kind of relationship God wants with you. God absolutely does want to give you your dreams, but your dreams must also match up with what God wants for you. You're a team, remember? He's got big dreams for you, and that's better than having a wish-list God.

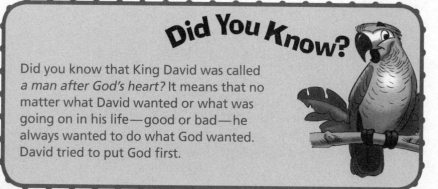

Did You Know?

Did you know that King David was called *a man after God's heart?* It means that no matter what David wanted or what was going on in his life—good or bad—he always wanted to do what God wanted. David tried to put God first.

February 21

So Talk

Tiffany stormed up to her room and slammed the door behind her, hard. She was never ever going to talk to her parents ever again. They thought she was a baby. She wasn't a baby! She *was* old enough to go to the shopping mall with her friends all by themselves. Her dad called to her from downstairs. "Tiffany, honey, let's talk about this."

She shouted back, "NO! I don't want to talk to you!"

Words to Treasure

Get rid of all hard feelings, anger and rage.

Ephesians 4:31

Not talking is *not* helpful. But talking about stuff in a calm way *is* helpful. That means no shouting, door-slamming, screaming, name-calling, and other unhelpful attitudes. By talking with her family, Tiffany could learn why her parents don't want her to go to the mall alone. By talking, Tiffany could show her parents that it might be time to give her some freedom. Maybe they could go to the mall together but let Tiffany and her friends go into her favorite store while her parents waited outside. That way everyone wins a little. Talking fixes problems.

Next time you are so angry you just don't want to talk, write out how you feel and make a list of the things you want to talk about with your parents, friends, or brothers and sisters. When you talk with them, keep to the list and don't get sidetracked. Have a good talk that is planned and thought out and that puts anger and hurt feelings in the backseat.

February 22

Show Time

The crowd clapped and whistled as Mark did another endo on his bike by riding on his front wheel only. Then he bunny-hopped a bench and finally ended his performance with an amazing tailwhip off a ramp where the only thing connecting him to his bike were his hands on the handlebars. His legs were out in space behind his bike. Just at the right moment, he pulled it together and had his feet back on the pedals ready to hit the ground.

Words to Treasure

Your gifts meet the needs of the Lord's people. And that's not all. Your gifts also cause many people to thank God.

2 Corinthians 9:12

Mark was part of a bike show that was raising money for people who had lost everything in a terrible flood. Everyone was showing off their moves, and the crowd loved it. They were raising a lot of money for needy families.

Did you know your talents or skills aren't there just to help you get famous or wealthy? You're also supposed to use them to help others. You can be a gift from God to the world.

Talk to your parents, friends, teachers, coaches, and pastor and ask them what they think are your outstanding talents and abilities. Make a list of what you're good at. Then make another list—a list of some of the ways you could use those talents to help others. That's one way of sharing God's love.

February 23

Why a Story?

Mac raised his hand. “If Jesus wanted us to learn about God and heaven, why didn’t he just tell us? Why did he tell us so many stories?”

Words to Treasure

He taught them many things using stories.

Mark 4:2

Mr. Lund closed his Bible. “Okay. In school you’ve just learned about space and the solar system. Pretty complex stuff, right? Planets, suns, black holes and galaxies.” The class nodded. “But you understand it because you’re in the fourth grade. Right? I wonder, how would you explain outer space to your two-year-old brother?”

“Not very easily,” Mac laughed, “He’s too little.”

His teacher leaned forward in his chair. “That’s right. But we might tell him a nursery rhyme about how a cow jumped over the moon. This teaches a little kid about the moon. And the moon is part of …”

Mac smiled, “our solar system. I get it. When it comes to understanding God … we’re like little kids.”

Jesus told easy-to-understand stories to help us learn about a really, really complex thing called the kingdom of heaven. Can you make up a story that teaches somebody else about God?

Did You Know?

Did you know that you can find 30 of Jesus’ parables or stories in the New Testament part of your Bible? Go ahead and read some of them, and then talk to someone about what you think those stories say about God, heaven, and you.

So Many

The small children skipped around them with their little hands out, but Marcus and Drew had run out of coins and little gifts. They were traveling with their parents in Africa, helping to build drinking wells for villages in the area. At each village, the boys gave the children gifts of candy, coins, or little toys. But today they didn't have enough to go around. Marcus wished he had more to give the children as he waved goodbye and climbed into the truck. "Mom," he said as he stared out the window of the truck, "there are so many families that need help. But we can't help all of them. What are we going to do?"

Words to Treasure

Anything you did for one of the least important of these brothers and sisters of mine, you did for me.

Matthew 25:40

His mom ruffled his hair. "A very kind lady named Mother Teresa said, 'If you can't feed a hundred people, then feed just one.' So, we just help one person at a time. Then that one person can help somebody else. We all need to help each other. Remember when people helped us when our river flooded?" The boys nodded.

Marcus rolled down the truck window, took off his favorite baseball cap, and tossed it to a young boy as they drove past. The boy put the cap on and waved as they drove away.

Jesus and his disciples were watching people donating money to the temple. A rich man came and put in a large amount, but a poor widow put in only two small coins. Jesus asked the disciples who gave more. His answer? The widow, because she gave away almost all the money she had (see Mark 12:41–44).

February 25

Right 'til It Hurts

Terry heard the noise of spinning tires on ice and snow. A lady was digging the wheels of her big car into a big snow bank. She was *stuck*.

Words to Treasure

Blessed are those who suffer for doing what is right. The kingdom of heaven belongs to them.

Matthew 5:10

The last ski shuttle bus pulled into the snowy parking lot. Terry boarded the bus, but his shoulders slumped as he glanced back at the lady. Now she was out of her car walking around in high heels on the ice. She was going to break a leg. Terry got off the bus and unloaded his board—no incredible snowboarding for him today. He walked over, "Excuse me. Can I help you?" She looked so grateful. Terry glanced over as the bus drove up the mountain to the ski hill.

Doing what's right sometimes isn't fun or convenient. Sometimes doing what's right can be the most difficult choice you're ever going to make. That's called "being dependable until it hurts *bad*." But, on the upside, God is absolutely impressed with you.

People in Bible Times

Doing what's right isn't always easy. Take our friend Noah, for example. He was a good man who did everything God told him to do. He even built this outrageously huge boat and packed it full of animals. You can be sure his neighbors thought Noah was one raindrop short of a flood. It was hard, but Noah did what was right (see Genesis 6:9–22).

Lonely at the Top

Pete climbed the hill that overlooked the playground. This wasn't his playground, and the kids below weren't his friends. Nothing good had happened since they moved here. Nobody talked to him at school. He was Mr. Invisible. Would he ever fit in? Pete climbed an oak tree to sit and watch the world go by, while he kept on being invisible. Being alone in a tree felt better than being ignored in a crowd.

Words to Treasure

But I am always with you. You hold me by my right hand.

Psalm 73:23

Everybody, no matter how popular they seem, feels alone sometimes. But we can't let that feeling take over our lives, because it will grow bigger and bigger. How do we shrink feelings of loneliness? Get out of your loneliness tree and go say hi to somebody instead of waiting for them to say it first. You'll be surprised at what might happen. Go out and take a karate class or join the swim club. Loneliness makes us think about ourselves all the time, so don't get caught up in it. Go out and think about other people by volunteering to help others. God's calling you out of your tree. Climb down and meet the world.

People in Bible Times

Zacchaeus the tax collector couldn't see over the crowd, so he climbed a tree to get a better look at Jesus. Jesus stopped, called to Zacchaeus, and told him to climb down out of the tree. Some amazing things happened after Zacchaeus climbed out of that tree. You can read about it in the Bible (see Luke 19:1–10).

February 27

Missing

Brad was cold, but he was completely prepared for the long night of searching the forest with his dad. They were volunteers with the Search and Rescue Society, and sometimes they were called out to find missing hikers. Brad always stayed close to his dad because his dad was an experienced rescuer. Tonight they were looking for two teenage girls who hadn't returned from their day hike. He hoped they were smart enough to bring warm clothes with them. It was one cold night. The team would do what it took to find them. Everybody is important.

Words to Treasure

"I tell you, it will be the same in heaven. There will be great joy when one sinner turns away from sin."

Luke 15:7

Hey, God feels the same way about us. Everybody is important. Jesus told this story about a shepherd who owned a hundred sheep. But one had wandered off and got lost. Even though the guy had ninety-nine other sheep, he still went to look for that one lost sheep. When he found it, he did shepherd cartwheels. Jesus said God's like that too. He doesn't want even one of us to be lost from him.

Did You Know?

Did you know that people have been caring for sheep for about 10,000 years? That makes shepherding one of mankind's oldest known jobs! Did you know sheep can be milked like cows to make cheese and that today's sheep aren't as smart as their ancient cousins? They have smaller brains. Go figure.

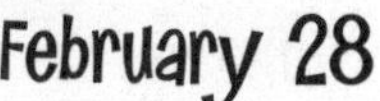

February 28

Me, Worry?

She picked up the dog toy and gave it a little squeak. Suddenly every doggy eye in the dog park was riveted on her.

Tina's mom whispered in her ear, "Throw it, quick." Tina did, and the dogs chased it in a frenzy. Her mom watched the dogs. "It won't be long before you get your new puppy." Tina was quiet. "Don't you want your puppy?"

Words to Treasure

"I tell you, do not worry. Don't worry about your life."
Matthew 6:25

"I want him so bad that it makes me worry." Tina frowned, "What if something happens to me before then ... like an accident? What if I never get him?"

Her mom hugged her. "Tina, you're not going to get in an accident before you get your puppy. Chase that thought right out of your head."

Worry can make us think some pretty weird stuff. Sometimes stuff that can't possibly happen. Worry is like carrying around a huge backpack full of rocks. God doesn't want you to feel crushed by worry. In your mind, give all your worries to God to take care of. He can, and he will, help you with your problems. You're not alone. Go talk to God about your worries and then talk to someone you trust.

When you feel worried or uncertain about the future, read these verses and remember that God is talking to *you*. "'I know the plans I have for you,' announces the Lord. 'I want you to enjoy success. I do not plan to harm you. I will give you hope for the years to come'" (see Jeremiah 29:11–13).

March 1

Laugh Out Loud

Duncan wasn't sure what Su-Yung was saying in Korean, but she seemed to think that the way he used his chopsticks was kind of funny. Duncan watched Su-Yung show him how to do it again, but his big fingers just couldn't get the hang of eating with the thin sticks. This time he almost got the piece of fish to his mouth, but then he dropped it in his lap. He sheepishly looked around the table while Su-Yung and her family giggled in a nice way. He relaxed and laughed too. It didn't matter that they couldn't understand each other. It didn't take Duncan very long to decide that eating Korean style wasn't easy—and that his Korean hosts were very nice about his mistakes.

Words to Treasure

A cheerful heart makes you healthy.

Proverbs 17:22

The amazing thing about laughter is that everybody in the whole world laughs. Everybody! We don't have to speak the same language to understand laughter. Laughing together tells others that you like them and you're having a good time being with them. The world should do a whole lot more laughing together. God loves it when we laugh.

Did You Know?

When you laugh, your entire body laughs. Laughing is really good for you. It makes your heart, muscles, and brain stronger. Laughing can help you fight off sickness, and it helps you feel less pain. Laughing really is the best medicine of all.

March 2

Right Turn

Myles read and reread the competition rules carefully, line by line. He didn't want anything to go wrong. He wanted to know exactly what he could and couldn't do before he started building his robot for the Robotics Kids' Multinational Competition. He would never do anything wrong intentionally, but he didn't want to do something to disqualify himself without knowing it. That would be total stupidity and total annihilation.

Words to Treasure

Blessed are those who are hungry and thirsty for what is right. They will be filled.

Matthew 5:6

Before he even started on the design for his robot, Myles was making sure he had every detail in the rule book covered. Doing it right from start to finish is the smartest move of all.

Part of doing what is right is wanting to do what is right. Just like Myles. Even Satan knows the Bible really well and knows what's right and wrong. He just doesn't *want to do* what's right. Jesus wants us to know God's rules by heart, and in our hearts, and he wants us to follow them. Reading your Bible is the start to knowing what's right.

People in Bible Times

Satan decided to try and tempt Jesus into doing wrong things. He was pretty clever and even used words from the Bible to back up his moves. However, Jesus not only knew the Bible, but he also knew God's heart. He busted Satan simply by knowing what's right. No score for Satan. (See Matthew 4:1–11.)

March 3

I Reject Your Rejection!

Wayne didn't know what to say. The guys didn't want him to snowboard with them. Apparently he wasn't good enough. He was still learning some things, but he wasn't the slowest guy on the hill either. He wanted to say a bunch of stuff, but instead he just shrugged. "See you later." The guys took off without looking back. Now Wayne felt horribly lonely and wasn't sure who he'd spend the afternoon with.

Words to Treasure

I have chosen you.

Isaiah 41:9

Suddenly a new kid from school slid to a stop beside him. "Hey, I found a new trail. You want to try it with me?"

Wayne smiled, "Yeah. I'd like that."

It hurts when people don't want to be your friend. But, you're not the only one on the rejection rollercoaster. Everybody has felt rejected at one time or another. It happens. Jesus was rejected and understands every bad feeling that goes with it. His advice is the best you're going to get. When you feel ignored, dumped, or rejected, you just have to shake it off and move on. You have nothing to prove to anybody. If you have to talk people into being your friend, that doesn't make them good friends, anyway. Think of it this way: rejection puts you on a road to discover new and better friendships.

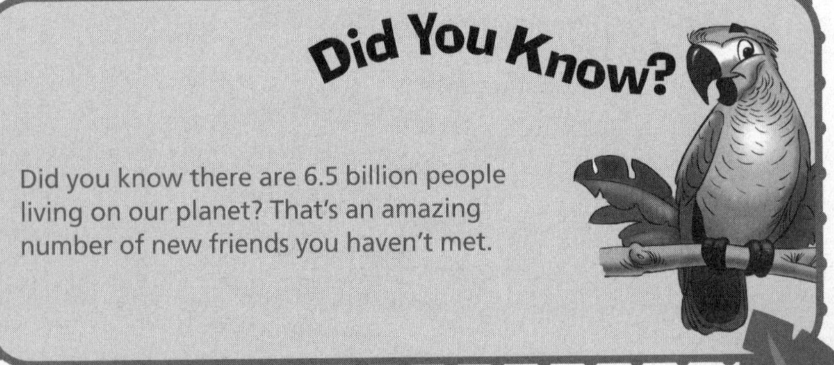

Did you know there are 6.5 billion people living on our planet? That's an amazing number of new friends you haven't met.

March 4

Action Word

On the television the children looked so hungry and sick. Abby turned to her dad. "They shouldn't go hungry just because of a war. It isn't their fault. It isn't fair."

Her dad peered over his reading glasses. "What are you going to do about it?"

"Me?" Abby blinked. "Me? I'm just a kid. What can I do?"

"That's not a very good excuse. What do you think you can do?"

Abby thought about it. "I could use some of my babysitting money to help sponsor a family that needs help."

"Tell you what." He put down his book, "If you give half, I'll pay the other half."

"I tell *you* what," Abby stuck her hand out. "I'll sponsor one child all by myself, and you sponsor another child."

"Deal!" They shook hands.

It isn't enough to want to see things get better in the world. You have to become part of what changes the world. That's called *love in action*. Don't just talk about helping others—*Do it*.

Words to Treasure

Dear children, don't just talk about love. Put your love into action. Then it will truly be love.

1 John 3:18

Did you know that 400 kids went to the United Nations to talk to world leaders about how to change the world for the better? Think about ways you can get involved to help your community or the world. Adults are waiting to help you make a difference. All you need to do is get involved.

March 5

Word of Mouth

Megan was a communication master. She could handle more gadgets and buttons than anyone she knew. At this very moment she was on video chat, updating her online photo page, listening to music, and texting on her phone. Could a kid get more connected?

Words to Treasure

"So you must go and make disciples of all nations."

Matthew 28:19

Did you ever wonder what they did in ancient times to communicate long distances? How did people get the word out about Jesus? Well, Jesus started with twelve guys and sent them out into the world to talk to people. They traveled by foot, horse, or boat to all kinds of cities in the ancient world. They talked to people in temples, in homes, and on street corners. Then those people talked to other people, and soon the things Jesus did and said were spreading all over the place. It may not have been our kind of social media, but it worked. How can you talk to people about Jesus? Sometimes, just talk face-to-face—no batteries needed. People have been doing it for thousands of years. Give it a try.

Paul's journey to tell the world about Jesus was a little more dangerous than just picking up the phone. The guy was whipped, beaten, imprisoned, almost stoned to death, and was shipwrecked three times. Ancient people played rough. (See 2 Corinthians 11:25.)

March 6

The Point

Jason stared at the little pills in the older boy's hand. "So?" asked the boy. "Do you want to try it or not? They'll make you feel good." Jason's friends looked at him because he was the unofficial leader of their group.

Words to Treasure

My son, listen and be wise. Set your heart on the right path.

Proverbs 23:19

Jason shook his head, "No thanks. I'm not into drugs." The boy looked at Jason's friends. "How 'bout you guys?"

Jason shook his head again while his friends just stared at the boy with blank faces. "My friends don't do drugs either."

The boy slipped the pills back in his pocket and walked away as if it didn't matter to him anyway. "Your loss," he said over his shoulder.

There comes a point in every kid's life when you face that monster moment of whether to do drugs or not. Don't take that moment too lightly, because it can be a life-changing event. If some older kid starts offering you drugs, walk away. Stop before you start and keep to the path God wants for you. Be exactly who you are, with no chemicals added.

There are some pretty important talks you need to have with your parents. If someone offers you drugs, talk to an adult in your family. Even if you just have questions, talk to your mom and dad, because they care about you and will answer any questions you have.

March 7

To Look or Not to Look?

Mary knew where her parents had hidden some Christmas presents. The problem was, she had promised not to snoop. To look or not to look—that was the question. She was so curious that it was painful. Her parents would never actually know if she looked. She danced on her tip toes trying to decide. Promises were important. She knew that. Finally, she headed downstairs with a heavy sigh. Christmas wasn't that far away. She could wait.

Words to Treasure

My honesty will be a witness about me in days to come.

Genesis 30:33

The Bible tells us people like and respect an honest person, not someone who breaks promises and sneaks around. If you are honest about everything, do what's right and keep your promises, people will notice. That's a promise.

A symbol of honesty in ancient times was that of a scale and weights. In the market, people used scales to weigh things. You put what you wanted to buy on one side of the scale and used weight stones on the other. Then both you and shopkeeper would know how much you should be charged. Scales made everything fair and honest.

Throw It Away

Trish sat in the parked car in her driveway, silent and sad. They had just returned from a day at the amusement park. Her mother had asked her to hold onto her little brother's hand just for a moment, but she had gotten distracted, and when she turned around, her brother was gone. They searched for him, and finally they found him by the bumper cars. But it made Trish feel bad for the rest of the day. It was her fault.

Words to Treasure

Turn to God. Then your sins will be wiped away.

Acts 3:19

Trish's mom opened the car door and sat beside her. "Aren't you coming inside?" Trish shrugged. Her mom passed her a candy. "Everything's okay. You learned to keep a better eye on your brother, and he learned not to wander off. Stop worrying about it."

Sometimes when we make a mistake or do something wrong, we just keep replaying it in our heads. We go over and over it, feeling even worse each time. Jesus doesn't want us to go over and over our past mistakes. When we talk about our mistakes with Jesus and he forgives us, it's as if it never happened. It is like rewinding and starting over, and that's the way it should be.

Do you feel guilty about some things? Talk about them to the people who love you. Then write them down on a piece of paper. Ask God to forgive you, then rip up that paper and throw it away, because you don't need to carry around guilt anymore.

March 9

STOP!

Every day it was the same. David would watch the five boys tease the smaller boy. They threw clumps of dirt at him and called him names. But every day the kid just walked home and went inside his house. Every day David felt sorry for him, but he never did anything about it.

> **Words to Treasure**
>
> One person could be overpowered. But two people can stand up for themselves. And a rope made out of three cords isn't easily broken.
>
> Ecclesiastes 4:12

One day after school, David walked up to him. "Hey, kid, can I walk home with you?"

He looked so grateful. "Sure."

As they left the playground, David turned to the five boys and gave them a look that meant *the bullying stops now*.

It takes courage to stand up to bullies. Bullies can be guys or girls who use words or actions to disrespect or scare someone. Does somebody at school make you feel that way? Talk about it with your parents, teacher, or church leaders. They will help the bully understand that you are not the problem, but his or her behavior is. Nobody has the right to make you feel bad. Bullying can only happen if we won't help each other.

Live IT!

Jesus prayed for the people who were hurting him. He said, "Father, forgive them. They don't know what they are doing" (Luke 23:34). Jesus is our example, so even when people bully you, don't forget to pray for them. They may bully others because they are having a hard time and just don't know how to act.

Do They Have to Live Here?

Simon went into his room and found every one of his car models on the floor, and his Lego castle was in pieces. How many times did he have to tell P.D. and his friends to stay out of his room?! Simon surveyed the damage. It would take him all afternoon to rebuild what they had taken apart. "MOM! P.D. did it again!"

Words to Treasure

Do not hate your brother in your heart.

Leviticus 19:17

Sometimes living with brothers and sisters can be a complete pain. They seem to exist only to mess up your stuff and drive you crazy. In fact, it's kind of hard to see what your parents actually like about them in the first place. You're neat, and they're messy. When you want them to play a board game, they won't. And then when you have friends over, they won't leave you alone. They never do what you want them to do.

Important house memo: brothers and sisters aren't supposed to be a mini-you. They have their own interests and personalities, and that's a good thing in the long run. Someday what makes them so different from you may be exactly what you need.

People in Bible Times

When God asked Moses to go speak to Pharaoh, Moses explained that he wasn't very good at speaking to a crowd. But Moses' brother Aaron was good at public speaking. So God made the two brothers a team. Both started doing what they did best. It worked.

March 11

Too Thin Is Not In

Lindsey looked in the mirror and didn't like what she saw. She wanted to be super thin. The only problem was that she liked to eat a normal, healthy breakfast, lunch, and dinner. To stay thin, some of her friends threw their lunches away at school. Her mother said Lindsey looked beautiful and sporty. Her mother explained that being too thin is not good for you.

Words to Treasure

What you have done is wonderful. I know that very well. None of my bones was hidden from you when you made me inside my mother's body.

Psalm 139:14-15

Sometimes, instead of looking at the things we like about our bodies, we only look at what we don't like. Then pretty soon that's all we see. We compare ourselves to the people in movies or television. News flash—some of those people are also very unhealthy and unhappy people. With negative thinking, we can actually make our brains dislike our own bodies even though we *are* beautiful. Do you know what? You are amazing just the way you are. Perfect in every way God made you.

How we see ourselves and how other people see us can be two completely different things. Sometimes all we see are the things we don't like about our bodies. But that's not what other people see. Ask a good friend to describe the way you look. Did you hear? Yup, that beautiful person is you!!! Believe it!

March 12

Pssst, Want to Be a Christian?

Cindy's friend Francisco went to her church a couple of times, but he decided that church, Jesus, and all that stuff just weren't for him. Now, Cindy sat in church feeling kind of sad because she wanted Francisco to believe in Jesus like she did. Why couldn't she make him believe? Why didn't God make him believe? She was so disappointed.

You can bring a friend to church, but you can't force him to believe in Jesus. It just doesn't work that way. Everybody has to have his or her own special first time with God. Don't worry, because Jesus knows just the right time to talk with your friend, and that might be later, not now.

All you can do is invite your friends to church events they may enjoy. You can't make a God thing happen, but you can pray for your friends and continue to talk to Jesus about them.

Words to Treasure

We loved you so much. So we were happy to share with you God's good news. We were also happy to share our lives with you.

1 Thessalonians 2:8

People in Bible Times

Philip had met Jesus and believed in him. He told his friend Nathanael all about him. Nathanael wasn't too sure about this guy named Jesus, but he went to meet Jesus anyway. When the two talked, Nathanael was amazed by Jesus, and he also came to believe in him. Philip brought the two men together, and the rest was up to Jesus and Nathanael. Good job Philip! (See John 1:43–51.)

March 13

Fast Seems Slow

As he ate his hamburger, Daniel thought about how Jesus fasted (went without eating) for forty days. He didn't think he could go four *hours* without eating something. He slurped the last of his vanilla shake as he puzzled about how people say that being hungry helps you get closer to God. He didn't get it.

> **Words to Treasure**
>
> "But when you go without eating, put olive oil on your head. Wash your face. Then others will not know that you are fasting. Only your Father, who can't be seen, will know it. Your Father will reward you, because he sees what you do secretly."
>
> Matthew 6:17–18

When people fast they combine three things: praying or talking with God, thinking about God, and deciding not to do certain things. Some people fast by not eating for a short time or by not eating certain things they like such as snacks or sweets. People also "fast" by avoiding things that distract them from God, such as watching television or doing something they enjoy. Fasting reminds you throughout the day that you are thinking about God today. Remember, God doesn't want you to make yourself sick or do something harmful to yourself; he just wants your full attention. When your attention isn't on food or entertainment, you can focus it on God. (Kids should not fast without talking to an adult first.)

Many things we do with God are meant to be personal and private. Jesus said that fasting, praying or even being seen at church isn't about impressing people with how spiritual we are. Just quietly being with God is enough.

Talk Is Cheap

Toby pointed to the big oak tree in his backyard. "I am going to build the biggest, most amazing tree fort in the world. It's going to be three levels with a swing bridge, a telescope, and secret passages. Just wait and see. It will be great."

His friends rolled their eyes. "Like the snow fort last winter or the go-cart last summer?" Evan shook his head. "Man, you're all talk." Mumbling, the boys left to go swimming. Toby sat down, embarrassed by his big talk.

Words to Treasure

All hard work pays off. But if all you do is talk, you will be poor.

Proverbs 14:23

His dad stopped gardening and sat beside him. "Maybe we should draw up some plans for that tree fort. You up for it?"

Toby studied the tree. "Could we build the most amazing tree fort in the world?"

His dad tilted his head, "In due time, maybe ... if you work hard." Toby couldn't answer because he was off to get some paper and pencils, so they could draw up plans.

God knows that big talk doesn't make big dreams happen. You have to pray about it, plan it, and work hard to make dreams come true.

Discovering Archaeology

Scientists figure it took the Egyptians roughly 20 years to build the great pyramid of Khufu. It took the Chinese hundreds of years to build what we now know as the Great Wall of China. It took 14 years to carve the faces on Mount Rushmore, and it took 22 years to build India's Taj Mahal. Hard work equals amazing things.

March 15

God Is Listening

Wilson ripped open his report card and found out that he didn't do as well as he had hoped. How could that be? He had prayed for a better report card every night. Didn't God hear him? What's the point in praying if nothing happens? Wilson headed for the exit door, but Mr. Wu stopped him. "Good work this term, Wilson. But I do think you could do better. I have some ideas that might help how you study. I'll be in my classroom after school on Tuesdays if you'd like some help."

Words to Treasure

Even before they call out to me, I will answer them.

Isaiah 65:24

Wilson sighed, "Thanks, Mr. Wu, I'll stop by."

First off, God always hears our prayers. There's no problem with God's hearing. The difficulty comes when we've already decided what the answer to our prayers should be. Wilson had decided that the answer to his prayer should be a straight-A report card. But that's not the way God had it worked out. Maybe God's answer was putting Mr. Wu in Wilson's life to help him learn how to study better. God *is* listening and helping us—*his* way.

When the Israelites were in the desert, they got kind of tired of eating manna (the food God gave them) every single day. So they prayed for a change. God's answer was to dump a whole ton of little birds called quail on their camp. But he wasn't too pleased with the complaining. Be content with God's answers to your prayer. What God gives you should be enough.

March 16

Science Needs Faith

Laurie had wanted to be a scientist as long as she could remember. Her dad had made her a room in the attic where she could study things. Today she was looking at microscopic creatures in pond water. Little one-celled animals buzzed around in the drop of water she was studying. The thing that worried Laurie was that scientists and Christians didn't seem to like each other very much. Could she still be a Christian and a scientist?

Words to Treasure

The heavens tell about the glory of God. The skies show that his hands created them.
Psalm 19:1

Science is about asking questions and finding answers. Faith is about asking questions and trusting God will help you with the answers. The important thing is to understand that God does know everything, and science is about learning about everything. If God is your teacher, can that be a bad thing? We know a lot about our amazing world, but there is still so much more to learn. There are still a lot of mysteries to solve both in science and about God. Many scientists have a strong belief and faith in God. Many believe that science helps them to become closer to God. So go explore the world with God as your guide and teacher.

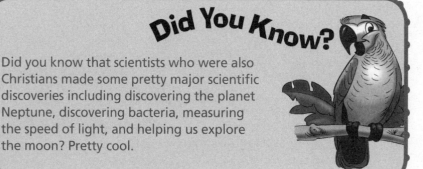

Did You Know?

Did you know that scientists who were also Christians made some pretty major scientific discoveries including discovering the planet Neptune, discovering bacteria, measuring the speed of light, and helping us explore the moon? Pretty cool.

March 17

Extreme

On TV, Allen watched the mountain bikers race down the hillside. They were riding over logs and splashing through deep mud holes. They were *awesome*! They were the toughest bunch of extreme athletes he had ever seen. Allen looked around the family room and turned off the television. He wasn't going to be an extreme biker if he sat around inside all day. He swung open the garage door and saw his own bike waiting for him there.

Words to Treasure

Young men are proud of their strength.

Proverbs 20:29

Allen was cruising the dirt trail behind his house. It wasn't a mountainside but it was a start. He hit a mud puddle and rode hard to get out of it. *Doing* was way better than watching it on TV.

Keeping your body healthy and working at peak performance is important. Your body is an amazing gift from God that allows you to go snowboarding, hiking, kayaking, mountain biking, or whatever you like to do. Being fit gives you staying power, speed, strength, great reflexes, and a positive outlook. And that goes for both guys and girls. Being fit doesn't require training for the Olympics every day, but it does mean getting off the couch and discovering exactly what kind of amazing athlete is in you.

Extreme sports aren't new! Wrestling was a hugely popular sport in ancient times. In some cities breaking your opponent's fingers was fair game. *That's* an extreme sport. And not very nice. Don't try that at home.

Don't Get You?

Coach Dave didn't look very happy. "I don't know what to say, Gary. Practice will be on Sunday morning. If you don't make practice every week, you can't play first string. I don't see why it's a question—the team needs you."

Gary felt his heart sink. He had worked hard to be first string on his hockey team, but he also felt he needed to be at church. He gave a heavy sigh. Now it came down to God or hockey? Gary wished he didn't have to make this choice. "Sorry, I won't be able to make Sunday practices, Coach."

Words to Treasure

Love the Lord your God with all your heart and with all your soul. Love him with all your strength and with all your mind.

Luke 10:27

Coach Dave looked disappointed. "Gary. I thought you were committed."

Gary picked up his skates. "I am. To church."

There will be times when people won't understand your close relationship with God. But that's not your problem. Putting God first in your life is never the wrong choice. When faced with choices, pray for God's direction, talk to Christians you respect, and then do what is right.

Did You Know?

Did you know sometimes even Jesus' own family didn't understand him? Jesus was constantly surrounded by crowds of people, and his family felt they had to take charge and rescue him. Some of them thought Jesus was out of his mind. So if people don't get you and your relationship with God, you're in good company. They didn't get Jesus sometimes either. (See Mark 3:20–21.)

March 19

The Reason Why

Donna was handing out baseballs at the dunking tank. Her youth pastor sat in the seat, waiting to splash down into the ice cold water in the tank. Donna had worked really hard to help make this the most amazing carnival they had ever had. They were raising money for a hospital in South America. She was proud of her hard work, but she was also hoping that people would notice how hard she worked. She took being a Christian more seriously than anybody else in her youth group, and she wanted people to notice that too.

Words to Treasure

Everything a person does might seem pure to them. But the LORD knows why they do what they do.

Proverbs 16:2

Stop that thought before it swells any bigger. Donna's pride is making her head the biggest thing at the carnival. Is she helping out to get attention, or is she there to make a difference? The *reason* we do something is the most important thing to God. Showing off is never a good reason to do anything, even something good.

A long time ago some people got together to build a really amazing city with an impressively tall tower. Sounds like a good idea, but let's look at the reason why. They wanted to show off and make a name for themselves. This city was all about pride. God was pretty unimpressed with this sky-high pride. In the end, the tower never got built, and God scattered the people in the city to far off places. He kind of busted their proud plans. (See Genesis 11:1–9.)

Leadership

Hinto looked at the compass, and Sally studied the map. If they had done everything right, there should be a bridge just over the hill. They were in a cross-country hiking race. Hinto, Thomas, and Sally climbed the steep path to the top and looked over the edge. Below was the bridge with race officials waiting to give them their next set of directions. The team slapped hands with great big smiles. Hinto put away his compass. "Good job, everybody. We're the first team here. We can rest at the bridge or keep going. I think we should keep going. What do you think? How do you feel?"

Words to Treasure

David cared for them with a faithful and honest heart. With skilled hands he led them.

Psalm 78:72

Sally handed out water bottles. "You're the team leader, Hinto, I go with what you say."

Thomas agreed.

"Let's get going." Hinto led the team down to the bridge to the shouts and claps of the people waiting.

An important part about being a leader is inspiring people to do their best. It's about listening to ideas and making sure everybody feels involved and respected. A good leader knows that he can't do it all alone and that his team helps him be a good leader. You can't lead if nobody wants to go where you're leading.

People in Bible Times

God offered Solomon *everything*: wealth, fame, and a powerful army. But Solomon asked only for wisdom to be a good leader. God gave him that and everything else. And Solomon ruled Israel with wisdom. (See 2 Chronicles 1:7–12.)

March 21

Humble Is

Rick stood on the theater stage looking a little nervous, but when he began to sing he completely forgot to be nervous. He remembered everything his singing teacher had said. He dropped his shoulders, relaxed, and had a good time just singing. He almost forgot he was singing in front of important people. When he finished, he waited for them to say something.

Words to Treasure

But he gives grace to those who are not proud.

Proverbs 3:34

"Rick, do you want to say anything?" the director of the play asked, looking very serious.

Rick cleared his throat. "Thank you for letting me try out for your play. I hope my best was what you are looking for."

The director sat back in his chair and smiled for the first time. "Well, Mr. Campbell, your best is exactly what we're looking for. Welcome to our show. We would like you to sing in our play."

Humble is not about bragging, trying to impress people, trying to get attention, or needing to be first. *Humble* is just being what God made you. And that's impressive enough without you saying a thing. Let people discover the amazing person you are without big talk. God loves a humble heart. Humble looks very good on you, and it goes with everything.

Did You Know?

Did you know that Moses was the most humble guy on the face of the earth? The guy just didn't know how to be too proud. And God took that humble man and stood him before kings. Humility looked good on Moses too.

March 22

New Neighbors?

Becky," her mother said as she handed her a tray of homemade lemon tarts. "We're going to take these over to the new neighbors."

Becky pulled a face, "I don't know what to say to them. They talk funny."

Her mother gave her a look. "They don't talk funny. They speak Greek. They just moved to this country, and they could use some friendliness. You don't have to speak the same language to be good friends and neighbors."

Words to Treasure

Love does not harm its neighbor.

Romans 13:10

The new neighbors, Mr. and Mrs. Papadis, insisted on inviting the entire family for dinner. Becky had to admit she had a great time. Becky even liked the squid, or calamari, with tzatziki sauce. Sometimes we're scared to meet people who are different from us. But that's not how God wants us to be. He wants us to be good neighbors to everyone we meet so we can share our differences and find lots in common.

Invite your friends over for an international potluck dinner and ask them to bring a favorite family dish that represents where their family came from. You could also bring some old family photographs and a good story to tell. Good food and good friends with a global twist.

March 23

Knockout Fear

The pictures on television were upsetting. Trish watched from the doorway of the family room, not wanting to get too close to them. Her parents watched the news every night, and every night the world seemed to get scarier and more dangerous. Weren't there any good people left in the world, and wasn't there any good news at all? Trish was so tired of feeling scared all the time.

Words to Treasure

Even though I walk through the darkest valley, I will not be afraid. You are with me.

Psalm 23:4

The world has always had hard and scary times. But now, we have instant television news showing us every bad thing that happens every day, everywhere around the world. But that's not the whole story. There are also many good things happening in our world. Really good things are happening every minute of every day. People are helping each other and taking care of our planet. And God is in charge of all of it. God doesn't want you to live in fear, because he is with you every minute of every day.

For two weeks, cut out of the newspaper only positive news about the world and watch only positive television shows. After you have a collection of good stories, go through them with your family. Talk about what you discovered and how you feel about the world now. Fear can't grow if you focus on what's good and hopeful in the world.

March 24

Come on In

Allison looked around the little apartment above their garage. Everything was ready. She left the basket of muffins and fruit on the table. Her family had made this little apartment for a very special reason. Her father was a doctor at the children's hospital, and he knew that many families from out of town needed a place to stay while their children were being helped at the hospital. So they invited families to stay here when they needed to be in town. It was her family's way of sharing what God had given them.

Words to Treasure

Don't forget to welcome outsiders. By doing that, some people have welcomed angels without knowing it.

Hebrews 13:2

Hospitality is showing strangers and friends kindness in your home. And hospitality is something God's really into. After all, he's sharing his world with billions of people … us. The Bible says not only should we share with people, but we also need to do it with a good attitude—no grumbling. Think of ways you and your family can spread a little kindness in your community. Who can you welcome to your home for a meal or a visit?

People in Bible Times

People in Bible times felt they should always offer kindness to strangers. In some areas, the land was very hot and very dangerous, so a traveler often needed protection, food, and water. Not to invite someone into your home was considered pretty rude. And not to accept someone's offer of hospitality was even ruder. (See Genesis 18:1–8.)

March 25

Wave-O-Rama

Moe was on the threshold of awesome. This was the largest indoor wave pool in the world. Five acres of indoor tropical paradise with water slides and bungee jumping. The pool was like a lagoon. The waves rolling across the pool were at least six feet high. The person who thought up this place had to be the coolest person on the planet. Even though it was snowing outside, it was wave-o-rama under the big glass ceiling.

Words to Treasure

I reached out my great and powerful arm. I made the earth. I made its people and animals. And I can give the earth to anyone I please.

Jeremiah 27:2

Pretty impressive all right. Now, imagine something even more amazing. Glaciers that touch the sky, huge oceans, massive rivers, deep jungles, and sand dunes like mountains. Our planet—our own amazingly colossal home created for us by God. Man makes some cool things, but God's creativity is ginormously beyond it. He makes everything wonderful. No competition.

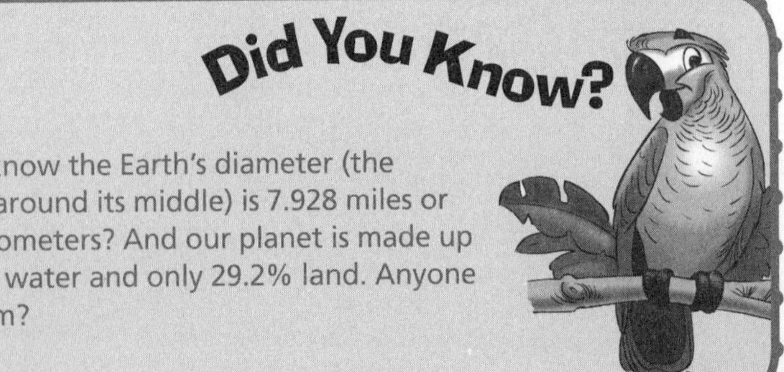

Did You Know?

Did you know the Earth's diameter (the distance around its middle) is 7.928 miles or 12760 kilometers? And our planet is made up of 70.8% water and only 29.2% land. Anyone for a swim?

March 26

What's Evil?

Phil and Min hardly noticed the other people leaving the movie theater because they were busy talking about the movie. Both agreed that the bad guy was pretty evil. He was pretty much all evil. But they started talking about what made him evil, and they couldn't decide what evil is. Is evil a person or a thing or what? Can you touch evil? Can you see evil?

Words to Treasure

So make sure that the light inside you is not darkness.

Luke 11:35

Evil isn't actually a thing or a person. It is kind of like darkness. What is darkness? Darkness can only happen when we don't have any light—no sunlight or light from a lamp. Darkness happens because there is a lack of light.

Same with evil. Evil is the lack of good. Evil can only happen if we shut out good the same way we do light. People can choose not to do right things, and that's a lot like sitting in a dark room in the middle of the day. Evil happens when people shut out good.

People in Bible Times

Jesus said we should be the light of the world. To put it another way, the *good* of the world. He said that we should let our light or goodness be seen in how we love God, love other people, and do things. When people see the light or good inside you, they will thank and praise the God who made you that way. (See Matthew 5:13–16.)

March 27

My Hero!

The smell of breakfast in the morning had to be just about the best smell in the whole world. Sarah slid down the banister and cruised into the kitchen—it was a good day. She glanced at the paper her dad was reading. Her good day just came to a bad stop. The person she most admired in the entire world ... the person she wanted to be exactly like ... the person whose poster was on her bedroom wall ... had cheated in a world sports competition! The thought made her not want to eat breakfast.

Words to Treasure

Some people in Jerusalem were thought to be important. But it makes no difference to me what they were. God does not treat people differently.

Galatians 2:6

We can admire famous people, but that doesn't mean we actually know them. Sometimes the person you admire may not be who you thought he or she was. Admiring famous people is fine, but don't stop there. Look around and see the amazing people right in your own family, school, and church.

There are people in your own town who aren't famous, rich, or successful. You won't find their pictures on bedroom walls, but they do amazing things to help others. They're heroes!

Talk to your parents, pastors, teachers, and coaches and ask them who they admire in your town or neighborhood. Ask them *why* they admire these people. Find out who the heroes are right in your neighborhood and school.

Kids Rock

Susie's uncle was practically falling into the open hood of his car and wasn't very happy about it. Her neighbor Thomas walked across the lawn and stood by the car. "Excuse me. Can I help?"

Susie's uncle glanced over his shoulder. "Help? Help with what? You're just a kid."

Thomas shrugged. "A kid that's been helping in his dad's auto repair shop since he was two. I can help if you want me to."

The man stopped working and sized up the kid beside him. "Really? You know about engines? Do you know why it's making that weird noise?"

Thomas grinned. "Sure do."

Don't let your age stop you from doing extraordinary things at school, at home, and at church. In fact, when it comes to being a good example and doing right things, age *just doesn't matter*. Ready or not, God's got an adventure waiting for you. You're an amazing person *right now,* so be prepared to do amazing things *right now*. Later is for the other guy.

Words to Treasure

Don't let anyone look down on you because you are young. Set an example for the believers in what you say and in how you live.

1 Timothy 4:12

Take the case of Jeremiah. One day God made Jeremiah his special prophet. But Jeremiah freaked out because he was just a kid. He wasn't ready to talk to nations and kings. But God thought being a kid was a good thing and just what he had in mind. Jeremiah was a kid *and* God's messenger.

March 29

Family?

Greg looked around the church. Some interesting looking kids were here. The girl with the purple hair, the kid with the strange shirt, and the little kid that never stopped talking. And now a seriously big guy was walking over to him. Was this a good thing or bad thing? Greg looked up—way up—and big giant dude looked down. What was going to happen now?

Words to Treasure

Be joyful with those who are joyful.

Romans 12:15

The big guy pulled out a cloth napkin. Okay, why is he doing that? And then, he made it disappear right before Greg's startled eyes. Greg stared at his huge, empty hands. Where did it go? Greg looked up, impressed, "How did you do that?" This supersized magic trick guy was all right. Okay, maybe coming to this youth group wasn't going to be a total nightmare waste of time.

Going to a new church can be like going to a family reunion with strangers. You're just not sure if this is the right family for you. Before you write somebody off at first glance, stop and get to know them better. That person could be your next lifelong friend.

Did You Know?

Did you know there's an idea that everybody on earth is connected to everybody else by knowing somebody who knows somebody else who knows somebody else who knows somebody who knows you? It's called "six degrees of separation." Confusing? In other words, you may be only five people away from knowing anybody on the planet.

Too Good for Whom?

Summer had waited in the line at the music store for two hours. She was waiting to have her autograph book signed by her favorite singer in the entire world. It was a long, long wait but now she was nearly at the front of the line. She had rehearsed and rehearsed what she was going to say to him. Then suddenly she was standing in front of him. But he was talking to a person beside him and, without even looking at her, he signed her book and slid it back. He didn't ask her name. She didn't talk to him. They didn't even make eye contact. He didn't know she existed!

Words to Treasure

Be willing to be a friend of people who aren't considered important.

Romans 12:16

Being ignored never feels good. Did you know that there might be people who look up to you too? It might be a younger brother or sister, someone in a younger grade at school, or someone in an activity you do. There are people who admire you and may be looking for an opportunity to talk with you. Take the time to be interested in other people, famous or not. God's watching how you treat others.

Do you know somebody at school, church, or in sports who might be having a hard time making friends? Take the time to get to know him or her. Maybe invite them to hang out with you and your friends. Take the time to be a friend to somebody who needs a friend.

March 31

First Impressions

Taylor watched the dolphins swim past in their lagoon. One dolphin swam up and chattered at him. Taylor was glad, but he felt uncomfortable. The collar of his best shirt made him hot, and his good shoes pinched because he had almost outgrown them. He wanted to put on his shorts and T-shirt, but this was his interview to try out for the junior volunteer program at the aquarium. The program director walked toward him with an impressed smile on his face. Suddenly a wall of cold water drenched Taylor's new shirt, best jeans, and tight shoes. The dolphin surfaced, pretty pleased with the results of his mega tail splash. The director laughed, "I guess Slick approves of you. Need a towel?" Taylor smiled and nodded.

Words to Treasure

Show proper respect to everyone.

1 Peter 2:17

Okay, not everybody is going to get a soaker when trying to make a good first impression. But first impressions are important. When we take the time to care about how we look, it tells people that we respect them and want them to think well of us. It tells people they can trust us to do a good job. First impressions are always the first step into new things.

Did You Know?

Did you know it takes only a few seconds for people to form ideas about you based on how you look and your body language? They can tell whether you look friendly, interested, or fun to be with, all before you even say a word.

By the Book

Chris heard the *thump, thump* of his friends playing basketball next door. He wanted to be out there, but he had homework. Chris stared at the blank piece of paper in his notebook. It was so white, so empty. He absolutely had to have a story written for class tomorrow morning. He had put it off for two days, and now his brain was empty of any ideas at all. *Thump, thump* went the basketball outside. Imagination, don't fail now! Suddenly Chris had a thought and started to write. "A strange thing happened while I was playing basketball the other day ..."

Words to Treasure

No prophecy in Scripture ever came from a prophet's own understanding of things.

2 Peter 1:20

Do you think the people who wrote the Bible had the same problem? Not really, because the Bible is different. God selected very special people to write down ideas, thoughts, and things that happened, things that God felt were important for us to know about. These people only wrote down what God told them, so even though the Bible is made up of different parts written by different people, all of it is God's own words and thoughts. It's God's gift to us, written with the help of some friends.

Discovering Archaeology

The Dead Sea is a very salty lake near Jerusalem. In eleven caves near there, people found over 800 scrolls written by people in Bible times. Those ancient books are called the Dead Sea Scrolls, and they are some of the oldest-known Bible writings in the world.

April 2

Easter

In her mind, Sophie traveled back two thousand years and imagined the soft wind in the trees, the feel of the pathway under her feet, and the other women quietly talking as they approached the burial grounds. How would she have felt that first Easter as they stood before angels sitting on the large stone that had once covered the entrance of Jesus' tomb? The heavenly creatures shone like lightning, and beside them were guards so frightened they shook. But the angel spoke kindly to the women, "Don't be afraid. I know that you are looking for Jesus, who was crucified. He is not here! He has risen, just as he said he would." Sophie imagined her sadness being lifted away. She had seen his lifeless body days before but now Jesus wasn't dead. He was ALIVE!!! Everything he had said was true!

Words to Treasure

"Why do you look for the living among the dead? Jesus is not here! He has risen!"

Luke 24:5–6

That morning is as important today as it was thousands of years ago. It was God's amazing surprise for mankind. Jesus took away our sins when he died, rose again, and allowed us to have a closer relationship with our heavenly Father. Stop and think about it this Easter.

In Jesus' time people often buried their dead in caves. Rich people would have caves or tombs carved in the sides of hills and poor people would have been buried in the ground.

Good Morning World!

Skye held on tightly. When the camel walked, it felt like she was riding waves. Skye liked the smell of the desert as they headed up the mountain. Her camel was named Pepper. The moon was out, but soon they would be at the summit. This mountain in Egypt is where people say Moses went to meet God. The Bible calls it Mount Sinai. Skye watched the sun rise over the Sinai Desert. The world below her turned to shades of red, orange, and yellow as the desert greeted a new day. It was so beautiful she almost cried. She wondered if Moses felt the same way when he saw the morning from way up high.

Words to Treasure

The Lord came down to the top of Mount Sinai. He told Moses to come to the top of the mountain. So Moses went up.

Exodus 19:20

Sometimes it's hard to imagine that people in the Bible like Moses, King David, or Joseph were real people doing real things and feeling real emotions just like us. But they did. They walked They hiked. They smiled. They cried. Check out their stories in the Bible.

Arabian camels have been used for transportation for thousands of years. They can travel huge distances with very little food or water. In the Bible, Abraham had his own herd of those desert traveling marvels and Job had an epic number of 6,000 camels.

April 4

Pray for You

His dad had on more gear than a gladiator in Rome. He had bought a helmet, wrist guards, knee guards, shin guards, elbow guards, and shoulder and chin guards. Troy and his dad stood at the top of a long, winding steep road. Troy had serious doubts about his dad's new interest in longboarding. "Are you sure you want to do this, Dad?"

Words to Treasure

In all my prayers for all of you, I always pray with joy.
Philippians 1:4

Troy's dad furrowed his eyebrows, "You boys ride this hill all the time? It's a good ride, right?"

"Sure, but I don't think you're ready for this." Troy had a bad feeling about this. His dad put on his expensive sunglasses and pushed off down the hill. Troy called after him. "I'll pray for you, Dad. Big prayer!" Troy pushed off to follow his dad. "You'll need it."

Did you know that the adults who love you usually spend some time praying and talking to God about you? That's right, you have your own personal fan club, with the Lord of the universe as president and chief of operations. Your club wants good things for you in the future.

Do you spend time praying for the adults in your life? Maybe it's time to include a little prayer time for adults when you are talking with God.

Hey, ask your parents if they have some things they'd like you to pray about for them or the entire family. Then every night you can talk to God about those things.

Ordinary People

Christa was very, very quiet for a very long time, but still she couldn't hear anything—nothing, nada, zip, silence. This wasn't going to work. She wasn't hearing God. She didn't even know what he was supposed to sound like. Why did God talk only to those special guys in the Bible?

Words to Treasure

God spoke to Israel in a vision at night.

Genesis 46:2

Those special people were called prophets. They were special but also pretty ordinary people—ordinary people who happened to hear from God. They were fisherman, shepherds, farmers, slaves, tentmakers, and kings. They were ordinary people like you but with an extraordinary close friendship with God. They loved God, and hey, so do you. That works!

God *does* talk to us even today. Sometimes we hear him in our minds and hearts, and sometimes God talks to us through the things people say to us or through things that happen to us. Sometimes he talks to us through what we read in the Bible or through answers to our prayers and the prayers of other people for us. God is talking to us, but we have to learn to listen in new ways.

A prophet named Amos wasn't a priest or a person with religious training; he was a farmer, shepherd, and merchant. But God gave Amos an assignment, and he was ready for the job.

April 6

We Have to Talk!

Jack looked at his book report. He was so angry. It was a masterpiece, perfect in every way, but he had only gotten a B-minus. It was mind-boggling that Mrs. Carter couldn't see the brilliance in his work. This was unfair, a travesty of justice ... although he wasn't sure what that meant.

Words to Treasure

I will make a covenant with you that will last forever. I will give you my faithful love.

Isaiah 55:3

"Jack?" Mrs. Carter noticed his upset face. "Would you like to talk?" He sure did!

Can you be mad at God in the same way that you can be upset with your teacher or parents? Can you be upset with God? Moses, Elijah, and Job all were. Did they quit believing in God or ignore him? No, they talked to God about their unhappy feelings.

God understands our feelings and wants us to be honest with him about everything. But that doesn't mean he'll change the way things are going. Because sometimes we simply don't see the big picture of why God does things the way he does. Just keep trusting in God's love in all situations. He knows what's best, and he's there when you need to talk.

People in Bible Times

The prophet Elijah was having a hard time because he was the center of a prophet manhunt. Everybody wanted to kill him, and he wanted to quit being a prophet. God listened to Elijah's fears and complaints. He sent angels to take care of Elijah, and then he had a heart-to-heart with his prophet. Elijah was both humbled and encouraged. (See 1Kings 19:1–18.)

What Is Heaven Like?

The giraffe reached up and with long lips pulled at the leaves of the tall savannah tree. Not far away, little gazelles flicked their tails as they grazed. The guide, Neo, pointed to a leopard sleeping in a tree across the clearing. Wow! His eyesight was amazing! Meg could hardly see the cat sleeping in the shade. Neo passed Meg the binoculars. She took in the scene and wondered if heaven could be this beautiful. Could anything be this beautiful?

Words to Treasure

Do not let your hearts be troubled. You believe in God. Believe in me also.

John 14:1

That's a question people have been asking for thousands of years: What is heaven like? And where is it? Nobody knows the answers, because that's one of the mysteries of life. Think of the most beautiful place on earth, and know that heaven will be even better. Heaven will be *amazingly everything good.* Jesus said that in his Father's house are many rooms. And God is preparing a place for the people he loves, a special place for each of us. Jesus asked us not to worry, but to trust our entire future to him. The one thing we can be sure of is that heaven won't be a disappointment. In God we trust.

Did You Know?

The prophet Elijah didn't experience death as we know it. Instead, he was suddenly taken up to heaven on a horse-drawn chariot that rode on a strong wind. What an incredible and surprising exit for an incredible and surprising man of God. (See 2 Kings 2:11–12.)

April 8

Girls Plus

Girls can't be heroes." Randy said it as if it were a fact. He adjusted his snow goggles while he sat on the chair lift.

Words to Treasure

In those days, I will pour out my Spirit on my servants. I will pour out my Spirit on both men and women.

Acts 2:18

"Excuse me?" Amy couldn't believe what she was hearing.

Alex shrugged. "He's right."

Amy shoved her hands in her jacket pockets. "He is not."

Randy started to rock the chair. "Women are weak and scream all the time. Heroes don't scream."

Alex nodded. "He's right."

Amy held onto the swaying chair. Randy continued to swing the chair. "Scared yet, Amy? Going to scream?"

"Yes," she said as she adjusted her helmet in frustration. "I'm sitting with gorillas."

Heroes come in all sizes and sexes. It might surprise Randy that the Bible is full of female heroes. God uses both men and women to change the world and spread his word. So move over Samson, Gideon, and Joshua and make room for women such as Esther, Miriam, Mary, and Deborah, to name a few. Check out their stories in the Bible. There's nothing weak about them.

Did You Know?

Did you know that a woman named Deborah was a wife, a prophet, and the leader of Israel? Not only did she lead an army against a bad-news Canaanite general named Sisera, but with God's help and her strong leadership, Israel beat him fair and square. Women heroes—God's got them covered. (See Judges 4:1–23.)

Smart Guy

Tommy was about to open the door to the Learning Assistance Room. A kid behind him sniggered. "That room's for dummies."

Tommy turned around, "I'm dyslexic, which means my brain works differently than yours. But if I'm stupid, so are Albert Einstein, John Lennon, Thomas Edison, and Henry Ford. If they're dummies, so am I." The boy didn't know what to say.

Words to Treasure

Then the Lord God formed a man. He made him out of the dust of the ground. God breathed the breath of life into him. And the man became a living person.

Genesis 2:7

The simple truth is that we're not all made the same way. But that's all good. Some people are great at some things and not at others. Some people can sing, some are good at sports, and some people learn different ways. It doesn't mean one person is better than another; it just means we do things differently. Tommy mentioned some extraordinary people who learned in different ways. They may have had trouble with some things like reading but were incredible at other things such as inventing things, acting, or unlocking some of earth's mysteries. They were creative, talented, and successful at what they loved doing. God made you exactly the way you are with no mistakes. If you ask God, he will show you how to turn your brain into the most amazing machine around. You've got what it takes!

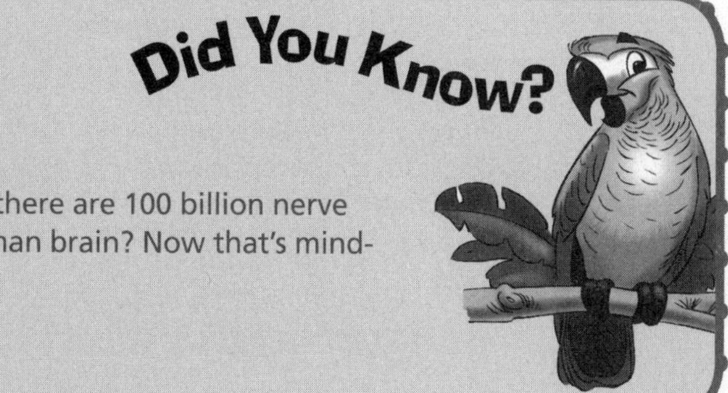

Did you know there are 100 billion nerve cells in the human brain? Now that's mind-boggling!

April 10

All Dogs?

Max walked slowly, letting his dog Scout catch up. The old dog still liked a walk, but not very far and not very fast. His parents had told Max that someday soon Scout would die of old age. It didn't seem fair that you can love dogs so much but they die before you want them to. A dog should live as long as you do. Scout finally caught up, and Max stroked his dog's head as they walked in the park. Max wondered, *When I am old and die, will Scout be waiting for me in heaven?*

Words to Treasure

Who can tell whether the spirit of an animal goes down into the earth?

Ecclesiastes 3:21

That's a good question, but it's kind of unanswerable. The Bible doesn't really tell us if animals go to heaven or not. Some Christians believe they will see their pets in heaven, and others feel they won't because animals are different from humans. Animals don't have the same type of soul that God gave people. The only thing for sure about this question is that only God knows the answer. So love your pet and give it a good life with you. The Bible does say, "Those who do what is right take good care of their animals" (Proverbs 12:10).

Today's Canaan dogs are direct descendants of the dogs used in ancient Israel for herding sheep. They are smart, quick, and very protective.

Taking Care of Business

Judy and Rosa walked carefully along the riverbank carrying jars with small baby salmon in them. They had hatched them from eggs in their classroom. The little fish were now ready to be released back into the stream. Judy had named her fish Fido, and Rosa had named her fish Willy. Their teacher said that Fido and Willy would swim downstream to the ocean to live and then swim back later to have babies. Because Chinook salmon are an endangered species, Judy felt good that she was doing something to help baby Fido and the environment.

Words to Treasure

God saw everything he had made. And it was very good.
Genesis 1:31

God made our planet, and he expects us to take good care of this awesome gift. There are many areas in our world where animals and natural areas are in danger of being destroyed. What can we do? We have to do our part by doing things such as recycling and getting involved in programs or organizations that help our natural world. Judy is helping salmon in her community. What are you doing?

Did You Know?

God decided that man was pretty wicked (and he didn't mean that in a cool, good way), and he decided to flood the world to get rid of all the evil people. But God wanted to protect the animals he created, so he told Noah to build a huge ship to save two of each animal. God had an ecological super plan, and so should we. What can you do to help our world and the animals in it? (See Genesis 6–9.)

April 12

Wrong Move

Teddy leapt into the air and landed hard on Mike. He did the wrestling move exactly right, but he wasn't exactly expecting the funny snapping noise and Mike's howls of pain. "Get off! Get off me!!" Mike cried loudly. Teddy got off and saw Mike's arm looking kind of odd and twisted.

Words to Treasure

Increase my knowledge and give me good sense, because I believe in your commands.

Psalm 119:66

Mr. Lucas raced into the bedroom. "What happened?" He looked at his son's arm and asked again. "What happened?"

Teddy looked worried, "We were just wrestling like on TV."

"Well," Mr. Lucas said as he helped Mike sit up. "Looks like we'll be taking a trip to the hospital."

Important information: Many, many of the things we see on television should stay on television. Professionals on television do all kinds of things that are dangerous and should never be tried by kids. They know how to make stunts look real, or they have special equipment to help them. Television or movie stunts may seem like cool things to try, but getting hurt isn't impressive. Making good safe choices is all about having good judgment. God made you smart, so making smart choices should be your first move. Play safe!

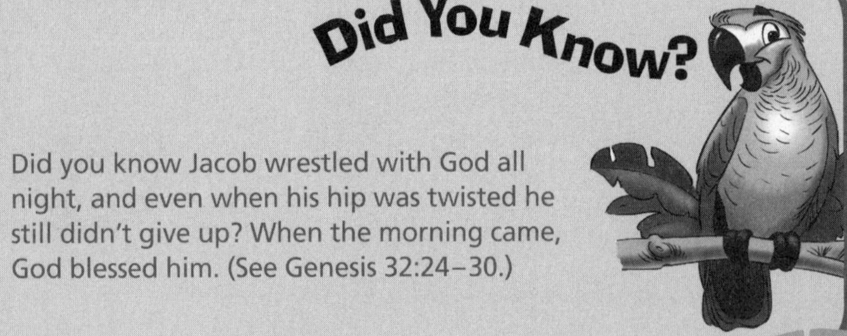

Did you know Jacob wrestled with God all night, and even when his hip was twisted he still didn't give up? When the morning came, God blessed him. (See Genesis 32:24–30.)

Something Fishy

Sheila sat on a rock staring down at the huge fish trying to swim up the river. Salmon were heading upstream to lay their eggs. Her friend James and his people had been fishing this river for thousands of years. James' uncle walked by with a huge forty-pound fish in his hands. He smiled at them, "This one is for tonight. Sheila, you staying for dinner?"

She nodded, "Yes please. We just buy our fish at the store."

James leaned on her shoulder. "We like it old school like how our ancestors did it. Except Uncle Jack buys his BBQ sauce from the store. Ssssh, don't tell anyone. He claims his sauce is an ancient family secret."

In Jesus' time, people had been fishing for thousands of years just like James' family. It was a tradition passed on from family to family. Do you have some family traditions? Ask your parents how they started? One tradition that's been handed down generation after generation is telling Bible stories and sharing God's truth. Will you help pass it on?

Words to Treasure

"Honor your father and mother. Then you will live a long time in the land the LORD your God is giving you."
Exodus 20:12

In Jesus' time, the place to fish was the Sea of Galilee. Funny enough, the Sea of Galilee is actually the largest freshwater lake in Israel. There were over twenty different types of fish in the lake. Would you like your fish roasted or pan-fried?

April 14

Things Happen

Jordan was exhausted from the long hike, but he stopped short at the edge of the parking lot where they had left their car. Their car was rocking back and forth as a fat black bear was halfway into their destroyed front window. Each move of his back legs scratched more paint off the car.

Words to Treasure

Brothers and sisters, don't ever get tired of doing the right thing.

2 Thessalonians 3:13

"Oh, no!" His dad took off his backpack.

"Dad." Jordan watched the bear disappear inside their car. "He's trashing our car. Shouldn't we go scare him away?"

"No, it's safer to wait here until he's done." His dad took a photograph. "We're going to have one good story to tell when we get home."

"But Dad." Jordan watched as the bear pulled himself out of the window. "We didn't leave any food in the car. We did everything right."

"I know. But some people do leave food in their cars and that attracts bears." His dad dialed his cell phone. "Hello, I'd like to report a bear breaking into cars. Thanks, I'll hold. No, we won't go near the bear."

Sometimes even though we do everything right, things can still go wrong. Life's like that. Just keep doing what's right even when things go wrong. Doing right is always right.

Brown bears were pretty common in ancient Israel. When King David was a shepherd, he protected young lambs from hungry bears.

Best Advice

Coop called Samuel over to the group. Airplanes buzzed over their heads. The skydivers stood beside their plane. Coop put his hand on Samuel's shoulder. "These are my top two pieces of advice for you. Always check your rig before you go up, and always pray before every jump." The group formed a circle and prayed.

Words to Treasure

But those who are wise listen to advice.

Proverbs 12:15

Coop and Samuel were jumping in tandem, meaning they were jumping together with one parachute. Samuel felt the rush of air and the big space outside the plane as he jumped out the door. Samuel glanced up to see the plane flying away and looked down to see the world far below. He *was* flying! Okay, falling. With a sudden jerk, the parachute opened and he was drifting on the air far above a world of little farms, cars, and roads.

Before we do anything new, taking good advice from experienced people is important. They know important stuff that we need to know. Wise words can change your world and give you a better landing.

People in Bible Times

Before King David died, he gave his son Solomon these wise words on being a good king and ordinary guy. "Do everything the Lord your God requires. Live the way he wants you to. Obey his orders and commands. Keep his laws and rules. Do everything written in the Law of Moses Then you will have success in everything you do" (1 Kings 2:3).

April 16

New Start

The man on the street corner pointed at Cheng with his worn-out Bible. "You need to be born again!"

Words to Treasure

Jesus replied, "What I'm about to tell you is true. No one can see God's kingdom without being born again."
John 3:3

Cheng was a little afraid of the wild-eyed man and turned to his dad. "Born again? How can we do that?"

His dad laughed. "It's a different kind of being born. Let's go have hot chocolate and talk about it."

Being born again has nothing to do with the birth of babies. So relax, there's nothing to get grossed out about. Jesus said that when we are born as babies, that's the birth of our bodies. But when we are born again, that's a new start for our souls or spirits. We don't really have a choice about whether we want to be born or not, but we do have a choice about whether we want to be born again in Jesus. Being born again means giving your entire self to Jesus by believing in him. It means wanting a close relationship with God, Jesus, and the Holy Spirit by loving God with all your heart, mind, and spirit forever.

The apostle Paul wrote that when we decide to be born again we receive a brand-new spiritual connection with God, Jesus, and the Holy Spirit. It's as if we are adopted by God. Our parents love us, and now God also becomes our heavenly parent. Being born again means we become God's kids too. (See Romans 8:14–17.)

Take My Advice

The boat was bobbing in the current and drifting down the slow, lazy river. Leo was getting a little nervous while his grandfather tried to fix the boat motor. "Grandpa, have you tried—"

Grandpa snapped back, not letting Leo finish. "Don't tell me about motors. I know everything about motors."

"But Grandpa ..." Leo tried to talk again but got a big grumpy "Sssssssh-hhhhh!" from the older man. It was growing too dark to be out on the water. "Grandpa, would you listen to me one minute?" Finally, Grandpa turned around and listened. "Did you check the gas tank?" Leo asked.

"Of course, I checked the—" Grandpa stopped short. He tapped the gas gauge and then opened the tank and stuck a rod in it. He pulled it out and examined the gas level. Empty. The gas gauge was broken. They put more gas in the tank and were soon heading for home. Grandpa chuckled to himself. "I guess I should listen to my grandson more often."

Always remember that even though you're young, you have important things to say.

Words to Treasure

Plans fail without good advice. But they succeed when there are many advisers.

Proverbs 15:22

People in Bible Times

A great general named Naaman was very sick, but he was smart enough to listen to the advice of a young slave girl. She told him to go visit a prophet to get healed. She was just a slave girl, but her advice came from God. Naaman was healed because of a girl with good advice.

April 18

Too Much Yelling!

Sandy closed the door to her room and flopped down on her bed with her pillow over her head. Her brothers and sisters were fighting again. At her house everybody yelled. They were always having fights—loud ones. She yelled at her brothers and sisters; they yelled at her. Everything just seemed so jumbled and angry all the time. Was this the way all siblings acted? When would the yelling stop?

Words to Treasure

People should listen to the quiet words of those who are wise. That's better than paying attention to the shouts of a ruler of foolish people.

Ecclesiastes 9:17

Sometimes fighting, yelling, and getting angry becomes a bad family habit. How much yelling is too much? That's hard to say. But you can start to change this habit by not yelling at your brothers and sisters. Talk to your parents about how this loud fighting makes you feel inside. Programs through your school, your church, or your community can help your family find a different way of talking to each other. Talking about it can be the best way of turning down the volume on conflicts.

In ancient times, families tended to be large and might include grandparents, parents, and children living in the same home. Most family disputes were settled by the grandfather or father, and what they said was the last word.

People Notice

Peterson ran off the field to get the soccer ball, but instead of handing it to the other team, he just dropped it on the ground and walked away. That was *rude*. Coach Dillon watched Peterson, and he didn't like what he saw. Peterson had scored three goals, but his behavior was terrible. He had argued with the referee, yelled at his own teammates, hogged the ball, and called the other team's players names. Peterson was a walking, talking bad attitude. The fact that he was the highest goal-scorer on the team just gave him an enormous ego and even more of a problem.

Words to Treasure

But his heart became very stubborn and proud. So he was removed from his royal throne.

Daniel 5:20

After the game, Coach Dillon called Peterson over. "You scored a lot of goals today. But you're not a team player. In fact, your behavior out there is rude and embarrassing. I can't have a team captain acting like that, so I'm going to make Rick the new team captain. You need to clean up your act." Peterson was shocked all over.

Being good at something also means having a good attitude and treating other people with respect. Good sportsmanship in everything you do makes you the best.

People in Bible Times

God gave success to the tough guy king, Nebuchadnezzar. His Babylonian empire was huge and powerful. But this king got proud, so God took away every good thing he had blessed Nebuchadnezzar with, and then some. Neb went from a powerful king to living like a wild donkey. Attitude counts!

April 20

Don't Go There!

Stacy showed her mom the party invitation. Brittany was having a fortune-telling birthday party. A lady would be there to tell their fortunes, and then they would play with an Ouija board, a game that asks spirits to talk to you through a board with numbers and letters. All the birthday guests were supposed to come dressed up like fortune-tellers or ghosts. These were all things that Stacy knew that she should avoid. She was disappointed not to go to the party, but she wanted to do what was right.

Words to Treasure

But anyone who lives by the truth comes into the light.
John 3:21

Fortune-telling, practicing spells, playing with Ouija boards, and doing séances are all things we should stay away from completely. They are not cool or fun but connected to dark things. Jesus talked about being a godly light to everyone around you. That makes God proud. So dark is out, and light is right.

Here's a list of things God hates and doesn't want you to do:

- Don't practice evil magic.
- Don't use magic to try to explain warnings in the sky or other signs.
- Don't worship evil powers.
- Don't talk to dead people.

It's fun to do scary things like going to a suspenseful movie or riding a roller coaster. But trying to get scared by doing wrong things is clearly off limits. Go ride a roller coaster instead. (See Deuteronomy 18:9–12.)

Where's the Meat?

Douglas was eating a ham sandwich just the way he liked it when Patty sat down beside him. She opened her tub of pasta, but she didn't look very happy. "How can you eat meat? You're eating a poor defenseless animal. Pigs are very smart, you know." She looked down her glasses at him. "I'm a vegetarian. I don't eat dead animals."

Douglas took a bite of ham and smiled, "How nice for you. If you're trying to make me feel guilty, it's not working." He talked with his mouth full, "I *love* meat."

Words to Treasure

He gives you crops in their seasons. He provides you with plenty of food.

Acts 14:17

Ask people what the Bible says about whether we should eat only vegetables, and they'll all have a different answer. It is one of those gray areas where it appears God has left it up to us to decide what is best. The important thing to know is he has provided you with a world that is designed to give your body all the things it needs to stay strong and healthy. So whether you grab a burger or a carrot stick, the bottom line is to respect other people's choices, and they will respect yours.

In ancient times, fruit and vegetables were eaten fresh, cooked, or often dried so they could be stored for later use. Meat was eaten, but certainly not as much meat as we eat today. People ate fish, goat, lamb, beef, and birds.

April 22

Problems Can Be Good

Why do bad things always happen to me?" Grace climbed back on her fun board and looked at her foot. She had cut her foot on some coral, and it was bleeding all over. Razor sharp coral was all over the waters of the Hawaiian Islands. It wasn't a big cut, but it needed attention. This was such a downer, because today was one of those perfect spring vacation windsurfing days. Now she'd have to sail in. Grace watched the other kids zip over the waves. Her aunts and uncles waved as they tried to get their sails out of the water. You could tell they didn't live by the ocean.

Words to Treasure

It was good for me to suffer. That's what helped me to understand your orders.

Psalm 119:71

Her mom examined her foot. "Well, you won't be going back out today. Actually, this could be a good thing. I could use some help with your little cousins until your aunts and uncles come back in from their sail lesson. They don't get a chance to windsurf every day like we do. So it's nice that we can babysit for them."

Not all "bad" things that happen to us are evil and wrong. Sometimes God allows things to happen so we learn something important. Grace learned that maybe today was more about sharing her beach with family than enjoying it by herself.

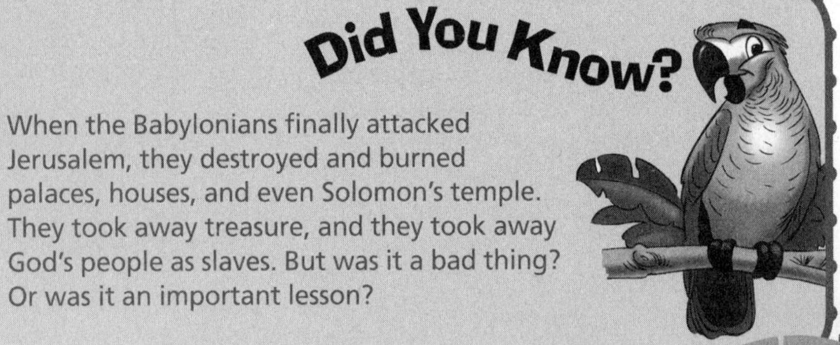

Did You Know?

When the Babylonians finally attacked Jerusalem, they destroyed and burned palaces, houses, and even Solomon's temple. They took away treasure, and they took away God's people as slaves. But was it a bad thing? Or was it an important lesson?

Not Just One in a Crowd

One minute Amy was one person alone in a strange, crowded airport, afraid she had been forgotten. The next minute a huge man was hugging her right off her feet. Her Uncle Ronnie swung her around. "Welcome to England, love!" Soon a mob of relatives was hugging her and talking to her all at once. She was swept away by aunts, uncles, and cousins all happy to see their Canadian cousin. She wasn't alone in the crowd—she was the reason there *was* a crowd.

Words to Treasure

My door was always open to travelers.

Job 31:32

Some people think that God created our world and then just kind of took off to parts unknown; that he's only interested in creating stuff and not in sticking around to love each of us every day. But that's not true. God lives in the small details of his world, and you're one of them. You are front and center in his thoughts. God's got your picture on his desk.

Jesus was walking through a huge crowd of people when a sick woman reached out to touch his cloak, believing that action would heal her. It did! But Jesus felt the power of healing leave him and turned suddenly, looking through the crowd to find her. She fell at his feet, afraid, but Jesus was pleased with her faith and blessed her. He cared about that one woman in a crowd of people. God cares about you in a world full of people. (See Mark 5:25–34.)

April 24

The Mission

The Mexican afternoon was hot, and Pedro was feeling the heat up on the roof of the small house they were building for a needy family. As he worked he watched one of the girls on the team play with the children of the neighborhood. And the more she played, the more it bugged him. He was working hard to help get this house finished, and she was goofing around doing kid stuff. He wanted to climb down and tell her off. This house wasn't going to build itself.

Words to Treasure

We are God's creation. He created us to belong to Christ Jesus. Now we can do good works.

Ephesians 2:10

Pedro is right and Pedro is wrong. Building a home for a needy family is fantastic, but getting to know the family is also just as important. We need both. Doing good works without good friendships with people doesn't really work, because building the house ends up becoming more important than the people who will live in it. To do good things we need both work and love in equal parts.

People in Bible Times

A woman named Martha opened her home to Jesus and his friends. She was busy being the perfect host while her sister Mary sat at Jesus' feet listening and enjoying the company. This really bugged Martha, because she was doing all the work. Finally she asked Jesus to tell Mary to help her. But Jesus told Martha to stop worrying about things. Mary's choice was a good one. (See Luke 10:38–42.)

April 25

A Lot to Learn

Zac looked up the palm tree, a little uncertain. His friend Adan laughed as he quickly climbed to the top of his tree, the bottoms of his feet firmly pressed against the tree trunk. Zac started his climb, but he only got a few feet up and had to jump down. His climbing skills needed work.

Zac wished he didn't have to leave Adan's village so soon, because he had learned so many new things from his friend, such as fishing with a net and how to use a machete to clear a path in the forest. Adan's people had been living this way for thousands of years. Zac had learned one important thing: having computers and video games didn't make his world better or more important—just different. When we start thinking that the way we live and where we live is the best, it's time to go explore the world and do a little rethinking. God created a big world, and there are lots of different ways to live in it.

Words to Treasure

Or is God the God of Jews only? Isn't he also the God of Gentiles? Yes, he is their God too.

Romans 3:29

Discovering Archaeology

Archaeologists digging at Herod the Great's palace in Israel found 2,000-year-old Judean date palm seeds. In 2005 they planted some of the seeds, and one of them sprouted and is still growing today. Wow, a 2,000-year-old plant! What's the expiration date on those dates?

The E Word

Wes only intended to go over and check out Brendon's new mountain bike. It was absolutely Wes' dream bike, and here it was, just dumped on the wet lawn. Brendon didn't deserve a bike like this. Before he knew what was happening, Wes was riding the bike down the road. Only a test drive. But he was so distracted that he didn't see the car pulling out of the driveway. He hit the car and flew over the hood onto the ground. He knew without looking that both he and Brendon's new bike were trashed.

Words to Treasure

A peaceful heart gives life to the body. But jealousy rots the bones.

Proverbs 14:30

Envy is wanting something that somebody else has. It's a big bad dog of an emotion that, when out of control, can bite us when we least expect it. It can make us do crazy wrong things because we get full of jealousy and anger. How do we stop it? Be content with what we have and work hard to follow our *own* dreams.

People in Bible Times

Genesis 4:1–16 is the story of two brothers, Cain and Abel. Cain was a gardener, and Abel was a shepherd. Both men presented offerings to God Abel always made sure he gave God only the best from his flock. God was very pleased with him but not so much with Cain. Instead of giving God his best crop Cain offered his worst stuff. And, then he got the worst case of brother jealousy and envy in history and killed his brother Abel in a rage. Envy = evil.

Ignore It!

Joey, Wendy, and Sandra felt sick as they walked through the community garden they had made in a vacant lot. They had gone through a lot of trouble to get permission to make the garden. Yesterday they had tomatoes, bean plants, and boxes full of flowers. But last night somebody destroyed it all.

"What are we going to do? Everything's wrecked." Wendy said.

Joey eyed some teenagers watching from across the street. They were smirking and looking pretty pleased. Joey started cleaning up. "We replant what we can, and we get some more seeds. We don't give up." He looked across the street at the teens. "If we give up, they win."

Words to Treasure

Sanballat heard that we were rebuilding the wall. So he became very angry and upset. He made fun of the Jews. He spoke to his friends and the army of Samaria. He said, "What are those Jews trying to do? Can they make their city wall like new again?"

Nehemiah 4:1-2

Joey, Wendy, and Sandra were trying to do something good for their neighborhood, but not everybody shared their good intentions. There were people in the Bible who wanted to do great things for their cities and ran into problems just like Joey, Wendy, and Sandra. But Joey had the right idea! Just keep trying no matter what.

People in Bible Times

Nehemiah and his gang were rebuilding the wall around Jerusalem, but not everybody thought it was a good idea. They didn't want a strong city again. First they made fun of the workers, and when that didn't work, they planned to kill the workers. Did they stop building? Find out in the Book of Nehemiah.

April 28

Watch It!

Joey, Wendy, and Sandra went back to the neighborhood garden only to discover it completely trashed *again!*

> **Words to Treasure**
>
> From that day on, half of my men did the work. The other half were given spears, shields, bows, and armor.
>
> Nehemiah 4:16

Joey picked up a broken bean plant. "We can't keep rebuilding the garden every morning."

Sandra looked at the apartment buildings overlooking the garden and got a brilliant idea. "What if we did a block watch? People could take turns watching the garden from their apartment windows."

They knocked on doors and talked to neighbors about the garden. People were willing to watch over and protect the garden. Now it wasn't just their garden anymore; it was everybody's garden!

Wendy painted a big sign and posted it on the garden fence. "Garden Under 24/7 Surveillance. Vandals Will Be Promptly Reported to Police." Would this plan work?

When good people work together, evil finds it harder to get in there and mess things up. When God is on your side and you work together, anything is possible.

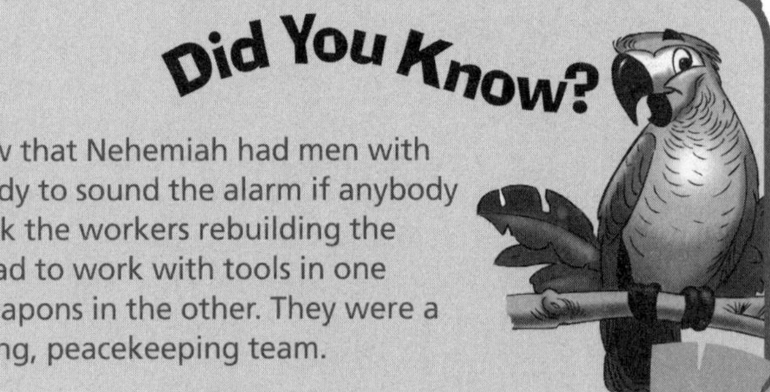

Did You Know?

Did you know that Nehemiah had men with trumpets ready to sound the alarm if anybody tried to attack the workers rebuilding the wall? They had to work with tools in one hand and weapons in the other. They were a wall-rebuilding, peacekeeping team.

What Do Heroes Do?

It was midnight. In the garden, the guys were pulling up plants and joking around and having a good time. Suddenly the garden was flooded with light. The vandals blinked as dozens of flashlight beams completely surrounded them. They had no place to go and no place to hide. They had been caught in the act of garden destruction. A figure stepped out of the light. "Smile!" Joey took a couple of photographs and gave a little wave. "How about a group shot?" The guys didn't know what to do or say. Suddenly a police car pulled up with lights flashing. Now the guys had a lot of explaining to do to everyone.

Words to Treasure

Speak up for those who can't speak for themselves. Speak up for the rights of all those who are poor.

Proverbs 31: 8

Heroes stand up for what's right. They fight all kinds of wrongs—big ones and little ones. That doesn't have to mean physical beat-'em-ups. Usually, it means finding peaceful ways to help others and stopping evil from happening.

In Bible times, many leaders were greedy and made their people pay more taxes than they could afford. Some moms and dads had to sell their children into slavery to pay their debts. This was happening in Jerusalem but, our hero Nehemiah stood up to those bad leaders and made them promise to stop. They did. It helped that Nehemiah had God and powerful King Artaxerxes on his side.

April 30

Together at Last

Joey, Wendy, and Sandra and the neighborhood of "good Samaritan" guardians not only protected the community garden from vandals, but also started working in the garden. Now, the neighbors felt that it was their garden too. People bought more seeds, brought in new plants to plant, and hammered together more garden boxes. Someone even donated a fountain for the middle, with a couple of benches to sit on.

Words to Treasure

So my God gave me the idea and encouraged me to gather the people together.
Nehemiah 7:5

Soon birds, butterflies, and even little frogs had found their way to the pretty neighborhood garden. And every evening, people would stroll and talk in the garden. Neighbors got to know neighbors they had never met before. The garden soon became the gathering place for everybody.

Where there had once been just trash and dirt, now there was a little bit of paradise in the big city. All because of neighborhood heroes and the never-give-up threesome: Joey, Wendy, and Sandra!

A garden isn't really a garden until people enjoy it together. After all, God created our planet to share with each other.

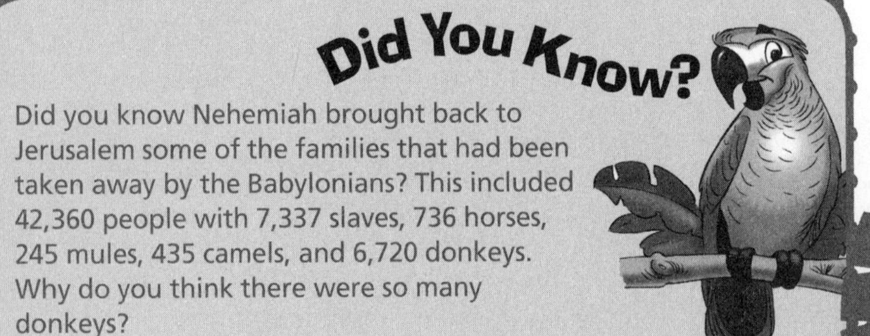

Did You Know?
Did you know Nehemiah brought back to Jerusalem some of the families that had been taken away by the Babylonians? This included 42,360 people with 7,337 slaves, 736 horses, 245 mules, 435 camels, and 6,720 donkeys. Why do you think there were so many donkeys?

May 1

Plan A

The bear cub rolled on the ground at Henry's feet. The other cub grabbed the giant-sized bottle and began to slurp milk formula all over everything. It wasn't fair that they couldn't keep these two cubs because there just wasn't enough room at his aunt's ranch for any more orphaned baby bears. They would need to make the bear enclosure bigger, and they didn't have the money this year. Henry prayed for some way to help them. He watched them wrestle with his dog Dakota, thinking how cute they were, just like two little stuffed bears. Henry stopped—God had just given him a plan.

Words to Treasure

Then the LORD said to Noah, "Go into the ark with your whole family. I know that you are a godly man among the people of today."

Genesis 7:1

Henry's booth was full of adorable, black teddy bears. He had made a sign telling everybody at the shopping mall about his aunt's wildlife rehabilitation ranch. People just couldn't get enough of the toys. A few days of this and they'd have enough money to enlarge the bear enclosure and maybe a bit more.

God can use you to be the start of something really big that will help others. Be prepared to hear from God and then go out and change the world.

It started when God told Noah to build an ark (a kind of boat) to save the world's animals. Then Noah's entire family also got into the eco-friendly plan. One person like Noah who listens to God can change the world. (See Genesis 6–9.)

May 2

Write Stuff

The cliff went down and down and down to the thin blue line of river below. This crazy high canyon was out of some action adventure movie. The cable car docked on the ramp ready for another load of people and supplies. The car swung from a delicate line of steel cable. Fran's knees began to shake, and she clung to the edge of the car as it sailed across the gorge to the far side. She looked down, both thrilled and terrified. When she got off the cable car, she was never so grateful for solid ground.

Words to Treasure

So write down what you have seen. Write about what is happening now and what will happen later.

Revelation 1:19

While she waited for everybody to cross, Fran took out her journal and began to write about her adventure in Ecuador. Her diary was full of thoughts, feelings, little prayers, and pictures she had drawn. She liked to write things down and get her feelings out. Sometimes she wrote letters to God in her journal. It helped to tell him everything, and it helped her to look back at all the amazing things God had done in her life. It was her own personal reminder diary of God's greatness. You can start one too!

Discovering Archaeology

God held back the Jordan River from flowing down to allow Joshua and the Israelites to cross safely over the dry riverbed. God told Joshua to pile stones from the river to make a marker that would remind people in the future of God's Jordon River miracle. It was kind of an ancient way of writing in a journal. (See Joshua 4:1–9.)

May 3

Dunking Fear

He remembered the feeling of being underwater in the cold and dark, and the feeling of his lungs burning because he needed air. He still had nightmares about the time he almost drowned at the lake. Austin stood at the edge of the pool fighting the fear inside him. This was his first swimming class, and he would have to go into the water. He repeated to himself, "Water is my friend. Water is not a scary monster that wants to *kill* me. Water is my friend."

Words to Treasure

The Lord turned to Gideon. He said to him, "You are strong. Go and save Israel from the power of Midian. I am sending you."

Judges 6:14

His swimming teacher waited for him to get in the pool. Austin asked God to help him not be afraid. He could do this because God didn't want him to be afraid either. Learning to swim was going to punch fear right in the nose.

In the Bible, a guy named Gideon was really afraid of the enemies of his people. He was so afraid that he was hiding out, but God helped Gideon become one of the bravest warriors in the Bible. Gideon faced his fears and won.

Sometimes when we give something new a try, we find out there's nothing to be afraid of after all. Austin didn't jump into the deep end of the pool right away. Instead, he started out slowly in the shallow end. Beat fear one step at a time.

May 4

No Problem

Savanna hiked all the way up to her grandmother's cabin. Her grandmother was wise. Whenever she had a problem at school or at home, Savanna would hike to her grandmother's cabin and talk to her about it. Savanna knocked on the door, and her grandmother answered it.

Words to Treasure

Why are you coming to me only when you are in trouble?

Judges 11:7

Savanna burst inside and fell into a chair in an unhappy heap. Grandmother sat down by the fire. "Something wrong, Savanna?"

"Yes! My BFF doesn't understand me. We had this terrible argument—"

"Wait!" interrupted her grandmother. "I'm not hearing problems today."

"What?" Savanna didn't understand.

"Savanna, the only time you come to visit me is when you have a problem. It would be nice if you came here just to visit me." Savanna's mouth hung open, confused. "So if you would like a cup of tea and some cookies, we can have a nice, normal visit. If you like, you can come back tomorrow and we'll talk about this BFF problem then."

God, your friends, and your family don't want to be your personal problem-solvers all the time. If you only talk to them to complain about life, that's not fun for them. Sometimes a visit should be just about spending time together.

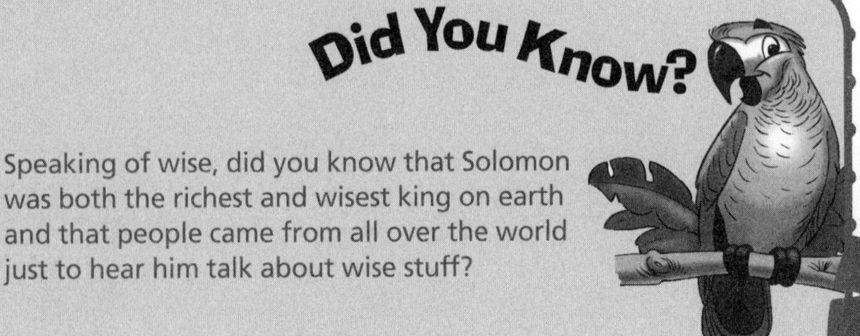

Speaking of wise, did you know that Solomon was both the richest and wisest king on earth and that people came from all over the world just to hear him talk about wise stuff?

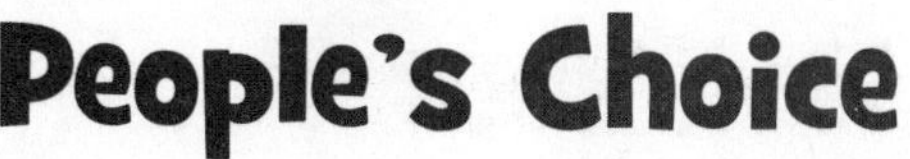

May 5

People's Choice

Vince studied the TV screen, almost ready to rent his movie. His dad came in with the popcorn and looked at Vince's selection with a little frown. "So, can I watch this one?"

His dad read the description. "What do you think?"

Vince reread the description and looked at the picture. "Vampire zombies take over New York and only one man can stop the carnage. Total annihilation of humanity or one man's battle to save the world." Vince shrugged, "Sounds good to me."

His dad grimaced. "You're joking, right?"

"Nope."

"Okay, this is your pick," his dad warned. "If we rent it and it isn't appropriate, *no* movie tonight."

Vince did lip twists with his mouth. "Okay, I'll find another one."

Learning to make smart choices is important. Not just in movies but in all kinds of things like games, books, websites, and a ton of other activities. Our choices tell the world what we value and what we think is worthwhile. When we make smart, right choices that's called good judgment. And that's impressive.

Words to Treasure

God made Solomon very wise. His understanding couldn't even be measured.

1 Kings 4:29

Did You Know?

Did you know we make hundreds of little and big choices all day long, from when to wake up in the morning to whether or not it's a good idea to stuff peanut butter in your sister's shoes? (For the record, nixes on the peanut butter. Do that, and your sister's anger can't be measured.)

May 6

Not Your Fault

Your fault?" Grandpa Joe shook his head. "Honey, your parents getting divorced isn't your fault."

A tear trailed down Sandra's cheek. "Maybe if Adam and I didn't fight so much or ..."

Words to Treasure

LORD, have mercy on me. I'm in deep trouble. I'm so sad I can hardly see. My whole body grows weak with sadness.

Psalm 31:9

Grandpa Joe looked her in the eyes. "You listen to me, honey. Your parents are good people who find living together too hard. But that has nothing to do with you or your brother. Don't you ever forget that your mom and dad love you both very much. That won't change. Want to pray about this together?" Sandra threw her arms around Grandpa Joe's neck.

When a wife and husband don't want to live together anymore, it is a sad, sad thing for a family. It makes God sad too, but he loves your family very much. The important thing to remember is that divorce is a grown-up problem, which means there is nothing a kid could have done to make it happen or to fix it.

Remember, divorce doesn't make your family bad or not as good as other families. It just means you have two parents who love you but live in different homes.

Divorce makes for mixed-up feelings of anger, sadness, and worry. It isn't wrong to feel any of those feelings. If your family's going through a divorce, talk to someone you trust—your grandparents, uncles or aunts, or youth pastor. Remember, you're never alone, and you're always loved.

May 7

It Isn't about You

Drew wasn't exactly doing his work with a good attitude. He was helping to paint the church, but he didn't want to be painting at all. He looked up at the men climbing above, nailing the new roof in place. That's where he wanted to be—pounding nails with the older guys, up there climbing around the roof. Instead he was painting outside walls. Sure, the church was in a needy village where they didn't have enough money to take care of it, but this was *boring*!

Words to Treasure

God loves a cheerful giver.
2 Corinthians 9:7

Pastor Michael walked over. "How's it going?"

Drew decided to let fly. "Why do I get stuck painting all the time? I'd rather be doing the roof. It isn't fair."

"Well," Pastor Michael frowned a little, "we need you to paint."

"I didn't sign up to paint all the time," Drew fumed.

Pastor Michael put his hand on Drew's shoulder. "This isn't about what you want to do. It's about wanting to help somebody else."

God wants us to help others, but he wants us to do it with a good attitude. Pitch in and help anyway that helps. It's *so* not about us, and so about other people.

Did You Know?

The Bible says this about generous people:

- Good things will come to them (Psalm 112:5).
- They will succeed (Proverbs 11:25).
- They will be blessed (Proverbs 22:9).
- They will be made rich in every good way (2 Corinthians 9:11).

May 8

Pals?

Yvette threw her book bag on the sofa and slumped down, almost in tears. Aunt Lucie looked up from her computer. "Bad day?"

Words to Treasure

PDon't be proud at all. Be completely gentle. Be patient. Put up with one another in love. The Holy Spirit makes you one in every way. So try your best to remain as one. Let peace keep you together.

Ephesians 4:2-3

Yvette tried to pull off her snow boots. "Nadia and I had the worst fight and now we're not friends. She said she is never going to talk to me ever again. This is the worst day of my life."

Aunt Lucie pulled at Yvette's boots and managed to pull her socks off as well. "Everybody has fights sometimes, even good friends. I bet—" The front doorbell rang. Aunt Lucie opened the door and there, looking just as unhappy, was Nadia.

Nadia sniffled, "Is Yvette home?"

Everybody has disagreements, and that's okay. Disagreements don't have to end friendships if both sides are willing to forgive and forget, and if both sides still want to be friends. In fact, sometimes disagreements make our friendships stronger because we learn how much that person means to us. We also learn that we can disagree and still be friends.

People in Bible Times

Long-time friends Paul and Barnabas had one big disagreement over whether they should take a guy named John Mark with them on a trip. They just couldn't agree, so Barnabas went one way with John Mark, and Paul went another. But that wasn't the end of their friendship. Later they forgave each other. Fights happen, but what happens after the fights is what makes a good friendship even better. (See Acts 15:36–41.)

May 9

Plenty of Room

Patrick and Desmond were watching their dad put together the baby crib in Desmond's old room. The boys weren't sure if they liked this idea or not. Desmond sat on the rocking horse, which was way too small for him now. "Will he cry a lot?"

Their dad was crawling around under the crib, looking for his wrench. "I suppose so. Babies cry."

"A lot?"

Their dad leaned back against the wall. "Yes, a lot. You boys still good with this? Getting a foster baby?"

Words to Treasure

Anyone who welcomes one of these little children in my name welcomes me.

Mark 9:37

Desmond sat against the wall next to his dad. "Will he spit up all over everything? Buckets of baby vomit everywhere?"

"Gallons," his dad said as he passed Desmond a wrench. "Tighten that side, will ya? Patrick, hang on to it here so it doesn't come apart." Desmond and Patrick went to work.

Many families all across the world have made the choice to open their homes to a child who needs a family to love and care for them. It isn't just that kids need foster moms and dads. They also need foster brothers or sisters. You can be a hero to someone who needs somebody like you to be part of his or her family for a long time or short time.

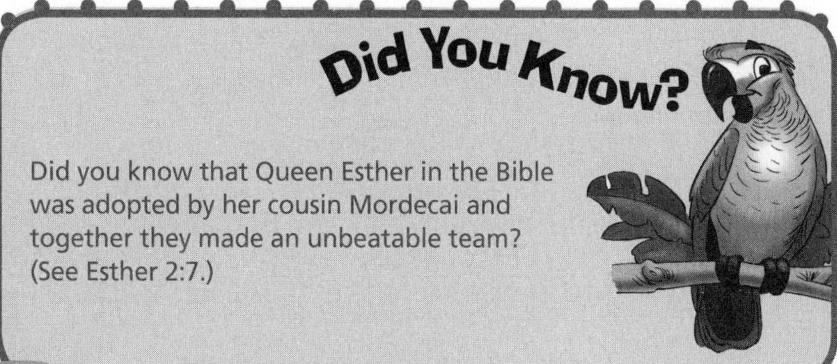

Did you know that Queen Esther in the Bible was adopted by her cousin Mordecai and together they made an unbeatable team? (See Esther 2:7.)

May 10

Love You Lots

Papa had gotten a sickness that made him forget things, even people he loved. Dianne gave him a box of chocolates, and he smiled at her, but he didn't remember who she was. He didn't remember that they used to go fishing together or sneak out for ice cream during family get-togethers. It was like Papa was gone and only part of him was left. It made her very sad that he couldn't be who he used to be. But she knew it wasn't his fault and that if he could do it, he would still be taking her fishing. Her grandfather couldn't love her the same way as before, but she could still love him the same way and just as much. In fact, he needed her love now more than ever. Every time she visited, she looked at the photograph beside his bed of the two of them fishing together. It reminded her who Papa was inside.

Words to Treasure

tand up in order to show your respect for old people.

Leviticus 19:32

It's really hard when people we love get sick and change. Sometimes they're not as active as they used to be, need help doing things, or don't remember as well as they used to. But that shouldn't change how much we love them.

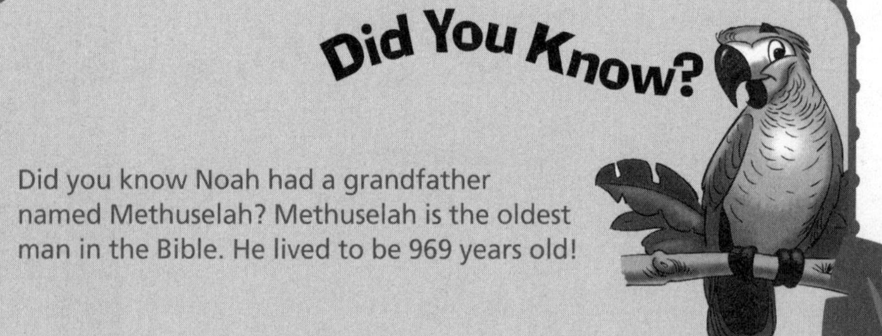

Did You Know?
Did you know Noah had a grandfather named Methuselah? Methuselah is the oldest man in the Bible. He lived to be 969 years old!

How Many Times?

The big horse moved at a steady pace around the ring. Tina's instructor was standing in the middle as the horse and girl circled her. Tina was kneeling on the broad back of Storm. Her legs felt shaky. She started to rise but knew she was going to lose her balance. So she went back down to her knees. Mrs. Romeyn nodded. "That was better … almost. Try again."

Words to Treasure

But be strong. Don't give up. God will reward you for your work."

2 Chronicles 15:7

Tina sat down with a groan. "How many times is it going to take before I can do this?"

Mrs. Romeyn stopped Storm and walked over. She looked up at Tina with an encouraging smile. "As many times as it takes." Tina grunted in frustration but was ready to try again.

As many times as it takes. Whenever we try something new and challenging it may not come easy. Not the first try or the second time. Maybe not even after a hundred tries. So be patient with yourself; don't give up. When you do succeed … awesome will describe the feeling inside.

Did You Know?

Horses aren't just a one trick pony. Apparently horses love to learn new things their entire lives. King Solomon really, really liked horses. He had 12,000 horses and 1,400 chariots.

May 12

Inspired

Tina sat in the front row watching the beautiful horses race past her on the stage. The riders were just as beautiful in their colorful costumes. The way they rode was everything Tina dreamed about. One rider stood on two white horses with one foot firmly planted on each horse's back.

Words to Treasure

Instead, let us encourage one another with words of hope.

Hebrews 10:24

Mrs. Romeyn leaned over and whispered. "Do you think he learned to do that in one try?"

Tina's mouth hung open as she watched the riders and horses move under the big white tent. "No, I sure don't." Tina couldn't wait for her next lesson.

Sometimes when we feel a little discouraged, a little inspiration can keep us going. The Bible says that patiently trying and practicing produces endurance. Endurance inspires others—just like the rider on two horses inspired Tina. Ready to get up and try again?

When Moses and his people left Egypt, the pharaoh or king chased after them with an earth-pounding 600 chariots. But don't worry, God had an inspiring plan for escape. Find out how in Exodus 14.

May 13

Smile

Macy was in the famous art museum in Paris called the Louvre. The crowd was packed in so tightly that Macy had a hard time pushing through to the front. When she got there, she stared at the famous painting. The woman with that funny crooked Mona Lisa smile. The famous artist Leonardo da Vinci painted this real lady who lived hundreds of years ago. And it became one of the most famous paintings in the world. The Louvre was full of other amazing art from all over the globe. Macy loved all kinds of museums—science, space, art, natural history, and more. They were full of stories, facts, and adventures just waiting to be discovered.

Words to Treasure

So I went down to the potter's house. I saw him working at his wheel. His hands were shaping a pot out of clay.

Jeremiah 18:3-4

The Bible is kind of like a museum on paper. It tells the stories, facts, and adventures of countries, rulers, boys, and girls from thousands of years ago. God is waiting for you to discover their adventures. Next time you have a day off, check out one of the adventures in the Bible.

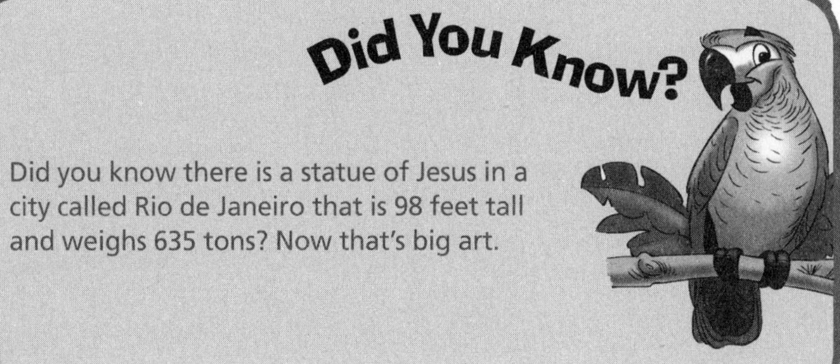

Did you know there is a statue of Jesus in a city called Rio de Janeiro that is 98 feet tall and weighs 635 tons? Now that's big art.

May 14

Next Floor, Please

Tiffany walked into the girl's washroom and stopped. There was her friend Anne, leaning close to the bathroom mirror, putting on eye makeup. She already had lipstick and blush on. "Where did you get that? Your parents don't want you to wear makeup yet!"

Words to Treasure

While our sons are young, they will be like healthy plants. Our daughters will be like pillars that have been made to decorate a palace.

Psalm 144:12

Annie put on a little more eye shadow in another color that had glitter in it—way too much. "I want to look like a teenager."

Tiffany looked at her friend's face. "Well, I never saw a teenager who looked that, ummm, colorful. Maybe you should learn how to use makeup first. You look like somebody's color-by-numbers picture. You're sort of a makeup explosion."

Annie studied her reflection in horror. "Really?"

Mrs. Cole walked in and took one look at Annie. "Oh, dear."

Next floor: makeup, high heels, and boyfriends—but not yet. Trying to be older means you will miss out on all the fun things that happen at the age you are now. Go ahead and have fun and be who you are *now*, and not someone you will be in a few years.

Did you know that in ancient Israel both women and men wore makeup and used perfume? Some kinds of eye makeup helped to keep flies from their faces. Now that's multi-purpose.

I Am Me

The field was full of dozens of gigantic hot-air balloons. Amy and her dad were entered in a balloon race, and they were busy getting their own balloon ready. Soon they'd be up in the air with all the other colorful balloons. It would be an amazing sight. Amy watched as their balloon filled with hot gases, and a beautiful Celtic cross unfolded for the world to see. She thought it was one of the most beautiful balloons in the whole field. Amy wasn't embarrassed about having a cross on the balloon. Being a Christian was just part of who she was and not something she wanted to hide.

It's okay to be a person of faith, and it's okay to share your feelings about that. Don't do it because you feel you have to, but because loving Jesus is a natural part of who you are, inside and out. Be proud of your relationship with God.

Words to Treasure

Come, let us sing for joy to the LORD. Let us give a loud shout to the Rock who saves us.

Psalm 95:1

People in Bible Times

King David had God's Holy Ark brought to Jerusalem. As they were carrying it into the city, David danced with everything he had. He didn't care if he looked silly or wasn't acting kingly. He just wanted to show God how much he loved him. David was proud of God and proud to love him with all his heart. David rocks! (See 2 Samuel 6:14–23.)

May 16

Let Me Get Back to You

The lights had been turned down low, and the teacher was about to put the DVD into the player. Nick raised his hand. "Mrs. Dale, I don't think that's a movie my parents would want me to watch."

Words to Treasure

Children, obey your parents in everything. That pleases the Lord.

Colossians 3:20

Mrs. Dale motioned for Nick to come over to her so she could talk with him. "Nick, if you want to, we can fast-forward through anything that makes you feel uncomfortable."

Nick scratched his chin, uncertain about what to say. "What's the rating on this movie?"

"It's rated PG, which means Parental Guidance."

Nick sighed, "Then I'd like to phone my mom."

Nick was very courageous to stand up for what he felt was the right thing to do. When you feel uncomfortable about a situation at school, at a sports event or practice, or even at your church, you have every right to talk to your parents about it—right away, if you feel you need to do it quickly. Checking with your mom or dad on something you're unsure about is never a wrong choice. Your parents will be proud of you for doing it, and so will God.

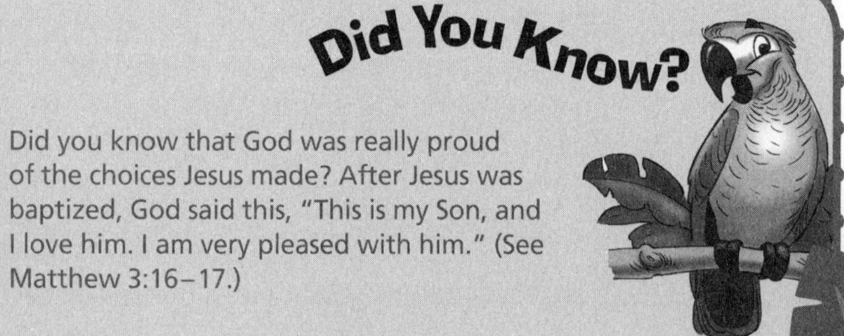

Did You Know?

Did you know that God was really proud of the choices Jesus made? After Jesus was baptized, God said this, "This is my Son, and I love him. I am very pleased with him." (See Matthew 3:16–17.)

The Ark

Todd's little brother sucked his root beer up and down inside his straw. "Does it really melt people's faces off, and is it in a warehouse with dead rats?"

Todd raised an eyebrow, "Bobby, what are you talking about?"

"The ark. You know, the gold box thing in that movie. The telephone-to-God thing. Is it real?" Bobby slurped so loudly that people turned to stare.

"The ark? Of course, it's real." Todd slid down in his seat, embarrassed. "Stop slurping, will you?"

Words to Treasure

Send the ark of the god of Israel away. Let it go back to its own place. If you don't, it will kill us and our people.

1 Samuel 5:11

God told Moses to build a special chest called the ark. Inside this beautiful gold box, Moses put the Ten Commandments, a pot of manna, and Aaron's shepherd's rod. The ark was kept in the Israelites' tent church, called the tabernacle, and later in the temple in Jerusalem. It was like God's throne on earth—the most holy thing in the world.

Sometimes it was carried into battle by the Israelites. When the Philistines captured the ark, it caused so much sickness and death that they sent it back. The ark was powerful and holy.

Discovering Archaeology

Where is the ark today? *Mystery time*! After the Babylonians trashed Jerusalem, the ark disappeared from history. Some say the Babylonians destroyed it or that the Israelites hid it under Jerusalem somewhere. Some think the Israelites took it to Egypt or Africa for safety. Some think God took it away. But don't expect to find it in a warehouse.

May 18

Little Thing or Big Mistake?

Wayne, Mel, and Brad were never ever allowed to ski out-of-bounds past the ski runs. They thought it would be okay to follow some older guys, but they hadn't planned to go this far. Somehow they had taken a wrong turn. Now they were lost, and to make matters worse, Brad had fallen down a snow well around a tree. It was deep, and they couldn't seem to get him out without snow falling down on top of him. It was getting dark, and they were in big trouble.

Words to Treasure

Teach me. Then I'll be quiet. Show me what I've done wrong.

Job 6:24

Little wrong things can turn into life-threatening big mistakes. Where did the boys go wrong? When they figured they could get away with a little wrong choice. They can't! Now they're in a very scary situation and need a rescue team to find them. They're in for one long cold night and one long talking-to by everybody. Wrong is never right.

People in Bible Times

When Joshua and company finally took the city of Jericho, God told them not to take anything with them from the city. But a guy named Achan ignored God's order and took a few things for his tent. This upset God, so when they had their next battle, guess what? They lost big-time. Joshua couldn't figure out why, because God had promised only victory. Well, Achan's little wrong thing turned out to be a big problem for everybody. (See Joshua 7.)

May 19

Junk Pirate

It was like a treasure chest that was never empty. It was the candy machine across the street at the gas station. Rows and rows of candy bars, potato chips, and gum. Nigel loved everything about it. The sound of his change going in and the thud of the candy as it fell to the bottom of the machine. Then reaching in and pulling out the candy. Every afternoon Nigel did the same thing—he bought candy. Lots of candy.

Nigel, did you ever hear of an apple, orange, or any kind of fresh vegetable?

Candy is great, but only sometimes—not all the time. Your body *cannot* live on sugar and chocolate. And that goes for other junk food too. It just isn't healthy. God made your body to be like a high-performance sports car. You don't want to clog it up with bad fuel. You won't be racing anywhere with a gummed-up engine. As tempting as it can be, walk away from that coin-eating candy chest and find some high-performance food. Go get some muscle-building, brain-boosting, naturally good-for-you food. Junk the junk food.

Words to Treasure

Then God said, "I am giving you every plant on the face of the whole earth that produces its own seeds. I am giving you every tree that has fruit with seeds in it. All of them will be given to you for food."

Genesis 1:29

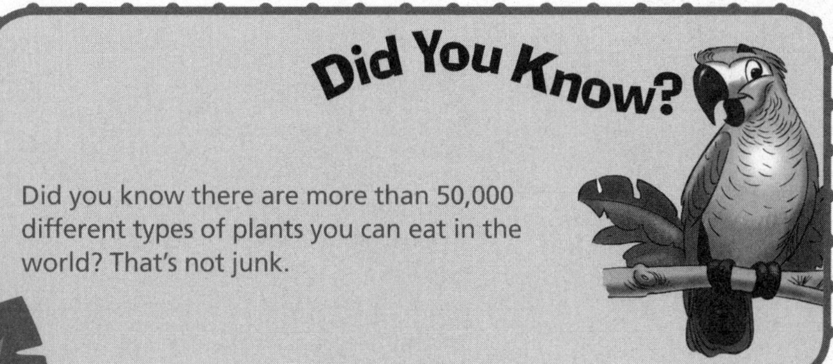

Did you know there are more than 50,000 different types of plants you can eat in the world? That's not junk.

May 20

Changing

Tom had done two major things today. He had made a huge model castle with all his plastic building pieces, *and* he had made an important decision. He had decided that he didn't want to have any more birthdays, because the older he got, the more he would change. Tom was worried that someday he wouldn't like his toys anymore and wouldn't want to build forts in the backyard anymore. Tom didn't want to grow up and be a teenager. He didn't want anything in his life to change—ever. He liked being a kid.

Words to Treasure

When I became a man, I put the ways of childhood behind me.

1 Corinthians 13:11

Change isn't a bad thing! Growing up isn't an instant *ZAP! You're different*! You kind of grow into growing up. That's the way God made it to be. Sure, your interests will change, but you'll want those changes when the time comes. You'll want to try new things, because you'll be ready for them. Someday driving a real car will be a whole lot better than playing with a toy car. Don't freak out. Just take one day at a time. Change is good.

There are all kinds of really good stories about kids facing the big mystery called "growing up." A world of books and movies about great adventures you can have when you're a little bit older. Check them out. A lot of kids feel the same way about growing up, but it's an action adventure you'll want to be part of.

May 21

Salvation

Pastor Duane prayed with Mark in a corner of the room. All around them was the noise of the youth meeting. Kids were laughing and talking loudly, but for Mark everything was quiet inside. He could feel Jesus' love surround him like a warm glow. Pastor Duane talked softly. "Mark, do you love Jesus?"

"Yeah," Mark prayed, "Jesus, forgive me for being a mess-up and doing wrong things. Tonight I just want to ask you to be with me, and I want to love and believe in you for the rest of my life."

Words to Treasure

Jesus answered, "I am the way and the truth and the life. No one comes to the Father except through me."
John 14:6

Mark just made a big choice to accept salvation. But what is it? Why do we need it?

God is perfect. He can't ever do anything wrong because he is holy. That makes it hard for God to have a close friendship with us, because he's so holy and we're not. But God's son Jesus came to earth and allowed himself to be killed even though he never did anything wrong. When he came back to life, he took the world's badness away. He made us holy. When we believe in Jesus, God doesn't see the bad things (the sins) we might have done in the past or will do in the future—he just sees somebody he loves. That's salvation! Cool, huh?

Did you know salvation means "to save"?

May 22

Ready? Go!

The sun was just rising at 6:30 in the morning. Dean shivered in the morning chill as he shoveled sand into a bag. His rain hood kept slipping down as the rain poured down in sheets, and his hands were covered with enormously gross blisters. When his pastor had phoned at 4:30 in the morning, his family jumped out of bed to help. The next town over was facing an ugly flood. The river was overflowing, and everybody was stacking up bags of sand to hold back the river from the houses. Dean didn't know any of these people, and it didn't really matter. What mattered was they needed help and their church was here.

Words to Treasure

"It will be good for those servants whose master finds them ready. It will even be good if he comes in the middle of the night or toward morning."

Luke 12:38

Nothing is nicer than a warm bed on a stormy cold night, but sometimes we have to be prepared to get uncomfortable if that's what God wants. Jesus said that we should be dressed and ready to serve like servants waiting for their master to return. It's kind of like a superhero waiting for the superhero signal in the sky. When God signals, be ready to be a hero for him.

In Bible times, servants were people hired to work for a family. They got paid a certain amount to work around the home or at the family business. They were free servants, not slaves.

Right, Wrong, Then, Now

Mercer quietly walked through the stone arches to the sunny balcony. He looked down into what was left of the rooms and chambers that had once been hidden by a wood floor and covered with sand. So this was the famous Coliseum of Rome. He tried to imagine the gladiators fighting all kinds of different animals while the Romans watched and cheered for their favorite fighter. It made him wonder why Romans didn't know killing people or animals for fun was wrong.

Words to Treasure

We know that in all things God works for the good of those who love him. He appointed them to be saved in keeping with his purpose. God planned that those he had chosen would become like his Son.

Romans 8:28–29

There are many things that happened in the past that we know are wrong today, things such as slavery or fighting to the death in the Coliseum of Rome. What changed? Why do we know those things are wrong today, but the Romans didn't know back then?

Well, we've changed. Jesus taught us how to treat other people with kindness and love. Hopefully some of the things we still do wrong today will one day be things of the past. Jesus taught us to love God and each other with all our hearts, and that just keeps changing the world for the better.

Live It!

How can you help change the world for a better future? In everything you do and say, think about how Jesus would have acted. Then follow through and do it.

May 24

If Everybody Hated Them

Sidney watched the movie on television while eating buttery popcorn. The beautiful horses and chariots raced round and round the track. There were great big chariot crashes, and she wasn't sure who would win the race—the good guy or the bad Roman guy. Nobody seemed to like the Romans in this movie. Nobody seemed to like the Romans in the Bible either. How come?

Words to Treasure

In those days, Caesar Augustus made a law. It required that a list be made of everyone in the whole Roman world.

Luke 2:1

Okay, so if everybody hated them, why were the Romans hanging out in Jerusalem and all of Palestine during Jesus' time? Well, the Roman Empire had the most powerful kingdom-kicking army in the world. In a very short time, Rome had gone from an ordinary city to an empire that ruled most of the known world. Romans fought and took over some kingdoms, but some countries wanted to be part of a powerful empire and joined up. Israel was one of the kingdoms that got conquered or taken over by Rome. Soon the Romans were walking around as if they owned the place and were demanding that the people pay heavy taxes to support the growing Roman Empire. That didn't go over too well, and everybody was upset and angry with the Romans and thought they were bullies.

Slavery was just part of life in ancient times. Many slaves were from defeated kingdoms like Israel. At one point in ancient Rome, more than 80 percent of the people were slaves.

Dead Sea

Jerry waded around in the thick waters of the Dead Sea. A man warned him not to go in if he had any cuts because the salt in the water would really sting. No cuts, so he was good to go. He knew the Dead Sea was way saltier than the ocean, but he was surprised by how slippery and oily the water felt. This was crazy thick water. Jerry lay back in the water like the other swimmers. His dad handed him a comic book, and Jerry let the salty water keep him afloat with no swimming needed. He just sat back and relaxed while his mom took a photograph. His dad gave him a little splash, and suddenly Jerry's eye stung like crazy. "Dad!" The salty water had gotten in his eye. Jerry ran for his towel and bottled water. "Hey, that stings!"

"Sorry, kiddo, I forgot."

The Dead Sea is actually a salt lake that was once part of the ocean a long, long time ago. The lake has been shrinking over the years. In the Bible, the Dead Sea is also called the Salt Sea. People call it *dead* because the water is so full of minerals that animals can't live in it. No fish or anything. People have been visiting this Bible spot for thousands of years.

Words to Treasure

You are the salt of the earth.
Matthew 5:13

Ancient people used salt to add flavor to food and also to preserve and dry out things like fish. Salt was so valuable that ancient people often used it like money. Being the salt of the earth means you're special and indispensable.

May 26

Helping Kids Be Kids

Brendon looked at all the toys on the store shelves. He had birthday money in his pocket and knew where to spend it. His uncle Toby stood beside him and examined a box. "Hey sport! Is that the birthday gift you want to buy?"

Words to Treasure

But you have not practiced the more important things of the law, which are fairness, mercy and faithfulness.

Matthew 23:23

Brendon glanced at him, "This is the one. This is the perfect gift."

"Do you ever research toys?"

"Sure, I ask my friends what they like." Brendon picked up another box.

Uncle Toby pointed to the box Brendon was holding. "I'm looking at where this toy was made. I try to choose toys that were made in fair ways. Some kids in the world don't get to play with toys. They spend their time in factories making toys."

Brendon looked concerned. "Kids shouldn't have to work in factories."

Uncle Toby shook his head sadly. "I know," he said. "That's why I try to do a little research before I buy something."

In some countries, kids have to work like adults do. When you buy toys or clothes, you can actually purchase them from companies that are fair to everybody. By doing this, you can help a kid you don't even know by buying with care.

The Bible talks about fairness. That means making decisions or choices that are good and right for everybody, not just for a few people. Are you fair in the way you treat other people? Talk about it with your family.

Never a Wrong Move

It was the first time C.C.'s dad had let her help round up cattle in the high country. It was a tough job, with long, hard hours riding horseback and in trucks. Her grandpa wasn't sure a kid should go at all. But, C.C. was hoping someday she'd own the ranch. She sat on top of the corral fence and prayed quietly to herself. "Dear God," C.C. whispered, "please help me do the best job I can. Protect everybody—the horses, the dogs, the cattle, and Grandpa. Amen."

Starting anything big or small with prayer is always a good idea. It means we put God first in everything we do and that we want him involved from the very beginning. Prayer is always the first and right move.

Words to Treasure

Don't worry about anything. No matter what happens, tell God about everything. Ask and pray, and give thanks to him. Then God's peace will watch over your hearts and your minds. He will do this because you belong to Christ Jesus.

Philippians 4:6–7

People in Bible Times

Nehemiah was a cupbearer to the Persian Emperor Artaxerxes. But Nehemiah's heart was for his homeland and his people in Jerusalem. He had heard reports that the people were having trouble and the city was kind of destroyed. He was very sad and prayed to God about the people of Israel day and night. Nehemiah's first prayer was the first step in an amazing adventure God had planned for him. Nehemiah the cupbearer was going to rebuild a city. Imagine that! (See Nehemiah 1:4–11.)

May 28

Polite Works

Garth and his aunt Carol stood where her car used to be parked. Then they spotted the sign. *No parking after 3:00 p.m.* They had been longer at the flea market than they had expected. "We've been towed," Aunt Carol sighed. "I don't even know where the tow yard is. It could be miles away."

Words to Treasure

A person who has a pure and loving heart and speaks kindly will be a friend of the king.

Proverbs 22:11

Garth spotted a tow truck a block away. "Come on!" They started to run down the block.

The tow truck driver was listening to a really angry lady. She was calling him all kinds of names for towing her car. "Excuse me, sir," Aunt Carol interrupted. The pair stared at her. "I'm terribly sorry, I parked too long. It was my fault, and I think you towed my car. Could you please tell me how to get to your tow yard?"

The driver smiled at her. "Because *you're* so polite, I'll drive you and the kid to the yard. I'm just heading back. Climb in." The angry lady didn't know what to say as they drove away.

Being polite is always the best way to handle any situation. Aunt Carol's good attitude was rewarded. Having a good attitude and respecting others is God's way. Politeness rocks.

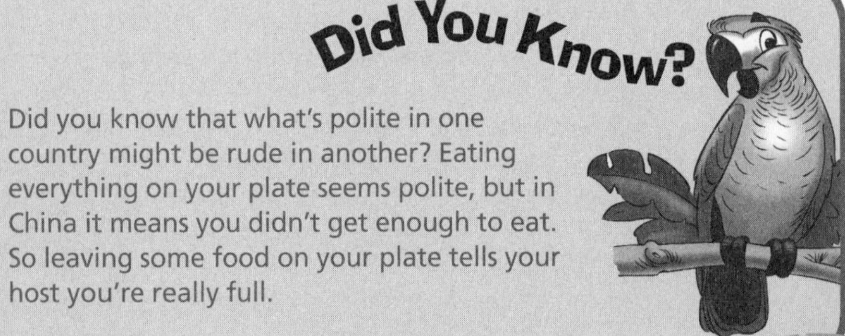

Did You Know?

Did you know that what's polite in one country might be rude in another? Eating everything on your plate seems polite, but in China it means you didn't get enough to eat. So leaving some food on your plate tells your host you're really full.

Lord's Prayer

Murray knew the prayer, but he wasn't sure what it meant:

"Our Father in heaven, may your name be honored.

May your kingdom come.

May what you want to happen be done on earth as it is done in heaven.

Give us today our daily bread.

Forgive us our sins, just as we also have forgiven those who sin against us.

Keep us from falling into sin when we are tempted. Save us from the evil one."

Words to Treasure

On one of those days, Jesus went out to a mountainside to pray.

Luke 6:12

Jesus taught his disciples this prayer so that we could tell God that we love and respect him. What does this prayer teach us? First off, that God is our Father in heaven and that he rules everything. And someday we will be with him in that heavenly kingdom. Just as everything in the universe obeys God's will, we want to as well.

Our daily bread means that we understand everything we have is from God, because he takes care of us. In this prayer we also promise to forgive people who do us wrong just as God forgives us. We also want God to help us do right things. Only God can and will protect us from evil. It's a simple prayer with a whole lot in it. When you need to pray, try memorizing the prayer Jesus taught us.

Discovering Archaeology

Jesus prayed often. Today, many people go to the Western Wall in Jerusalem to pray. It is thought to be the only remaining part of Jerusalem's third temple that wasn't destroyed by Rome's General Titus when he completely destroyed the city.

May 30

You Are What You Do

"I thought you were my friend." Owen fidgeted in the seat waiting to talk to the principal.

Words to Treasure

YYou can tell each tree by its fruit.

Matthew 7:16

"I am." Jack drummed his fingers on his leg.

"Then why did you hide your fireworks in my locker? Now, *I'm* in trouble." Owen couldn't believe this was happening. His parents were coming, and he was innocent in all of this.

Jack stretched. "Now, *I'm* in trouble because you told them the fireworks were mine."

Owen was speechless for a moment. "They *are* yours! I should never have given you my locker combination. You used me and my locker."

"Well," Jack yawned, "you told on me. What kind of friend does that make you?"

"I don't think we're friends anymore." Owen moved over to a chair on the other side of the office.

Jesus warned us that you can tell the character of a person, not by what they say but by what they do. Actions speak louder than words. Is Jack a good friend? Not really. His actions tell a whole different story. When making friends, look for the people who do right things, because they are what they say they are.

Jesus asked an important question: Do you get figs from vines or grapes from thorn bushes? Nope. You can tell what kind of tree it is by the fruit it grows. A good person does right things and a bad person does bad things—what they do is their fruit. (See Matthew 7:16–19.)

How Many Temples?

Jewel put the finishing touches on her model of King Solomon's temple. Her older brother Richard inspected it. "Looks like a parking structure."

"Very funny." Jewel removed the roof to show the inside of her temple.

Richard peered inside. "No cars?" He picked up a figure. "Your horse is kind of lumpy."

"It's a camel. Give it back before you break it."

"Don't get all touchy." Richard put the camel back. "So? Did you download some actual photographs to do this?"

Words to Treasure

"Do you see these huge buildings?" Jesus asked. "Not one stone here will be left on top of another. Every stone will be thrown down."

Mark 13:2

She rolled her eyes. "Considering it was destroyed thousands of years ago, no."

There were actually three temples built in Jerusalem. The first temple was built by King Solomon but was completely destroyed 340 years later by the Babylonian bad boy, King Nebuchadnezzar. When the Israelites came back from being slaves in Babylon, they built a second temple. Then later, King Herod the Great did a home-improvement thing and made one really impressive *big* temple. That would be the temple Jesus visited in Jerusalem. Herod built his temple to impress people, especially the Romans. But it was destroyed by the Romans only six years after it was completed. They didn't seem overly impressed. After that, no one rebuilt the Jerusalem temple.

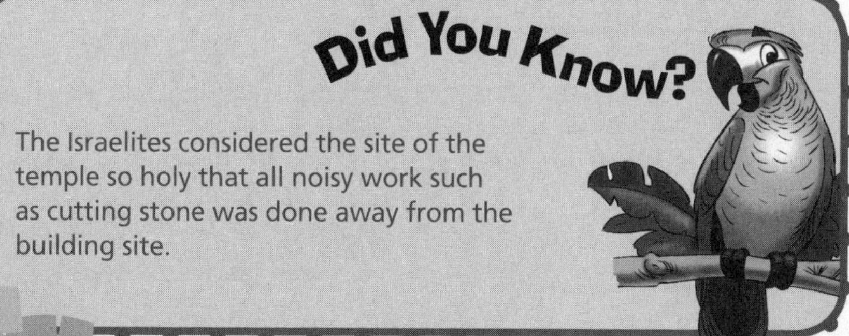

Did You Know?
The Israelites considered the site of the temple so holy that all noisy work such as cutting stone was done away from the building site.

June 1

Courage

Fern walked into the hospital with shorts on. After her surgery, it had taken her a long time to dare to wear shorts. But now she didn't care. She peeked around the corner to see a little girl in a big bed. Fern walked in with a warm smile. "Hi, I'm Fern." The little girl stared at Fern's artificial leg. Fern knocked on her leg with a shrug. "I lost my leg to a disease. I heard you had an accident." The little girl nodded shyly. "Pretty soon you'll be getting a leg like mine—a prosthesis. Big word, huh?" The little girl nodded again. Fern sat softly on the bed. "I do all kinds of stuff like rock climbing and snowboarding. It will be okay. I'm going to visit you lots until you're completely sick of me." The girl smiled.

Words to Treasure

Be strong and very brave.
Joshua 1:9

Fern is a special kind of hero, somebody who has faced a really tough situation and has decided to help other people face the same kind of challenges. She wasn't going to let losing her leg stop her. Life is full of all kinds of challenges. How we handle them is what makes us heroes.

Joshua was taking God's people into the Promised Land, and there would be hardships and huge battles to fight. God just kept telling Joshua to be strong and brave. And do you know what Joshua told his people? You guessed it. Be strong and brave. So whatever situation you face, be strong and brave. Pass it on.

Expect the Unexpected

Willa and Sal sat on the rock with the swirling current below them. They hadn't noticed the tide coming in until it was too late. The sandbar they had hiked along to get to this great fishing spot was now gone, and the water was rising up the rock. Willa prayed that the tide would stop and that it wouldn't cover the rock before somebody noticed them. The tide crept up and up, covering the barnacles and mussel shells. The sky was getting dark, and she worried nobody would see them from the shore. They had shouted until their throats were hoarse.

Words to Treasure

He does wonderful things that can't be understood. He does miracles that can't even be counted.

Job 5:9

A voice called out of the growing darkness. "What on earth are you kids doing there?" A kayaker slid by silently. "I thought I heard somebody shouting. I'll go back and get my rowboat. Crazy kids."

Billions of people pray different prayers every day, and God answers them all in different ways—sometimes the way we expect and sometimes not. But the important thing is that God hears each of our prayers. You're never alone. God can and will do amazing things. Little and big miracles happen every day.

When Joshua went into battle, he wasn't alone. When he talked, God listened. One battle with the Amorites, God made armor-denting hailstones storm down, killing most of Joshua's enemies.

June 3

Miracles

Jesse's mom rubbed the newborn puppy vigorously with a towel. The little pup looked kind of blue and wasn't breathing. Jesse stroked his dog as the new mother licked her other pups. "Do you think it's dead?"

Words to Treasure

ou are the God who does miracles.

Psalm 77:14

"Well," his mom kept rubbing. "Sometimes they just need a little jump start." Jesse said a quick prayer in his head. The pup suddenly did a little twitch and made a soft squeak. His nose and mouth turned from blue to pink. "There we go. That's it, baby," said Mom.

"Was that a miracle?" Jesse took the little puppy and placed him beside his wriggling brothers and sisters.

His mom smiled. "I don't know, maybe."

What is a miracle? A miracle is something wonderful that God does for us. It can be big like parting the Red Sea or small like helping a little puppy take its first breath. (Yes, even that could be a miracle too.) All we have to do is believe in God and Jesus. Miracles happened in Bible times, and God causes wonderful things to happen today as well.

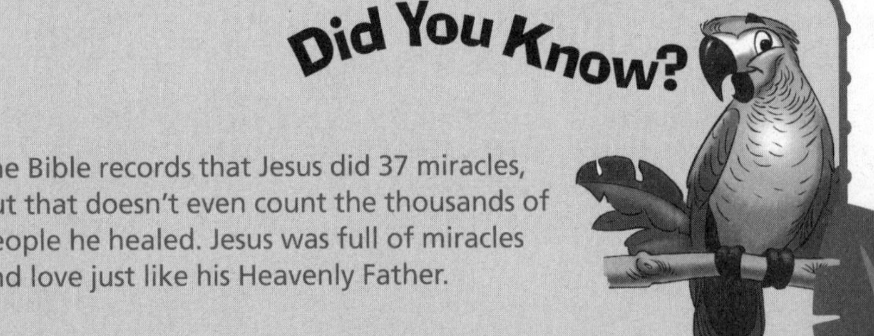

Did You Know?
The Bible records that Jesus did 37 miracles, but that doesn't even count the thousands of people he healed. Jesus was full of miracles and love just like his Heavenly Father.

June 4

Stepparent

Amber hit the choppy wave and suddenly lost her balance. She did a face-plant into the water, and that sent water right up her nose. Her water ski came off, and soon she was just floating, snuffling to get the water out of her nose, waiting for the boat to circle around. Her stepmom pulled alongside. "Okay, that's it for the day. You're too tired to keep skiing."

Words to Treasure

Love never fails.

1 Corinthians 17:6

"Come on, just one more, please," Amber pleaded.

"Nope." Her stepmom caught up the floating ski. "In the boat. Now, please."

Amber reluctantly climbed up the ladder. "Okay."

The Bible clearly says that we are to respect and obey our parents. And that includes stepparents. Nobody says that having a new parent in your life is always easy. It's a whole new person you have to get to know, and it can be kind of overwhelming. But like a new friendship, getting familiar with a stepparent takes time—talking together, doing things together, and showing each other lots of respect both ways. Your stepparent can become a really good friend and parent if you're willing to let them be a part of your life in a really *real* way. Give 'em a chance!

Although Jesus was completely the Son of God, he also had a very earthly adoptive father in Joseph. Joseph wasn't Jesus' "real" dad, but Jesus loved, respected, and obeyed him completely. (See Luke 2:41–52.)

June 5

Blasted

Abby knew she wasn't supposed to go past the out-of-bounds markers, but the dunes looked so much better over there. Leaving safety behind, she went zooming up the side of a forbidden sand dune. She got to the top, only to find a big cliff-like drop-off on the other side. Her ATV was airborne and heading downward for a crash. She fell off her machine and lay on the ground, spitting sand. Rick sped over. She sat up and waved to show she was okay.

Words to Treasure

Why did you turn your back on what I told you to do?

2 Samuel 12:9

"Abby, you know you're not supposed to be over here. You know better. What am I going to do with you?"

"Ban me from the dunes?" Abby felt her stomach drop, because she loved riding dunes. "I'm really sorry I let you down. I won't do it again."

Together they pushed her ATV out of the sand. "You're a good kid and a good rider. You can spend the rest of the day helping me with the new riders. But do this again and you're banned."

Abby did something impulsive, but Rick understood she was sorry and she wanted to do better. If you do make a mistake, God may be disappointed but he still loves you because he knows your heart.

Incoming sandstorm! Yup, sandstorms were a problem in ancient Israel. Wind picked up and blew sand everywhere. Sometimes strong sandstorms looked like a solid wall of sand heading straight for you.

Boring!

Mitchell slumped on the bench, oozing attitude. He was determined not to have a good time at the amusement park. When he got off the fastest, most looping rollercoaster, he acted as if he didn't like it. When he tumbled out of the Pirates Cove, he said it was boring. He didn't like his food at lunch, and he couldn't find anything good to buy. This might be the happiest place on the planet with the most amazing rides going, but he was not going to have a good time. This was all boring.

Words to Treasure

Be filled with joy in the sight of the Lord your God. Be joyful in everything you do.

Deuteronomy 12:18

Mitchell thought everything in his world was boring. He had decided that acting bored was a cool attitude. Nobody can make fun of you if you don't like anything or anyone first. People go out of their way to try and please you, especially your parents—being bored works.

Being bored *doesn't* work. Being constantly bored or negative on purpose sucks all the fun out of your life. It also makes *you* kind of boring to be around. Nobody wants to hang out with someone who is down on everything. That's no fun! Soon people will stop inviting you to do things. So stop acting bored! God wants you to get excited about life and the amazing world he created for you. Go have *fun*. Bored is boring.

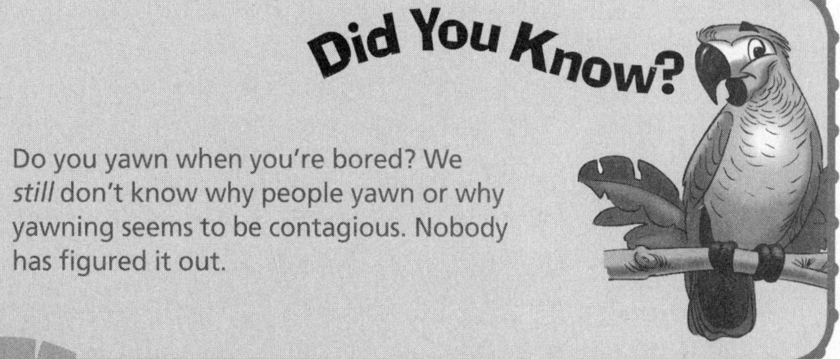

Do you yawn when you're bored? We *still* don't know why people yawn or why yawning seems to be contagious. Nobody has figured it out.

June 7

Click

The school bus jerked to a stop, and Brooke jumped out and headed for the tall grass. She had felt sick all day long and now, in front of the entire school bus, she was going to be sick. This was the most embarrassing moment of her life. Or was it?

Words to Treasure

Do to others as you want them to do to you.

Luke 6:31

At home, Brooke was resting in bed, feeling awful, when her brother passed her a piece of paper. It was a printed photograph of her throwing up. She looked at her brother, horrified. "Where did you get that?"

"The Internet. Gordon used his cell camera. Now that's nasty." Brooke wanted to hide under a rock forever. It just wasn't fair!

Clearly the Bible doesn't say anything about cellular phone cameras or other types of modern stuff. But it does have a whole lot to say about kindness and respect for others, which would fall under the heading, "*Just Because You Can Doesn't Mean You Should.*" Be considerate of others and respect that there are some things and situations people do not want captured for the world to see. Think before you click or post.

Stuff like cellular phones, digital cameras, little tiny video cameras, and other spy gear is amazing and so much fun to use. But never, ever use them to be disrespectful to other people. Use 'em for good, not for evil.

June 8

A Family Thing

Quinn hit his alarm clock with his dirty sock. Then he hit it with his shoe. Then he hit it with his baseball glove and knocked it clear off the dresser. It stopped. He didn't want to go to church anymore. He wanted to stay home and sleep. He'd been going to church since he was born. How much more did he need to learn about God anyway?

Words to Treasure

I am the good shepherd. I know my sheep, and my sheep know me.

John 10:14

Well, here's the truth: if Quinn studied every day for the rest of his entire life, he'd still be learning new mysteries about God. God's a very big subject. Best of all, there is one more important thing Quinn needs to know, and you need to know too.

Important study note: Jesus and God are completely into you. They want to know everything there is to know about *you:* what you're thinking, how you're feeling, and how it's going. God doesn't find you a boring subject. God wants to learn more about *you* every day. Be the same way back!

Jesus came to earth to teach us about his heavenly Father so we can understand and love God more. Jesus also wanted us to know that God loves us exactly as a good father loves his son or daughter. God loves us the same way he loves Jesus. You are God's adopted kid! Very cool. (See John 17:25–26.)

June 9

Root of the Problem

"Bobby," yelled Uncle Mort loud enough for the whole sci-fi convention to hear him. "Look who's here. Dennis! Dennis, the kid who used to go to our church."

Words to Treasure

They believe for awhile. But when they are tested, they fall away from the faith.

Luke 8:13

Bobby nodded to his old friend. "Hi, Dennis."

Dennis looked about as uncomfortable as a cat at a dog show. "Hi, Bobby."

A huge green alien on stilts walked past. "Will you look at that guy?!" Uncle Mort was loving his first sci-fi convention.

Bobby smiled at Dennis. "I was just going over to the costume contest. I heard that if the Klingons lost again this year, things were going to get interesting. Want to come?"

"Sure." Dennis nodded.

They walked past the comic book section in silence. Finally Bobby spoke. "Are you ever coming back to church?"

Dennis looked uncomfortable again. "Maybe. Maybe not."

"If you want to talk, call me." They could already hear the Klingons protesting loudly. Both boys smiled. They loved Klingons.

The truth is, not everybody who goes to church will always go to church. Some will drift away. Love them, pray for them, and never stop being their friend.

Jesus said some people are like seeds that fall in a rocky place. They start to grow but their roots dry up. That's like people who believe for a little while and then drift away from God. But remember, God never forgets about anybody. He'll always be there for them and so should you. (See Luke 8:4–15.)

June 10

Old Gear

Logan glanced into the other fishing boats as he walked down the dock. They were new boats with new fishing rods and the best gear you could imagine. At the end of the dock was his uncle's old boat and their really old tackle. Logan climbed into the boat very discouraged. "Uncle Rich, how are we going to win with old stuff like this? Those other guys have fish sonar, GPS, and out-of-this-world rods. There's no way we can win this fishing derby."

Words to Treasure

By your power we walk all over them. I put no trust in my bow. My sword doesn't bring me victory. But you give us victory over our enemies.

Psalm 44: 5-7

Uncle Rich started the engine and pulled away from the dock. "Have a little faith in something more important than gadgets." Logan put on his life jacket. Uncle Rich tapped his head. "Fish smarts," he said. "I know where the fish like to go."

They were anchored in a little cove all alone. Nobody knew about this spot, because it was hard to get to. They hadn't had their rods in an hour before Logan felt a huge pull on his rod. He knew right away that this fish was big, maybe even trophy-winning big.

Uncle Rich was right; you have to have faith in the right things.

Israel had a hard time when it came to enemies with new gadgets. They were fighting battles against an enemy with better stuff. While the Israelites had weapons made mostly of wood and leather, the Philistines knew how to make weapons out of iron. So King Saul and the boys had to put their faith in God instead of in their weapons.

June 11

Hello

Dustin and Gordon were waiting at the airport for their Uncle Marty. They held up their homemade "Welcome to Ireland" sign. They waved to all the travelers who entered the arrival lounge. Their friendliness brought big smiles.

Words to Treasure

If you greet only your own people, what more are you doing than others? Even people who are ungodly do that.

Matthew 5:47

One man walked over and shook their hands. "Thank you for the welcome!" he laughed. A little girl ran over and hugged Dustin's knees.

"Hey!" Uncle Marty shouted from the doorway. He walked over and playfully wrestled with his nephews.

Everybody wants to feel welcomed and appreciated sometimes. So whether it's at church, school, your sports team or the airport, say hello to someone else who could use a smile. Using signs is, of course, optional.

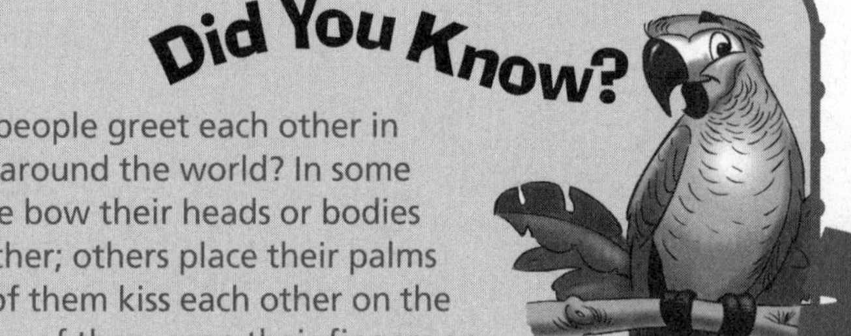

Did You Know?

Did you know people greet each other in different ways around the world? In some cultures, people bow their heads or bodies toward each other; others place their palms together; lots of them kiss each other on the cheek; and some of them snap their fingers or even back-slap.

June 12

Inside Out

I don't like my size." Wyatt ate a chocolate bar in two bites as they walked along.

His best friend, Alton stopped, and looked up. "You've got to be kidding me?"

Words to Treasure

So accept one another in order to bring praise to God.
Romans 15:7

Wyatt shrugged. "I'm too big for a kid. I'm bigger than most adults. I'm big and clumsy. People stare. I always have to play Goliath in the church plays. I always get killed."

"You never told me that."

Wyatt shrugged again. "That's because you're a little person. I thought you wouldn't understand."

"Believe me, I understand. I'm less than four feet. You want to talk about people staring. I can tell you about people staring. But I never thought someone could feel bad about being big. That's incredible. Thanks for telling me, man. We so get each other." Wyatt extended his arm for a fist bump.

People come in all shapes and sizes. Sometimes we just see what's on the outside and don't think about the person on the inside and how they're feeling. Being a friend means wanting to know about the person on the inside as well as the outside.

It is never cool to make fun of someone's height, weight, cultural background, or anything about the way he or she looks. Losers put down others to make themselves feel better about themselves.
You're not a loser, are you?

June 13

Slow to Anger

Is that all of it?" His dad scanned the ingredients on the table. "The whole stink bomb kit?"

Words to Treasure

His anger lasts for only a moment. But his favor lasts for a person's whole life.

Psalm 30:5

Leo slumped into a chair. "Are you mad?"

"Mad that you stunk out your Sunday school class for the entire morning? What do you think?"

People get angry, but does God get angry? Yeah, God does get angry, but always for a good reason, never because he's just being grumpy that day. God is extremely patient with the people he loves; even when they continue to do wrong things. God will always give them chances to do better.

God's anger is never out of control, because he really doesn't want to be angry. Sometimes he will do things to get our attention and to teach us what's right. God is always ready to forgive when we're ready to listen. Nothing you will ever do will stop God from loving you.

Over and over again, the Israelites disobeyed God. They refused to listen to him. God put up with it for a long, long time. He even sent prophets to talk to his people. They didn't listen. But God didn't destroy them or desert them. He just sent them for a much-needed time-out with the not-so-nice Babylonians. God was patient and fair. He loved his people and was slow to anger. In the end he brought them home again and all was forgiven. (See Nehemiah 9:29–31.)

List

The assignment was tough and diabolical. Only masterminds of cruelty could have come up with it. His parents had sent him into his bedroom to make a list of the things that everybody did for him, everyone from his brother and grandparents to teachers and coaches. Each person's list had two sides. One side was what he did for them, and the other side is what they did for him. He hated to admit it, but their side was a whole lot longer than his side. The list of the things his mom did for him was enormously long. So was his dad's.

Words to Treasure

None of you should look out just for your own good. Each of you should also look out for the good of others.

Philippians 2:4

Nathan was beginning to get the point. People in his life did a whole lot for him. And he was taking them *completely* for granted. He needed to do more for everybody he knew, and he needed to be a whole lot more thankful. It didn't take a rocket scientist to tell him he was taking from people a lot more than he was giving back. He had to change. The worst part was admitting his parents were right. Okay, maybe they weren't masterminds of cruelty after all. Lesson learned.

Are people doing a lot for you and you're not exactly giving back the same? Make a list of nice things you can do for the people you love. Give a little bit more back! Be a giver, not just a taker.

June 15

Gum Factor

Denny was giving a great talk to the little kids at Sunday school. He looked good and sounded really smart. Denny was feeling pretty proud and impressed with himself. "Do you have any questions?"

> **Words to Treasure**
>
> But your proud heart has tricked you.
>
> Obadiah 1:3

A little girl raised her hand. "How come you have gum stuck in your hair?"

Denny touched his head, and she was right—there was gum in his hair. He turned beet red. "I don't know why. Maybe because this morning I thought I was so much older and smarter than you. But none of you have gum in your hair do you?" They giggled. "Looks like you're smarter and cooler than me. I don't have it all together like I thought."

Everybody is just stumbling along, learning about God and trying to do the right things. Nobody (not even your pastor) has it all together. Let's learn about God together. Remember that the next time you think you're *so* great. You may have gum in your hair and not know it.

Jesus asked the disciples what they had argued about while they were walking along. They grew kind of quiet because they had argued about which one of them was the most important person in the group. Jesus explained that if you want to be the first, you have to be willing to be the last. In other words, stop worrying about being the greatest. Being humble, helpful, and honest are great attitudes. (See Mark 9:33–35.)

King or Queen of the Hill?

"Boys are lame, and girls are brains," Page yelled down from their tree fort. The other girls giggled.

Brian shouted back. "Guys have brains and guys have muscles, so you better go get some help from your mothers."

The boys all yelled, "YEAH!!" Everybody laughed. They were having fun teasing each other.

Brian started to climb the ladder. "We're coming up. It's our tree fort too." Soon water balloons came crashing down on the boys. They didn't care because they had brought their own and were soon throwing balloons up at the fort. The water fight was on, and everybody was getting wet and having a good time.

So which are better, boys or girls? In God's eyes, neither. He created male and female and loves them both. Boys and girls *are* different from each other. That's okay. We're supposed to be different. But those differences don't make one better than the other. Be proud to be a guy. And be proud to be a girl. God, your Father, is equally proud of you both.

Words to Treasure

So God created human beings in his own likeness. He created them to be like himself. He created them as male and female.

Genesis 1:27

Discovering Archaeology

Skeletons all pretty much look the same. Right? Not to scientists. By measuring certain bones, archaeologists can tell you whether the skeleton is a male or female. Sometimes they can also tell you how old the person was when he or she died, and sometimes even how he or she died. Our bones tell a story about us.

June 17

Harvest

Natalie felt very small beside the big combine that was going to harvest the family wheat field. A combine is a big cutting tractor that cuts down, thrashes, and loads wheat into grain trucks. Her dad climbed up and threw open the door. "Natalie, you want to make the first round with me? I might let you drive a little."

Words to Treasure

Before long the grain ripens. So the farmer cuts it down, because the harvest is ready.
Mark 4:29

"Really!" She climbed into the cab.

"Maybe." He started the engine, and she felt the big machine move forward. In front of them was a sea of beautiful golden wheat. Natalie had helped plant the seeds, and every night she had prayed for good weather for a good harvest. Someday Natalie would be in charge of the farm, and she wanted to learn everything about being a good farmer.

We may not realize it, but God has planted in each of us a seed of love and understanding of him. Then God gives us everything we need to grow and learn—a family, teachers, and pastors. Jesus and the Holy Spirit also help us understand heavenly things. God is patient like a farmer knowing that someday we will grow into grown-up believers. That's God's kind of harvest.

In Bible times, the harvesting machines of the day were oxen-, donkey-, and manpowered. A farmer cut down the wheat by hand with a big blade called a sickle. Then the wheat was loaded onto donkeys or oxen and taken out of the field. Animal and man working together.

Little Bit More!

Mr. Stroud admired the mural Mia had painted on one inside wall of the old hardware store. Mia had used an old, old photograph of the store to paint a picture of what the inside of the store looked like in 1885. Women in long dresses and men in top hats filled the painting. "Come with me." Mr. Stroud took her outside the store and pointed to the massively big blank side of the building. "What do you think? The entire side of the building one big painting? Can you do it?"

Mia's mouth hung open. "I don't know. I think I can."

Words to Treasure

You have done well, good and faithful slave! You have been faithful with a few things. I will put you in charge of many things.

Matthew 25:23

When you are faithful or do a good job in small things, God will give you bigger things to accomplish. It means God and people trust you to do what you say you'll do. So do a good job in little missions, and be ready for those big adventures.

People in Bible Times

Joseph's brothers sold him into slavery. Joe did an awesome job of serving his new master, but then Joe got framed and thrown in jail. You guessed it; he did an even more amazing job helping his guards. Then he got taken to the palace when Pharaoh needed a little help. Joe was amazing again and became Pharaoh's right-hand man. Being faithful in little things works.

June 19

Prejudice

Sid was just about to pet the really whopping big tan dog when his bigger brother Randy threw himself in front of him. "DON'T! He's a bad kind of dog."

Words to Treasure

Whoever loves other people has done everything the law requires.

Romans 13:8

Sid peered around his brother and waved at the panting, wagging dog. "Why is he so bad?"

"He's a ..." Randy spelled out, "P-I-T B-U-L-L."

The dog's owner came up behind them. "You're safe. Muffin can't spell." The owner stroked his dog. "Muffin's a really friendly dog. You can pet her. You can't judge every dog by the actions of some bad dogs. But ..." he looked at Sid, "you should always ask a dog's owner if you can pet his dog." Sid stroked Muffin, and he giggled as she licked his hand.

Sometimes we can believe wrong things about people based on how they dress, the color of their skin, their religion, or stories we've heard about their traditions. Treating people differently based on any of those things is wrong and is not the way God wants you to be. We're supposed to love and give *everybody* a chance to be our friends, because everybody is unique and special. Being prejudiced is wrong *every* time.

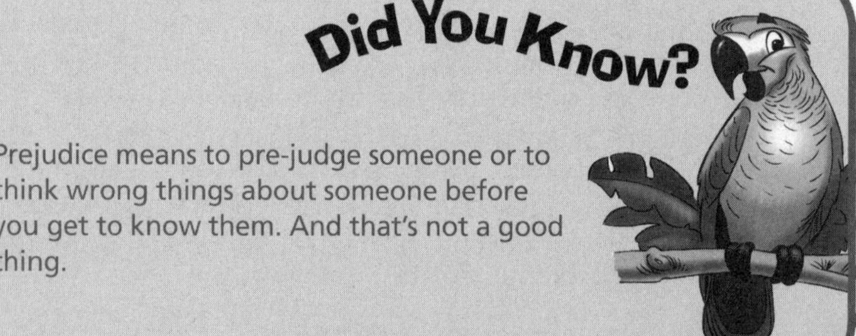

Prejudice means to pre-judge someone or to think wrong things about someone before you get to know them. And that's not a good thing.

Blessings

Liam got his coat and was ready to go home, but his mother called him back into the room. "Great-Granny wants to say something to you."

The very old woman smiled at Liam. "May the road rise up to meet you, may the wind be ever at your back. May the sun shine warm upon your face and the rain fall softly on your fields. And until we meet again, may God hold you in the palm of his hand." Liam nodded politely.

Words to Treasure

May the Lord bless you and take good care of you.

Numbers 6:24

Going out the door Liam whispered to his mom, "I don't own any fields."

His mom laughed. "It's a very old blessing."

Blessings come in all kinds of forms.

God can bless people, which means he gives them special help or gifts. People can also pray a blessing, which is asking for God's special love and care for other people or situations.

We often will say a blessing before we eat, which is a short prayer giving thanks to God.

You can also say blessings to God, which means to worship and thank him for everything wonderful he is. Blessings are never out of date.

People wanted Jesus to touch and bless their children, but the disciples told them to stop. After all, Jesus was busy doing important stuff. When Jesus saw this, he got angry and told them to let the children come to him. He took the children in his arms and blessed them. Kids are important! (See Mark 10:13–16.)

June 21

Kick the Dog

"I mean it, young man. It is your job to clean your fish tank. Those poor little fish are swimming in soup." His mom was very unhappy. "Go down and get a bowl to put your fish in while you clean it."

Words to Treasure

A foolish person turns their back on their parent's correction. But anyone who accepts correction shows understanding.

Proverbs 15:5

Molson slumped down the stairs and walked straight into a doll tea party. Liana had every doll in the house sitting around the hallway waiting for tea. Cody their dog was licking jam off a doll's face. Molson kicked one of the dolls clear across the room. The doll hit the wall with a soft plop. "You shouldn't have all your dolls out." Molson stomped through the party.

Liana started to cry. When she saw Cody licking the doll, she yelled. "*Go away, Cody*!" Poor Cody left the room with his tail between his legs.

We call what Molson and Liana did "kicking the dog." Someone gets upset at you. You then go and get upset at someone else, usually someone smaller than you. Then that person (or pet) gets upset too like poor Cody. Molson kicked the doll because he was a little angry at his mom. Liana yelled at Cody because she was mad and knew the dog couldn't yell back. It's an anger chain reaction. Break the chain with mercy and kindness.

A servant was having trouble paying back the money he borrowed from the king. The king wasn't happy, but showed understanding and mercy. This upset servant immediately went out and got mad at another servant who owed *him* money. But he didn't show any mercy. When the king found out, things weren't looking good for Mr. No-Mercy. Kicking the dog, Bible style. (See Matthew 18:21–35.)

Funny Names

Forrest inspected his new baby cousin. "What's her name?" He hoped it was a pretty name, because this was one funny looking baby. Her head was pointy on top. She'd have to wear a hat for the rest of her life.

Words to Treasure

Saul was also known as Paul.
Acts 13:9

His mother held the new baby. "Elizabeth or Lizzy for short. And don't worry, her head won't be pointy for long."

Forrest studied the pointy head again. "Lizzy the lizard. Lizard, that's a cool name." None of the adults looked very happy.

Names are funny things, and they're even funnier in the Bible. Some people in the Bible changed their names. What's with that? Just when you think you know who's who in the Bible, they suddenly change their name. Saul was suddenly called Paul. Or Abram became Abraham. Or Simon was renamed Peter. Why?

Sometimes God gave someone a new name with a special meaning because it marked a change in that person's life. God promised Abram that he would be the start of a whole country of people. So God changed Abram's name to Abraham, which means "Father of Many," just a little daily reminder of God's promise that someday Abraham would be a father. Jesus changed Simon's name to Peter, which means "rock." Jesus knew that this guy's faith would be rock solid. What's in a name? Apparently lots. What does your name mean?

Live It!

There are books that have lists of first names and the meanings behind them. Check one out of the library and look up what different names mean and where they're from. What does your name mean?

June 23

Learn This

Penny really wanted her black belt in Karate. "Mr. Cho?" she asked. He nodded to her, "Yes?"

"What's the fastest way to get a black belt?"

"Be a good student. Listen and learn," he said.

"But that'll take a long time."

Mr. Cho smiled and nodded. "Yes. I teach and you learn from me."

We know that Jesus had twelve disciples, but what exactly is a disciple? The word *disciple* means "learner or student."

Jesus chose twelve men to be his students. Some of his disciples were simple fisherman, and one was even a tax collector. These disciples left their homes, families, and jobs to travel with Jesus and learn from him. Like any student, sometimes they did smart things and sometimes not-so-smart things. But Jesus saw something very special in each of them.

Words to Treasure

Jesus went up on a mountainside. He called for certain people to come to him, and they came. He appointed 12 of them so that they would be with him.
Mark 3:13-14

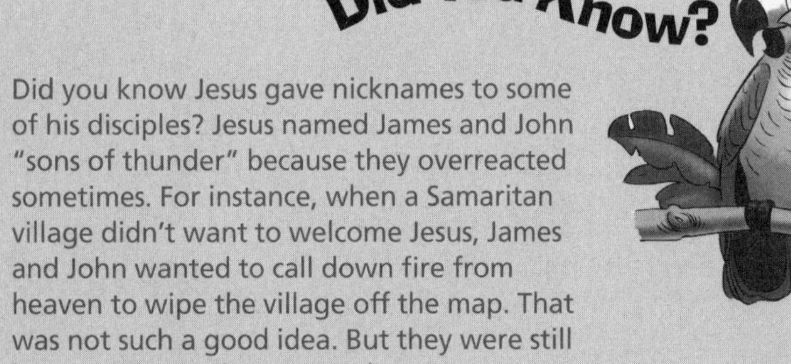

Did You Know?

Did you know Jesus gave nicknames to some of his disciples? Jesus named James and John "sons of thunder" because they overreacted sometimes. For instance, when a Samaritan village didn't want to welcome Jesus, James and John wanted to call down fire from heaven to wipe the village off the map. That was not such a good idea. But they were still learning. (See Luke 9:54–55.)

Get Going

Kayley," Mrs. Meza called her to the front and pulled four raw, dead fish from a cooler. "You did so well when we did our Japanese fish-printing class. Do you think you could help teach Mr. Lambert's class how to do it? He really could use your help. I won't need you back until after lunch."

"Sure thing." Kayley headed out to help teach her first art class.

Kayley just might be a fish-print *apostle*. What's an apostle? An apostle is someone who is sent out to teach or show other people what they know. In the Bible, apostles were people sent out to teach about God.

Words to Treasure

I, Paul am writing this letter. I serve Jesus Christ. I have been appointed to be an apostle. God set me apart to tell others his good news.

Romans 1:1

Disciples are students, but at some point they become *apostles* when they are sent out on their own to teach. When Jesus sent his disciples out to teach about God, they became apostles. Jesus was also called an apostle because his heavenly Father sent him to the world to teach us. Disciples and apostles become a long unbroken chain of students learning to be teachers. We're still doing it today.

Jesus had some instructions for his apostles.

- Go teach, heal the sick, raise the dead, and drive out demons.
- Don't take money, extra clothes, sandals, or walking sticks. You will be given what you need.
- Stay where people want you, and leave if they don't.

(See Matthew 10:1–42.)

June 25

Thankfully Thankful

The wind rustled the tent roof, but the boys didn't notice because they were listening to a story. It wasn't a ghost story but it was a scary story. "One day," Zuberi said, sitting on the sleeping bag with his friends, "men came into our village. We were very afraid. They took all the food we had in the entire village. We didn't know what to do because we were so hungry. So my father said, 'Let's pray for our daily bread.' You know, let's say the Lord's Prayer we say at church. But in Africa we were really praying for bread for that day to eat. It was not just a thing to say; it was a real prayer. We really needed food."

Words to Treasure

Lord, I will give thanks to you, because you answered me. You have saved me.

Psalm 118:21

"What happened?" The chocolate bar in Amos's hand was melting.

"My father walked many miles to look for food. At last he found a bag of sweet potatoes sitting in the middle of the road. It must have fallen off a truck. It was a miracle. We thanked God."

For many people around the world, the prayers that we take for granted—such as saying a prayer before we eat dinner—have a whole different meaning. So when you thank God today, be really, really thankful.

You can say, "Thank You" in over 200 different languages. Each time you pray say thank you to God in a different language. Your parents can help.

June 26

Staffs with Stuff

Jay ran the sandpaper down the walking stick he had just carved out of a tree branch. Great-Uncle Morgan was finishing his fifth stick of the morning because he sold them at craft fairs. "This," Jay tested his stick, "is the greatest walking stick ever made."

Great-Uncle Morgan examined Jay's work. "Good stick, but can it turn into a snake?"

"What?"

Jay made a good stick, but it wasn't in the league with the snake-morphing, plague-making, Red-Sea-splitting shepherd staffs of two brothers in the Bible. Moses and Aaron were shepherds before God sent them on a pharaoh-busting mission to save God's people. Their tool of choice: a shepherd's staff. God used everyday items to do some of the most amazing miracles the world has ever seen. It just doesn't get bigger than causing the Red Sea to part so that the Israelites could cross through to safety, while deep-diving the pharaoh's army that tried to follow.

Those simple shepherd staffs became a sign of God's power to protect the Israelites and reminded people that Moses was God's pick for leader. Aaron's staff was later put in the Ark of the Covenant, God's throne on earth. Simple wood stick or amazing tool of God? Kind of like you—simple kid or amazing person for God?

Words to Treasure

But take this walking stick in your hand. You will be able to do signs with it.

Exodus 4:17

Did You Know?

Did you know that in some countries today a single flock of sheep may have up to 4,000 individual sheep? Talk about counting sheep!

June 27

Now That's a Whale

The large dorsal fin rose out of the ocean right next to their little boat. George didn't know whether to be terrified or thrilled. Then the killer whale slipped back down into the dark water. Next, a tiny fin emerged. A baby whale followed his mother. George's dad was taking pictures like crazy. Suddenly, they were in the middle of a family of killer whales, or orcas, teaching their baby how to hunt. They swam under and around the boat. George could feel the spray of water as they exhaled through their blowholes. The big male was bigger than the boat—maybe twenty-six feet long and over five tons. (Some elephants weigh that much.) What an unexpected surprise by nature.

Words to Treasure

So God created the great sea creatures. He created every kind of living thing that fills the seas and moves about in them.

Genesis 1:21

How awesome for two of God's creations to be sharing the same ocean on the same day.

A man named Jonah tried to make a quick escape from God's plans for him. What happened? Crazy storm, sinking ship, upset sailors. They tossed Jonah into the deep ocean and then he was swallowed by a whale. But was that the biting conclusion of Jonah? Check it out in the Book of Jonah in your Bible.

June 28

Now You Know

Cody Reed didn't want to make eye contact with his dad or the lifeguard. Cody's initials were carved deeply into the picnic table by the water park. There was no doubt about it. And it didn't help that he was caught in the act of carving it.

"Well?" His dad wasn't so happy.

"The older kids were doing it, and I just did it too. You never told me it was wrong."

His dad's mouth hung open. "I never told you vandalism is wrong! That carving into someone else's furniture is wrong! I figured that goes *without* saying. Some things, Cody Michael Reed, you should know without being told."

"I didn't know. Nobody told me," is an excuse lots of people use to explain away their bad behavior—even grown-ups. That excuse doesn't wash with God, because he's given us his Son Jesus, the Holy Spirit, the prophets, and the Bible so we *do* know how we should behave—no excuses allowed.

Words to Treasure

He shows those who aren't proud how to do what is right. He teaches them his ways.

Psalm 25:9

One day Jesus sat down on a mountainside and began to teach people how God wants us to behave and the best way to live our lives. This important talk is called the Sermon on the Mount. Jesus wanted us to understand important godly things so we could never say, "I didn't know. You never told me." *Yes, he did!* (See Matthew 5–7.)

June 29

I Can't Do Perfect!

Meg melted down into a heap beside the crossed swords on the smooth floor. Her Highland dancing teacher, Mrs. Brown, passed a bottle of water. "I spotted a few mistakes that I think we should go over, Meg. This time, you kicked the swords twice."

Words to Treasure

My grace is all you need. My power is strongest when you are weak.

2 Corinthians 12:9

Meg lay down, enjoying the feeling of the cold wood dance floor. "I'm never going to get it perfect. I practice and I practice, but I'm never going to get it perfect."

Mrs. Brown laughed. "Whoever said you could? I just want you to do your best. I know you can do that." She clapped her hands. "Right, off the floor." Meg groaned.

God never expects you to be perfect. God just wants you to work at doing your best. That's not hard. Don't worry, Jesus and the Holy Spirit are here to help you every step of the way. They love you when you do right things, and they love you even when you mess up. Nobody's perfect. God knows that.

Sometimes we try so hard to have everything perfect. We want to have a perfect room, have perfect clothes, or be the perfect student or the top athlete. Sometimes we get so focused on having everything perfect that we forget to enjoy the things God's given us. Wanting to do your best is good, but always remember that your best is good enough. Perfection isn't required.

You in the Back!

Okay!" Sammy inspected the junior campers on the boat dock. "Who canoes with me? I have mystery stuff stashed in my canoe, and the person who paddles with me can plot the ultimate practical joke on the rest of my crew. So who should it be?" The kids rushed forward, hands waving to be the chosen one. They shouted out reasons why they'd be the best pick. Shy Ivy (everybody called her that) stood in the back, quiet and hopeful. Sammy pointed at her. "Ivy, you are my co-pilot for the day. Come on up here."

Words to Treasure

Blessed are those who are humble. They will be given the earth.

Matthew 5:5

Shy Ivy was so surprised. "Me?"

Jesus said that heaven belongs to the poor and the ones who are needy in spirit, in other words, the humble guy, the person who understands that he or she doesn't deserve anything and who is thankful for everything God sends. When you understand that God's love isn't something you have a right to have, but something God wants to give you, then you are on the path to being Jesus' co-pilot. Being humble rocks!

People in Bible Times

AND the winner of *The Biggest Pride Award* in the Bible goes to the Pharaoh of Egypt. Give him a big hand. He went toe-to-toe with the most humble man on the planet, Moses. Pharaoh wouldn't listen to God and got smacked with twelve really disgusting plagues until finally the royal guy got a big dose of humble pie and let God's people go.

July 1

Not Ever Alone

It was so fast that Janelle didn't really know what had happened until it was all over. Her brother grabbed her hand and dragged her into the storm cellar with her family. Then it sounded as if a train drove right over their house. It was so loud she covered her ears. She never wanted to hear something that terrible again. She felt the house shudder and heard wood crack and splinter. Then as quickly as it came, the twister passed.

Words to Treasure

Blessed are those who are sad. They will be comforted.

Matthew 5:4

Now Janelle was standing in front of a pile of rubble that had been her house. It was like a dollhouse that somebody picked up and shattered into a million pieces. She started to cry. A fireman walked over and pulled a teddy bear from his coat. Janelle fell into his big arms and cried and cried.

Life can be full of hard, hard things that come and turn our world upside down in minutes. But Jesus said if you're sad you will be comforted. Not only is Jesus there for you, but God will also send people to help you. You're never ever alone, because God promises to bring friends to help you and comfort you.

In Bible times, when people were sad or upset, they often put on clothes made out of uncomfortable material and walked around barefoot. Sometimes they tore their clothes or cut their hair to show how sad they were. They also put ashes on their heads.

July 2

Meek

What would you like me to do?" Holly really wanted to work at the petting zoo when she was older, but right now she was ready to volunteer for any chore at the zoo. The zookeeper thought about it for a moment. "The gutters in the barn could use cleaning out. It's kind of nasty work, though."

Words to Treasure

"Blessed are those whose hearts are pure. They will see God."

Matthew 5:8

Holly's friend Kerri did not look very happy. "Could we groom the ponies instead?"

"We'll clean the gutters if that's what you need done. Come on, Kerri." Holly headed for the barn. The zookeeper smiled, impressed with Holly's attitude.

Holly is what the Bible would call meek. That doesn't mean timid and shy, which is how we usually think of meek. In the Bible, meek is being willing to serve God without complaining, doing whatever he wants us to do. No job is too hard or too small for the meek! Holly knows that if she works hard and proves herself in every task, good or gross, she'll be the best zookeeper she can be in the future. We should have that same attitude with God. The mighty meek!

Did You Know?

Did you know Jesus was meek? He did everything that God told him to do, even to the point of dying on the cross for our sins. Jesus said, "I do exactly what my Father has commanded me to do." So should we. What is God telling you? Talk with your family about it.

JULY 3

Friend in Need?

Porter and Richard walked along the gravel road carrying their bats and gloves. "I just knew you wouldn't make the team," Richard said smugly. Porter was so upset he didn't even want to talk. Richard just wouldn't stop talking about it. He talked about how Porter had a weak throw and how he wasn't the fastest guy on the field. Porter was feeling worse and worse about himself.

Words to Treasure

They said many things to give strength and hope to the believers.

Acts 15:32

His other friend Anton caught up. He wrapped his arm around Porter's shoulder. "You know, your throw's not so bad. We can work on it together ... and then next year you'll make the team for sure." Porter felt better.

When you're feeling sad, you need friends who want to find ways to make you feel better—friends who want to help you fix problems. If a friend is just way too happy about your unhappiness, it's definitely time to get a new friend. God will put people in your life who want to encourage you, not discourage you. So pick your friends wisely, and they will be good friends when you need them the most.

Not long after Jesus, there were believers living in different places and countries. It was a constant job for the leaders of the early church to send letters of encouragement to all of their far away friends. They knew it was important for everybody to feel wanted, loved, and valued, especially when hard things were happening. Do you have a friend who might like an encouraging email or letter?

Giving Back

"Why are you helping us read better?" Winter flapped the pages of her book impatiently.

"Because somebody helped me when I was having a hard time learning to read," Paul said as he leaned back in his library chair.

"Who?"

"Mr. Crowe. He was very old, but every Saturday he'd sit in the library and help kids learn to read." Paul pointed to a bronze sign on the wall. "The city put up that sign to thank him."

Words to Treasure

"Blessed are those who show mercy. They will be shown mercy."

Matthew 5:7

"He doesn't come anymore?" Winter selected a new book.

Paul looked a little sad, "He died a couple of years ago." Paul turned and pointed to five other older kids helping little kids to read. "He helped all of us, and now we come to the library every Saturday to help you. When you're older, maybe you'll come here and help somebody else read better."

Part of a personal trait called mercy is showing kindness to someone else—just like Mr. Crowe and Paul.

People in Bible Times

Two blind men were sitting along the side of the road. Jesus and a large crowd walked past. The two men called to Jesus and asked him to have mercy on them. But the crowd told them to shut up. The two guys yelled even louder. Jesus called, "What do you want me to do for you?" They shouted back, "We want to be able to *see*." Jesus touched their eyes and gave them their sight. (See Matthew 20:29–34.)

July 5

Only Takes a Second

Sharon saw the wave heading toward the beach. She could see that it wasn't dangerously wild, but it wasn't embarrassingly little either. Her father pointed at the line of water and he nodded at her. This was the one! Sharon pushed herself halfway onto the boogie board and clutched the sides of it, waiting for the wave to hit. In a rush of water, she felt the surf pick her up and push her forward. For a few seconds she let the wave take complete control of her board, and it was as if she was flying across the water toward the beach. Then, just as suddenly, she was dropped into the sandy shallows. Laughing, she rolled off her board and sat up in the warm water. She looked across the beach at the colors of the setting sun. This had been a perfect day. She smiled and whispered, "Thank you, God."

Words to Treasure

Give thanks to the Lord, because he is good. His faithful love continues forever.

1 Chronicles 16:34

Did you know thanking God isn't just a Sunday-at-church thing? It can be an everyday thing. If you're enjoying something, take the time to thank God that very second of that very day. God wants to share your good times.

When the great King David was just a young shepherd hanging out with his sheep, he often looked up at the stars and was so thankful for the amazing universe God had created that he even wrote songs about it. Now, that's an example to follow.

Peace

Henry was really mad, "You can't have it both ways, Ryan. You have to pick. Who are you going to side with on this fight? Are you staying here with Trevor, or are you coming with me?"

Ryan looked from one friend to the other.

Trevor pushed the soccer ball around with his foot. "You're either with me or against me, Ryan. This is war, bro. Pick!"

Words to Treasure

"Blessed are those who make peace. They will be called children of God."

Matthew 5:9

Ryan frowned deep in thought. "Okay," he said, "this is my choice. Neither. You two are acting *so* lame. This fight is stupid. This is how it plays out. If the two of you want to be *my* friend, you'll have to work out your differences and then call me." Ryan walked away muttering, "*Pick sides*! You've got to be kidding me. *This is war* … this is crazy." Ryan smiled, pleased with his choice. Trevor and Henry didn't expect *that* move.

Jesus said that people who turn away from conflicts and help enemies find peace together are children of God. It isn't enough for us to avoid fights; God also calls us to help others find peaceful ways to solve their differences. Peacemakers follow Jesus, the Prince of Peace.

God granted Solomon wisdom to rule his people. Isn't it also interesting that during Solomon's rule it was a time of great peace, happiness, and success? Making peace just might be a wise move.

July 7

Fear or Trust?

Annette adjusted her helmet nervously as she glanced at the rolling, churning river beside her. The river guide pointed to the big yellow raft on the bank. "I know you've heard a lot of scary stories about this river. Before you get in that raft I have to know that you trust me with your lives. Trust that I know everything about this river and I know exactly what to do in every situation. *And* I have to trust you to do everything I tell you, when I tell you. If we do that, we are going to have the most exciting time of our lives whitewater rafting. Do you trust me?"

Words to Treasure

Some trust in chariots. Some trust in horses. But we trust in the Lord our God.

Psalm 20:7

The entire team screamed, "YES!"

"Do I trust you?"

Annette picked up her paddle and shouted, "Yes!" She helped push the boat into deeper water. They climbed in and let the whitewater take them to the most dangerous adventure she'd ever been on. Annette trusted her guide. She also trusted God in this adventure and in her entire life. Do you?

Before the days of high-tech gadgets, Joshua sent spies to check out the land God promised them. And even though they came back with some scary reports, they still put their complete trust in God to help them win the land. Trusting God even when you're totally afraid is just really smart.

Hassle-Free

The big guy flipped the book out of José's hand, and it fell to the grimy floor of the bus. The guy picked it up and laughed, "A Bible?"

José tried to take it back, but the guy pulled the book away. "Are you a Christian?" He snorted through his nose as he laughed again.

José exhaled. "Yes, I go to church."

"So, you'll forgive me when I do this." The guy tossed José's Bible out the window. José pulled the stop cord and walked toward the bus exit. The guy called, "Hey, aren't you going to say anything?"

José turned, "My name is José. See you tomorrow."

The next day on the bus, José walked up to the guy and his crew. "Here, I bought this for you." José passed him a new Bible. "Don't throw it out the window." The guy was very surprised.

Almost every Christian will get some type of hassle for being a Christian. Get in line, because people have been hassling God's people for thousands of years. Nothing new about it. How we handle it will tell the world about us. Tough it out, and know Jesus is with you all the time.

Words to Treasure

Blessed are you when people make fun of you and hurt you because of me.

Matthew 5:11

There are Christians all over the world who are suffering hard times because of their faith in Jesus. Pray for Christians around the world each day.

July 9

Don't Do As They Do!

Marianne and her friends were debating what movie they should see. All of her friends wanted to see a thriller, but Marianne had her little sister with her.

Words to Treasure

Practice and teach these commands. Then you will be called important in the kingdom of heaven.

Matthew 5:19

Her friend Cindy played with her ponytail. "It'll be okay. She won't get that scared."

Marianne looked at her friends and then at her trusting little sister. "No, she'll get scared. I'll see you after the movie. We're going to go see that new animated movie. You know, the one for kids."

Mariannc and her little sister settled into their seats when all of a sudden her friends piled in beside them. Cindy shrugged, "This sounded more fun."

Not only should we do what's right, but Jesus said we also have a big responsibility to teach others what is right. We set an example for other people including our younger brothers and sisters to follow. Did Marianne lead the right way? Jesus saw her actions as important. What do your actions say?

In Bible times, children mostly learned good examples from watching and working with their parents and other adults in their village. Girls learned how to run a good home from their mothers, and boys learned a trade from their fathers or were sent to learn a trade from a more experienced craftsman.

JULY 10

Make It Right

Joel walked into church and looked around for friends to sit with. He spotted Cam and Devon and made a mental note to sit on the side of the church far from them. He had had a huge fight with them this week. Now they weren't speaking.

Joel's pastor slid in beside him. "I notice you're not sitting with Cam and Devon. There a problem?"

Joel nodded his head knowingly. "They must have talked to you."

His pastor eased back in the pew. "A little. Before we get into worship, I'd like it if you guys worked it out. Make it right with each other." Joel glanced at Cam and Devon, and they glanced at him. "If you want, I can referee. Let's go talk with them." Joel followed his pastor to go patch up a broken friendship.

Jesus encouraged us to patch up problems with others before we go before God in church or in our prayers. Problem fixing is just the right thing to do.

Words to Treasure

Leave your gift in front of the altar. First go and make peace with your brother. Then come back and offer your gift.

Matthew 5:24

Are there some disagreements that need fixing in your life? Go make things right. You'll feel better, and you'll be glad you did. It's important to clear these matters up. Everything's better when friends are friends again.

July 11

Yes Means Yes

Are you going to help us deliver Mr. Mann's flyers as you promised?" Yoshio asked as he compared the old wheels of his longboard to the new wheels he was putting on.

Words to Treasure

All you need to say is simply 'Yes' or 'No.' Anything more than this comes from the evil one.

Matthew 5:37

"Yep, I'm there." Blair tested his board by bouncing up and down on it. Then he glided across the garage floor. He didn't even look at Yoshio.

"That's what you said last time, and you didn't show up." Yoshio spun a wheel to test the balance, then he stopped and studied Blair's face.

Blair looked down and flipped his board on his foot. "I'll be there. I swear."

Stop! Don't swear—just be there. Jesus made it very clear that we shouldn't make oaths or swear. An oath is agreeing to do something by promising God and that person you'll make good on what you said. Many people in conversation will say, "I swear to God." Don't do that. That's wrong and very disrespectful to God.

You don't have to involve God to make your promises seem more truthful or more real to someone else. Jesus wants your *yes* to mean *yes* and your *no* to mean *no,* all on your own. No swearing, no oaths.

Before you make a promise, think very carefully. Make sure you're able to keep that promise. If you're not sure you can—then don't promise.

What Does It Take?

Cindy looked at the fried worms and snails in the frying pan. "You're kidding me, right?"

Her camp counselor shook her head. "Two days living off the land—that's what it takes to get your survival badge. This is all we could find to eat."

Cindy picked up a hot piece of snail meat. "I'll eat the snail, but I'm *not* eating the worm."

Actually, Cindy was happy at this point just to be sitting by a warm fire. It had taken them ages to start a fire with no matches. She promised God that she was never again going to complain about dinner or anything else at home. From now on, she would be thankful all the time.

Be happy with the simple gifts God has given you, things such as the home you live in, the food you eat, and all things you have that make your life easier. After you become content, then you can be generous with somebody else who's in more need than you are.

Words to Treasure

When you have eaten and are satisfied, praise the Lord your God. Praise him for the good land he has given you.

Deuteronomy 8:10

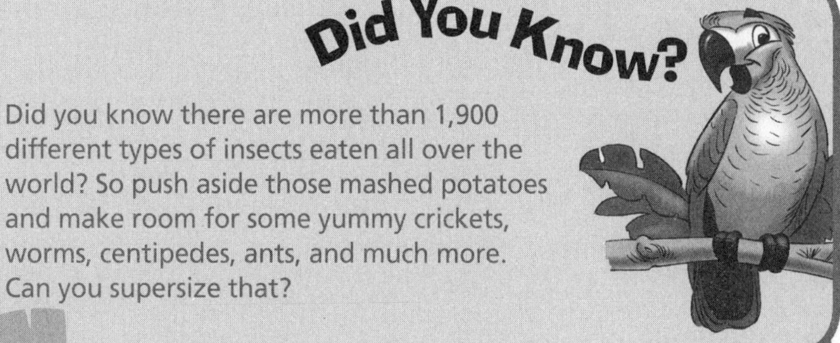

Did You Know?
Did you know there are more than 1,900 different types of insects eaten all over the world? So push aside those mashed potatoes and make room for some yummy crickets, worms, centipedes, ants, and much more. Can you supersize that?

July 13

Pray for Others

Dane sat on his bed thinking and thinking as he played chess with himself. He wasn't concentrating very well on his game. Instead, he was concentrating on his thoughts. He didn't really want to, but he knew he had to pray about this. "Lord, I want to pray for Jonathan Keese, also known as Trouble to the authorities and to me. I know he's a mean, self-centered bully and a compulsive gum chewer, but can you do whatever it is you do to people to turn them around? Oh, a personal request ... could you start with his gum smacking in my ear? Amen."

Words to Treasure

PPray for those who hurt you. Then you will be children of your Father who is in heaven.

Matthew 5:44–45

Dane did what we should all do and that is to pray for people who cause us trouble. It could be the hardest prayer to pray, but it just might be the most important prayer you can pray. People who do wrong or evil need our prayers. Jesus told us that kindness and prayer are stronger than evil, and they are.

Live IT!

Make a list of people you have some problems with, and start to pray for them every day. Prayer can do amazing things not just for the person you pray for, but in your heart as well. Remember, even when people were hurting Jesus—he still prayed for them.

Can You Hear the Love?

Kevin felt the cool grass against his back as he looked at the millions and millions of stars in the sky. Then a bright light streaked across the night, and then another. One after another and then another. Soon the entire night sky was filled with streamers of light. The meteor shower painted the sky. This was amazing! "Look at that big one!" His dad pointed to the west. A meteor raced across and faded away. "Do you hear that?" Kevin listened and heard frogs in the pond and some night bird, maybe an owl. His dad explained, "Everything you see and hear is praising God tonight."

Words to Treasure

Praise the Lord. Praise the Lord from the heavens.

Psalm 148:1

Kevin thought about that. "Why tonight? Because of the meteor shower?"

His dad laughed. "They do it every night and every day."

What an amazing thought! Everything that God created worships or thanks him all the time, maybe not in the same ways we do, but they do it. It's just a natural thing in nature to praise God. The Bible says the heavens tell about the glory of God and the skies show that his hands created them. They "speak" of it and make it known—even though they don't use words (Psalm 19:1–3).

Psalm 148 talks about how everything in nature praises God by being exactly how he created them—a frog by being like a frog or a lion being like a lion. But for humans it's different. Just *being* us isn't enough. We have to choose to worship God and follow Jesus. So choose to join all of nature and praise God today. You're in good company.

July 15

Stuff

The bed was tossed and pulled apart, all her drawers were dumped on the floor, and her little jewelry box was gone altogether. They had even taken her crystal horse. Abby began to cry. This wasn't fair! The burglars had stolen everything that was important!

Her father walked into the room. "I'm sorry, honey." He hugged her tightly. "But you know what? It's just stuff. We can get new things." Her cat crept out from under her bed. Abby picked her up, so relieved she was all right. Both she and her dad together petted the frightened cat. "See, love is the most important thing."

Words to Treasure

"Do not gather for yourselves riches on earth. Moths and rats can destroy them. Thieves can break in and steal them. Instead, gather for yourselves riches in heaven."

Matthew 6:19-20

That's right. We may like the stuff we own, but it is just stuff. Replaceable, useable, throw-out-when-it's-old stuff. Thousands of years ago Jesus told us that stuff rusts, rots, and falls apart, so our possessions shouldn't be our focus. Instead, we should focus on what's really important, like loving God, loving your family, loving your neighbors, and being God's person on earth. Those are heavenly treasures that never wear out or get lost.

People in Bible Times

Jesus told a story of a rich farmer who had great plans for his wealth, but those plans didn't seem to include being generous with the needy. Before he could use his wealth, he died. God called him a fool because he was not rich where it counts—in generosity. (See Luke 12:16–21.)

What about Tomorrow?

Carson passed another nail up to his dad. They were working hard to cover all the windows with plywood before the big storm hit sometime tomorrow. "So, what's really going to happen tomorrow?"

His dad snapped his fingers for another nail. "I don't know."

"Is our house going to get sucked out to sea or what?"

His dad had just hammered his finger and was shaking it around. "Carson, I don't know."

"Do you think we'll be safe at Grandma and Grandpa's? Is it far enough inland?"

"I don't know. I think so." His dad climbed down the ladder.

"Dad?"

"WHAT?"

Carson picked up the box of nails. "What *do* you know?"

His dad put the ladder against the bay window. "I know that we should worry about today before we worry about tomorrow."

That's right! Worrying about the future is kind of pointless and a bit of an energy-waster. Focus on today and what needs to be done today. Let tomorrow come and then deal with that day on *that* day. Being prepared is important—freaking out about the unknown isn't going to get you anywhere. What's going to happen will happen, and you'll be able to handle it when it comes.

Words to Treasure

So don't worry about tomorrow. Tomorrow will worry about itself. Each day has enough trouble of its own.

Matthew 6:34

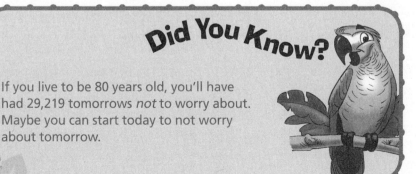

Did You Know?

If you live to be 80 years old, you'll have had 29,219 tomorrows *not* to worry about. Maybe you can start today to not worry about tomorrow.

July 17

Pearls of Wisdom

Wendy was a bit shocked to see the entire gang she wanted to hang out with at the swimming pool. The group didn't seem all that happy to see her. "I didn't know you were going to be here," said Wendy.

Words to Treasure

Do not throw your pearls to pigs. If you do, they might walk all over them.

Matthew 7:6

Fin shifted from one foot to another. "It was a last-minute thing."

"I was hoping to see you at church Sunday," said Wendy. "The car rally was great. Maybe you can come next time."

"Maybe." Fin was the leader of the pack. "We have to go. See ya." The gang walked away whispering. Wendy felt her heart drop.

Her mom stood beside her. "Your friendship is a special thing, sweetie. Make sure that whom you try to give it to are people who will treasure it. They may be popular, but they don't seem very nice." Wendy thought about that.

Wendy had tried to share both her friendship and her church with people that, let's face it, didn't see value in either one. That stings. Jesus warns us to be very careful whom we give precious things to. Give it to the wrong people, and you get hurt. Pick friends who are eager to be your friend and want to share adventures with you at school, home and even church. Friends of value *value* you.

Discovering Archaeology

Pearls, in ancient times, were considered a symbol of wealth and fame. Romans really got into pearls. The oldest-known pearl necklace belonged to a Persian queen and is well over 2,000 years old.

Around the World in One Bite

Cindy didn't know what to eat first. Tacos over there, sushi right here, or bangers and mash (British for sausages and mashed potatoes) on the next table. Then there was the deep fried cheesecake. Cindy stopped to look around at all the people at the international food fare. They were as different from each other as the food was. One person had tight curly red hair, another person had dark brown skin, and the kid over there had freckles all over his face. How come God made so many different looking people?

Words to Treasure

They came from every nation, tribe and people.

Revelation 7:9

Good question. God loves variety. Just look at the world around us. Nature shows such an assortment, from delicate butterflies to elephants the size of trucks. Wouldn't the world be boring if there were only one type of food to eat? Or one type of animal? Or one type of person? The world is full of all kinds of people, and that makes it a beautiful place.

Take a world tour right in your home. Have your parents help you find books or websites about different countries. Discover what they like to eat, how they dress or things they like to do. Sometimes great adventures start at home.

July 19

This Way

Bennett's lungs were burning with each step, but he was going to make it to the top of the mountain. When he looked out at the view, it was the most wonderful thing he had ever seen. Other mountains melted away into the hazy horizon. He felt as if he was on top of the world. He and his aunt Helen had trained for months for this climb. Ahead of them the trail narrowed to a thin line across a ridge of mountain. Both sides of the trail dropped away to steep rocky cliffs. Bennett's knees felt weak. This was scarier than he thought.

Words to Treasure

But the gate is small and the road is narrow that lead to life. Only a few people will find it.

Matthew 7:14

His aunt checked their safety gear. "You ready?"

"I think so."

"Take a look around. Not many people make it this far. Some turn back right here. Do you want to turn back?"

Bennett gulped air. "No way!" He headed for the ridge.

Jesus said that our walk to heaven is like a narrow path that few people find. Sometimes it isn't an easy path, and it will test all our courage and willpower. But Jesus will help us, because he's our experienced guide on that narrow walk through life.

Discovering Archaeology

Did you know one of the oldest-known manmade wood walkway is 6,000 years old and is called Sweet Track? It was a narrow, raised, wood walkway built over what would have been a swampy area in ancient England.

All Together Now

Will watched as their marshmallows flared up into sweet infernos of fire. Kevin and Sean were laughing themselves sick as they stuck their sticks into the heart of the campfire. So much for "toasting" marshmallows. Those things were cinders now.

Will had been pretty unsure about going to this Bible Camp Weekend. Spending three whole days with a bunch of kids from church that he didn't know very well hadn't seemed like a very good idea to him when he first heard about it. Turns out it *was* a great idea! The weekend was only half over, and already they had done all kinds of fun things together. *And* he had made two new friends. Kevin passed him a piece of chocolate with one hand while burning six more marshmallows on a stick in his other hand. The guy was seriously crazy but seriously fun. This could be the start of a good friendship.

Words to Treasure

So also we are many persons. But in Christ we are one body. And each part of the body belongs to all the other parts.

Romans 12:5

At church you hear the word *fellowship* all the time, but what does it mean? It just means being friends in a special God kind of way. God wants you to hang out and have fun with other godly people. Being lonely is never God's plan for you.

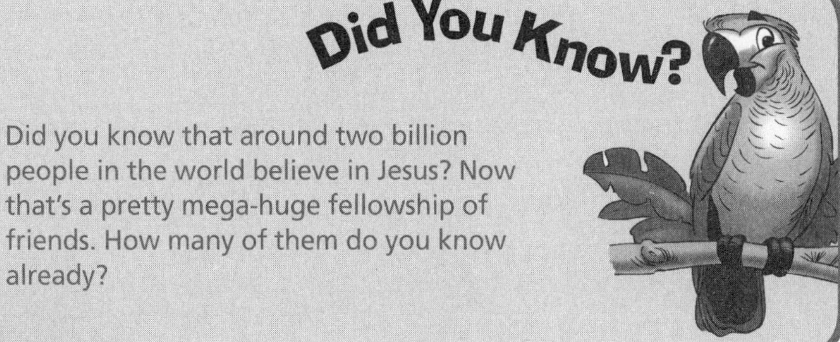

Did you know that around two billion people in the world believe in Jesus? Now that's a pretty mega-huge fellowship of friends. How many of them do you know already?

July 21

Rules Are Rules

The lifeguard put a bandage on Janna's forehead. "I called your mom, and she's coming to pick you up. You have a nasty bump on your head." The birthday party wasn't over for another hour, but it was over for Janna. The lifeguard checked her again. "You did see the *No Running* sign on the pool deck?" Janna nodded. "And you did hear me warn you twice not to run?"

> **Words to Treasure**
>
> Anyone who has my commands and obeys them loves me. My Father will love the one who loves me. I too will love them. And I will show myself to them.
>
> John 14:21

"Yes," Janna wrapped her towel closer.

"But you kept running anyway."

"Yes. I kinda forgot because we were having so much fun."

"Now you know why we have that rule, right?"

"Because you will fall on your face in front of an entire pool full of kids and look like a dweeb and get a bump on your face the size of a golf ball," Janna said. There's a really good reason for rules. Most rules are there not to wreck our fun but to keep us safe. God's got rules for us too, and they're there for the same reason—to keep us safe. Just think of the world as God's pool party—we can have fun and live right at the same time.

Spend a day noticing the different rules around us from traffic rules, to school rules, to household rules. Why do we have them? Talk about it. Hey, even your pets have rules to keep them safe.

I Get It!

Carey hadn't laughed so hard in a long time. Her sides hurt from laughing. Every kid at church was laughing. These guys were so funny. But they also understood kids. When they talked about God, Carey understood what they were talking about. Sometimes at church she didn't understand everything her pastor said because he used big words and he was a little boring. But these guys she could understand because they talked *kid.*

It was kind of like that for the people of Israel when Jesus spoke to them. He talked about things *they* understood. He explained things in ways they could understand. Suddenly they understood new and important things about God because Jesus understood exactly how to explain it to them. He wasn't boring. He told stories. People everywhere were amazed at his teaching. Jesus so got them. And they so got Jesus.

Words to Treasure

Jesus finished saying all these things. The crowds were amazed at his teaching. That's because he taught like one who had authority. He did not speak like their teachers of the law.

Matthew 7:29

Live IT!

If somebody is teaching you about God, Jesus, or the Bible and you don't understand what they're trying to say, ask to have it explained again in another way so you *can* understand. Wanting to understand or wanting to know more about God is important. You have a right to understand. Don't worry about looking foolish. The disciples were constantly asking Jesus to explain things over and over again until they understood it. You're in good company. So go ahead and say, "I don't understand. Could you please explain it a different way?" And somebody will.

July 23

That's So Me!

Nikki showed her mom the outfit she wanted to try on. Her mother's eyebrows came together, and that was never a good thing.

Words to Treasure

They should wear clothes that are right and proper.
1 Timothy 2:9

"That shirt won't even cover your belly button."

"Mom, all the girls on TV wear these. Please, please."

Her mom shook her head. "Honey, they dress like that because they're performing. It's like a costume. Real girls in the real world don't need to show their belly buttons at school. I want you to have girl power."

Nikki's lower lip hung down to her chin. "What's that?"

Her mother put her arm around her. "Being you, not somebody else. I thought you loved hoodies."

Nikki thought about that. "I do."

Her mom steered her toward a row of boarder hoodies. "Let's check these out." She pulled out one that was exactly what Nikki had been wanting. "What do you think?"

Nikki smiled. "Perfect. That's so me."

"Not those other girls?"

Nikki smiled. "Just me."

Not too much to add to that. Remember, be you, not somebody on TV. Dress with style, dress with personal attitude, but don't feel you have to dress in any way that makes you or your family feel uncomfortable.

Today it's popular to be critical about the clothes or styles people are wearing. They do it on television and in magazines all the time. Is it hot or not? Trashing is not right or cool. What you wear is your choice. Being critical of what other people wear really doesn't look good on anybody.

Forgive? Yes!

Martin looked at his black eye in the mirror. He looked like a one-sided raccoon. Billy sat on the bed looking miserable.

"I am so sorry," Billy said "One minute I was boarding the slope listening to tunes and the next minute you were right in front of me. Wham! You went down. You slid forever. I posted the video, and it already has a ton of hits. It was awesome." Martin turned and looked at his friend with his one good eye.

Words to Treasure

Forgive other people when they sin against you. If you do, your Father who is in heaven will also forgive you.
Matthew 6:14

Billy sheepishly shrugged. "Except for the whole eye thing. Which, by the way, looks cool. Really tough." Billy paused. "Sorry."

Martin sat down on the bed and studied his friend. "I know. I forgive you."

"Really?" Billy looked relieved.

"Sure. Bro, you're my best friend."

Dwelling on past hurts isn't good for you. It keeps all those bad feelings boiling up over and over again. It stops you from healing your hurt feelings. Forgiveness makes everything feel better. When somebody sincerely asks for your forgiveness, ask God to fill your heart with forgiveness and say yes.

People in Bible Times

Peter asked Jesus, "Lord, how many times should I forgive my brother or sister who sins against me?" Seven times seemed like a pretty fair amount to Peter. But Jesus had a much bigger number in mind—77 times. To put it another way: forgiveness is an all-the-time thing, not a sometime thing. (See Matthew 18:21–22.)

July 25

Namesake

Next!" The baseball coach looked over his clipboard, "What's your name, son?"

> **Words to Treasure**
>
> You must give him the name Jesus. That's because he will save his people from their sins.
>
> Matthew 1:21

"Michael Anthony Bishop Richardson-Phillips the Third." Michael waited for the expected reaction.

"Whoa." A kid behind him had never heard such a long name.

"You're kidding me." The coach searched for his name. "I have a Michael Richardson-Phillips."

"You can call me Mike. I'm a good shortstop."

The coach made a note and nodded. "Long name, good shortstop. Your uniform's over there. Next!"

Jesus also had several names. People called him all kinds of names or titles for different reasons: *Jesus of Nazareth* because Nazareth was the town he grew up in (not his last name). *Jesus Christ* because the word *Christ* means "anointed" or "Messiah." *Messiah,* which means "expected deliverer," or the person expected to save his people. Some called Jesus *Emmanuel,* which means "God with us." Jesus called himself the *Son of Man*. That was kind of a cool way of saying, "I'm human, but I'm also the Son of God." Jesus has dozens of names and titles in the Bible, and all of them tell us something special about him and what he did to save the world.

Did You Know?

- *Adam* means "man" in Hebrew.
- *Eve* means "life."
- *Moses* can mean "drawn out of the water."
- *Esau* can mean "hairy."
- *Joseph* means "God or Jehovah increases."
- *David* means "beloved."
- *Esther* means "star."

No Surprise

York knocked on the door loudly. A voice from inside called, "Let me guess. Don't say anything." There was a long pause. "It's York!"

"How'd you know it was me?" York talked to the door.

York's older cousin Tim opened the door. "Your mom just called to say you were coming over. Hey, you want to take a milk run in my new car?" York had been waiting for an invitation to ride in Tim's new sports car. Tim jumped straight into his convertible without opening the door. York was about to try. "Stop! Use the door."

Words to Treasure

We are going up to Jerusalem. Everything that the prophets wrote about the Son of Man will come true.

Luke 18:31

That's kind of like the way it was in Jerusalem when Jesus came to town. No, Jesus did not drive a convertible. But people should have been expecting him because they were given enough warning. For hundreds of years, God's prophets had been telling people exactly how Jesus would come to earth and what would happen. But when the time came, even though Jesus did everything the prophets and God's laws said he would do, people were still confused about him. They didn't expect him *then,* or they thought he'd look different. Hello! Heaven to earth—weren't you guys listening earlier?

People in Bible Times

A teacher and leader named Nicodemus had many questions about Jesus. Jesus seemed surprised that such a smart guy didn't understand what the prophets had said about the coming Savior. (See John 3:1–20.)

July 27

Wiser Than Most

The dog howled as the thunder rumbled down the valley. Ruthie sat on the porch with her family. Volts of electricity crackled and snaked across the sky, flashing downward as they hit the earth. The lightning strikes frightened her a little, but she couldn't take her eyes off the sky.

Words to Treasure

The star they had seen when it rose went ahead of them. It finally stopped over the place where the child was. When they saw the star, they were filled with joy.

Matthew 2:9-10

The thrilling power and beauty of nature sometimes makes us tourists of God's creation. We just have to watch.

We aren't the only nature tourists. Remember those wise guys, or magi (advisors to kings), following a strange star to a little town named Bethlehem? They believed they'd find a new and great king. For thousands of years people have wondered: What *was* that strange star or light they had followed to Bethlehem?

Today, some scientists think the wise guys may have followed the light of a supernova, which is like an explosion in space that stays bright for weeks or months. Or perhaps a brilliant comet. Or maybe it was planets—like Jupiter, Mars, and Saturn—coming close together to form a bright light in the sky. We may never know what was in the sky that led those ancient travelers to Jesus, but 2,000 years later we are still looking at the world with the same kind of wonder.

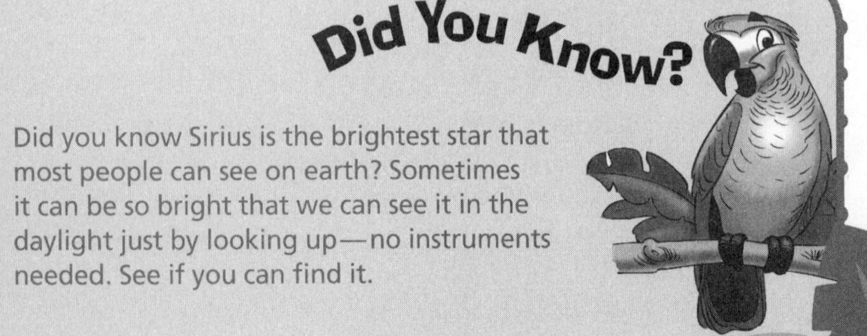

Did You Know?

Did you know Sirius is the brightest star that most people can see on earth? Sometimes it can be so bright that we can see it in the daylight just by looking up—no instruments needed. See if you can find it.

Doubt-Free

Thomas looked at the thin metal cables and the harness that would lift him up and allow him to swoop and soar above the stage as if he could fly. "Are you sure this is safe?" Thomas asked Ben.

"Absolutely," the big man answered while adjusting the harness. Ben smiled at Thomas's worried face and pulled out some coins from his pocket. "Why don't you go get us something from the machine downstairs?"

Words to Treasure

Show mercy to those who doubt.

Jude 1:22

When Thomas returned, the stage was empty. "Up here!" He looked up and there was big Ben flying around on the thin wires. His assistants Greg and Stan were working the wires offstage. The big man dove down and then lifted off like one gigantic flying turkey. "Now," Ben shouted down, "*I* can do this, and I'm absolutely huge. Are you ready to give it a try?" Thomas nodded, all fears and doubts gone. He was a believer!

Having doubts isn't a wrong thing, but there are times when we have to put them aside and make a choice to trust and believe the truth.

People in Bible Times

One of the disciples, also named Thomas, didn't believe it when the others told him that Jesus had risen from the dead. He told them that he couldn't believe until he saw Jesus and had proof he was alive. A week later Jesus appeared to Thomas and let him touch the wounds in his hands left by the nails that held him to the cross. Thomas never doubted Jesus again. (See John 20:24–29.)

July 29

Critical Mass

James shivered on the log watching Phil make their morning campfire. "You're not building the fire right."

> **Words to Treasure**
>
> Do not judge other people. Then you will not be judged.
>
> Matthew 7:1

Phil gave him a look. "I *am* doing it right."

James shook his head. "Fire needs air. You're choking it with too much wood. You'll never get it going."

Phil threw down the last piece of wood. "Same as how I didn't put the tent up right, I cook my hot dog weird, I don't paddle the canoe right, and I use the wrong fishing bait. Is there anything I do *right*?" Phil stormed away. "Build your own fire!"

James has a bad case of the criticals. Some people seem to think it's their job to tell everybody else what they're doing wrong. News flash! In real life you are not the celebrity judge on a reality television show. Finding faults with others is wrong and will really bug your friends and family. It doesn't make you look smart, important, or better either. God isn't critical of you, because he respects and loves you. So don't be critical of others either. A critical nature is critically wrong.

Being critical isn't new. Jesus actually had a lot to say about it. He put it this way. Before you point out your friend's sawdust-sized faults, make sure you get rid of your own giant plank-sized problems first. In other words, you probably have way bigger faults of your own that you ignore. (See Matthew 7:3–4.)

Close the Book

The cabin was a riot of flinging pillows and smelly pajamas. Cabin "Raptor Claw" was having a candy bar pig-fest and pillow fight. Boys were being knocked off bunks and dropping like flies. Candy wrappers littered the floor. But in the corner, Holland was reading his science book quietly. That's what Holland always did. There were some seriously good times that he was missing out on. There were lifelong friends waiting to be made if only he'd put down the book.

Words to Treasure

There is a time for everything. There's a time for everything that is done on earth.

Ecclesiastes 3:1

Jason sat beside Holland. "Do you want some of my saltwater candy?" Holland shook his head, not looking up. "Do you want to have a pillow fight?" Holland just turned a page. Jason snatched the book out of his hands and tossed it out the window.

Holland couldn't believe it. "What are you doing?!" Jason wrote something on his hand and showed it to Holland. His hand read. "Read this! I'm trying to be your friend."

Wanting to learn more about the world is great, but don't let that stop you from being part of the world. Balancing fun, friends, and study is important. Don't let one activity take over everything else.

Did You Know?

Do you know what a real bookworm is? Well, there are over 5,000 insects that you could describe as bookworms or book lice. But the most common is a little wingless insect that loves to eat the paste or glue used to hold books together.

July 31

Grandma Sadie

Hannah didn't want to go stay with Grandma Sadie for the entire summer! But her mother had to go away to work for a few weeks, so it was decided this was the best choice. Hannah put her suitcase in the trunk and climbed into the car.

Words to Treasure

Don't be afraid. Don't lose hope.

Deuteronomy 1:21

They drove over mountains and down twisting valleys until they pulled up to an old wood gate that read Crooked Creek Ranch. They drove down a dusty road to a big ranch house with a red barn behind it. An older woman stepped off the porch. Her face was leathery and looked older than the mountains around the ranch. She gave Hannah a crisp nod and quick hug. Everything Grandma did was quick and to the point. Part of Hannah was excited but most of her was scared.

New, unexpected things are scary sometimes. It is okay to feel scared, but the important thing is to face things with a positive attitude. Remember, the most exciting adventures aren't planned by you but are planned by God. So just go with the unexpected plan.

People in Bible Times

The king of Persia was looking for a queen. He ordered the most beautiful girls of his kingdom to be brought to his palace. Sort of a pick-my-queen beauty contest with only one judge. A young Jewish girl named Esther was taken to the palace, whether she liked it or not. This was the start of a very dangerous and unexpected adventure. (See Esther 1–2.)

Donkeys, Llamas, and Other Things

Words to Treasure

Everyone who saw Esther was pleased with her.

Esther 2:15

Hannah smelled breakfast cooking in her grandma's kitchen. She jumped down the stairs in shorts and sandals. Grandma looked up from the paper. "No breakfast until you do your morning chores." She frowned at Hannah's sandals. "I'll have to take you into town and get you some boots. Now, go outside. You'll find a bucket of feed by the door. Pour some in a line on the ground in the donkey-llama field."

Hannah found the bucket, found the field, and climbed over the fence. She called to the eight llamas and the two donkeys. Suddenly, they charged at her like some goofy stampede. Afraid, she dropped the bucket. The animals fought over the spilled food. The donkeys, being smart, kicked the bucket away from the others. Getting up her courage, Hannah tried to pet a llama. It lifted up its camel-like head and spit right in her face. Hannah was shocked! The spit stung because it was full of half-chewed food. Grandma Sadie whispered, "You'll get the hang of it."

Your first day doing anything is bound to be hard—you might say "spitting hard." But don't get discouraged. Just do your best. It will get easier.

Donkeys were like little pickup trucks—small but tough. Donkeys were used for riding, carrying heavy things, and for milking. Nothing like a frosty glass of donkey milk! Rich people had huge herds of donkeys.

August 2

Face It!

Hannah looked at the llama, uncertain. He was very tall. He gave a low moan, and this made Hannah nervous. Grandma Sadie held the halters. "Are you going to let him talk back to you? Hannah, you have to show him you're boss. You can't help me do llama treks if you're going to let the llamas tell you what to do."

Words to Treasure

Be brave. And may the Lord be with those of you who do well.

2 Chronicles 19:11

Hannah's new cowboy boots felt funny. In fact, this whole thing seemed funny. Here she was standing in front of a grumpy llama, not knowing what to do or say. Hannah walked up to Noble and shook her finger in his face. "No more spitting, back talk, or trouble from you! Behave yourself!" Hannah put a halter on the llama and led him to the fence to be groomed. To her surprise, he walked along without a grumble or complaint. Grandma nodded her approval.

Sometimes you just have to walk up to your problems and face them, and that takes courage—same as Hannah did with her llama. And God is big on helping you find that kind of problem-busting courage.

Is there a problem you're worried about facing? Maybe your homework's late, your room's crazy messy, or you did something wrong. Make two lists. One list is things that will happen if you avoid the problem. The other list is the good things that could happen if you face your problem. Big problems become small when you're the boss.

Flat Deal

Sandy stretched her muscles as she got ready for the bike race. She was excited because she had a good chance at winning. Her parents would have to hurry here with her bike, because they were already calling riders to the start line.

Words to Treasure

God, create a pure heart in me.

Psalm 51:10

"Honey." Sandy heard her mother call her over to the car.

Sandy looked but couldn't believe it. Somebody had slashed her bike tires. They were flat and ruined. Who would do such a thing? She looked around, but it could be anybody. How could she tell who did it?

Unfortunately, in real life it's hard to tell the good guys from the bad guys. Everybody looks the same on the outside. Only God can look into somebody's heart and mind to see what's going on in there. All you can do is work on doing right things yourself, and pray that God will help people who do wrong things to you. In the end, God will judge each and every person.

God asked his prophet Samuel to find a new king for his people. And what he saw in one young man was perfect. He didn't look on the outside. Instead Samuel looked at the young man's heart just like God does. And what he saw was a heart after God. "People look at the outside of a person. But the LORD looks at what is in the heart" (1 Samuel 16:7).

AUGUST 4

Treasure

Quincy dug like crazy in the sand. His grandpa had taken him treasure-hunting on the beach with a metal detector. His grandfather had found all kinds of old coins, war metals, rings, and things.

Words to Treasure

Won't she search carefully until she finds the coin? And when she finds it, she will call her friends and neighbors together. She will say, "Be joyful with me. I have found my lost coin."

Luke 15:8-9

Quincy searched through the sand and pulled out a beautiful diamond ring. "Look, Grandpa Joe! A ring! Do we get to keep it? Maybe I can give it to Mom or Grandma. Or sell it and keep the money." Quincy was all excited.

"First we put an ad in the lost and found. If nobody identifies it or claims it, *then* we can keep it."

Quincy was disappointed. "But Grandpa, finders keepers."

Grandpa put the ring in his bag. "Always remember that how you treat other people is more important than treasure."

A few weeks later Quincy showed a lady the ring. She immediately burst into tears, she was so happy to have it back. She pulled out a hundred-dollar bill and gave it to Quincy. He looked surprised, but his grandfather didn't.

Next time you find something that belongs to somebody else (even though you may want it) make every effort to return it to the rightful owner. Doing what's right is God's kind of riches.

Listening to Your Little Voice

Bridget's Auntie Rae was teaching her how to rock climb. She sat on a ledge above Bridget, coaching her up the cliff. It wasn't a huge cliff, but right now she was stuck and wasn't sure where to put her hands next. "Look up and to your right," encouraged her aunt.

Bridget was about to reach up but something inside her didn't quite trust that perfect-looking little ledge. "I don't want to use that one."

Words to Treasure

I only know that in every city the Spirit warns me.

Acts 20:23

"Why?" asked her aunt.

"I don't know. Just a feeling." Bridget found another way up the cliff and finally she sat beside her aunt.

Auntie Rae put her arm around her as they looked at the view below. "You learned an important lesson today. Always trust that little voice in your head. If something inside you tells you not to do something—listen. God gave you that little voice for a reason."

God designed us to be very aware of our world and to listen to the Holy Spirit inside us. Trust the feelings or instincts God's given you. Sometimes your *instincts* are God's way of giving you a message.

Did You Know?

Did you know that many people report that animals can sense dangers such as storms, earthquakes, or tidal waves long before humans? Some dogs can warn their owners of epileptic seizures before they happen, and in wartime, pets have sensed enemy air raids long before they happened. God designed animals to be high observers of their environments, and that's amazing.

August 6

Secret Weapon

The boys in the dugout began to laugh as Spencer took his place on the pitcher's mound. Spencer was the smallest kid in the league. He didn't look like a pitcher.

Words to Treasure

Man looks at how someone appears on the outside. But I look at what is in the heart.

1 Samuel 16:7

Spencer warmed up his arm as he sized up the first batter. With a confident nod, Spencer drew back and let it fly. A rocket-like fastball whizzed across the field. How did that much power come out of that little arm? The batter swung, but too late—the ball was long gone. Spencer focused again, and this time he released a knuckleball. Try as he might, the batter couldn't figure out where the ball was going. He swung and missed. Spencer held the ball close to his chest, and then another fastball headed down the field. Got ya! This fastball was really a slow slider. The pitcher swung fast, but the ball was slow. Strike three and out.

The boys in the dugout chewed gum quietly. This guy was a secret weapon.

Spencer was small on the outside, but he was full of heart inside. We judge things by what we see on the outside, but God looks at what's inside a person.

Discovering Archaeology

Kids have been playing ball games for thousands of years. Ancient Egyptians played handball. (Cat lovers stop reading now.) Ancient balls were made out of catgut, or intestines, wrapped into a sphere and then covered in leather.

Big Fat Hole

Paxton was sailing on the lake. It was a great day! The wind was perfect, the sun was shining, and his small sailboat was sinking. *Sinking*? How could that be? Water was seeping quickly into his small boat. Then he remembered he had lent his boat to his friend Simon.

Words to Treasure

Suppose you have not been worthy of trust in handling someone else's property. Then who will give you property of your own?

Luke 16:12

Paxton got on his knees and searched the floor of the boat. There it was: a big fat hole that was sort of, but kind of not—*patched*. Simon never told him he had damaged his boat. Paxton took out his cell phone. "Dad, this is Pax. I'm sinking. Do you think you could come out and tow me in? Thanks."

Paxton took out a coffee can and started to scoop out the water. Lesson learned: never lend Simon your boat—ever.

So how responsible are you? Can people trust you to take good care of their things? Putting a hole in Paxton's boat was probably an accident, but not telling him about it was no accident. When you make a mistake, don't hide it.

Discovering Archaeology

A 2,000-year-old fishing boat was found in the mud of the Sea of Galilee. Crazy, but because of a long drought, parts of the lake bottom were showing for the first time in thousands of years. And there in the mud were the remains of a 26-foot long wood boat, maybe even the same kind of boat Jesus sailed in long ago.

AUGUST 8

Measure Up

Mom, does this look cooked?" Mary was cooking the trout they had just caught in the river beside their camp.

Words to Treasure

He rules over all. He says to his people, "Treat everyone fairly. Show faithful love and tender concern to one another.

Zechariah 7:9

Her mom sniffed the good smell of lemon and butter in the pan. "It smells done."

Mary took it all in—their kayaks on the bank and their tent beside the waterfall. This was like paradise. "Mom, we have a good life, don't we?"

Mary's mother pulled their potatoes out of the fire. "A very good life."

"But there are people who don't have as good a life. How can we help?"

Her mom sat beside her and thought for a moment. "We can start by sharing our time and God-given talents with others. It may seem like a small thing, but it does make a difference. When everybody does what Jesus wanted us to do—love God and love each other with all our hearts—we won't be able to stop the world from changing for the better. We won't be able to count the number of people helping and the number of people being helped."

That's an amazing thought. God loves and helps people who love him and love others with all their hearts. God wants a world like that.

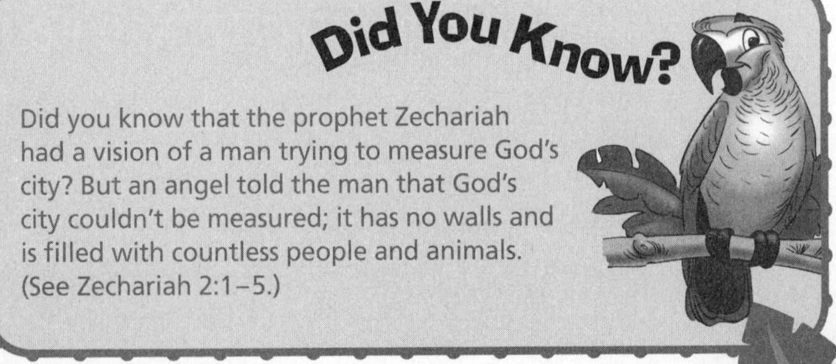

Did You Know?

Did you know that the prophet Zechariah had a vision of a man trying to measure God's city? But an angel told the man that God's city couldn't be measured; it has no walls and is filled with countless people and animals. (See Zechariah 2:1–5.)

Just Ask—A Lot

Page sat on the cabin porch quietly and patiently. The cabin door opened, and a beautiful woman with long gray hair stepped out on the porch. Cathy stared at Page and shook her head. "Are you going to sit on my porch every morning?"

Page handed her a donut and coffee from the corner store. "You're the best river kayaker I know. I want to be the best for the Olympics some day."

Cathy sipped the coffee. "So you're going to sit on my porch every morning and give me coffee and donuts until I agree to coach you?"

"That's the plan." Page smiled sweetly.

"Well," Cathy sighed with an amused smile, "you proved to me you really want this, and I think you'll work hard."

The next morning, Cathy's and Page's kayaks floated side by side in a quiet pool of the river. Cathy nodded. "Okay, let me see what you've got. I'll be right behind you." Page nodded and paddled out to catch the current.

Page's persistence worked. Sometimes showing people how much you care about something says a lot more than words.

Words to Treasure

So here is what I say to you. Ask, and it will be given to you. Search, and you will find. Knock, and the door will be opened to you.

Luke 11:9

People in Bible Times

Jesus told a story about a man who went to a friend's house late at night to borrow some bread. He knocked on the door so much that finally his friend got up and gave him what he wanted. Jesus said that knocking on God's door is okay. Pray often about the same thing because God doesn't mind. He *loves* your persistence. (See Luke 11:5–10.)

August 10

Queen of Llamas

Hannah matched each hiker with a llama she thought would suit them. They would trek up the narrow trail to a beautiful mountain meadow. After spending a month at the ranch, she knew each animal.

Words to Treasure

No one knows what lies ahead. So who can tell someone else what's going to happen?

Ecclesiastes 8:7

Hannah's boots were now well broken in from all the hiking and ranch chores she was doing. She had found muscles she never knew she had. Grandma shook her head in wonder. "I've never seen my llamas take to someone the way they've taken to you. Hannah, you're a natural with animals and hard work."

Hannah had the tourists lined up with their llamas, ready to follow her up the trail. She gave Noble a playful nudge to get him moving. The llama rubbed his goofy head against her. To think she had been scared of him only a few weeks ago!

A big part of faith is trusting God with your future, especially when you're not at all sure how things will turn out. Funny thing, if we knew how it would turn out, we wouldn't look to God for direction every step of the way. Mystery is good.

Go on the Internet with an adult and research adventures you've never tried before, such as llama trekking, horseback riding, bird-watching, or snowshoeing. See if you and your family can try something new and fun.

Right Moves

People were having a good time leading their llamas along the narrow trail. Hannah was in the front, and Grandma Sadie was taking the rear. All of a sudden, the llamas became frightened and skittish. The hikers had a hard time holding on to them. Hannah quickly searched the woods with her eyes, and what she saw sent a flash of fear through her body. She pulled out her bear spray, because just above them was the biggest cougar she had ever seen—actually, the *only* cougar she had ever seen.

Words to Treasure

Without guidance a nation falls. But many good advisers can bring victory to a nation.

Proverbs 11:14

Hannah froze for a minute, but quickly remembered what her grandmother had told her. Hannah shouted to the tourists, "Everybody, I want you to hold on to your llamas, but then I want you to shout—make lots of noise and wave your hands. Look really tall." The hikers weren't sure why they were doing this, but they followed her instructions. With an irritated grumble, the big cat leaped into the bushes and disappeared because of the noise.

Grandma waved her understanding to Hannah as they moved the group on up the trail. Then she quietly radioed for a park ranger.

Way to go, Hannah! She remembered what she had to do. That comes from listening to people with experience and doing what they teach you.

People in Bible Times

Wise Esther took the advice of people who knew the king. She only did what they suggested. That way she never made a mistake while in the palace or with the king. Listening would win the day.

AUGUST 12

Good Things

"Grandpa, I'm going to be late for my own birthday party." Trish followed her grandpa up the trail. Where was he taking her?

Words to Treasure

How much more will your Father who is in heaven give good gifts to those who ask him!

Matthew 7:11

"Just a little bit farther."

"Grandpa, we've been hiking for two hours!" He just smiled and nodded. They came to the top of a ridge. Trish was all out of breath, but Grandpa didn't seem tired at all. His eyes sparkled as he pointed to the grassy meadow below. There by his truck was his horse, Rusty. Trish looked, and she couldn't believe it! Also by the truck was a beautiful black and white pinto. It was the prettiest horse she had ever seen, and it had a big red bow on it. Her grandfather put his arm around her. "I thought maybe we'd ride back."

Trish didn't know what to say. "I only asked for new boots for my birthday." From behind the truck waved her mom, dad, and grandmother. This was the best day of her life.

Trish's family knew how hard she had been working and saving to buy a horse. They wanted to surprise her with this amazing gift. God is like that too—only a zillion times more. He wants to give us amazing gifts because he loves us.

Sometimes an amazing gift isn't a "what" but a "thing." Freedom. God helped Moses give his people the gift of freedom from slavery. Now that's a perfect surprise.

The Biggest Gift

It was Hannah's birthday, and Grandma Sadie had invited friends and family over for a big ranch BBQ. Hannah's mom got some time off to come for the weekend. Hannah had talked Grandma Sadie into hanging a big rope from the hayloft in the barn. It was almost like flying when she let go and landed in the soft hay below. This was the best birthday party Hannah could ever remember.

Words to Treasure

They should care for their own family. In that way they will pay back their parents and grandparents. That pleases God.

1 Timothy 5:4

Grandma Sadie watched the kids for awhile, and then called Hannah over. They took a walk on the dirt road behind the barn. Grandmother put her arm around her. "You like my ranch?"

Hannah chewed on some grass. "This is the best place on earth. I could live here and take care of the ranch forever."

"Glad to hear it." Grandmother brushed the hair from Hannah's face. "That's why I'm going to leave you the ranch when I die. Someday this will be yours. Happy birthday, Hannah!" Tears of happiness came to Hannah's eyes.

Hannah loved the ranch and loved her grandmother. She tried to do her best, and she got a big reward. She was God's gift to her grandmother and the ranch. And the ranch was God's gift to her. Funny how God's unexpected adventures can change your life forever.

Did you know King Xerxes picked Esther to become his queen over hundreds, perhaps thousands, of other young girls?

August 14

Without Being Asked

Lightning flashed like a bright whip across the sky, the wind howled, and the rain blew sideways instead of straight down. The storm had come up fast and hard. Weller and his two dogs were bringing in horses and cows from the east field. The horses were nervous and the cows unhappy. Weller pulled his hat down low and moved slowly so he didn't scare the animals. His dad appeared from out of the rain.

Words to Treasure

A voice from heaven said, "This is my Son, and I love him. I am very pleased with him."

Matthew 3:17

"You're already bringing them in. That's great, Son!"

Weller shouted over the wind. "Sometimes I know what you want me to do *without* you telling me."

His dad grinned. "I know. Let's get the horses in the stable. Then pizza—my treat." Weller wasn't going to argue with that idea.

Jesus also knew what to do without his heavenly Father telling him. One day Jesus went to his cousin John to be baptized, because he knew that it was the right thing to do and it was what his heavenly Father wanted. And God was really proud of Jesus for everything he did.

Do you always have to be asked to do things around the house by your parents? Want to amaze, surprise, impress, and totally blow their minds? Start doing stuff before they tell you. They'll wonder what happened, but let's just keep that a secret.

How Can I Help?

The little doe was stuck in the thick mud of the mudflats, and the tide was coming in. If the boys didn't help, the deer would drown. They ran to a construction site near the beach and talked to the workers. Soon workers and kids were carrying wood planks to the beach. One after another they placed the boards across the mud—creating a wood trail. A policeman and two construction workers walked across the boards to the frightened deer. Carefully they pulled the little animal from the mud, wrapped it in blankets, and carried it back to the shore. They unwrapped the deer, checked her over, and then released her. With a flick of her muddy white tail, she ran back toward the woods. She didn't even look back.

Words to Treasure

Two people are better than one. They can help each other in everything they do.
Ecclesiastes 4:9

The boys had pulled everyone together to help one little creature in trouble. When people pull together, amazing things can and do happen. Teamwork is all part of God's plan for us.

People in Bible Times

Jesus was teaching a whole crowd of people in a house, and it was standing room only. Four men brought a friend who couldn't walk to be healed by Jesus. But they couldn't get near Jesus because of the crowd. So they made a hole in the roof of the house and dropped the man down through the hole. Jesus was impressed and healed the man. Now that's teamwork and friendship! But don't try this at home. (See Mark 2:1–5.)

August 16

Shining Through

Sandy was going fast down the mountain trail right behind another bicycle racer. Suddenly the girl in front hit a tree root the wrong way, slammed into a tree, and then cartwheeled to the ground. She was seriously hurt. Sandy stopped to help her. The girl's leg was broken, and she moaned in pain. Other bikers whizzed past, not stopping to help. Sandy quickly pulled the bike off the girl and talked to her. "Don't move. Help will be coming soon."

Words to Treasure

Do you bring in a lamp to put it under a large bowl or a bed? Don't you put it on its stand?

Mark 4:21

The girl shook her head. "Go! You can catch up to the rest. Don't stop because of me!"

"There'll be other races." Sandy wished she had a jacket to keep the girl warm.

The girl shook her head. "You don't understand. I was the one who slashed your tires before the race. You can't help me after what I did!"

Sandy held her hand. "Looks like I am."

There are lots of ways to be heroes. Jesus wants our kindness to shine like a light so everybody can see.

If you broke your leg in Bible times, they would have used wood splints to hold your bones in place and then wrapped it with stiff bandages. Not too different from today. Wonder if people signed each other's casts the way we do today? Hey, Moses wrote, "Get better soon!"

No Room for Panic

Sandy talked to Krista quietly as they waited for help to come. No more bike racers whizzed past, and the woods were very quiet. Krista began to cry both from the pain of her broken leg and emotion. Tears streamed down her face. "I'm never going to be able to ride again. And you're going to tell on me for sabotaging your bike. My whole life is ruined!" She began to cry harder.

Words to Treasure

He got up and ordered the wind to stop. He said to the waves, "Quiet! Be still!" Then the wind died down. And it was completely calm.
Mark 4:39

"Ssssh." Sandy kept holding her hand. "I'm not going to tell on you, and you'll be fine." But Krista cried harder and couldn't catch her breath. "Dear Jesus," Sandy prayed, "please help Krista today. Help her to be brave and calm until help comes."

Sometimes we need to ask Jesus to help calm down a situation or even just our thoughts. And that's totally a right thing to do. After all, Jesus is the Prince of Peace. Sometimes we could really use some of his supernatural panic-kicking peace.

People in Bible Times

Jesus and his disciples were in a boat when a wild storm hit. The disciples were freaked out, but Jesus slept soundly. Finally he woke up and noticed his panicked disciples and the stormy lake. He got up and ordered the wind and the waves to be quiet and still. And before they could say, "We're going to drown," the storm stopped. (See Mark 4:35–41.)

August 18

Laughing at Life

Erin stared down at the fuzzy shark slippers she was wearing. She and her friends had been surfing that morning when a shark attacked. The shark bit Erin's leg, and now she was in the hospital getting better.

Words to Treasure

We accept good things from God. So we should also accept trouble when he sends it.

Job 2:10

Erin smiled at her friend Lucy. "I should be in church next week—on crutches."

Lucy was shocked. "You still want to go to church? Erin, God didn't protect you. You have a huge bite in your leg."

Erin sipped her juice. "How do you know that? Maybe that shark would have eaten all of me if it wasn't for God's protection. And that's something to be thankful for." The nurse brought in Erin's dinner. She peeked under the metal cover and started to laugh. She removed the lid. It was meatloaf shaped like a shark. Her family, the nurses, doctors, and kitchen staff were laughing from the doorway.

Sometimes how we handle hard times is all about how we look at it. Having faith in God no matter what *and* having a good sense of humor will get you through just about everything.

Even when Job was covered in gross, disgusting sores and life was so bad he didn't want to live, he never once said anything against God. He still loved him and had faith in him. Give that man a *big* pat on the back—but not too hard. (See Job 2.)

Good Reputation

Diego was helping his dad fix the boat dock at the cabin. He had worked really hard all day, hardly saying anything. Finally his dad asked, "What's on your mind?"

Diego swatted a mosquito. "I was wondering if maybe Pete, Jerry, and I could take the rowboat out to Jug Island and camp overnight?"

His dad rustled around in the bag of nails. "Just you three on the island alone?"

"Yes, sir."

His dad thought about it. "Well, you've always been a responsible camper. You've worked hard the last couple of weeks, helping with things around the cabin. Given your trustworthy reputation, I'll say yes. But you must have life jackets on at all times in the boat."

Diego reached for more nails. "Thanks, Dad."

"Thank yourself. You've always been responsible, and that calls for some type of reward."

How you handle yourself in the past also reflects on what you'll be able to do in the future. If you're not responsible and trustworthy in past things, chances are there'll be no cool rewards in your future either. Think about it.

Words to Treasure

God was kind to me and helped me. So the king gave me what I asked for.

Nehemiah 2:8

People in Bible Times

Nehemiah wanted to go home to help rebuild the city of Jerusalem, but he was worried about what the king would say. Good thing for him that he was a good and faithful servant to King Artaxerxes, because the king didn't hesitate to give Nehemiah permission to go.

August 20

Prepared!

Jerry's mom didn't look overly convinced about their plan to sleep overnight on Jug Island. But Diego was ready. "Mrs. Kibby, my dad and I go camping all the time. I'm one of the top scouts in my troop. I have first-aid training, and we're taking a radio with us. My dad has the other radio, and he's leaving it on all night. The island's only ten minutes away, and my dad's going to boat over to check on us before bed and in the morning. We promise not to use an ax. If you'd like to talk to my dad, that's okay."

Words to Treasure

"I also told them how my gracious God was helping me. And I told them what the king had said to me." They replied, "Let's start rebuilding." So they began that good work.

Nehemiah 2:18

Jerry's eyes pleaded with his mom. She nodded slowly, "It looks like you've got everything covered, Diego. I'll call your dad. Okay, Jerry, you can do it."

When you want people to believe in your plan, be very prepared. Think about what questions they might have and then be ready to answer them. Diego thought about what would make this a fun and safe adventure, and his knowledge was impressive. Next stop, Jug Island.

The first job on Nehemiah's list was to rebuild the wall around Jerusalem. A city couldn't defend itself if the people didn't have a strong protective wall to keep out monster armies and ugly bad guys. Or is that ugly armies and monster bad guys? Either way.

The End

Ben stood at the end of the dock and looked across the lake. The bats were just coming out, chasing bugs in the twilight. He liked watching them. He liked everything about the cabin—swimming, hiking, fishing, and boating. He wasn't ready to have the world end. And that thought worried him a lot. Uncle Thomas said he knew that the end of the world was coming soon. He talked about earthquakes, wars, and all kinds of things that pointed to the end of everything we know. Would it happen today, tonight, tomorrow, this week … next year?

Words to Treasure

But no one knows about that day or hour. Not even the angels in heaven know. The Son does not know. Only the Father knows.
Matthew 24:36

Jesus said that one day he would return and the world we know would end. But that isn't a bad thing. That will be one awesome, amazingly terrific day to celebrate because evil will be *defeated* and everything good that Jesus told us about God and heaven will *happen*.

Everything will be different but in a very good way. Nobody knows how mind bogglingly incredible it will be because our imaginations can't even picture that much good. Think of your happiest day ever, and it will be better than that. But nobody, not even Jesus, knows when that day will happen. If Jesus doesn't know, it's doubtful Uncle Thomas has the heads-up on it either.

The only thing you have to think about is loving God with all your heart, soul, and mind. God will take care of the rest. No worries.

August 22

Promises, Promises

"But you promised we'd catch some fish." T.J. pouted as he gave Marty his hook to bait. "We've been out in this boat all morning, and we haven't caught one fish."

Words to Treasure

I will make my covenant with you last forever.

Genesis 17:7

Marty baited their hooks with fat worms. "I can't make the fish bite, T.J."

T.J. sipped his can of juice, unimpressed. "But you promised we'd catch some fish."

Marty couldn't believe his brother was being so difficult. "Okay, okay. You're right, I shouldn't have promised something I couldn't make happen."

"You promised."

"Here's a new promise. And this one I can keep."

"What?" T.J. was curious.

"If you say 'But you promised we'd catch some fish' one more time, I'm going to throw you overboard and make you swim back." T.J. tightened his lips, not taking any chances.

God always keeps his promises—every single one. Nothing in the universe can stop God's promises from coming true. For example, take the promise that he'll love you forever. That's a keeper. Nothing can ever change God's love for you.

A covenant is an important promise or agreement between two or more people. God promised to bless his people and be their God forever.

Couldn't Wait

Suddenly the wheel wouldn't turn, and Ben was heading straight for a mailbox. His soapbox car was out of control. Ben held on tight as he heard the crunch of his cart hitting the box and felt the jerk of coming to a sudden stop. He got out of the car. The entire front was busted up. This was not good. He and his dad had only finished it last night and already it was wrecked.

Words to Treasure

"You have done a foolish thing," Samuel said.

1 Samuel 13:13

His dad inspected the damage. "Ben, I told you we had a few more things to check before you could test it. Why didn't you wait for me?"

Ben didn't have a good answer for that one. He had made a big mistake.

It's easy to make mistakes when we want to get something done in a hurry or we just don't want to wait any longer to do something important. Sometimes waiting is the most important thing you can do.

People in Bible Times

King Saul knew he should have waited until Samuel got there to make an offering to God. But the prophet was late, so the king did it himself. After all, he had a war to fight and he wanted to get started. But he disobeyed God, and that was a big lose-your-kingdom mistake. Obeying God from the start is never a mistake.

AUGUST 24

Trusting Friends?

People on the dock were watching kids and adults jump off into the water below. Jana climbed up on the railing of the high dock and sat down. "Come on, Jasmine, let's jump."

Words to Treasure

Jonathan said to David, "I'll do anything you want me to do for you."

1 Samuel 20:4

Jasmine wasn't sure about this. Jana's dad helped her sit on the railing beside Jana. "I'm not sure, Jana. This is high."

"Not as tall as the high dive at the pool, and you've jumped off that." Jana held out her hand. "We can jump together. Do you trust me?"

Jasmine took her hand, and she counted for them. "One, two, three, GO!" They both jumped off the dock hand-in-hand. Jasmine's long ponytail flowed behind her. They hit the water with a big splash. The crowd cheered, and Jana's parents took a photograph. The two friends swam to the lower dock and climbed out. Jasmine brushed her wet hair from her face. "Let's do it again!"

Do you have a friend you can trust like that? If you have one friend you can trust and go on adventures with, then you're rich where it counts. That's the way best friends David and Jonathan were in the Bible.

Most ancient cultures taught their kids how to swim. Swimming was an important part of a soldier's training. In ancient Greece if you wanted to upset a guy you made fun of the way he ran or swam.

Godly Cupbearers

The dolphins swam around the trainers in the lagoon. Taylor stood at the side of the tank and scratched at his new wetsuit. Tanya and David waved and swam over to Taylor. Tanya sat on the edge of the water. "James Haskell told me that you're a very good volunteer."

"I helped James fix up the otter pool," said Taylor.

"We need someone to help us with a few things around here. You up to working with us and Herbie and Oliver?"

Taylor couldn't talk. This was a dream come true. He felt weak in the knees. He squeaked, "Yes."

Tanya motioned for him to sit beside her. "I'll introduce you to the boys." She slapped the water, and the dolphins joined them. "Herbie, Oliver, this is Taylor. Taylor these are my guys." Taylor reached out and touched a real live dolphin for the first time. This was the start of the rest of his life, and he knew it.

Just like the cupbearer suggested to Pharaoh to send for Joseph, God is going to put people in your life who are going to help open amazing doors for you. They are going to say just the right thing to the right people at just the right time. When that happens, hold on for an adventure you never dreamed could come true.

Words to Treasure

So Pharaoh sent for Joseph. He was quickly brought out of the prison. Joseph shaved and changed his clothes. Then he came to Pharaoh.

Genesis 41:14

Did You Know?

Did you know Joseph spent 13 years as both a slave and prisoner before he became the second-in-command of Egypt?

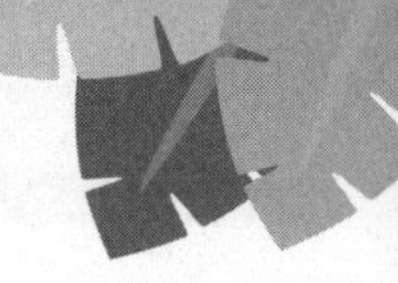

AUGUST 26

Wasn't All Me!

The reporter watched the bear cubs playing in their new enclosure. "They are so cute!" she said.

Words to Treasure

I haven't kept to myself that what you did for me was right. I have spoken about how faithful you were when you saved me. I haven't hidden your love and your faithfulness from the whole community.

Psalm 40:10

The television camera turned back to Henry, and he felt nervous. He gave the reporter a black teddy bear. "This is for you," he said.

"Thank you!" She showed the toy to the camera. "Henry, did you think so many people would buy these stuffed toy bears to help the orphaned cubs you raise here on the range?"

"No way," Henry smiled shyly. "People just keep buying them. We now take orders by Internet."

"This whole thing was your idea. Right, Henry?" The reporter stood very close to him.

"Well, I think it was an answer from God. I prayed about how to help the bears, and that's what came into my head."

"Really?" The lady reporter sounded surprised. "That's amazing!"

"Yeah," shrugged Henry.

When God helps you, don't be afraid to tell the world. Give God the thanks and credit he deserves.

Pharaoh had heard that Joseph could understand the meaning of dreams. But Joe set the record straight right away. Joe gave God all the credit and glory, and that was exactly the right thing to do. Check out Genesis 41.

Master Plan

Krista hopped along on her crutches as she approached the podium. It was the award night for mountain bike racers. Krista talked into the microphone. "I want to give this Sportsmanship Award to a very special person and friend tonight. At the semifinals I fell off my bike, and Sandy pulled over and stayed with me until help came. She gave up her chance to win to help me. She's both a hero and winner to me. But what you don't know is that I did something very unsportsmanlike to her at the beginning of the race, and she never told anybody. That makes her my idol and role model. I want to become an athlete and a person just like Sandy Newman." Krista wiped a tear from her eye as Sandy stepped up on the stage to claim her award. The girls hugged tightly, and the crowd stood up and clapped.

Sometimes when people do something for bad, God turns it around and makes it good.

Words to Treasure

"You planned to harm me. But God planned it for good."

Genesis 50:20

People in Bible Times

No kidding, Joseph's brothers were up to no good when they sold Joseph into slavery. But that evil plan got twisted around by God to make sure Joe became an extremely important person. And when a terrible famine came, Joseph had the power to help his family when they needed it the most. It was all in God's master plan for good.

August 28

On Track

Deacon, Angus, and Timothy were picking blackberries as they walked along the forest trail. After eating a gazillion, they began to throw berries at each other. They were dodging between trees and hiding behind rocks because it was an all-out blackberry battle zone.

Angus stopped and got a funny feeling. "Do you guys know where we are?" Angus climbed a rock to look for the trail. They were really lost. He took off his backpack. "Before we get even more lost . . ." He pulled out a trail map and his compass. He studied the map. "Okay, we're here. But we should go west along Goat Valley Trail." Angus led the way back on track.

Words to Treasure

The LORD your God has blessed you in everything your hands have done. He watched over you when you traveled through that huge desert. For these 40 years the LORD your God has been with you.

Deuteronomy 2:7

Sometimes we don't know we're going the wrong way or doing the wrong things until we're really lost. The Bible is kind of like a map, because it gives us directions to follow and helps us stay on the right path.

People in Bible Times

A young king named Josiah made a really important discovery. While fixing up the temple, they found an old scroll that had God's laws written on it. When the young king read the laws, he tore his clothes and wept with sadness because he knew his people were doing wrong things. God's laws had been forgotten. Right away, Josiah set about making things right with God. (See 2 Chronicles 34–35.)

August 29

That's Big of You

Richard and his friends were hanging out and looking brave as they slid down the scariest slides at the water park. Kenny tugged on Richard's arm. "I don't want to go down these slides anymore." Richard offered to take his little brother to the water park with his friends, but now Kenny was a big complaining pain. "You have to go down this slide because I'm going down this slide. And you have to do what I do."

Words to Treasure

Pharaoh's daughter saw the baby. He was crying. She felt sorry for him. "This is one of the Hebrew babies," she said. Then his sister spoke to Pharaoh's daughter.

Exodus 2:6-7

Kenny shivered, "Can't we go down the little slides for kids my age?"

"I'm going to look like a complete idiot hanging out at the little kid slides. Richard was trying to keep his cool, but it was hard.

"Pleeeeeease," begged Kenny.

Richard felt way too big as he stood in the water watching his brother slide down the little kid slides. Any *cool* he had was completely gone. He hoped Kenny appreciated this, because it was taking courage.

Being an older brother or sister sometimes takes a lot of courage. Take Moses' big sister, Miriam. When Moses was floating down the Nile in a basket, Miriam followed to see what would happen to him. When Pharaoh's daughter found the baby, Miriam the slave girl was brave enough to talk to a *princess*. That's courage!

Live IT!

Have you helped your brothers and sisters lately? Maybe they could use some help learning to tie their shoes, tell time, or count money. There's a hundred ways you can step up and help out.

AUGUST 30

God's Man Job

Erin sat on the beach looking out across the water. Someday soon she'd be all healed from her shark bite and could go back in the ocean again. She wondered how that would feel. Tonight, family and friends were celebrating that she was home from the hospital.

Words to Treasure

People who have an easy life look down on those who have problems. They think trouble comes only to those whose feet are slipping.

Job 12:5

Sometimes she wondered if this whole shark thing was God punishing her for something she did wrong or some bad thought she might have had. But then she laughed at herself. She knew God loved her and she knew that even though she made mistakes, she did try her best to be good. Does that count?.

Sure does. In the Bible, Job's friends thought the same thing. They thought that Job must have done something pretty bad to have *so* many bad things happen to him, and that God was punishing Job. But Job knew that he had a good relationship with God and that all this weird hard stuff was for a good purpose. He knew that this bad stuff wasn't about him being bad or God being mean. He knew his unhelpful friends were wrong. Job was a good man, and God was a good God. Check out Job's story.

Live IT!

Are you going through hard times? Always remember, God loves you no matter what! And that hard times like shark bites aren't your fault. Stuff happens, and sometimes troubles actually make us feel closer to God because we lean on his strength and love.

Mistakes Happen

The lifeguard sat Cody down in the office. "Last time you were here you vandalized our picnic table."

Cody didn't want to make eye contact. "Yes, sir. You took away my season's pass. But I'm really sorry. I saved up my allowance to pay for the damage." Cody gave him a big jar full of money. "And I was wondering if I could get my pass back and still swim here." Was it Cody's imagination or did the lifeguard start looking a little nicer? Maybe it was just around the eyes.

"We usually don't let vandals back in the park. But I think you made a mistake, and I'm going to give you one more chance. You can have your pass back."

Cody jumped up and started shaking the lifeguard's arm off. "Thank you! From now on you'll have no problems with me. I promise."

"Good. Stop shaking my arm."

Cody released him. "Okay, I'm sorry."

When you make mistakes, the best thing for you to do is to talk to the person you wronged. You'll be surprised how one talk can give you a second chance to make things right. God's a big believer in giving people second chances, and you should be too.

Words to Treasure

They must admit they have committed a sin. They must pay in full for what they did wrong. And they must add a fifth of the value to it.

Numbers 5:7

People in Bible Times

Samson made a few whopper mistakes in his life, but he prayed to God for help one more time. God answered by giving Samson back his strength for one last battle. Samson pushed down his enemy's temple with one mighty muscle-bulging push. (See Judges 16.)

September 1

Sing It!

Meg and Krista had bought their concert T-shirts and now were finding their seats. This would be the best concert they had ever been to. The lead singer was great and their music was always excellent. Meg was hoping they would play her favorite song. She liked that song because she understood what they were trying to say about how amazing God was. She would remember this night for as long as she lived. The arena went dark, and the crowd grew quiet. In a flash of light the stage was bright and the band began to play. And it was her *favorite* song.

Words to Treasure

I will sing praise to the LORD. He has been so good to me.

Psalm 13:6

People have been singing songs about God for thousands and thousands of years. King David was a music guy and constantly wrote songs and poems about his life with God. He wrote them when he was worried, afraid, sad, or incredibly happy. It was kind of like his way of talking with God. God loves it when we use music, writing, drawing, or other types of art to show how we feel about him.

Music was important to the Israelites, and they played all kinds of instruments. They had horns made out of animal tusks, wood or bone flutes, trumpets, drums, tambourines, rattles, harps, and other string instruments. They played music for fun, to worship God, and for battle calls.

Forget about It!

Cheri walked up to her sisters. "Candice and Cindy, do you remember when you took the dog's shaver and gave me a buzz cut when I was five years old? Or when you ate my entire Easter chocolate bunny? Or the time you broke my mouse watch? Or all the times we played hide and seek and you never even looked for me? Or the time you forgot to put my pet lizard away and then you sat on it at dinnertime? Or the time you drew happy faces all over my face, arms, and legs with permanent marker when I was asleep at summer camp? Or last week when you told Eric Hedley that I liked him and now he calls me every day? Do you remember all those things?" The sisters nodded. Cheri threw her arms around them. "I forgive you! I forgive you! Although I would like a new lizard."

Words to Treasure

So then, don't be afraid. I'll provide for you and your children." He calmed their fears. And he spoke in a kind way to them. Joseph stayed in Egypt along with all his father's family. He lived 110 years.

Genesis 50:21-22

Forgiving your brothers or sisters for stuff is hard, but it's the right thing to do. If Joseph could forgive his brothers for thirteen years of slavery and jail time, don't you think you can forgive your family for a few things?

Did you know that 400 years later, when the Israelites finally left Egypt, they took Joseph's bones with them?

September 3

Snake, Be Gone

The little corn snake crawled into the back of a small cupboard. Gracie's two sisters and her mother stood on the kitchen counter. Gracie quickly got the video camera. "This is my family terrified of a tiny little snake. Everybody wave for the camera!"

Words to Treasure

As he grew up, the LORD blessed him. The Spirit of the LORD began to work in his life.

Judges 13:24–25

Her mother gave her a warning look. "Gracie. Please."

"Okay, okay." Gracie slid her tiny body into the small space. She held the flashlight and searched for the snake. There it was, curled in the back. Gently Gracie picked up the bright-orange snakeling and squirmed back out. She held up the snake. "See, he wouldn't hurt anybody."

The three squealed. Her mother waved the snake away. "Gracie, take it outside. Please. Right now."

"Okay." She opened the back door and put the snake under a bush and watched it slither away.

Gracie was the perfect kid for this snake-catching mission. She was small enough to crawl in after it and, most important, she wasn't at all afraid. God designed each of us with special gifts and abilities to do things other people can't. From the day we were born, God knew what we would be good at and how we should use our abilities.

Before Samson was even born, God knew that he would be an incredible, fearless, muscle-bound, lion-killing, army-busting, temple-crashing strong man. And God had a very special save-my-people mission for Samson. (See Judges 13–16.)

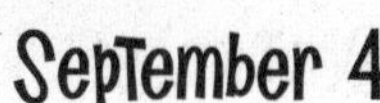

P.I.

Riley was having a lot of fun chatting on this kids-only website. She was allowed to chat for an hour after she finished her homework. She really liked chatting with a kid named Mason. He was really funny, and he liked the same music, went to church, and loved dogs.

Mason wrote, "Why are Dalmatians no good at hide-and-seek? Riley replied, " Why?"

"They're always spotted! Hey, Riley—what school do you go to?"

Riley wrote back. "LOL. Funny joke. As for school, that's P.I. stuff."

"What's P.I. mean?"

"Private Information. Sorry, can't tell you. Gotta go. Talk to you later." Riley signed off.

Riley's a smart kid. Never give out information about yourself to people you don't really know—especially online, even if you chat with them a lot. If you have any doubts about a question, just don't answer it.

Remember Samson in the Bible? He gave away P.I. stuff on how to defeat his strength, and look what happened to him. The Philistines captured him. Really not good. When you're online, be safe, smart, and hush, hush on private stuff.

Words to Treasure

Those who are careful about what they say keep themselves out of trouble.

Proverbs 21:23

Talk with the adults in your family about what type of information is okay to talk about online, on the phone, or with strangers, and what type of information should be kept private. If you need to, put a list of off-limits topics by the computer—P.I. stuff. And if in doubt, go ask your parents before you reply to any question.

September 5

Cat Got Your Tongue?

Faith didn't want to be doing this, but somebody had to stand up for what's right. People stopped and read her sign, which read, "No Free Kittens!"

Words to Treasure

"Who knows? It's possible that you became queen for a time just like this."

Esther 4:14

The pet-store owner came out very angry. "What are you doing, little girl?"

"My name is Faith Robertson," she introduced herself politely. "It isn't responsible to give away a free kitten with every fifty-dollar purchase. People should plan and research before they get a pet. Some of the kittens you give away for free will be abandoned because people take them without thinking ahead. That's wrong."

The store owner glared at her. "I'm going to phone your parents."

Faith pointed across the street. "That's my dad having coffee and watching me. He agrees."

"She's right," said one lady nearby. Another man agreed. Soon a crowd of people were gathered, all supporting Faith.

Sometimes God will pick you to speak for someone or something that can't speak for itself. You don't want to be rude or break the law, and you should always get your parents' help and support. Be brave when God calls you.

Evil Haman convinced the king to have all the Jews killed. So it was up to Queen Esther to save herself and her people. To do this, she would have to go talk to her husband. Small problem—you couldn't approach the king if he didn't send for you first. If she displeased him, she could die. (See Esther 4.)

September 6

No Matter What!

Sara walked around the old go-cart she had bought. It wasn't much to look at, because she didn't have a lot of money. It was going to take a ton of work to get it running before racing season. Her friend Hayden sat on an old tire in the garage. Sara rubbed at the rust and hoped it wasn't too deep. "I'm not going to get this fixed up in time."

Words to Treasure

But Ruth replied, "Don't try to make me leave you and go back. Where you go I'll go. Where you stay I'll stay."
Ruth 1:16

"Sure you are." Hayden was always encouraging, even if he didn't know what he was talking about.

"No, I'm not." Sara tried to start the engine, but nothing happened.

"You are, because I'm going to help you. Every afternoon until race day."

Sara passed him a root beer. "Hayden, I can't ask you to do that. Even if we get it running and looking good, I may not win anyway."

Hayden kicked a tire. "I know. I don't care about winning. I care that you care so much. I'm your friend, and that's what friends do."

Give Hayden a big cheer, handshake, slap on the back, and … let's go all out and give him a parade! He's exactly the loyal, I'll-go-where-you-go-and-I-don't-care-what-happens kind of friend to have. Can we clone that guy?

What kind of a friend are you? Write down your idea of what a perfect friend would be. Then be that kind of a friend to someone else.

September 7

Speak Up

"Well? Sandy, what can I do for you?" said the principal.

"Principal Collins, I think ..." she cleared her throat.

"Yes?"

"I think we are a really wasteful school. We should start a recycling program. If we want to protect the earth, we have to stop littering and start recycling. I wrote a report." Sandy placed her report on his desk.

Principal Collins sat back in his chair. Sandy was so nervous that she wanted to crawl under the carpet. Finally, he said, "You're right. This could be a great school project," he said.

Sometimes you may see a concern that no one else sees. God often calls people to stand up and help make a change—like prophets in the Old Testament. Whether the concern is big or small, ask God for the boldness to raise the question to the right people.

Words to Treasure

But the LORD said to me, "Do not say, 'I'm too young.' You must go to everyone I send you to."

Jeremiah 1:7

People in Bible Times

Queen Esther invited her husband and Haman to dinner. Her husband, the king, asked Esther what he could do for her. "Nothing really, just save me and my people from being murdered by a maniac man." *What!*? The king asked who would do such a thing. Esther pointed to her other dinner guest, Haman. Haman nearly choked on a meatball. The king was surprised and extremely angry. And Haman was soon to be road kill. (See Esther 7:1–6.)

September 8

My Room

Cameron walked into the strange house and wondered how long he'd be here. Would this ever feel like home? His new foster parents hugged him and took his suitcase. They looked nice, but were they the parents he'd been praying for? The family that would love him and take care of him for a long, long time?

Words to Treasure

He said to me, "You are my son. Today I have become your father."

Psalm 2:7

They led him to his bedroom. When they opened the door he froze. The entire room was painted like the night sky and covered in space posters. Constellations, planets, and galaxies filled the room. A telescope pointed out the window. Cameron didn't know what to say. He'd never had a room like this before. His new foster mom put her arm around his shoulder. "We heard you were interested in everything about space."

His new dad led him to the telescope. "I'm not sure if this is the right kind. We can take it back if it's not what you want." Cameron looked around at the room that was made just for him.

In Bible times, it wasn't uncommon for children to be sent away from home when they were very young to learn a job. In the Bible, a boy named Samuel went to live with a priest named Eli and his family. Samuel did odd jobs and took religious lessons from Eli. Sometimes his mother visited him, because she loved him very much.

Kids' Place

Seven-year-old Haley thought and thought about it. Finally she walked up to Pastor Owen. "Pastor Owen, can I talk to you about something I think would be good for our church?"

Words to Treasure

"Anyone who takes the humble position of this child is the most important in the kingdom of heaven."

Matthew 18:4

"Sure, Haley. What's up?" Pastor Owen smiled.

"Have a seat." Haley pointed to some chairs. "Not everybody has family to celebrate their birthdays with. I think every week we should buy some flowers and hand them out to everybody who's having a birthday that week. That way they won't feel so lonely. Birthdays are important, you know."

Pastor Owen thought about it. "That would be nice, Haley. If your parents want to help you, I can give you money each week, and you can buy some flowers to hand out each Sunday."

This time Haley thought about it. "Okay. I'll be in charge of birthday flowers."

Sometimes church can seem like a grown-up world. Adults, step back and make some room for *kids*. Kids are smart and creative, and they hear from God too. If you've got an idea for church, go talk about it.

People in Bible Times

Young Samuel was sleeping in God's temple outside the inner chamber when God called to him three times. Now God didn't often talk directly to people, so this was really special. God gave Samuel a very important mission. Even though he was just a kid, Samuel did what he was told. He kept listening to God and became one of the Bible's greatest prophets.

September 10

But I'm Good

A big red SOLD sign hung in their boat window. Abby was helping her dad clean the boat for the new owners. She loved this boat, but she wouldn't let her dad see her sadness. He had been laid off from work, and they couldn't afford to keep the boat. She understood how hard this was for him. This had been his dream boat.

"It's okay, Dad." Abby tried to cheer him up. "Maybe our next boat will be even nicer than this one. You'll get a new job soon. Besides a boat's just *stuff*. No big deal." Her father gave her a sad little smile and went back to cleaning the deck.

Words to Treasure

But reach out your hand and strike down everything he has. Then I'm sure he will speak evil things against you.

Job 1:11

It doesn't seem fair when hard things like losing a job, getting sick, or a death in the family happen. Bad things shouldn't happen to good people. Having a good attitude and still doing things God's way through hard times is really the biggest test of our lives. Abby's right. Hard times don't last forever, and good times could be right around the corner. Trust God.

People in Bible Times

A man named Job had a good life and loved God. But Satan argued that Job only loved God because God gave him good things. "Make Job's life unhappy, and he won't love you anymore," Satan teased. So God and Satan decided to put Job's love to the test. (See Job 1.)

September 11

Stop, Already!

Ross, Gavin, and Ali were playing darts. Ross hadn't ever played darts before. He threw one dart and it stuck in the ceiling. His next dart nearly jabbed the dog, and the last dart bounced off the wall and into the fish bowl with a big, wet splash. None of his darts came anywhere near the dartboard. His friends were killing themselves laughing. How could anybody be *that* bad?

Words to Treasure

How long will you crush me with your words?

Job 19:2

Gavin laughed, "Ross, you kind of throw darts like you're harpooning a whale. Just little throws—the way I showed you."

Ross gritted his teeth. "I know. I'm trying my best." His two best friends continued to make fun. "STOP IT!" shouted Ross. The boys stopped instantly. "For guys who are supposed to be my friends, you sure act like jerks."

There's having fun with a friend, and then there's making fun of your friend. Make sure your fun isn't at the cost of a good friend's feelings.

Discovering Archaeology

The game of throwing darts may have been invented by soldiers throwing their arrows at objects for training—or just for fun. Hey, it can be boring waiting around a battle camp. Ever wonder why there are feathers on arrows or darts? They're called fletchings, and they keep the arrow flying straight to where you want it to go.

You're God, and I'm Not!

Her dad was cleaning the garage when Samantha stomped in. "I've decided that we shouldn't move. My friends are here, I like my school, and I don't want to move to Dallas. Everything's perfect for me right here."

Her dad picked up his coffee. "I see. Just a few questions."

"Go ahead." She was confident she could make a good case for not moving.

"Do you have a job to support this family?"

"No."

"Do you know *all* the reasons why we're making this move?"

"No. Are you going to tell me all the reasons?"

Her dad sipped his coffee. "No. All you need to know is that it is important for our family, and *you,* that we move to Dallas. End of discussion."

"But, Dad!" Samantha complained.

"End of discussion," warned her dad. "I'm the parent, and you are the kid."

Sometimes your parents will make tough choices for your family. You have to trust that they've thought it out carefully and want what's best for your entire family. They may know parent stuff that you don't. That's okay. God's like that too. He knows stuff you don't. He's God, and you're not.

Words to Treasure

The Lord spoke to Job out of a storm. He said, "Who do you think you are to disagree with my plans? You do not know what you are talking about."

Job 38: 1-2

People in Bible Times

When Job questioned God's plan for his life, God gave him a short list of all the amazing things he did. In other words, God is Lord of the universe, and he knows what he's doing. He's God and you're not. His wisdom is something you can't question. But you can *trust* it.

September 13

Do It Now!

Dylan felt shy as the golfers walked by with their bags full of clubs. He sat on a bench and watched them play. Their golf balls seemed to float on air until they dropped gently onto the green. Dylan had thought and thought about learning to play golf.

> **Words to Treasure**
>
> Go in peace. The Lord is pleased with your journey.
>
> Judges 18:6

He walked bravely into the clubhouse and right up to the front desk. A man leaned on the counter. "What can I do for you?"

"I want to learn to play golf. I want to know what I need to do."

"You're smart, kid. Golf's the best sport in the world." The man pulled out a sheet of paper. "Here's the list of beginner classes, times, and prices. If you're going to do it—learn to do it right. Show that to your folks."

Dylan carefully folded the sheet and put it in his pocket. "I will. Thanks."

God wants you to explore his world and experience all kinds of new things. He wants you to discover amazing new talents and skills, because that's all part of the journey called your life. What new thing do you want to try?

Live IT!

Is there something new you want to learn or try? Do you want to learn to play a musical instrument, try a new sport, or volunteer somewhere? Go find out what it will take to do that new thing. You never know, it could be the start of an amazing new adventure. Don't wait until later—do it today. You could be the next incredible world talent.

Jealousy Web

The gigantic, hairy spider crawled up Sydney's arm. The entire class was quiet and impressed. Sydney's show-and-tell was a home run. Charles was pea green with jealousy. His homemade lava lamp wasn't the envy of all the class. It wasn't fair, because Sydney's mom was a zookeeper and brought home all kinds of cool animals. How can a guy compete with that? How can you bring a cooler show-and-tell than an enormous, blood-sucking, hairy spider?

"Would anybody like to hold my spider?" asked Sydney. "He doesn't bite. Just be careful not to pet him. It can damage the hairs on his body." The entire class waved their hands wildly. Even the principal came to have a look. Today was so disappointing. Charles just wanted to take his lava lamp and go home.

Words to Treasure

It really upset him. He said to himself, "They are saying David has killed tens of thousands of men. But they are saying I've killed only thousands."

1 Samuel 18:8

Charles could have enjoyed seeing and holding a spider with the rest of the class if he hadn't been so filled with jealousy. He missed out. And being jealous of what other people have or the things they do is like saying to God that you're not happy with the things he's given you. That's really disappointing for God. And it makes life disappointing for you too. So junk the jealousy.

People in Bible Times

David had defeated the giant Goliath, and the entire kingdom went David crazy. He was a superstar! They cheered him and sang songs about him. They treated him like a king! And that made King Saul very jealous. Who's king around here, anyway? Actually, God had decided David would be king, because David obeyed God and Saul didn't. (See 1 Samuel 18.)

September 15

Driving Brainless

The car looked kind of funny half off and half on the stone garden wall. Richmond's dad looked kind of funny as he surveyed the damage and waited for a tow truck.

Words to Treasure

But those who listen to me will live in safety.

Proverbs 1:33

Finally, his dad walked over to Richmond, Larry, and David. He gave them a serious gunslinger's squint. "It seemed like a good idea to get in my car, turn it on, and then gun it in reverse across the garden?"

Richmond looked everywhere but at his dad. "No," he answered honestly. "I knew it wasn't a good idea. We just wanted to drive the car down the driveway. We didn't think anything would happen."

"Thinking," agreed his dad, "was not a big part of today. And something did happen. My car is now a yard decoration."

"Sorry, Dad."

Everyone acts without thinking from time to time. Plenty of Bible characters did too—Adam and Eve, Moses, Samson, King Saul, and on and on. God gave us a brain to think before we act. But he's gracious when we forget to use it. There is always a chance to turn brainless into smart. Use it.

Kids have been getting in trouble for thousands of years, and it was no different in Bible times. Brothers tricked each other, sold each other into slavery, or teased a prophet so bad they got smacked by bears. You can read those stories in the Bible and learn from their mistakes. You can be 2,000 years smarter by listening to that wise, smart voice in your head.

Foul

This was get-even day. Allen had it all planned out, and it was the perfect revenge. Connor was always making fun of him at school, even though Allen had tried several times to be friends. Connor was the meanest bully in school, but today his rule of terror was coming to a big end.

Words to Treasure

Evil acts come from those who do evil.

1 Samuel 24:13

Allen had bought Stink Spray, and it was just about the most disgusting smelling stuff in the entire world. At lunchtime, he was going to spray it around Connor's locker and desk. When everybody came in, they'd think Connor was the stinkiest guy in the world. He'd never live it down.

Allen peeked around the corner, crept down the hall, and stood in front of Connor's locker. He held up the spray can, shook it well, and was about to pull the trigger. With one little push of a button, he'd have victory and revenge. He'd be the school practical-joke hero. Just one little spray. Allen stood there for a long time, but he couldn't do it. He just wasn't a revenge kind of guy!

It's pretty simple: doing wrong is never right. No matter the reason, doing wrong things makes you wrong in every way.

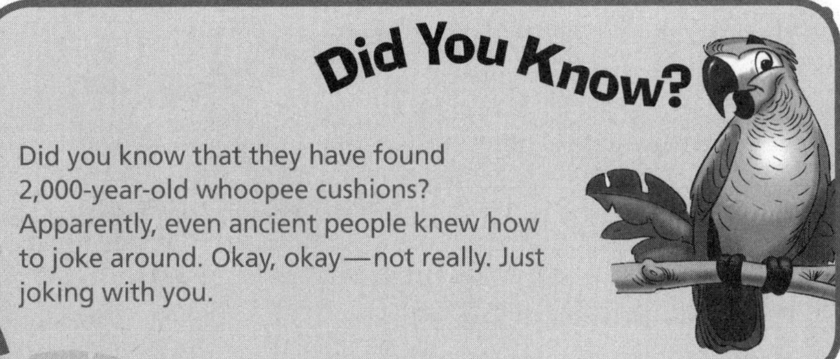

Did you know that they have found 2,000-year-old whoopee cushions? Apparently, even ancient people knew how to joke around. Okay, okay—not really. Just joking with you.

September 17

One More Time

Allen was dribbling the basketball down the court, and he was absolutely going to make a basket this time. He could feel it happening. This was going to be the most perfect basket ever. Suddenly, Allen tripped over something; his arms flew up, and the ball bounced away. He did a face-plant in front of his entire class. Allen had been purposely tripped. He looked around the gym. Connor smiled a mean smile as he slid his foot back. "Sorry about that, Allen."

Words to Treasure

TThe Lord rewards everyone for doing what is right and being faithful. He handed you over to me today. But I wouldn't lay a hand on you.

1 Samuel 26:23

It was lunchtime and Allen was standing in front Connor's locker *again* with the can of Stink Spray. He was so mad that *this* time he was going to do it. This was the day! This moment! This second! Right now! He was ready any second now. Spray away! But Allen couldn't do it. He just wasn't a revenge kind of guy.

Once again Allen did the right thing by not doing what's wrong. You know what? He's a hero in God's eyes.

Did You Know?

Jealous King Saul was riding around the kingdom looking to kill David. But two times David had the opportunity to hurt King Saul, and both times he refused to touch the king. David was doing everything in his power to obey God and do the right thing.

A What?

Aunt Sophie examined Kyle's rock."You found an artifact, Kyle. See how the sides have been thinned down to a fine edge. This end is pointed, and this end has notches in it. Did you know this rock is called obsidian and this is actually an arrowhead?. It might have been used as a spear."

Kyle's mouth hung open. "I found a spear! Awesome. Now what do we do?"

"Well, let's make it official. Measure your hole, and draw a diagram of it. Then we'll take a picture of the arrowhead and give it an artifact number. You are an archaeologist in the making."

Words to Treasure

"But ask the animals what God does. They will teach you. Or ask the birds in the sky. They will tell you."

Job 12:7

God's great big world is out there waiting to be discovered. From supernovas to ancient artifacts to creatures near and far. What will you discover? You're never too young to start exploring the world God created.

Did You Know?

Who in the Bible knows these answers?

- When mountain goats have their babies?
- Why ostriches are mean to their babies?
- Why horses have manes on their necks?
- How hawks know where to fly?

The simple answer is God. He knows everything about everything.

September 19

Put It Back

Kyle was filling in the hole he had dug in his backyard. His mom brought him a cold glass of lemonade. He drank it in four big gulps.

Words to Treasure

The earth is filled with the things he has made.

Psalm 104:3

"Thanks, Mom. Filling in the hole isn't as much fun as digging it. But Aunt Sophie said to make sure I put the dirt back the way it was before I dug there."

"She's right. Don't forget to put the grass back on top and then water it to help it regrow."

God created a beautiful world, so let's keep it that way. No matter what type of exploring you do, always leave the area the way you found it. For example, when you're hiking, pack out your garbage and leftover snacks. Or when you're exploring the beach and roll a rock over to see what's underneath, gently put it back after you're done. Explorers respect the world around them.

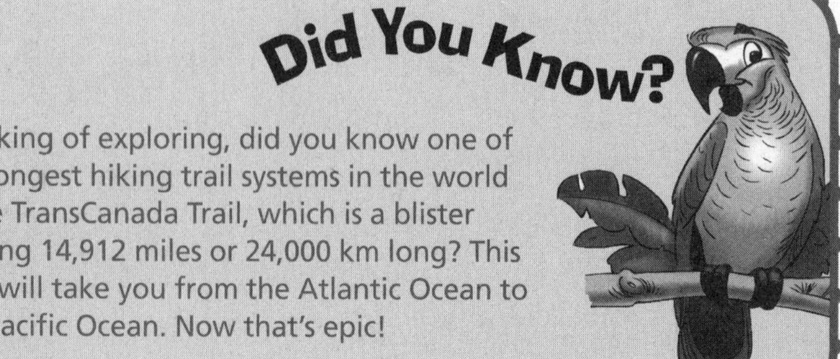

Did You Know?
Speaking of exploring, did you know one of the longest hiking trail systems in the world is the TransCanada Trail, which is a blister making 14,912 miles or 24,000 km long? This hike will take you from the Atlantic Ocean to the Pacific Ocean. Now that's epic!

Bragging Not So Good

The football team smelled, they were tired, and they had just lost the game. Thomas pulled off his football helmet. "I had a great game. Did you see me out there?" His teammates had just taken a beating, and they didn't want to hear it. For some of the guys, this had been the worst game they had ever played. Thomas grabbed the last bottle of water from the big Styrofoam barrel. "I did moves that I didn't even know I had."

Words to Treasure

Joseph had a dream. When he told it to his brothers, they hated him even more.
Genesis 37:5

Douglas slicked his sweaty hair back. "We lost, Thomas."

"Well, yeah. Because of you, not because of me."

You may be good at what you do. And maybe even God has told you that you're something special. But sometimes saying it to other people just might be the wrong move. Bragging about your present or future successes might not go over well with everybody.

People in Bible Times

Joseph was his father's favorite and that kind of upset his brothers. But to make matters worse, Joseph had these crazy dreams that revealed that some day he would be a really, really, really important person, more important than his older brothers. Joe's important talk didn't go over well with the bros. They sold the kid into slavery and packed him off to Egypt. (See Genesis 37.)

September 21

Not Again!

Larry, David, and Richmond stood on the railroad tracks. The train bridge stretched across the steep ravine. "Come on," encouraged Larry, "it will be fun. It won't take long."

Words to Treasure

Let your ears listen to wisdom. Apply your heart to understanding.

Proverbs 2:2

"I don't know," worried David.

"Believe me, a train's not going to come along. They hardly ever use this track anymore."

It would be fun and daring to step from one railroad tie to the next, seventy feet above the creek. It would be the way it was in the movies. "Well ..." Richmond looked down the long empty track that disappeared around the bend. "Okay. Let's do it." He took a few steps along the track and stopped. "I can't do this. This could be really dangerous. This could be the stupidest thing we've ever done. I'm going home." Richmond turned around and followed the quiet path back to the road. His friends caught up to him.

Larry moaned, "Richmond, you're a serious wimpnoid." The long, low wail of a train whistle sounded behind them as a train sped past toward the bridge. The boys looked at each other with big eyes.

Discovering Archaeology

Ancient Romans loved to build things, and they were really good at it. They built big stone bridges so that their armies could move around their empire quickly. If they couldn't go around a river or ravine, they built a bridge. Amazingly, some of those 2,000-year-old bridges are still being used today. Instead of chariots, cars are driving on them.

September 22

Mighty Friends

The guys pushed and pushed up the hill with all their strength. They'd been pushing for blocks. Finally they saw the building and turned into the parking lot. They rolled up alongside the building. A window opened and a woman poked her head out. "Can I take your order please?" Then she started to laugh.

Words to Treasure

"They put their lives in danger by going to Bethlehem to get it." So David wouldn't drink it.

2 Samuel 23:17

Oliver wiped sweat from his face. "We'd like three burgers, fries, and root beers." The two guys stood beside a boy dressed in a hospital gown and sitting in a wheelchair with a huge cast on his broken leg. Oliver shrugged, "Sometimes a guy just wants a burger. What's a friend to do?"

Jackson waved from his wheelchair.

Now that's friendship! When you pick your friends, find friends that are willing to go that extra mile to help you. Like David and his mighty men. David picked a crack team of fighting men to hang out with. One day David was in a cave surrounded by bad-guy Philistines. David mentioned he was kind of thirsty for water from a certain well. Three mighty men fought their way past Philistine guards camped at Bethlehem, got some water, and took it back to David. David was really, really touched by their love for him. That's order-in, military style!

Mighty men were pretty mighty. Take a guy named Josheb-Basshebeth. He took on eight hundred men with one spear and won!

September 23

Follow the Leader

This was Capture the Flag at its toughest. To top it off, this was a hidden-flag game. One scout from each game was allowed to see where the other team's flag was hidden and then describe it to his or her troop. "I'll be the leader and scout to see the flag." Finn put mud on his face.

Words to Treasure

"May King Solomon live a long time!" Then come back up to the city with him. Have him sit on my throne. He will rule in my place.

1 Kings 1: 34-35

"Why you?" Zane questioned.

"I'm the best man for the job. You have to be good at remembering things."

Zane didn't look convinced. He said, "Madison, turn around and, without looking, tell us what Finn's wearing."

She turned around. "He's wearing a black T-shirt, jeans with a hole in the left knee, a leather belt, white socks with the British flag on them, a leather shark-tooth necklace, brown hiking boots with green laces, a camouflage sports watch—and mud."

Zane raised his hand. "Everybody who wants Madison to be our leader and scout, raise your hand." Zane looked around. "That would be everybody. Sorry, Finn, looks like Madison's the best woman for the job."

There's a right way to become a leader and there's a wrong way. Saying you're a leader doesn't mean people will actually follow you. And that's embarrassing.

King David's son Adonijah was throwing a party for himself because he had made himself king. Well, wrap up the leftovers, because Adonijah had a surprise coming. God, King David, and the prophet Nathan had already made his brother Solomon the next king instead. Just a little embarrassing.

Secretly Glad

Tom was in big trouble for playing at the old abandoned farmhouse. He wasn't allowed in there because it was dangerous. Drew was sitting on the stairs listening to his big brother get a gigantically long lecture.

Drew smiled to himself and was kind of happy inside. He wasn't sure why, but when his brother was in trouble it made him feel as if he was the good, special kid in the family. He enjoyed it when his brother was in trouble.

His dad walked into the hallway and caught him listening on the steps. Drew looked up, trying to look as innocent as an angel. "I would never go to the farmhouse, Dad," said Drew.

Dad didn't look as impressed as he should be. "But you would sneak cookies from the cookie jar. We'll talk about that later." His dad started up the stairs but stopped. "Drew?"

"Yes, Dad?"

"Being happy about your brother being unhappy is wrong." Dad walked up the stairs.

That didn't work out quite the way Drew had planned. He wasn't the good, special kid after all.

Words to Treasure

Don't be happy when your enemy falls. When he trips, don't let your heart be glad. The Lord will see it, but he won't be pleased.

Proverbs 24:17–18

Speaking of ancient, old houses, how would you like to sleep on the roof in the summer or keep goats, sheep, and other animals in your basement in the winter? That's what many kids in ancient Israel did.

September 25

What's Best?

Sebastian stroked his dog. He didn't ever want to let go. The other family members waited quietly for his decision. It wasn't fair, because the animal shelter said that Henry was *his* dog. He had been his dog for five months! And now these people were saying that Henry was *their* dog. They had lost him in a park. This wasn't fair! He had done everything right to adopt Henry.

Words to Treasure

Love is patient. Love is kind. It does not want what belongs to others.

1 Corinthians 13:4

But Sebastian couldn't ignore how excited Henry was to see this family. Henry answered when they called him "Jett." He did tricks for them that Sebastian didn't even know he could do. He could see that Henry loved them and they loved Henry. This so stunk! Sebastian's mom touched his arm gently, knowing how hard this was.

Sebastian walked over to the girl and placed Henry—or Jett—into her arms. This wasn't about how *he* felt; it was about what was best for Henry. It was about doing the right thing even though it hurt.

Loving someone or something sometimes means caring more about what's good for them than what feels good for you.

Did You Know?

Did you know this? When two women both claimed to be the rightful mother of a baby, King Solomon ordered the baby cut in two, knowing that the real mother would give away her child first rather than see it harmed. The woman who gave her baby to the other woman was the true mother. The problem was solved with no bloodshed.

Mud Slinging

This was mud volleyball at its absolute best. It was a sunny day and the farmer's field was hosed down to make the thickest, deepest mud you could want. The area schools were having a mud volleyball tournament. All the players were completely covered in mud because they were diving and falling in the oozing ground. It was great!

If Hillary's team won this game, they would move up to second place and then maybe first. Everybody was tense as the other team was ready to serve the winning ball. The mud-covered ball skimmed over the net. Suzy dove for it but missed and landed face down in the ooze. The other team jumped up and down! They had won. Suzy sat up, wiping mud from her face. She was upset. Hillary sat down in the mud beside her friend. "Nobody could have gotten that serve. It was an impossible return. We came in third out of fifteen schools. All because of your rocket serves." Suzy flopped down in the mud and began to wave her arms and legs back and forth.

"What are you doing?" asked a puzzled Hillary.

Suzy giggled. "Mud angels. Try it." Soon the entire third-place team was making mud angels and having a good time.

Sometimes saying the right and kind thing makes for moments you never forget.

Words to Treasure

Kind words are like honey. They are sweet to the spirit and bring healing to the body.

Proverbs 16:24

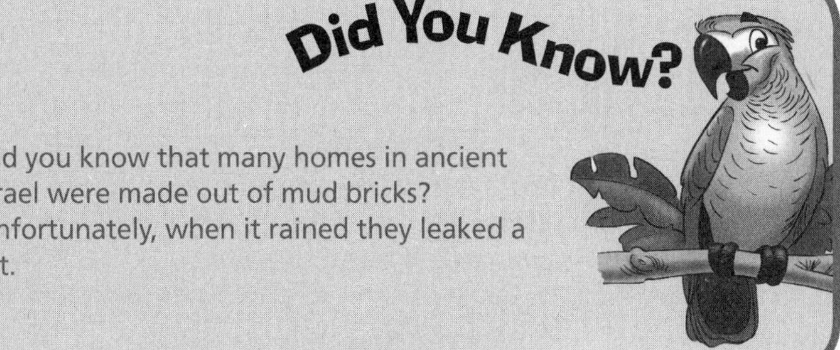

Did you know that many homes in ancient Israel were made out of mud bricks? Unfortunately, when it rained they leaked a lot.

September 27

Treetop Wisdom

Grandpa popped his head up in the tree fort and looked around. Joel quickly tucked something under the old rug. But Grandpa was pretty quick with stuff like that. He pulled himself up into the fort and carefully sat on the most secure part of the floor.

Words to Treasure

A man who loves wisdom makes his father glad.

Proverbs 29:3

"You've been up here a long time. What's up?"

Joel shrugged. "Nothing much ... you know, stuff."

Grandpa pulled two cold drinks from his pockets. "Here." Grandpa purposely put his hand down on the bump in the carpet. "What's under here?"

"Grandpa!" Joel protested.

Grandpa pulled out a Bible. He looked both puzzled and pleased at the same time.

Joel took the Bible back. "You're not going to make fun of me, are you?"

"Nope," Grandpa promised.

"Sometimes a guy just needs privacy. You know, for personal stuff. A guy doesn't need to advertise around the entire neighborhood that he reads the Bible."

"You're right," agreed his grandpa. "I'm making dinner in about an hour." Slowly and carefully the old man climbed back down the tree with a proud smile on his face.

Reading the Bible can be a very personal time you may not want to share with the world. And that's okay.

Jesus often went away by himself to pray and think about God. He wasn't ignoring people or being secretive. He just wanted to spend some quiet time with his heavenly Father.

Sharing Is a Big Idea

The little kid stared at the gumball machine and back at Lilly. He was like a puppy with shaggy long bangs. Where were his parents? She only had one quarter, and she really wanted a gumball.

She put the coin in, turned the knob, opened the flap, and pulled out a black gumball. The puppy-dog kid stared at the candy in her hand. Lilly pulled an oh-all-right face, "Go ask your parents if you can have a candy."

The little kid ran down an aisle and was back in a nano-second. "I can." Lilly handed over *her* gumball.

The store clerk glanced over. "Hey!" he said. "For a black gumball you get three free comics and five extra gumballs."

Lilly looked at the kid popping the black ball in his mouth and then turned to the clerk. "Really?!" She couldn't believe it.

Lilly walked home with her comics and red, yellow, pink, white, and blue gumballs.

Being generous with a little allows God to bless you with a lot.

Words to Treasure

Don't forget to share with others. God is pleased with those kinds of offerings.

Hebrews 13:16

For a long time there had been no water to grow crops. God's prophet Elijah asked a widow for food. She wasn't sure, because she was planning one last small meal of flour and oil before she and her son were out of food. But she decided to invite Elijah over anyway. God blessed her with flour and oil that never ran out until the drought ended. Her kindness with a little saved their lives.

September 29

No Call-Waiting

The airplane bounced around in the sky as the storm raged. Inside, Ava and her mom were holding onto their seats. This was like a roller-coaster ride, only it wasn't very fun, and you couldn't just get off to ride the bumper cars. A man beside them couldn't hold his drink steady enough to take a sip; the liquid just spilled all over.

Words to Treasure

Answer me. LORD, answer me. Then these people will know that you are the one and only God.

1 Kings 18:37

Her mother held her hand. "Baby, now would be a good time to pray." They bowed their heads and prayed quietly together. The plane took a sudden dip that made everybody in the plane give a little scream. But then everything stopped. The plane wasn't bouncing or diving anymore. Ava looked out the window. Behind them and all around them, dark storm clouds boiled and turned with wind and flashing lightning—but the skies around their plane were calm.

God is listening to your prayers—no ifs, ands, or buts.

Did You Know?

Elijah once challenged the priests of the god Baal to an altar-burning contest to see which god was stronger. Things weren't working out for the Baal team. Their god wasn't answering, and Elijah wondered aloud if their god had maybe gone to the toilet (no kidding). Then Elijah prayed, and God answered by not only burning the wet wood but also the stone and dirt around the altar. No competition. (See 1 Kings 18.)

Leave a Message

Emmy searched around trees, under bushes, and along the creek but couldn't find any animal tracks, not even a raccoon's. She sat down on a snowy log completely discouraged. There couldn't be an entire forest with absolutely no animals walking around. That was impossible! What was she doing wrong? She looked at her big brother, Paul. "I'm never going to be a good tracker like you. I'm stupid! I'm useless! I'm the only person in our family who won't grow up to be a guide. I'll have to go work in the city and sit in a stuffy office every day until I die." She looked around at the mountains and the trees. She loved her life here.

Words to Treasure

f any of you needs wisdom, you should ask God for it. He will give it to you. God gives freely to everyone and doesn't find fault.

James 1:5

"Ssssh. Do you hear that?" Paul looked around.

"What?" Emmy couldn't hear anything.

Paul pretended to pick up an invisible phone. "Hello?" He handed her the imaginary phone. "It's for you. It's discouragement calling." Emmy rolled her eyes. Paul ordered, "Off the log; go track some more. And this time, think like an animal. Where would you go?" Emmy got up and searched the snowy ground again.

Being discouraged means feeling bad about yourself or what's happening in your life. It's okay to feel that way, but don't let that feeling hang around too long or make important choices for you. Hang up on discouragement or take a message.

Did you know that when Elijah was really discouraged and tired, God sent an angel to look after him?

October 1

Truth

It was only an exhibition chess tournament, and Fran wasn't too worried about it. It was good practice, and it was a sunny afternoon in the park, with a picnic after. Ryan was losing the game and wasn't happy about it. He waved his hand for an official. Mrs. Noble came over.

Words to Treasure

A dishonest witness will be punished. And those who pour out lies will not go free.

Proverbs 19:5

Ryan pointed at Fran. "She cheated. She touched a piece and didn't move it."

"I did not!" Fran was completely shocked and surprised. She hadn't gone anywhere near touching a piece. Fran knew she hadn't cheated. But she also knew that if she was accused of cheating, it would damage her reputation as a good and honest player.

The woman whispered, "Sorry, Ryan, I've been watching this game, and I didn't see her touch a piece like that. Be very, very careful about making claims against other players. You could be the big loser."

Ryan thought about it. "Maybe I was mistaken."

Being dishonest to get ahead is never a smart move.

It can be very tempting to say one little lie. But remember, if people discover you lied, they will never trust you again. They will always doubt what you say. They will be disappointed, hurt, angry, and lose a ton of respect for you. You may even lose friendships. A little lie can be the start of big problems. No fooling or lying.

Making Fun Not Fun

Alton was walking out of the corner store, and three guys followed to stare at him. Alton got a lot of this because he was shorter than most people. One guy called out, "Hey, kid, where's Snow White and the other short dudes?" They began to sing, "Hi ho, hi ho …"

An unhappy, deep voice came from behind them. "I don't know where Snow White is … but you can guess where the giant is." The three guys turned and looked up to see Alton's taller-than-average best friend, Wyatt. "It would make me really, really happy if you apologized to my friend." Wyatt passed Alton his soda.

Alton took the drink. "Believe me, you *want* to make Wyatt happy." The guys mumbled an apology as they headed in the opposite direction. The two friends walked home drinking cold sodas.

People may pick on you, call you names, and act like jerks, but if you have one good friend, that's all you need. One true friend to hang out with is worth a billion jerks.

Words to Treasure

He makes fun of proud people who make fun of others. But he gives grace to those who are humble and treated badly.

Proverbs 3:34

A big gang of teens were making fun of the prophet Elisha because he had very little hair. But Elisha prayed, and two bears came out of the woods and made chew toys out of 42 of the guys.

October 3

Just Doing My Thing

Julie wiped her hands with a rag. "Hey, Dad, my dirt bike's stored for the winter. I replaced the oil, removed the battery and spark plugs, drained the gas tank, and waxed the paint."

Words to Treasure

We have only done our duty.

Luke 17:10

"Good," her dad said without looking up.

"Good? That's all you're going to say? That was a lot of work."

Her dad sat back. "It is your dirt bike, right?" Julie nodded. "It is your job to get it stored and ready for next season. Right?"

"Yeah."

"Now when you do something really out of the ordinary, like painting the entire house, I'll have something big to say."

Julie rolled her eyes. "Okay, I get the point. I shouldn't expect praise for something I should do anyway."

Her dad smiled. "You're one smart kid."

Don't expect a big parade or party for doing right things. Why? Because that's the way we're supposed to behave all the time. You don't expect your parents to throw you a party every day for brushing your teeth. Doing what's right is just an everyday, ordinary thing.

Kids in ancient times had daily chores too, such as gathering fuel for the fire or carrying water from the well. Children also weeded and watered the grape vines or gardens. Many children spent their days herding and watching over the family's sheep and goats.

Star Treatment

Myles walked into his science class as if he were a hero expecting a big welcome. He had won the Robotics Kids' Multinational Competition. He had a trophy the size of a small car, and today he didn't care if he was the biggest nerd in the world. He was a nerd with a monster trophy. Hold the applause. No autographs please.

Words to Treasure

So don't be proud if you want to be honored.

Proverbs 18:12

The room was quiet, as it usually was, and everybody was busy doing their science projects. No clapping, no handshakes, nothing. Mr. Cheng walked over. "You're late. Take your seat."

Myles took his seat, kind of disappointed. He was a nerd with a trophy the size of car, and nobody cared. Mr. Cheng leaned over, "Congratulations, Myles. We didn't want you to get a swelled head."

Myles shrugged. "No chance of that."

Sure there was. We all want to be treated special and important. But sometimes that's not the best for our egos because they can swell up and burst. Not a pretty sight. Messy. Very messy.

People in Bible Times

The chariots rolled in, and the important-yet-sickly General Naaman stopped at Elisha's house for some prophet-style healing. To Naaman's surprise, the prophet didn't even greet him. He sent out a note telling him to go jump in a river to get healed. Not the kind of service this important guy was used to. His big ego wanted a big welcome.

October 5

Kind of Embarrassing

Her ski instructor didn't look impressed with Zoe's new ski style. "Okay, I tell you what. Why don't you go to the Little Mountain run and work out some of the bad habits you've picked up skiing with your friends. I'll see you tomorrow."

"What!" Zoe dropped her poles in surprise. "That's the bunny hill. That's for beginners! Totally embarrassing."

Noel looked over her sunglasses at Zoe. "Well, it's embarrassing for me to ski with you while you're doing all those goofy things with your arms and legs. Seriously, go work it out. Trust me, you'll be glad you did."

Zoe had been busted down to the easy run, but she had to trust that her instructor knew best. Kind of like the way General Naaman had to trust that the prophet Elisha knew how to cure his skin problem. As embarrassing as it was, Naaman rode his chariot to the river and jumped in seven times and got cured. And Zoe worked all afternoon and improved her moves on the bunny slope. Sometimes a little embarrassment is exactly what we need.

Words to Treasure

"What if Elisha the prophet had told you to do some great thing? Wouldn't you have done it? But he only said, 'Wash yourself. Then you will be pure and clean.' You should be even more willing to do that!" So Naaman went down to the Jordan River. He dipped himself in it seven times.

2 Kings 5: 13-14

Discovering Archaeology

Chariots were the expensive "sports cars" of the ancient world. The rich liked to drive them, and everybody loved a good crash-'em-up chariot race. We know so much about chariots because some ancient people liked to have their chariots buried with them. And we found them.

Epic Behemoth

Polly felt tiny looking up at the gigantic bones in the history museum. Even her dad seemed small when standing next to it. The sharp teeth and the huge claws screamed *dangerous* with a capital D. "Dad?"

"Hmmm?" He was reading the sign in front of the skeleton.

"Are there dinosaurs in the Bible?"

"That's a very interesting question." Her dad pulled out his phone and pulled up a Bible passage from the Book of Job (40:15–16).

Look at Behemoth. It is a huge animal. I made both of you. It eats grass like an ox. Look at the strength it has in its hips! What power it has in the muscles of its stomach! Its tail sways back and forth like a cedar tree. The tendons of its thighs are close together. Its bones are like tubes made out of bronze. Its legs are like rods made out of of iron. It ranks first among my works.

"What do you think?" her dad asked.

Molly looked back at the bones above her. "It sounds like a dinosaur, doesn't it? And there aren't any Behemoths around now."

Whether a Behemoth was a dinosaur or not is a question that Bible researchers are trying to figure out. It may be one of those mysteries we'll never solve. Whether you say yes or no. God created the Behemoth to be one amazing creature. Hey, just like you.

Words to Treasure

Can anyone capture it by its eyes? Can anyone trap it and poke a hole through its nose?

Job 40: 24

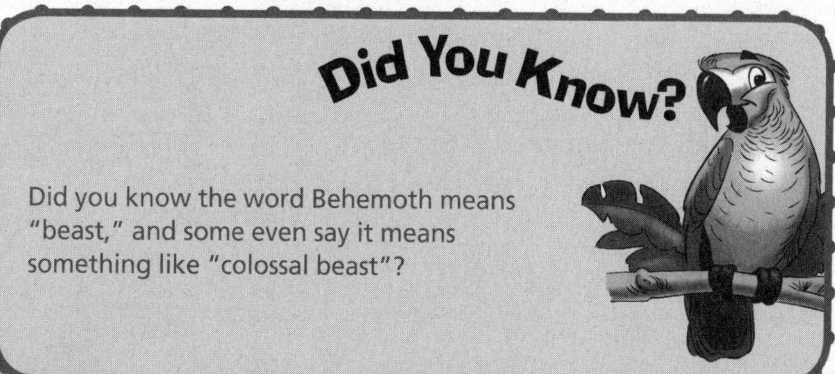

Did You Know?

Did you know the word Behemoth means "beast," and some even say it means something like "colossal beast"?

October 7

A Little Fixing Up

The work was hard with the muddy ground, but the last two weeks of fixing up the trail had been the most fun Toby and Phil had ever had. They had volunteered to be part of a team to build small bridges, walkways, and stairs. Toby cut some more wood for the next little bridge over a swampy patch. As he walked through the mud, his feet sank until his boots were almost covered. *Cool.* Phil was hammering the boards in place when Toby picked up a big handful of mud and threw it at him. Phil's hair was covered in mud. Soon the entire team was flinging mud until they looked like swamp creatures. It just doesn't get any better than that.

Words to Treasure

Then Hezekiah worked hard repairing all the broken parts of the wall. He built towers on it. He -built another wall outside that one.

2 Chronicles 32:5

Work can be fun! It feels great to be part of a team that is working together to make a difference in your town or city. There are lots of volunteer projects you and your family can get involved in. You don't have to have a lot of skills; just work hard and have fun.

Discovering Archaeology

Hezekiah had a long tunnel built to allow water to flow from one part of Jerusalem to another. Ancient writing tells us that two gangs of workers started at each end and dug toward each other. But the two teams almost didn't meet. They almost dug past each other. But one smart crew heard the sound of digging from the other team and dug toward the sound.

October 8

The Hook

"Is that all the candy you took? If it is, I'll let you off with a warning." The security guard for the store stared with big eyes at the boys. Aaron and Melker sat in hard metal chairs in the back office. The boys looked at each other sheepishly and pulled more candy from different pockets. They placed it on the table. The security guard shook his head sadly. "Okay, I'm going to give you one more chance." He pulled out two sheets of paper and two pencils. "I want you both to write me an essay on why I shouldn't call the police. Tell my why you deserve a second chance. Make it good, boys. I'll be back in an hour."

Words to Treasure

Manasseh prayed to him. When he did, the Lord felt sorry for him. He answered his prayer. The Lord brought Manasseh back to Jerusalem and his kingdom.

2 Chronicles 33:13

The clock ticked loudly as the boys wrote the most important letter of their kid lives to Mr. Security Officer. Would they get a second chance?

King Manasseh of Judah had done so many wrong things that finally God allowed him to be taken captive by the mighty Assyrians. They put him in prison, in chains, and put a hook in his nose. But the nose hook wasn't a fashion thing. Manasseh called out to God asking for forgiveness and help. He was a changed man. God believed him and helped him return to Jerusalem.

If you were Aaron and Melker, what would you have written to convince the security guard to give you a second chance?

Water Rescue

Crista and Paul were flying kites on the windiest beach in the world. The day was sunny, and their families had hiked there to enjoy a picnic. Crista liked the feel of the sand between her toes as she ran with her eagle kite. Then suddenly—*ouch!* She felt something sharp. Glass! Her foot had a nice-sized cut. No one could find the first aid kit. Then they saw a dark and shiny figure rising out of the ocean. A scuba diver. He waved at the family as he took off his flippers. He was carrying a net bag full of shells and coral. When he saw Christa's bleeding foot, he came over.

Words to Treasure

CThere the angel of the LORD appeared to him from inside a burning bush. Moses saw that the bush was on fire. But it didn't burn up.

Exodus 3:2

"Hey, I got something for that." He pulled out a waterproof bag that held a tiny first aid kit.

Wow! God does work in mysterious ways. Nobody could have predicted that.

Live IT!

God loves to surprise us with the unexpected, the amazing, and sometimes kind of unusual. Like talking from a burning bush, or having a donkey actually have a conversation with a man named Balaam. God is never boring. Check out this donkey talk story in Numbers 22:1–41. Are you ready for the unexpected?

Just a Lot of Respect

Jamie, Liam, and Emma were sitting up in the balcony at church. They had a guest speaker who used a lot of big words and long sentences. Soon they were making fun and got a bad case of the giggles. They got so loud that everybody could hear them. Soon the threesome realized the entire church was looking at them, and that wasn't so funny. They sank low in their seats, hoping the floor would open up and swallow them.

Words to Treasure

But God's people made fun of his messengers. They hated his words. They laughed at his prophets.
2 Chronicles 36:16

After church their youth pastor walked up to them with a shake of his head. "I don't know what to say. You guys were really rude. I'm disappointed in you. You'll have to work hard to get back the respect you lost today."

Your pastors, Sunday school teachers, and the people who come to your church have things to say about God and the world. God is saying important things to you through them. So listen, and show respect.

The Babylonians were powerful neighbors of Jerusalem. They were becoming bigger, badder, and bolder every year. No kingdom could stand up to them. And now the Babylonians had their eye on the kingdom of Judah. God was not very happy with his people's behavior towards his prophets and a mess of other bad habits. So he must have thought that a hard time with the Babylonians was just what his people needed as a tough lesson.

October 11

Too Much of a Good Thing

Words to Treasure

I knew how stubborn you were. Your neck muscles were as unbending as iron. Your forehead was as hard as bronze.

Isaiah 48:4

The rollercoaster came to a stop. Scott got out, but his little sister Ruby stayed in her seat. "Come on, Ruby." Scott waited for her.

"I don't want to get out. I'm staying right here. I want more rides."

Scott hated when his sister got like this. "Ruby, stop being stubborn. Get off the ride. Everybody is waiting."

"Nope." She wouldn't budge.

"Fine!" Scott walked over to the ride attendant. "Here's a roll of tickets. Let her ride as often as she wants." The man nodded.

Scott waited as Ruby rode the rollercoaster over and over. When she got off, she didn't look so good. She rushed over to a trashcan and threw up. Scott wasn't feeling sorry for her. She looked up at him with sick eyes. "Why didn't you stop me?"

"Some things you have to learn for yourself. Do you want lunch?"

She held her stomach. "I never want to eat again."

Ruby's stubbornness had gotten the better of her. She soon learned that too much of a good thing isn't a good thing.

Discovering Archaeology

The Bible describes a stubborn person like Ruby as being like iron. People have been making things out of iron for 5,000 years, but it's really hard to find those ancient iron objects. Why? When iron's left outside, what happens? It rusts! After thousands of years, iron objects completely rust away. Today iron is still the most common and most useful metal in the world.

Big Prize

Ruby sat on the bench beside her brother Scott. She was feeling better now. She would never ride the rollercoaster that many times again. Being stubborn was just stupid.

"Scott," Ruby said as she leaned against him. "I'm sorry for not listening to you. It won't happen again."

Scott nodded as he watched the kids throwing baseballs at stacked milk jugs at the game booth. "Follow me." He gave the man money and got five baseballs. He aimed the first ball and knocked down all the jugs. Soon a crowd of kids was watching as Scott kept knocking down milk jugs.

Words to Treasure

I would gladly treat you like my children. I would give you a pleasant land. It is the most beautiful land any nation could have.

Jeremiah 3:19

The man at the booth shook his head. "Kid, you have a rocket arm. Which prize do you want?" Scott pointed to the biggest, pinkest stuffed bunny Ruby had ever seen. Scott gave it to Ruby.

"I don't deserve it," Ruby talked from behind the gigantic toy. "Thanks, big bro." Brother, sister, and pink bunny walked together down the midway.

God is like that too. When we ask for his forgiveness and stop doing wrong things, he wants to give us the biggest and the best things in the world.

In the Bible, a good place to live is described as "flowing with milk and honey." Kind of weird, but in ancient times honey was an expensive and special sweet. So it was a way of saying the place was full of good things. Why flowing with milk? Well, it meant that the pastures would make your animals strong and healthy. Which meant lots of milk.

October 13

May or May Not

Katherine ran down the dock. A whole group of boys was getting into one rowboat. They wanted to fish together. There were arms, legs, fishing poles, and boat oars sticking out everywhere.

Words to Treasure

They might listen, or they might not. After all, they refuse to obey me. But whether they listen or not, they will know that a prophet was among them.

Ezekiel 2:5

"Guys!" Katherine shouted at them. "You all can't fit in that boat!"

"Sure we can!" shouted a voice from somewhere in the middle of the tangle.

"No you can't. Believe me." The boys laughed, and soon they were rowing away from the dock. Katherine called after, "You have to listen to me!"

One boy stood up. "See, we're fine!" But then the boat started to rock, and the boys started shouting and yelling. Then the entire boat flipped over. They all landed in the chilly water. Katherine had never seen so many boys swim so fast to the dock.

They climbed out shivering and shaking. Katherine walked back down the dock without saying a word.

People may not listen to your wise advice, but give it to them anyway. Never say, "I told you so," because they already know you were right. Being right is enough.

People in Bible Times

The Babylonians took 10,000 people with them as prisoners. These people became servants in Babylon. They were strangers in a strange country. But God gave his people a prophet like Ezekiel to go with them to comfort them during the hard years far away from home. To find out about this amazing prophet, read the book of Ezekiel.

God to the Rescue

Abigail loved the old Smith house with the stained-glass windows and the tall gabled roof. She was sad that the city was going to bulldoze it down. The Historical Society tried to buy the house, but they didn't have enough money. Now it would be gone. She wished there was something she could do. But the city had made their decision, and she was just a kid.

Abigail talked to her parents about it over dinner. "What do you like about the house?" asked her dad.

She toyed with her food. "I like to imagine what it would have been like all new. Something that beautiful shouldn't be destroyed just because it's old."

Words to Treasure

The king said to Daniel, "I'm sure your God is the greatest God of all. He is the Lord of kings. He explains mysteries. That's why you were able to explain the mystery of my dream."

Daniel 2:47

Her mother played with her potatoes as well. "Sweetie, unfortunately not everybody feels the way you do. It's a real shame. I like old houses too."

That night, Abigail talked to God about it and prayed for some way to save the house. Then she went to sleep.

When you talk to God about something, he does listen, and sometimes his answers will amaze everybody.

People in Bible Times

King Nebuchadnezzar had a wild dream and wanted his wise guys to explain the dream. But nobody could figure it out. This bugged him so much that he ordered all the wise guys in his kingdom killed. This would, of course, include Daniel, Hananiah, Mishael, and Azariah. When Daniel found out, he prayed for God's help. (See Daniel 2.)

October 15

Greatest

When Abigail woke up in the morning, she was amazed by her dream. She had dreamed about the old Victorian house. It was moving day, and a family in old-fashioned clothes pulled up in a big wagon with a beautiful team of horses. In her dream, the house was brand-new. Suddenly, Abigail knew what God was saying to her through this dream. "Thank you, God!"

Words to Treasure

"The great God has shown you what will take place in days to come. The dream is true. And you can trust the meaning of it that I have explained to you."

Daniel 2:45

Two months later, the gates of the old house were open, and the front yard had tables with white lace on them. Women in long dresses and men in funny suits served tea, sandwiches, and little desserts to tourists and townspeople. It was an old-fashioned garden party. Horses lined the streets ready to give rides around the block.

All the actors in town got together with the Historical Society put on this fundraising tea party. They had raised enough money in two weeks of tea parties to save the old house. It would become a museum, with tea parties in the front yard every day in the summer.

Because Abigail cared and prayed, God gave her a brilliant idea. He knew she was just the right person to save the day.

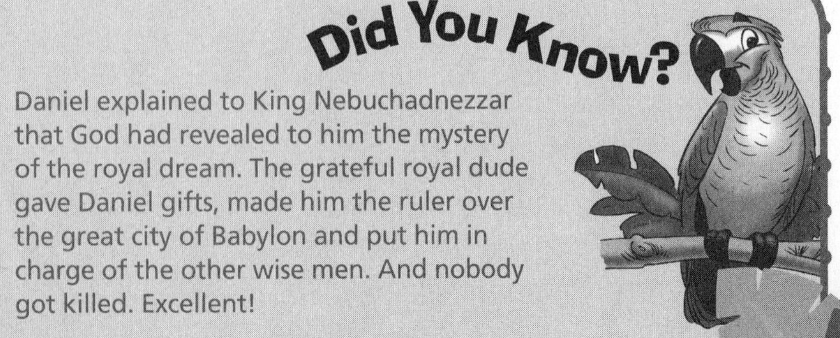

Did You Know?
Daniel explained to King Nebuchadnezzar that God had revealed to him the mystery of the royal dream. The grateful royal dude gave Daniel gifts, made him the ruler over the great city of Babylon and put him in charge of the other wise men. And nobody got killed. Excellent!

Means What?

Thomas and Kai walked home from the movie theatre. It had been a really good movie, but the boys couldn't agree on what the story meant.

Thomas tried to explain again. "It was about the friend that stood by him through the whole thing. The movie's about friendship no matter what."

Kai shook his head. "The movie is not about friendship. The movie is about how good fights evil and wins. That's the most important part of the film. Who cares if his friend went along or not?"

Words to Treasure

"Does anyone believe in me? Then, just as Scripture says, rivers of living water will flow from inside them."
John 7:38

"What are you two arguing about?" They turned around to see their friend Emily behind them.

Thomas gave Kai an irritated look. "We can't agree on what the message of a movie is. Good vs. evil or friendship?"

Emily licked her popsicle. "Did you both like the movie?" The boys agreed on that. "That's the most important thing. Besides, maybe you're both right." Emily continued her walk down the street. The boys looked at each other. Could they both be right?

That's kind of like the last chapters of Daniel. People can't agree on what it all means. They have different ideas, just as Thomas and Kai had different ideas. But the important thing is that they all love the Bible.

Did You Know?

Did you know there are 31,173 verses in the Bible? That's a lot of important verses to read and think about. But don't worry. You have the Holy Spirit to help you understand the over 773,692 individual words you read in the Bible. Phew.

October 17

Warning Signs

Tess, Brandon, and Shane stood on the edge of the little pond. It was full of broken furniture, tires, and lots of trash. Tess picked up an old bottle of car antifreeze. You didn't need to be a rocket scientist to figure out that in a few years it would just be a swampy garbage heap. The warning signs were already here. They couldn't hear any frogs or insects buzzing. The pond water already smelled stale and stagnant. But a bright-colored hummingbird zipped past and hovered with fast little wings. Maybe it wasn't too late to change this.

Words to Treasure

The LORD announces to his people, "Return to me with all your heart. There is still time."

Joel 2:12

The pond was giving out help signals for anybody who would stop and listen. In ancient days God was doing the same thing with his people. He was sending them signs warning them that they had better change their evil ways or the future would be a tough ride. God sent prophets such as Hosea and Joel to talk to them, and he even sent an army of plant-eating locusts to get their attention. But they didn't listen.

Did You Know?

Locusts are grasshoppers that can travel in swarms of 40 million or more. They can travel long distances in a single day and can eat their own body weight in food every day. So when you have millions of bugs that equals tons of destroyed crops. They were bad news. But ancient cultures also ate locusts and had lots of different ways to prepare them. Anyone for locusts on a stick?

Change

With the help of the community and some really smart experts, the pond was cleaned up. They restocked the pond with fish, frog eggs were placed in the reeds, and even turtles were released. Bird nest boxes and bat boxes were built. Butterfly plants were planted around the edge. Everything was done to make this a beautiful home for people and animals. The pond was a pond again because people were willing to change their bad habits. They listened and cared.

Tess, Brandon, and Shane watched a slow-moving turtle climb out of the water onto a rock to enjoy the sunshine. A dragonfly darted past, inspecting the new place. This was the start of a very good thing.

Words to Treasure

Jerusalem will be my holy city. People from other lands will never attack it again. At that time fresh wine will drip from the mountains. Milk will flow down from the hills. Water will run through all of Judah's valleys.

Joel 3:17–18

God didn't like being upset and angry with his people. He didn't want to punish them! He just wanted to love Israel and give them a good life in a beautiful home. They just needed to care about what was right and stop doing evil. That would make things right again. Just like the pond.

What the prophet Joel was telling his people is that God loves you and will reward and bless you now and in the future if you just change. How hard can that be?

October 19

Prayer Warrior

Phil and Mark were heading out the door of the church. They saw Grace quietly sitting in the church garden by the fountain. Phil walked over. "Grace, are you coming? We need to sell 300 chocolate bars to pay for our youth trip."

Words to Treasure

Brothers and sisters, pray for us.

1 Thessalonians 5:25

Grace smiled up at them. "Pastor Owen asked me to stay behind today and pray that everything goes well and we get the money we need for the mission trip. I'm a prayer warrior."

Mark scratched his head. "A what warrior?"

Pastor Owen walked over. "Someone who commits to praying about certain events or situations."

The boys looked at each other. Phil shrugged, "We need all the prayer we can get. We didn't sell anything yesterday."

Some people commit their lives to prayer and worship. They pray like they are preparing for battle. The world needs lots of prayer warriors.

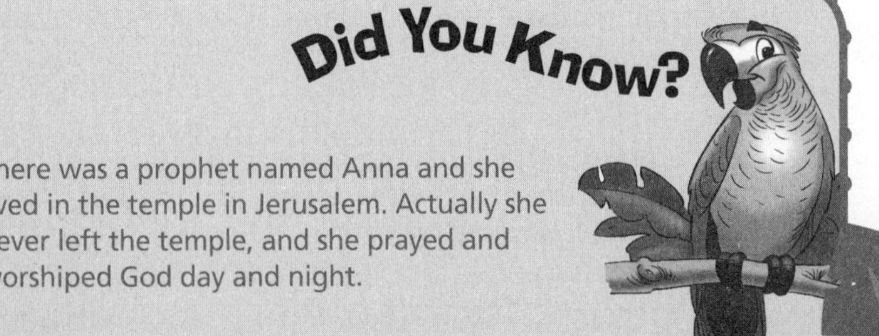

Did You Know?
There was a prophet named Anna and she lived in the temple in Jerusalem. Actually she never left the temple, and she prayed and worshiped God day and night.

October 20

Warning You

The paddleboat was a lot of fun. It was kind of like riding a bicycle on the water. Four people could sit in the boat with two people peddling to move it along. Hugh, Peter, Jade, and Erin had explored most of the little coves along the shore. They had fed the swans and had spotted a muskrat slipping out of its den in the bank.

Words to Treasure

The Lord and King never does anything without telling his servants the prophets about it.

Amos 3:7

"Hey!" The teenager in a boat didn't look happy as he motored up. "You're late bringing the boat back in. If you don't come back right now, I'm going to have to fine you for more time. Consider this a warning. If you got a watch, *use* it, for crying out loud."

They had completely lost track of time. Hugh waved back and said, "We'll come right back."

Ancient Israel was off doing their thing, forgetting all about their responsibilities to honor God. So God sent out prophets to tell them to come back to him. The prophets warned them that there would be some heavy penalties to pay if they didn't get right back to being godly people again. Remember, God always gives us plenty of warning. In the end, Israel listened and paddled right back to God.

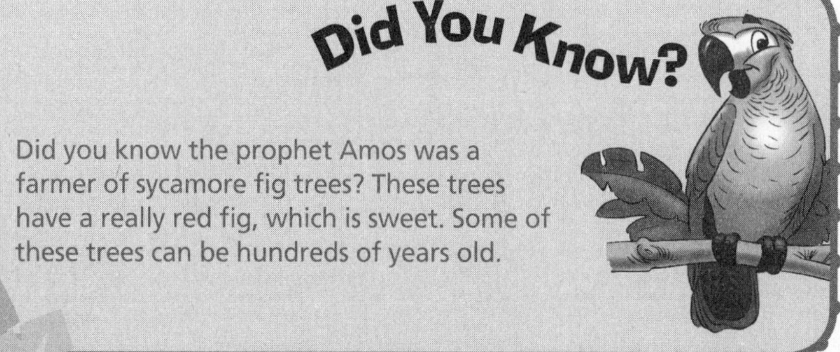

Did you know the prophet Amos was a farmer of sycamore fig trees? These trees have a really red fig, which is sweet. Some of these trees can be hundreds of years old.

October 21

Seriously Messed Up

Doug stuck his hand under the water tap again, but his hand still hurt like crazy. The burn was really bad. His parents had warned him not to fool around with fireworks. But he did, and now everything was seriously messed up. His mom knocked on the door. "Are you okay in there?" Doug opened the door a crack and shoved his hand out. He heard his mother exhale. "Oh, Doug! Don't tell me! Fireworks."

Words to Treasure

"Blessed are those whose sins are taken away. Blessed is the person whose sin the Lord never counts against them."

Romans 4:7-8

Doug fought back tears of pain. "Yeah."

Doug's troubles started when he didn't listen to his parents. Our troubles can start when we don't listen to God. That's called sin. *Sin* is behaving in ways that don't go along with how God wants us to be. First off, God is perfect and right all the time. God is never ever sinful. Nobody on earth is perfect or sin-free like God. We all fail at being perfectly good all the time. But we can admit our sins to Jesus and ask for forgiveness. Jesus forgives all our past, present, and future sins or wrongs. When that happens, perfect God doesn't see our sins, he just sees us. And he loves what he sees.

Jesus' forgiveness for all our future sins isn't some kind of a get-out-of-jail-free card so we can do wrong things whenever we want. That's not the point. The point is wanting to do right things that please God now and in the future.

October 22

By Design

The lava flowed down across the ground like a black blob monster. Cracks oozed red-hot lava. It was a slow sluggish lava that inched across the ground. Martin's dad was taking pictures of it for a science magazine. Martin watched through binoculars as plants in front of the lava burst into flames. He had never seen a real volcano before. Slow as it was, this lava was destroying everything in its path. His dad told him lava was really hot, between 1300 and 1650 degrees Fahrenheit. The hottest the kitchen oven could get was 550 degrees Fahrenheit, and that was hot. Nothing was going to stop this lava flow.

Words to Treasure

In the beginning, God created the heavens and the earth.

Genesis 1:1

Despite the damage volcanoes do, they're good for the world. They create mountains, islands, and soil for plants, and they put important gases and moisture into the air. God designed everything for a purpose and a reason. Even the position of our planet in the galaxy is not too far from or too close to the sun so that we have just the right amount of light and heat for a world full of living things. It's all in his plan.

Live IT!

Hey! Take some time to look at the world around you. Look at how animals or plants are designed. It's amazing! Compare how things are different or the same. How is a butterfly the same or different from a whale? What do lizards have in common with birds? Nature by God's design is a world where everything is important and connected together.

October 23

Making It Right

Allison turned down the car radio. "Dad, did you ever steal anything when you were a kid?"

Words to Treasure

Anyone who has been stealing must never steal again. Instead, they must work.

Ephesians 4:28

Her dad drummed his fingers on the steering wheel for awhile. Suddenly he turned the car around, and drove into the parking lot of the corner store near their house. "Come on."

She followed her dad into the store. He pulled out fifty dollars from his wallet and approached the old store owner. "Mr. Faye, when I was a kid I shoplifted a few things from your store. Mostly candy. This should cover it, with interest. I'm sorry. I was just a dumb kid."

Mr. Faye's old face crinkled into a smile, and he slapped Allison's dad on the shoulder. "You're a good man. A good man."

What Allison's dad remembered was that Mr. Faye was just a hard-working man who needed every penny he could earn from his store. Stealing is always wrong. Allison learned an important lesson. It isn't just enough to admit you did something wrong. You have to go back and make things right.

Have you ever stolen something from a person or a store? Are you feeling a little guilty about it? That guilt is a good thing. Go talk to your parents, and then go make it right with the person you stole from. It takes a big person to face big mistakes. And that rocks!

Blizzard

The telephone rang late at night, and it woke up Hannah. She heard her mom talking on the phone. Hannah crept out of bed and tiptoed into the living room of their apartment. Mom hung up the phone. "Your grandmother's sick and has gone to the hospital."

Hannah looked out the window at the winter blizzard raging outside. "Who is looking after the ranch?"

"Palmer is looking after things right now."

Words to Treasure

Tell those who do what is right that things will go well with them.

Isaiah 3:10

Hannah pulled her suitcase from the closet. "It takes more than one person to look after the ranch. We have to go right away, Mom."

"Honey there's a blizzard out there. The roads will be bad."

She started filling the suitcase. "Grandma and the llamas need us."

Hannah was ready to face some dangers and do what it takes to come to the rescue because she loved Grandma Sadie, the ranch, and the animals. That's called commitment—being there all the time, not just when it's fun. That kind of giving makes God proud.

Hannah loved her grandmother and the ranch. Create some art or a scrapbook that shows the things you really care about. What do you have a strong commitment to? How do these people or things make you feel?

October 25

Falling Star

Okay, everybody! Lunchtime!" Ms. Richards clapped her hands to get their attention. Jody pulled at her costume because it itched around the neck. She was glad to be part of the community play, but this costume was really horrible. Nevertheless, she was a trooper, and the show must go on. Jody found a place to sit so she could eat her lunch. Mary walked past with her lunch in hand, and Jody made room for her to sit. "Mary, you can eat lunch with me."

Mary gave her a superior look. "Jody, I'm the star. I don't eat with the cast. I eat in my dressing room."

Jody took a bite of her sandwich and said, "Mary, it takes everybody to make a play happen … not just the star." Mary walked past with a click of her red shoes.

Mary was expecting star treatment when she should be happy to be like everybody else. Feeling important about your self is never an attitude that God likes. Self-importance should not be important to you.

Words to Treasure

Haman noticed that Mordecai wouldn't get down on his knees. He wouldn't give Haman any honor. So Haman was very angry.

Esther 3:5

Haman was an important guy around King Xerxes' kingdom, and he liked that feeling a lot. He liked it way too much. In fact, he thought about it *all* the time. He wanted everybody to look up to him and to show him honor all the time. Pride had made Haman an evil man.

October 26

Overreaction

Mary stomped up to Ms. Richards and pulled her by the hand over to where Jody was eating her lunch. "I don't think that Jody is respecting me enough as the lead and star of this play," Mary complained. "Either she apologizes for what she said, or I want her off the play."

Jody sipped her juice box. "Everybody knows your mother made Ms. Richards pick you as the lead."

"Girls!" Ms. Richards wasn't very happy. "Jody, Mary is the star of this play, and that's not an easy job. So be supportive. Mary, you can't fire people off this play. The best actors are humble. We all have to work together. That's what makes a play great."

Mary's head was going into overreaction mode because her pride was running the show. Wanting bad things for other people because you want them to treat you a certain way is not a good thing—ever. Pride can make small things seem way too important.

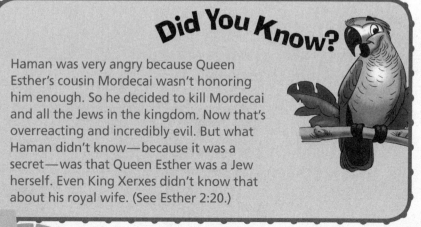

Words to Treasure

He also looked for a way to destroy all Mordecai's people. They were Jews. He wanted to kill all of them everywhere in the kingdom of Xerxes.

Esther 3:6

Did You Know?

Haman was very angry because Queen Esther's cousin Mordecai wasn't honoring him enough. So he decided to kill Mordecai and all the Jews in the kingdom. Now that's overreacting and incredibly evil. But what Haman didn't know—because it was a secret—was that Queen Esther was a Jew herself. Even King Xerxes didn't know that about his royal wife. (See Esther 2:20.)

October 27

Special Day

Henry got out of the car and couldn't believe all the people gathered to do the Buddy Walk. His dad helped his brother Joshua out of the car. Joshua had Down syndrome, a condition he was born with. It means that even though he was older than Henry, sometimes Joshua acted younger. Sometimes Joshua had a harder time learning things, but he was the guy with a million jokes to tell, and he always seemed to know what Henry was feeling. If Henry was having a bad day, Joshua would bring him a soft drink and they would talk. He was the best brother.

Words to Treasure

But the fruit the Holy Spirit produces is love, joy and peace. It is being patient, kind and good.

Galatians 5:22

Joshua waved at some friends he knew. "Can we walk with Ruth and BJ?" Joshua asked. Their dad nodded. Joshua ran over. "I have a new joke. You're going to laugh sooo hard." Joshua stopped suddenly and turned. "Henry, you can walk with us. You don't have to walk alone."

Joshua knows something that some people have a hard time understanding. Everybody wants to feel liked and accepted. Everybody *should* feel liked and accepted. This world would a better and wiser place if everybody was as kind as Joshua and told more jokes.

Live IT!

Kindness and acceptance are very powerful things. You and your friends can look for ways to do random acts of kindness at school, church, or in your neighborhood. Little things make people feel good and accepted. Spread kindness around.

Small Ride

Noah jogged up the hill feeling every inch of muscle burn. He was training for hockey, and this was good for him. Coming down the hill were some teenagers who were messing around on some little kid's plastic trike. They were standing on it and going down the hill. It clearly didn't belong to them. Noah jogged past, not wanting to make eye contact with the troublemakers. He turned around to see one boy throw the stolen trike into the bushes. Noah kept jogging but then turned around and pulled the toy out.

Words to Treasure

Suppose you see your neighbor's ox or sheep wandering away. Then don't act as if you didn't see it. Instead, make sure you take it back to him.

Deuteronomy 22:1

It took him over an hour knocking on neighborhood doors searching for the rightful owner. Finally a woman with a little boy came to the door surprised to see Noah and the trike. "Hey!" The little boy took the trike. "That's mine." Noah explained what happened. The woman and her son were so thankful to have his favorite toy back.

Some people would have just kept walking and ignored the whole thing. But Noah went out of his way to make sure that stolen toy got home. Good guys don't keep walking. They take action.

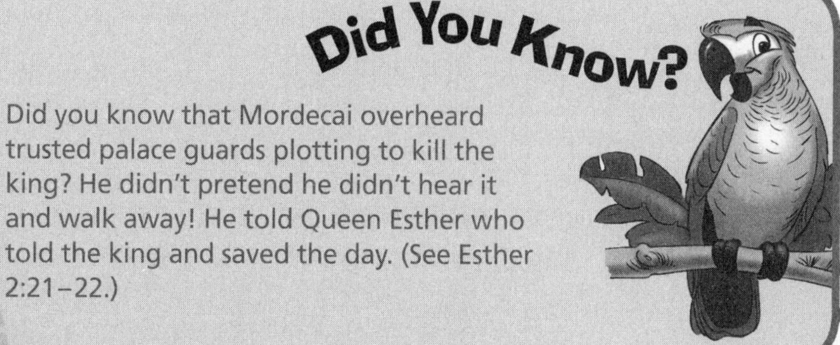

Did You Know?

Did you know that Mordecai overheard trusted palace guards plotting to kill the king? He didn't pretend he didn't hear it and walk away! He told Queen Esther who told the king and saved the day. (See Esther 2:21–22.)

October 29

Nice It Forward

Finn looked through his photo album before he went to bed. Finn lived with his mom because he didn't have a dad. Sometimes that made him sad. But he did have a Big Brother named Brian. Brian spent time with him doing things like going to baseball or hockey games. Finn looked at the photographs of them on the rollercoaster, whitewater rafting, going to the dinosaur museum, and having dinner on a train. He could talk about guy stuff, and Brian listened. He was a good friend.

Words to Treasure

"What great honor has Mordecai received for doing that?" the king asked.

Esther 6:3

Finn climbed out of bed and wandered into the living room. "Mom." She turned down the television. "Can we throw a party for Brian to thank him for being my Big Brother?"

Her eyes got all kind of sparkly, and she smiled. "I think that would be a really nice thing to do."

"Okay." Finn went back to bed.

Okay is right. When somebody does nice things for you, hey, you should do nice things back. That's kind of like a no-brainer. Makes everybody and God proud of you.

King Xerxes wanted to reward Mordecai for saving his life. There are all kinds of people who do amazing things for you, such as your parents, grandparents, teachers, friends, coaches, and club leaders. It's a crazy long list. Make sure you take some time to thank them for everything they do.

October 30

Not for Me?

"What would be the perfect birthday party?" Rory's mom asked as she was cooking dinner. Rory thought, *This has got to be for my birthday*!

He set the dinner table. "Well, with ten best friends, we could do go-carting and mini-golfing at Fun Palace. Then we'd come home, order some pizza with everything on it—except those fishy gross things. Hate those. Then we'd watch a movie, maybe even two, and have a sleepover. Then we'd have pancakes in the morning."

His mom tossed the salad. "Great, that's what we'll do for Danny's birthday next month."

Words to Treasure

Haman entered. Then the king asked him. "What should be done for the man I want to honor?" Haman said to himself, "Is there anyone the king would rather honor than me?"

Esther 6:6

Rory put a fork down. He had forgotten that Danny's birthday was next. His brother was getting *his* perfect birthday. That was kind of twisted and warped.

The sad fact of life is that not every birthday party is going to be your birthday party. Sometimes some other kid, even your brother, is the kid of honor. You just have to go with the flow and be happy for somebody else.

Haman was pretty eager to tell the king how to honor somebody important, because he thought that somebody was going to be him. Sorry, evil dude, he was actually talking about Mordecai. But here's how a Bible king honors somebody. Put a royal robe on the guy; put him on a king's horse, and have royal, important people lead him around town telling everybody how great he is. That's a party ancient style.

October 31

Who Is the Devil?

The devil looked at Bill, and Bill looked right back. He was pretty ugly. "I know you," Bill said as he took a closer look at the rubber mask. "You've been to our house before."

Words to Treasure

The God who gives peace will soon crush Satan under your feet.

Romans 16:20

The devil shrugged, took off his mask, and gave Bill his change. "It's me, Tom. Cool mask, huh?"

Bill took his purchase. "Isn't the devil a bad guy? I'd rather be a good guy." Halloween was such a weirdo holiday.

The name *Satan* means "adversary or enemy." The Bible tells us the devil was an angel created by God. When he sinned, God threw him down to earth and he became a fallen angel. Since then, Satan (also called the devil) has been plotting against God at every turn. He's basically at war with God and would like people to believe he has power equal to Jesus and God. But that isn't true. Satan will use tricks to lead people away from God. But the important thing to remember is that God has more power and control, and he is protecting you. Satan can plan all he wants, but Jesus is watching over you every minute of every day.

People in Bible Times

Jesus was teaching in a synagogue when a man controlled by a demon started to shout at him. Jesus spoke firmly to the evil spirit and demanded he be quiet and leave the man alone. The demon had to obey; people were amazed by Jesus. That's because nothing is more powerful than God, Jesus, and the Holy Spirit! (See Luke 4:33–37.)

Not a Fake Kid

Ricky was snooping in the attic for hidden early Christmas presents. It was totally wrong but he couldn't resist just a quick check. Surprises were for little kids. He liked to know what he was getting. Ricky pulled out a metal box that was pushed way under an old dresser. Inside were a bunch of papers and photographs. He took out a piece of paper and read it. This was a surprise Ricky wasn't counting on. He was *adopted*. His parents weren't his real parents. He was a fake kid.

Words to Treasure

Love never fails.

1 Corinthians 13:8

Rick isn't a fake kid, and his parents are real. They had wanted to be parents very much but couldn't have a baby of their own. So they prayed that God would give them a baby a different way. God gave them Ricky through adoption. Loving somebody isn't about sharing DNA or genetics. Your real family is the one you care about and live with every day. So it doesn't really matter whether you share DNA with your parents, grandparents, uncles or aunts, or foster parents. Love is in living together and sharing everything—that's as real as it gets.

Did You Know?

- Love is patient.
- Love is kind
- Love does not brag
- Love is not proud or envious.
- Love cares for others.
- Love isn't rude; it doesn't become angry easily.
- Love doesn't hold a grudge.
- Love wants what is right and truthful.
- Love protects and trusts.
- Love always hopes and never gives up. (See Corinthians 13:4–8.)

November 2

What Makes You Happy?

Cara sat in her room and surveyed her kingdom. She had a flat-screen television in her room, a DVD player, a pink computer, video games, and an electric guitar with silent-mode headsets so she could play quietly. But Cara was bored, bored, bored. She had all this stuff, but all her friends were away for the holidays. All this stuff, and she still wasn't happy. Stuff, she decided, didn't mean a whole lot if that's all you have. People are so much better than stuff.

Words to Treasure

Turn my eyes away from things that are worthless.

Psalm 119:37

God designed us to want to be with other people. We need family and friends to feel happy and complete. God wants us to value people way above other stuff in the world. People vs. stuff is no contest. People win every time.

Job had seven sons, three daughters, 7,000 sheep, 3,000 camels, 500 pairs of oxen, 500 donkeys, and lots of servants to take care of everything. Why so many animals? Raising animals was the major business. The Bible often lists how many animals a person owned because that told you how rich they were. Money sure has made things easier. Try putting a camel through a bank machine money slot. Watch out—they spit.

November 3

Rescue Me!

"Come on, Edgar, come on! You can do it." Lee encouraged his dog to sniff the ground and search the snow. Edgar loved this searching game. The dog walked right past a snow mound, but then suddenly turned around and got all excited, barking and digging. Lee's dad popped up out of the snow mound and gave the dog a big hug. "Good dog! You're a good dog. You found me."

> **Words to Treasure**
>
> The LORD takes care of those who are not aware of danger. When I was in great need, he saved me.
>
> Psalm 116:6

One day, Edgar would have to go with Lee's dad to a real emergency and save people's lives. Lee's family owned and trained service dogs, dogs that were bred and trained to help find people and things. His family and their dogs traveled all over the world helping find people trapped or lost after earthquakes or avalanches or storms.

Helping people caught in natural disasters was what Lee and his family did. But you don't have to be an on-the-spot rescuer to help. You can send money, blankets, food, or clothing to rescue organizations. Or you can give blood when you're older to show you care. Be there because you care.

Did You Know?

Speaking of disasters, did you know that Job experienced many disasters? Raiders stole Job's oxen and donkeys, then his sheep got zapped by lightning, more raiders came and stole his camels, his servants all got killed, and then a strong wind blew down his house on top of his kids. This *all* happened in one day, but Job still loved God. (See Job 1.)

November 4

Boast the Most

Carlos stood on the top of their snow castle built on the edge of a steep hill. This was the strongest snow fort he had ever built. He looked down at the kids throwing snowballs at them. Their snowballs weren't even coming close. He yelled down, "Even my grandmother could defend this snow fort. You guys don't have a chance. I could stay up here all day and not get hit by one snowball! You guys might as well give up and go home."

Words to Treasure

The Jebusites said to David, "You won't get in here. Even people who can't see or walk can keep you from coming in."

2 Samuel 5:6

Carlos felt something whack the back of his head. It was really hard and cold. Icy water was going down his neck. He turned around to find fort attackers standing right behind him. Another snowball got Carlos right in the ear. "Hey!" He dug out snow from his stinging ear. "How'd you get up here?"

Tony smiled. "Caught ya!"

Be careful when you say boastful words. You just might have to take them back sooner than you think. Sometimes the person who boasts the most is also embarrassed the most. The Jebusites were embarrassed when David captured their city fort, Jerusalem. Read all about that sneaky city in 2 Samuel 5.

In ancient times, people built their cities in places that were hard to attack, such as on the tops of steep hills. To capture Jerusalem, David's men climbed a tall, very narrow water shaft to sneak inside for a surprise attack.

Two Too Many

Carlos and Hunter just couldn't see eye-to-eye on how to run the snow fort. So after lunch, Hunter decided to take half of the kids and make a new fort. Carlos wasn't sure that was a very good idea. If they stuck together, it would be better. But Hunter went off with five other kids, and they built their fort down the hill by the forest. It didn't take long before the other team realized that instead of one big fort there were now two little ones to attack. Snowballs were flying everywhere until finally Carlos surrendered their fort and then Hunter surrendered his new and only half-built fort. They had been completely snowed-over by the other team.

Words to Treasure

"If a kingdom fights against itself, it can't stand."

Mark 3:24

Sometimes we can let arguments, different ideas, and other negative stuff separate good friends. That's not the way God wants things to be. Working together on something is the best way to do things. When we let disagreements get in the way, things happen. Sometimes they're not good things—such as a snowball blizzard attack that destroys your fort.

Wise Solomon started out following God, but slowly over the years he started to disobey God. For the world's smartest guy, not so smart. This upset God. So after Solomon died, he decided to allow the mighty kingdom of Israel to be separated into two smaller kingdoms with two different rulers. One kingdom was called Israel, and the other kingdom was called Judah.

November 6

Same Rule for Everybody

Carlos ducked behind the wall of their new snow castle. "Okay, Todd, Mary, and Peter, you go through the woods and come up behind their fort. You guys attack from the sides. Farhud and Leah, you make some more snowballs for the battle."

Words to Treasure

Both you and the king who rules over you must obey the Lord your God.

1 Samuel 12:14

"Wait a minute," Peter protested. "What are you going to do?"

"I'm the leader, so I'm going to stay here and watch the fort."

Mary smoothed a snowball in her hand. "But we said we'd all attack the fort. That was rule number one—one for all and all for one."

Carlos tied his snow boots. "That's before I became leader. It's not the same for me."

"I don't think so," argued Peter. "Good leaders follow the rules just like everybody else."

Peter's right—rules are the same for leaders as for everybody else. When Saul became the first king of Israel, the prophet Samuel warned him that rule number one was that the king would serve God just like everybody else.

The Israelites had never had a king before and really wanted one. All the *other* kingdoms had one. Samuel the prophet knew that God should be the only leader. But the people kept complaining and asking for a king. Finally, God gave them King Saul. Be careful. What you ask for may not be what you need. The leader you want must obey God like everybody else.

November 7

Be There or Be There

Jacob found Heather sitting on a log beside where they had buried her cat in the forest. He didn't know what to say to her, so he had avoided her for days. Her eyes were red from crying, and she gave him a brave smile as he sat down beside her.

"I really miss her," Heather whispered. "She was my best friend."

Jacob nodded. "I'm sorry that Skeena got hit by a car."

Heather smiled again. "Thanks for coming out here to sit with me."

"I should have come sooner. Sorry.

They sat some more. Then Heather laughed. "Do you remember when she chased that squirrel into the house and we couldn't get it out?"

"Yeah," Jacob said. "Or the time she fell off the entertainment center and landed in the bowl of popcorn."

"Yeah." The two friends talked for a long time about Skeena.

When a friend is going through a hard time, sometimes it's hard to know what to say to help the hurt go away. Just *being there* as a friend says everything without saying a word.

Words to Treasure

The LORD is close to those whose hearts have been broken. He saves those whose spirits have been crushed.

Psalm 34:18

Discovering Archaeology

Scientists think cats have been friends with people for over 9,000 years. Cats would have helped people by killing mice and other pests that would get into grain and other food stores of ancient homes.

November 8

More Bad

What are you doing?!" Brooke couldn't believe what her brother was doing.

Words to Treasure

Children, obey your parents in everything. That pleases the Lord.

Colossians 3:20

"I'm watching television." Robert ate a candy bar.

Brooke looked out the window, worrying her parents' car would pull in. "We're grounded from television and from going out for a month. If they catch you, you're going to be in bigger trouble."

"We're already in big trouble for having friends over without asking. What more can they do to us? Ground us for *two* months? They're not going to do that. Face it. We've hit the punishment limit. So we might as well live it up."

"Oh, really?" Dad and Mom stood in the doorway, looking unimpressed.

Robert turned the television off. From the look on his dad's face, he knew that his life had just gotten a *whole* lot more uncomfortable.

Does it make a whole lot of sense to do more wrong after you're already in trouble? Not really. Punishment is supposed to teach us what is right. Then we can do right things because we *want* to do them.

Pretend that you are Robert's parents. What would you do? Talk about it with your family. Think of ways you can help Robert understand that doing right is his best and only good choice. After all, Robert needs all the help he can get because he is soooo busted!

You Jazz!

Justin put the brightly wrapped gift on the music rack of Uncle Bill's piano. His uncle stopped playing, and the rest of the jazz band stopped playing too. His uncle gave him a puzzled little smile. "What's this?"

Justin picked up his trumpet and fiddled with the mouthpiece. "A thank-you gift for letting me play in the band and for taking the time to teach me about jazz. I really admire you, Uncle Bill. And I want to learn to play the trumpet as well as you play the piano."

Uncle Bill played a little tune. "You don't know how happy that makes me." Uncle Bill nodded to the band. "Let's play some music."

Is there somebody in your life that you want to be like? Somebody you respect and admire? The important thing is to tell those people what they mean to you and that they've made a difference in your life. You don't have to buy them a gift; just go ahead and thank them.

Words to Treasure

"The student is not better than the teacher. But everyone who is completely trained will be like their teacher."

Luke 6:40

People in Bible Times

The great prophet Elijah was training a young man named Elisha. Elisha admired and loved Elijah very much and asked God to give him a double portion of the spirit his teacher had. God answered his prayer and then sent this new and great prophet on many adventures just as he had done with his teacher before him. (See 2 Kings 2:9.)

November 10

Time to Stop

Cole stood by the 9,000-pound monster truck. It was the most beautiful thing he had ever seen. It was big, it was shiny, and it could squash cars like a kid stomping on ants. Cole had a special pass to walk around the arena floor to look at the trucks and talk to the drivers. Cole's dad owned a car repair shop, so Cole had grown up with trucks. A mechanic was working on the truck. "Not working?" asked Cole.

Words to Treasure

I'm putting my hand over my mouth. I'll stop talking.

Job 40:4

"Something's not right," the mechanic laughed.

Cole stood beside him, "Did you check the—"

The mechanic answered before Cole could finish his sentence. "Yup."

"Or maybe the—"

"Yup."

Cole tried again, "It could be the—"

The mechanic turned and gave him a look. "I've got it covered, kid." Cole knew it was time to shut up. He didn't need a monster truck to drop on his head. He got the hint.

Job got the same kind of hint from God. He had no right to judge God's actions or plans for the world. Job understood that God didn't need his thoughts, advice, or comments on anything. God had everything covered. Time for Job to be very quiet.

In Bible times, elephants were the monster trucks. They were caught in the wild and transported all across the ancient world. people used them to fight in battles, the Romans used elephants to fight in their gladiator sports, and royalty gave each other elephants as expensive gifts.

What Did I Say?

Shelley, Reed, and Justin sat watching the other kids mess around with their bows and arrows, trying to shoot at the targets.

A big voice boomed, "FREEZE!" The entire archery class froze and faced their instructor. Mr. Rayner walked down the row of archers and pointed at kids. "You go stand over there. You too. And you and you. " He stopped and winked at Shelley, Reed, and Justin. "You three stay where you are." He turned to the group gathered beside the shooting line. "What did I say before I left the range?"

Words to Treasure

"The angels will come. They will separate the people who did what is wrong from those who did what is right."

Matthew 13:49

One guilty looking boy answered. "You said not to do anything until you got back."

Mr. Rayner crossed his arms. "And what were you doing?"

"Shooting my arrows at the target."

Mr. Rayner didn't look happy. "Okay, the people who listened to my instructions will get to take their lesson. The rest of you can go sit on the wall and watch. Breaking my rules isn't a good idea."

Doing the right thing gets big rewards. That's the same in heaven! When you do right things, God wants to reward you.

In Bible times, bow and arrows were used both for hunting and war. Ancient archers had to have lots of muscle strength. If you want to experience how hard it is, go to an archery club and see how many times you can shoot a bow before you're pretty tired.

November 12

Play It

The school band was rocking the building down. They were loud, they were good, and they were giving everybody a good show. Then the band stopped playing, because it was time for Matthew to do his trumpet solo. Now it was just him, his trumpet, and the audience. He started out really slowly, but soon his fingers were flying as the music got faster. It felt like the whole world was just Matthew and his trumpet, and everybody else had melted away. Then it was over, but Matthew realized the crowd was silent. He got worried for a minute. They didn't like it? Then suddenly the crowd stood up and went wild.

Words to Treasure

Sing a new song to him. Play with skill, and shout with joy.

Psalm 33:3

Mr. Higgins, the conductor, walked over and told Matthew to take a bow. Matthew did. When the crowd had quieted down, Mr. Higgins talked into the microphone. "What you just heard was composed by our talented trumpet player, Matthew Carson." The audience clapped wildly again.

God created a world full of natural music such as birds singing, rivers roaring, and rain pattering on tree leaves. But God made people special. We want to create music and write songs.

Do you sing or play an instrument? Try to write a song of your own the way that King David wrote songs to God. You could also write in your journal or compose a poem about how you feel about God.

I'll Do It

The kids stared at the most perfect sledding hill in the world. Best of all, there was nothing at the bottom to crash into. The only problem was it was Mr. Rex Calder's property. He didn't like anybody or anything—except his seven dogs. And everybody knew they were all trained to eat kids. Olivia headed toward the house with her sled dragging behind her.

Landon ran after her. "Where are you going?"

"To ask Mr. Calder if we can sled down his hill."

Landon grabbed her sleeve. "Are you crazy?"

Olivia marched up to the porch and knocked on the door. Mr. Calder opened it. They talked, and then he slammed the door. She walked back to the gate.

"Told you," Landon smirked.

"We can sled on one condition. That we let his dogs play with us for the exercise." Olivia smirked back. Suddenly seven dogs came running toward them with tails wagging.

Sometimes you just have to do what you think is right. Olivia ignored all the gossip about Mr. Calder. Just like warrior hero Deborah who fought the Canaanites when everybody else thought they shouldn't. She did, and she won.

Words to Treasure

"All right," Deborah said. "I'll go with you. But because of the way you are doing this, you won't receive any honor. Instead, the Lord will hand Sisera over to a woman."

Judges 4:9

Did You Know?

Did you know Deborah led the army to defeat Sisera's army and his 900 chariots?

November 14

Dance

Victoria listened to the quiet encouragement of her ballet teacher. She loved the feeling of complete freedom when she was dancing well. She felt strong and in control. When she went up on her toes, it felt just right. She had practiced this dance so many times that she didn't have to think about the movements. She just allowed her body to flow through the dance as if she had nothing to do with it. Although sometimes her body felt sore and tired, nothing in the world felt as good as dancing. She didn't mind practicing hard, because it only made her dancing stronger and better.

Words to Treasure

Let them praise his name with dancing.

Psalm 149: 3

When God gives you a talent that you love, then you should make sure you do everything to help make that talent grow. That means learning and practicing so that you can be the best you can be. Practicing is hard sometimes, but don't stop—keep going. God has a plan to use your talent for something amazing.

In Bible times, people danced in a we're-so-happy-with-God-we-just-have-to-dance sort of way. They danced on special occasions, such as weddings, and they danced when something amazing happened, such as God covering Pharaoh's army with a trillion gallons of Red Sea. But in Bible times, men and women usually didn't dance together.

Time Flies?

Jason flopped down on the sofa, exhausted. His mom and dad joined him with an exhausted sigh. "Thanks, Mom and Dad. That was the sweetest party ever. Man, did it go by fast," Jason thought about that. "How come time does weird things? I mean, why does time go by super-fast when you're having fun, but other times it can seem sooo slow? Like in math class. "

His dad and mom glanced at each other and laughed. His dad explained, "Time doesn't change speeds. When we have fun, we don't notice time passing because we're so busy. When we're bored, we notice time more. But there was that one time …"

"What time?"

"When time stood still."

"Tell me." Jason leaned forward.

"Well," his dad continued. "God made time, right? But one day, he decided to stop time for a very important reason …"

Words to Treasure

"Sun, stand still over Gibeon. And you, moon, stand still over the Valley of Aijalon." So the sun stood still. The moon stopped. They didn't move again until the nation won the battle over its enemies.

Joshua 10:12–13

People in Bible Times

A warrior leader named Joshua was fighting a really important battle. But the day was ending and soon it would be too dark to fight. Joshua asked God for more daylight. More time to win the battle. God stopped the sun and moon giving Joshua more time to win the day. That was the only day where time ever stood still. (See Joshua 10)

November 16

Faith Zone

Cam was snowboarding down a big hill. Not only that, but he was fast and confident. He knew what he was doing and how to do it. He was good!

Words to Treasure

Then Jesus said to her, "Woman, you have great faith! You will be given what you are asking for."
Matthew 15:28

He remembered his first class on the baby hill. He had fallen so many times his backside was black and blue. He didn't think he'd ever be able to get the hang of it. But every afternoon for the last three winters Cam went to the ski hill by his house and practiced. Every time he fell down, he got back up and tried again and again and again. All that hard work paid off. Not only could he snowboard, but someday he hoped to teach snowboarding. And now he had the faith to believe he could do it.

Faith is about believing and trusting in someone or something. It took everyday hard work for Cam to believe in himself. Sometimes it takes everyday hard work to build a big faith in God too. Two important faiths in action.

Do you have goals like Cam did, but you just don't believe that God can help you achieve them? Get a calendar and make a faith plan. On each date, write one thing you can do that day to help you reach your goal, whether it is learning to snowboard or doing better with your homework. Big challenges get smaller when you and God work on them together every day. Your life is a big faith construction zone.

November 17

Mystery

Rickie looked up from his Bible. "So, Joshua and his army walked around that city …"

Mrs. Peters nodded. "Jericho."

Rickie continued, "… Blowing their trumpets, then the city's wall fell down. And they won the battle. How is that possible? "

Words to Treasure

Do you know how deep the mysteries of God are? Can you discover the limits of the Mighty One's knowledge?

Job 11:7

"People have been wondering that ever since it happened. The Bible is full of amazing and wonderful events that only happened by God's power. Can you name other mysteries in the Bible?" The class started talking all at once. Creation. Noah's ark. The Red Sea parting. Gideon's victorious battle.

Mrs. Peters quieted the class down. "Sometimes when we can't explain a mystery through science or logic, we must have faith that God is bigger, stronger, and can do anything. Miracles make our faith stronger. Mysteries make us even more curious about God. Don't they?" The class nodded.

Can you make a list of some of the mysteries or miracles in the Bible? How many can you name? It might take a long time to find them all.

November 18

Tantrum

Amber tore her horse posters off her wall and ripped the covers off her bed. She smashed one of her favorite horse figurines into a million pieces. Amber had never been so angry. She had slammed her door and completely trashed her room. It was the most out-of-control tantrum she had ever had. She absolutely *couldn't* wait another year for a horse. It just wasn't fair!

Words to Treasure

A wise woman builds her house. But a foolish woman tears hers down with her own hands.

Proverbs 14:1

She was all tired now and sat quietly, kind of shocked by what she had done to her poor room. She had worked hard to buy those posters and now her favorite horse figurine was in bits and pieces.

Her brother opened her door and looked in. "Brilliant, Amber. Well done." She threw a pillow at him. But he was right. She still won't get her horse this year. Now her parents think she's really irresponsible. And she destroyed her own stuff, stuff she really liked.

Temper tantrums don't solve *any* problem, and you'll wish you never got so mad. Anger can be this out-of-control monster that destroys things, friendships, and feelings. Next time you get mad, take a fast walk around your yard or paint a picture with lots of crazy colors. Put that energy into an activity that won't wreck the house or someone else.

When you're angry or frustrated, there are lots of ways to get all that energy and unhappiness out. Write about how angry you are, talk to a friend, and go do something active: play basketball, play your drums, listen to music, or go build something that requires lots of hammering or pounding. Just find better ways to let out all that energy.

Promise Keeper?

"Marcus! Come on down. We rented a movie for tonight. *Captain Courage*! The one you've been waiting to see. We got pizza," his mom called up the stairs.

Marcus walked slowly down the stairs and glanced at the big tennis trophy on top of the fireplace mantel. "I can't watch the movie with you." Marcus looked about as unhappy as cat in a bubble bath.

"Why?" his mother brushed hair from his face. "Are you feeling sick?

Marcus talked to his feet. "I made a promise to God that if I won the tennis tournament that I would never watch television again. I won."

"Well, that is a problem." His mom sat on the stairs. "We have to be very careful about what we promise God. That doesn't sound very careful."

"Mom, what should I do?"

God is not someone you should play let's make a deal with. Promising to do or not do things to get God to give you something good in return is never a good idea. Especially if the promise is almost impossible to keep. It's okay to pray to God about things, but promises are very special. Take them very seriously.

Words to Treasure

A person is trapped if they make a hasty promise to God and only later thinks about what they said.

Proverbs 20:25

What would you do if you were Marcus? Talk about it with your parents and friends. Have you ever made a promise you wish you could take back? Have you ever made a promise you've broken?

November 20

Huge Thanks

The dogs were barking inside the kennels and cages. Sayen searched the building, but she didn't see her dog Brazen. When the flood came, they hadn't been allowed to take her dog on the rescue boat. But some nice people went out and collected all the left-behind pets. Sayen prayed with all her heart that her dog would be here.

Words to Treasure

He threw himself at Jesus' feet and thanked him.

Luke 17:16

She heard a familiar bark and turned. A man had Brazen on a leash. "Is this your dog, sweetie?" Brazen was pulling to get to her. The nice man let go, and Brazen charged across the floor.

"Brazen!" Sayen knelt down, filling her arms with wiggling happy dog.

Her family happily put Brazen in the back of their car. Sayen took out two big baskets and ran back to the shelter. One was full of pet treats, and the other was full of people treats. She gave them to the volunteers. "Thank you for finding my dog." Sayen wiped a tear from her eye and ran back to the car.

Never forget to thank people who are kind to you. And don't forget to thank God for the people who have been kind to you.

People in Bible Times

While Jesus was traveling to Jerusalem he came across ten men with a pretty disgusting skin disease. Jesus sent them to see the priests, but on the way they were healed. Only one man turned around, went back, and thanked Jesus. So which guy do you want to be? (See Luke 17:11–19.)

Rusted Out

Brock pulled his bike out of the garage, but he wasn't happy. This was not a bike to be proud of. How could he go on a bike trip with the guys with this rusted junkyard bike?

"Dad!" Brock called his dad over from waxing the car. "I need a new bike for this weekend. Look at mine! It's all rusted and gross-looking. The guys are going to laugh at me."

His dad looked the bike over. "It wouldn't be rusty if you didn't leave it outside in the rain all the time would it? Would rust have something to do with the way you take care of your bike?"

Words to Treasure

I went past the vineyard of a man who didn't have any sense. Thorns had grown up everywhere. The ground was covered with weeds.

Proverbs 24:30–31

This talk wasn't going well. Brock bit his lip. "No new bike."

"No new bike. But you have all week to fix up this bike. I'll help you. But you have to learn to take care of what you have. This bike isn't that old."

Lesson learned: it's important to take good care of the things you have. Respect the gifts God's already given you before you ask for more or newer ones.

Discovering Archaeology

We have wheels on everything from cars and trains to airplanes. The first "wheels" were probably logs. people put a heavy object on logs and rolled it over the top of the logs. As the object rolled along, someone pulled a log from the back and moved it up front. Try it as an experiment at home by lining up a series of pencils.

November 22

Give It Up

Ernst touched the huge snake the men of the village were carrying. It was an anaconda, and it was over twelve feet long. They had found it in the river by the village. Ernst and his family had come to Venezuela in South America to work in a medical missionary hospital. Ernst got along with the kids of the village, and every day seemed like an adventure. Today it was a gigantic man-eating snake adventure. The men let Ernst have a photograph taken standing beside the snake. They told him anacondas could get up to 26 feet long!

Words to Treasure

"Come and follow me," Jesus said. "I will send you out to fish for people." At once they left their nets and followed him.

Matthew 4:19-20

"Do you miss movie theatres, fast food, and all that other stuff back home?" teased his dad as they backed away to let the researcher and his team measure the snake.

"Dad, I'm really glad we came here. I know I gave up some stuff, but I'm never ever going to forget coming here. This is great!"

Sometimes we have to give up things to go on the adventures God wants us to go on. Are you willing to do that?

Jesus told a story about a pearl merchant who found the most beautiful pearl he had ever seen. He sold everything he had to own that pearl. God is like that beautiful pearl; we have to be willing to give up everything or change the way we live to do things God's way. (Matthew 13:44–46.)

November 23

Record Clean

Nick crossed off another day on the calendar. He looked around his spotlessly clean room. He was going for a record. Fifty days so far! His mom didn't have to remind him to clean up his toys, make his bed, or feed his fish. He was the master of clean, the hero of organization, the duke of dusting. He turned around to head downstairs. There was his mom holding a plastic bag.

Words to Treasure

Hands that work hard will rule.

Proverbs 12:24

Nick peered at the fish. "No way! An x-ray fish!!" He could see the fish's skeleton right through the skin.

His mom sat down on the tidy bed. "You've worked hard keeping your room clean, so here's a new friend as a reward. What are you going to call him?"

Nick beamed. "Mr. Clean, of course."

Can you beat Nick's clean room record? If you already keep a spotless room, what can you work hard at? Try it. You may like it.

Did you know ancient Egyptians kept pet fish? Well, they also ate some of their pet fish. Don't try that at home.

November 24

What About Me?

Rose shifted her long white dress to the side. Aunt Becky sat down beside her. "Are you going to come help me with my bouquet of flowers?"

> **Words to Treasure**
>
> A friend loves at all times. They are there to help when trouble comes.
>
> Proverbs 17:17

"No," Becky stared at her white dress shoes. "Everything's ruined. You're marrying Bobby. I probably won't see you anymore. "

"What?" Aunt Becky wrapped her arms around Rose. "You are my shopping buddy. Didn't you help me pick out my wedding dress?" Rose nodded. "And when I want to watch a chick flick , who am I going to call?"

Rose looked up, "Me?"

Her aunt smiled. "Absolutely you. Just because I love Bobby doesn't mean I don't love you too. I have room for both of you—always. Now, you want to come help me throw these flowers?"

Rose shook her head. "I want to try and catch them."

Love has room for everybody. True friends love each other like God loves us. He loves us the same no matter how many new people become part of his family.

Did you know that in Bible times boys could get married as young as 14 years old and girls as early as 12 years old?

Using Your Head

The boys stood on the slope of the biggest jump on the mountain ready to make boarding history. Three boys waited at the bottom to take photographs and videos. Jonathan took off his helmet and passed it to Bailey. "I know you don't like helmets, but you're going to get mega airtime on this jump."

Words to Treasure

Wise people see danger and go to a safe place. But childish people keep on going and suffer for it.

Proverbs 27:12

Bailey laughed, "No thanks. I'm good." With that he pushed off. He pretty much knew that everything was going wrong at the top of the jump. He was off-balance and heading to one spectacularly bad landing. He wiped out for all the cameras to record for history.

The boys waited for Bailey to move. But he wasn't moving. He was out cold with blood running down his forehead. Jonathan joined them. "David, go get help."

After one sled ride down the hill, one ambulance ride to the hospital, one cutting off of a favorite shirt, one uncomfortable session of x-rays, and one long lecture from the doctor, Bailey was ready to go home for several days in bed.

Simple rule—extreme sports need extreme headgear. Wear your helmet. God gave you a great brain, so use it and protect it.

Hey, soldiers wore protective gear for the same reasons. The first helmets were probably made of thick leather and metal. The idea was to protect your head, face, and neck from all types of nasty damage. After all, your brain is your best weapon. Protect it!

November 26

Just My Parents

Piper, Bethany, and Lillian were eating an entire box of sugar cereal on the way home from the movies. They were throwing the pieces into the air and catching them in their mouths. A car pulled up beside them. It was Piper's dad, and he looked fairly unhappy as he rolled down the window. "Piper, you told me that you didn't have enough money to go to the movies."

Words to Treasure

Anyone who steals from his parents and says, "It's not wrong," is just like a man who destroys.

Proverbs 28:24

Suddenly Piper was looking kind of guilty. "Well … I borrowed some money."

"From whom?" questioned her dad.

Piper suddenly looked very guilty. "From Mom's purse."

"Did you ask her first?"

"No, not really." Rapidly this was turning out to be not such a good day after all.

"I'm sorry, girls." Piper's dad opened the door for his daughter to get in the car. "Piper has to go home now."

Actually, Piper has to go home to face the music. Taking money from your parents, grandparents, brothers, sisters, or friends without permission is stealing. It may not seem like stealing, but yes, it is stealing. So keep your hands off other people's money unless you're given the okay.

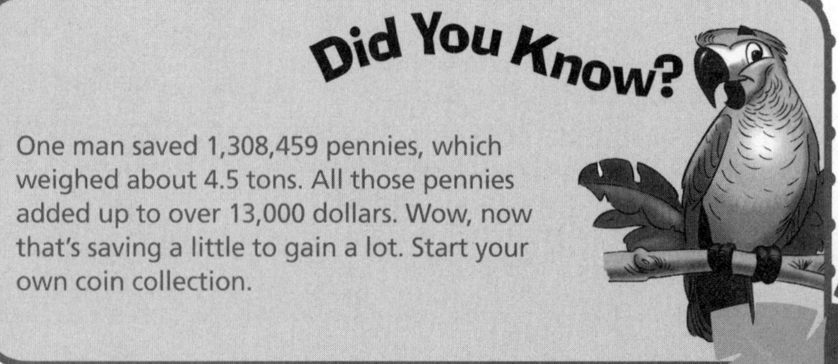

Did You Know?

One man saved 1,308,459 pennies, which weighed about 4.5 tons. All those pennies added up to over 13,000 dollars. Wow, now that's saving a little to gain a lot. Start your own coin collection.

November 27

Good Knight

The little boy pushed the little girl aside as he wedged his way to the water fountain. The kid turned around to find Mr. Jackson staring down at him. "I've been watching you. Let's have a talk."

The boy wiped water from his chin. "About what?"

"About you." Mr. Jackson took the boy aside. "You have two choices. You can be the bully of the school and have kids be afraid of you. Or you can be more like a knight. A knight like the ones in the story King Arthur and the Round Table—a guy that kids go to for protection. A good guy that everybody looks up to. So which do you want to be? A bully or a knight? Your choice."

Words to Treasure

Those who are kind benefit themselves.

Proverbs 11:17

The boy wrinkled his nose. "What are you?"

"I'm a knight."

"I want to be a knight too."

"Put it there." They shook hands. "Okay, you're an official knight in my round table. No more rough stuff. " The boy ran down the hall excited to tell his friends.

You have a choice to be hero or a villain, and that choice is completely up to you.

How do you treat others at school? Maybe it's time to think about being a knight too. Start your own Round Table and become like King David's mighty men, doing what's right all the time.

November 28

Change of Mind

Bruce's friends were throwing snowballs and sledding at the end of the road. Bruce walked right past the snowy driveway he had promised to shovel and salt and headed down the road to join them.

Words to Treasure

Let us not become tired of doing good. At the right time we will gather a crop if we don't give up.

Galatians 6:9

Bruce was just packing down a snow jump when Jonathan came running down the road. "Hey, Bruce, some guy just slipped on your driveway and he looks dead!"

Bruce ran back up the hill and saw his grandfather's car parked out front. Oh, no! Grandpa was sitting on the slippery driveway rubbing his head. Bruce's mother was helping him up, and she didn't look very happy. Bruce was so busted.

Jesus told a story about two brothers. One brother promised to do some chores for his father but didn't. The second brother said he *wouldn't* do the chores, but later he changed his mind and did them. So which brother did what his father asked? And which guy do you want to be like? That's kind of a no-brainer! The brother that had a change of attitude and did his chores, right?

When you think of ancient Israel, you probably think of a hot desert. Did they have snow days? Mount Hermon is the highest mountain around, and it has snow on it in the winter and spring. It's also known as *mountain of snow* or *gray-haired mountain*. Today, you can snowboard at a ski resort there!

Smart Shopping

Kate opened up the folder with all her notes and information in it. She was buying the biggest, most important purchase of her life. She was buying her very first dog, with her own money. She had spent months researching what type of dog breeds she liked. She had narrowed it down to three dog breeds. Then she had read everything she could about them. She made an appointment to talk to a veterinarian about them. Then she went to three dog shows and talked to people there. She got more information and some names of good breeders. She even researched dog-obedience classes.

Words to Treasure

She considers a field and buys it.

Proverbs 31:16

After all that, she picked the type of dog she wanted and phoned the breeder. They had some puppies ready to look at today. Kate pulled out her list of questions to ask the breeder. She had done everything possible to be a smart shopper and responsible owner.

Kate's mom called up the stairs, "Ready to go, sweetie?"

Kate closed her file. "I'm so ready."

Wise people never rush into important decisions.

Have you ever bought anything on a whim and really regretted it later? Lots of people buy pets because they're cute but give them away later because they're just too much unexpected work. Or they buy expensive things that they never use, like that unicycle covered in cobwebs in the garage. So be wise, plan ahead, and be shopper smart.

November 30

Don't Know Him

Judd played on the drum set in the music store. Some boys from school walked in, but they pretended they didn't even know him. The storeowner, Mr. Wakemen, glanced over with a frown at the boys' behavior. Mr. Wakemen was letting Judd practice in the store until he could buy his own drum set.

Words to Treasure

What about someone who says in front of others that he knows me? I tell you, the Son of Man will say in front of God's angels that he knows that person.

Luke 12:8

The shop door chimed open and in walked Yager. The boys turned and stared. He was a drummer for a pretty famous rock band. Mr. Wakemen shook Yager's hand, and the two men chatted. After a while, Yager walked over to Judd. "Hey, Judd! You've improved since I was last here."

Judd shrugged. "Trying."

Yager pulled up a chair. "Play some more. Don't be shy." Soon Judd was getting a drum lesson from a famous drummer. The other boys watched in complete awe. Yager looked over. "You know those fellas?"

Judd shook his head. "Not really. I don't think they like me."

"Oh! Their loss." They went back to drumming.

Those boys missed out on a great opportunity because of their exclusive behavior. Don't make the same mistake they did.

Live IT!

If you tell people you know you love Jesus, guess what? Jesus is going to say he knows and loves you in front of all God's angels. But if you pretend as if you don't know Jesus, guess what? In front of God's angels, Jesus isn't going to know you either. And that's not good. (See Luke 12:8–9.)

December 1

Nobody Important

The boy was nervous in front of all these important people. "Hello," he said, "my name is Joseph. I have known what it's like to be very hungry. My family was very poor."

The audience gasped as a photograph of a skinny, sickly boy came up on a screen. Joseph turned and looked at it. "That was me. But I don't look that way anymore because people like you came to my village to help us. I am here tonight to tell you to keep helping villages like mine. I'm here to tell you that if you had not helped, I would be dead today. I would not have survived and neither would my sisters and brothers. You have so much, and it takes so little to help someone unimportant like me." Joseph smiled at the audience. "My mother thinks I am a very fine fellow. Please listen to the words of this fine unimportant boy. God bless you." The audience was silent and then they cheered.

God doesn't just speak through important people, movie stars, and rock stars. Sometimes he speaks the loudest through everyday people with a really big message.

Words to Treasure

These are the words of Amos. He was a shepherd from the town of Tekoa. Here is the vision he saw concerning Israel. It came to him two years before the earthquake.

Amos 1:1

The prophet Amos was just an ordinary shepherd and farmer, but God gave him big visions. A vision is like a dream you have when you're fully awake. God often talked to prophets in visions by giving them pictures to see in their minds or words to hear. God makes the ordinary extraordinary.

December 2

And So On!

The people in the van all stared at each other in awe. Jonna was quite happy to have a captive audience. "Then we went to Africa, which was really hot, but we got to see lions. And can you believe it, the monkeys were just crazy? They stole stuff. And I was, like, *get out of here*. Then we went to Rome, which my aunt Tracy just hated, but I liked it. Because, like, I did this book report on Rome. Did I tell you my dog is named Caesar? After that Roman king guy. Not like the salad. I personally like regular salads better with Thousand Island dressing. Speaking of islands, we went to Hawaii. I, like, surfed the entire time. Well, not exactly the entire time. We went out to dinner and shopped and stuff. If you want shell jewelry, that is totally the place to buy it. There's a little store two blocks from our hotel. Can't remember the name of it. But if you want, phone me and I'll get my mom to tell you the name. I have, like, the worst memory. It's crazy! Did I tell you we just got a new bird?"

Words to Treasure

Many words result in foolish talk.

Ecclesiastes 5:3

Uncle Jim reached for the CD player. "Anybody want to listen to some music?"

Everybody said at once, "YES!"

Talking nonstop isn't the best way to communicate with other people. Good talks include everybody.

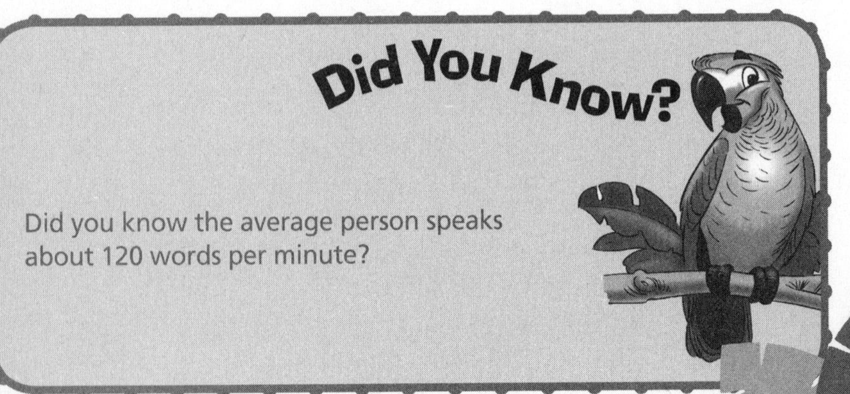

Did you know the average person speaks about 120 words per minute?

December 3

Name It!

James walked right up to the skipper of Red Sea Reef Cruises. Captain Kohen ran a fleet of glass-bottom boats and fishing charters. "Hi, my name's James Simmons. My uncle said I should come talk to you."

> **Words to Treasure**
>
> A good name is better than fine perfume.
>
> Ecclesiastes 7:1

Captain Kohen immediately broke into a smile. "Is your uncle Max Simmons?"

James nodded, "Yes, sir. He said that maybe you could use another weekend deckhand. I'm good on boats, and my uncle taught me all about the coral reefs. I can answer any questions your guests might have."

"Well," Captain Kohen said, and reached out and shook James's hand. "If your last name's Simmons, that's all I need to know. You come from a good family. Your family knows these waters just as well as anybody around. Sure, I could use a deckhand on Saturdays for the glass-bottom boat tours."

How you behave doesn't reflect only on you. It also reflects on your entire family. James's family had a good reputation that people respected. That was a big help to James. Make sure that you help maintain a good family name by doing right things too.

Did You Know?

Did you know that the Red Sea has amazing coral reefs? Over 1,100 different types of fish are swimming around. Take a dip in the Red Sea, and you'll be swimming with venomous lionfish, lively clownfish, giant moray eels, hammerhead sharks, and don't forget those crazy seahorses. And that's just for starters.

December 4

Haven

The sailboat climbed the crashing waves. Wind whistled through the rigging. This was the worst storm Hayley and her grandpa had ever been in. Soaked by cold seawater, she was glad to be wearing her full-body survival suit. They had taken the sails down and were using the motor, searching the shoreline for the hidden entrance to the little cove.

Words to Treasure

He will be like a place to hide from storms.

Isaiah 32:2

They had to be careful the wind didn't blow them onto the rocks. Finally they slipped into the protected cove. Hayley threw out the anchor when her grandpa gave her the signal. When everything was secure, they gratefully went down below into the cabin.

"Nothing to do but wait out the storm." Grandpa put the kettle on for hot chocolate and found some cookies. The quiet waves of the cove rocked the sailboat softly. The cabin was warm and they were safe from the storm.

You know, hanging out with God is a safe place. Like a quiet place to hide from storms or a shady place on a hot day. It just feels good.

Isaiah was one of God's prophets who lived during the time the kingdom was divided into Israel and Judah. But the really amazing thing is that Isaiah told people what Jesus would be like hundreds of years before he was even born. How'd he know Jesus was like a safe haven? God told him, of course!

December 5

Who Made God?

The brilliant red Siamese fighting fish watched his bubble nest very carefully. Inside the patch of air bubbles were his eggs. When an egg sank down to the bottom of the tank, he quickly gathered it in his mouth and spit it back into the nest. Nigel watched his fish. For a fighting guy he was a pretty good dad! Nigel's mom walked into his room. "Have any eggs hatched yet?"

"Nope. But Will Scarlet and I are standing guard. Pretty cool that I made baby fighting fish."

His mom put his laundry on the bed. "*You* made baby fighting fish? I think Will Scarlet and Sapphire made baby fighting fish."

> **Words to Treasure**
>
> So the heavens and the earth and everything in them were completed. By the seventh day God had finished the work he had been doing.
>
> Genesis 2:1–2

"Yeah sure," Nigel admitted, "but I provided them the right kind of tank, water temperature, food, and stuff. I mean I'm in charge of everything."

"If you're doing all the work, maybe the fish are training you." His mom whistled as she left the room. Nigel had to think about that.

Try to answer this question. If God created humankind—who created God? Got ya! Nobody can answer that. One of the gigantic, unanswerable mysteries of life. We just have to have faith that God exists and that it was his super big, creative intelligence that created everything else.

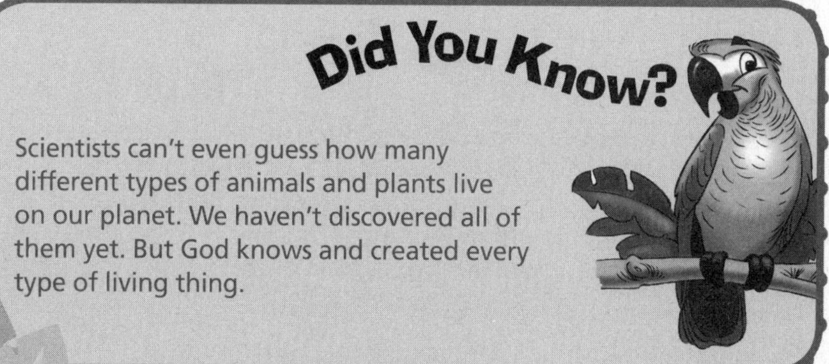

Did You Know?

Scientists can't even guess how many different types of animals and plants live on our planet. We haven't discovered all of them yet. But God knows and created every type of living thing.

December 6

Looking Good!

Words to Treasure

Then God said, "Let us make human beings so that they are like us. He created them to be like himself.

Genesis 1:26

Great-Aunt Mavis inspected Lilly as she served tea. "My, haven't you grown! And I'd say your eyes are your mother's, but your mouth and ears are certainly your father's."

My *ears*! Lilly wanted to scream. Dad's ears stuck out. Lilly wanted to die. She absolutely did not have her father's ears. Did she?

"Speaking of ears." Great-Aunt Mavis chuckled as she passed a neatly wrapped present to Lilly. "My birthday gift to you." Lilly opened the little box and inside were some beautiful pearl earrings. Great-Aunt Mavis sipped her tea. "For your pretty little ears."

"My ears don't look like my dad's?"

"Certainly not!" Aunt Mavis passed her an almond cookie. "Your father's ears stick out like satellite dishes."

We all have things about us that remind us of our parents—the way we look or talk. But did you know that God created us to look very much like him? We don't know exactly what God looks like, but if the Bible says we look like him, that's a big hint.

Did You Know?

The amazing thing about Jesus is that today nobody knows exactly what he looked like. There are no paintings of Jesus from when he was on earth. The paintings you see today are all what the artists imagined Jesus would look like.

December 7

Be One!

The cave was beautiful, with thick pillars of stone hanging from the roof and strange formations dotting the floor. They had formed over hundreds of years. The school group stood in the cavern completely awed by the beauty. Jerry stared at the milky blue pond in the middle of the room.

Words to Treasure

Think about what you see. Search through the market. See if you can find one honest person who tries to be truthful.

Jeremiah 5:1

"You!" The park ranger pointed at Jerry.

Jerry jumped about five feet in the air. "Me?" Every kid in his class stared at him.

"Do you remember what I said about touching the cave formations at the beginning of the tour? That just by touching them you can damage them?"

"Yes," Jerry said. "I haven't touched anything. I've been real careful."

"I know that. You are the only person on this tour who hasn't touched anything." He smiled at Jerry. "What's your name?"

"Jerry."

"Jerry, I'm going to give you a cave T-shirt and free tickets to bring your family next time. Well done." The rest of the kids were so bummed.

Are you doing the right thing even when everyone around you doesn't seem to follow the rules? If you are, then you totally ROCK!

Did You Know?
Did you know that there are still hundreds of unexplored caves yet to be found and waiting to be discovered?

December 8

Is This Fair?

Tony Lyons walked up on the stage and accepted his Academic Achievement Award. He smiled broadly at the audience of parents and students. Everybody clapped as he left the stage.

Words to Treasure

Lord, when I bring a matter to you, you always do what is right.

Jeremiah 12:1

Daniel slumped in his chair. *This is so cheap,* he thought to himself. *Tony has the worst attitude in the school. He's rude and makes everybody around him feel small. Am I missing something or is this truly lame that he gets an award?*

Daniel held his smaller Athletic Award and thought about how hard he had worked to earn this award. Then, he got the best thought. He couldn't control what other people did, but he could control what he did. Daniel had joined basketball, football, and the swim team. He had played fair, and people respected him. He always tried to do what was right. That's the biggest reward of all. He knew his actions honored God. That made him smile.

Jeremiah had those same thoughts thousands of years ago. And he talked to God about them. "But now I would like to speak with you about whether you are being fair. Why are sinful people successful? Why do those who can't be trusted have an easy life?" (Jeremiah 12:1).

Do you ever wonder stuff like that? Why does it seem like doing wrong gets people good things? Stop wondering, because whether *you* do right is all that matters. Having God's respect is the most important thing in life.

What to Do with Sadness

Amy came home from the airport. Her best friend was moving halfway around the world . She didn't know what to do with all the sad feelings she had inside, so she wrote a poem and drew a picture about her friend Sylvia. Amy decided she would write a letter to Sylvia about all the good times they shared. When you feel sad, write a poem or draw a picture about how you feel and then put it away. Sometime later when you want to remember that time, take it out and look at it. There is no right or wrong way to write a sad poem. Just write what you feel. Having both sad and happy times is normal.

Words to Treasure

Tears are flowing from our eyes.

Lamentations 1:16

The book of the Bible called Lamentations is really a book of sad poems. Many think these poems were written by the prophet Jeremiah after the Babylonians destroyed Jerusalem. Writing poems helped Jeremiah get all his feelings out.

December 10

Christmas Indie

Martin couldn't take another step. He couldn't shop in another store or stand in another long line. This was painful! He thought Christmas shopping should be listed as an extreme sport. He didn't know his mother could move that fast. And driving around the mall parking lot was like a cross between an Indy car race and a demolition derby. Martin just wanted to go home. Was Christmas really supposed to be like this?

Words to Treasure

A child will be born to us. A son will be given to us. He will rule over us. And he will be called Wonderful Adviser and Mighty God.

Isaiah 9:6

Good question. The answer is *no*! Celebrating Christmas is good, but not if you get so worn out that you can't enjoy the real meaning of Christmas.

Christmas should be a time to slow down, relax more, and enjoy the most important birthday celebration in the world. Jesus was born to save the world from sin, and you can't buy that at a store.

This Christmas, plan some activities that are fun and celebrate Jesus' birthday at the same time. Get your friends together and go caroling around the neighborhood. Sit down as a family and watch a movie about Jesus' birth. Go for a winter walk in nature with a thermos of hot chocolate. Play a family game together on a cold night. Just slow down and have some fun. And remember, Jesus wants you to enjoy his birthday party.

Problem-Solver

Miss Halley," Alexis caught up to her dance teacher. "Miss Halley, I have a real problem with the music you selected for our performance. I don't think it respects girls, and I think it makes crime look cool."

"It's a very popular song, and the other girls like it." Miss Halley glanced at her watch impatiently.

"I know. But it doesn't feel right for me."

Her teacher nodded as she headed out the door, "I respect that. Sorry to lose you on this."

"Wait." Alexis followed her outside. "Can I design my own dance and enter a solo dance?"

"Would that be fair to the other girls?" questioned her teacher.

Alexis was ready for this. "Yes, because I'm putting in the time to do it. If they want to do the same thing, they can."

Miss Halley got into her sports car. "Okay. Better be outstanding."

"Yes!" Alexis did a little jump.

Alexis was bold enough to talk about her concerns with her teacher, but she was also ready with a solution to the problem.

Words to Treasure

Daniel decided not to make himself "unclean" by eating the king's food and drinking his wine. So he asked the chief official for a favor. He wanted permission not to make himself "unclean" with the king's food and wine.

Daniel 1:8

People in Bible Times

Daniel was a young Jew who was taken from Jerusalem to Babylon to serve in the house of King Nebuchadnezzar. Daniel didn't want to eat meat already offered up to Babylonian gods. So, he asked if could eat only fruits and vegetables. He promised that he would remain healthy. He got the okay. Daniel was a godly man and a problem solver. (See Daniel 1.)

December 12

Don't Stay Silent

Alexis was dancing to her music in the dance studio. Tina and Ray were watching her. They liked her moves and they liked the music. In fact, they thought Alexis's dance was amazing. Tina handed Alexis her water bottle. "Alexis, your dance is really, really good. I didn't have the courage to say anything, but I don't like the song Miss Halley picked. Would you consider making your solo a trio? We'd love to join you."

Words to Treasure

Please test us for ten days. Give us nothing but vegetables to eat. And give us only water to drink. Then compare us with the young men who eat the king's food. See how we look.

Daniel 1:12–13

Alexis didn't want to cause any more trouble for Miss Halley. "If you go talk to Miss Halley and she says *yes*, then we'll do it together."

Miss Halley looked from one girl to another. "Why didn't you tell me you didn't like the song?"

"We didn't know how to say it."

Their teacher sighed. "Maybe I was wrong about this."

When people stay silent and don't talk about how they feel, things can't be changed. But if you're respectful and join together to solve the problem, things can change.

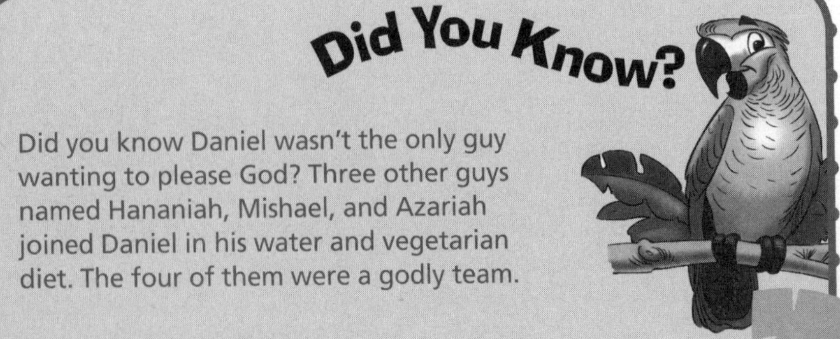

Did You Know?
Did you know Daniel wasn't the only guy wanting to please God? Three other guys named Hananiah, Mishael, and Azariah joined Daniel in his water and vegetarian diet. The four of them were a godly team.

December 13

God's Favor

The audience was clapping with the music, and the girls on stage were doing everything right. They looked strong and athletic. Alexis had designed everything about the performance. She had picked a popular song with *good* lyrics, and she had designed the dance and the costumes. And when she ran up a wall and did a back flip, the crowd clapped wildly.

Words to Treasure

God gave knowledge and understanding to these four young men. So they understood all kinds of writings and subjects. And Daniel could understand all kinds of visions and dreams.

Daniel 1:17

The girls stood in a line and bowed to the standing audience. They left the stage, but the audience kept clapping. Miss Halley gathered them together. "Go back out there. Take another bow."

The girls rushed back on stage, and the audience clapped louder. It was like a dream come true, all because Alexis was bold enough to put both her faith and talent on the line.

When you put what God wants ahead of everything else, you have to know that he's pleased with you. God wants you to succeed, but he wants you to succeed the right way, by doing what's right in his eyes.

Great kings became great because they gathered all the brightest and wisest men from their kingdom to advise them on important matters. King Nebuchadnezzar found Daniel and the boys to be the wisest of all, and he trusted their advice. From servants to kingly advisors—it's all in God's plan.

December 14

Never Forget

The smoke was thick and black, and it burned their lungs. Yukio, Johanna, and Kitt couldn't find their way out of the old church building. They were crawling on the floor when suddenly out of the smoke came a big fireman. He wasn't wearing a mask, but the smoke didn't seem to bother him. "Grab my hand and hold onto each other. Don't let go!" They held hands and followed the fireman through the smoky halls. He threw open an exit door, and the kids tumbled out. They turned around but he was gone.

Words to Treasure

There in front of them his appearance was changed. His clothes became so white they shone. They were whiter than anyone in the world could bleach them.

Mark 9:2-3

Another fireman rushed over to help them. Yukio, Johanna, and Kitt sat down on the grass by the fire truck. Kitt coughed, "A fireman helped us out."

"What?" The fireman gave them a puzzled look. "Son, we just got here. Nobody's gone in there yet." The kids looked at each other. Who helped them?

There are going to be moments in your life when God's unseen heavenly world touches your everyday world in the most amazing way. Those are moments you'll never ever forget, and they build your faith in God.

People in Bible Times

Jesus took Peter, James, and John up a mountain. Suddenly the way Jesus looked changed. His clothes became so white they glowed like nothing on earth. Peter, James, and John got a glimpse of the real Jesus—the Son of God. It was a heavenly moment they'd never ever forget. (See Mark 9:2–8.)

December 15

Christmas Glitter

Adrianna and her mother walked through the Christmas-glittered mall. They walked past Santa's Magic Mountain Train Trip to Wonderland. Her mom stopped to look in a shop window.

Words to Treasure

"Today in the town of David a Savior has been born to you."
Luke 2:11

"Mom," Adrianna said as she stopped beside her mom. "Do we actually know that December twenty-fifth is Jesus' birthday? Was his birthday written down somewhere?"

Her mother smiled at her. "I don't think so."

"Then how do we know for sure?" Adrianna studied the manger scene in the mall right beside Santa's train.

Here's the inside story on the date of Jesus' birth: We don't know the date. Some Christians even celebrate Jesus' birthday on January seventh. No big deal, though, because what day it falls on isn't really the point. What is the point is that on whatever day you celebrate Christmas or in whatever way, you stop and remember the most important birthday in history.

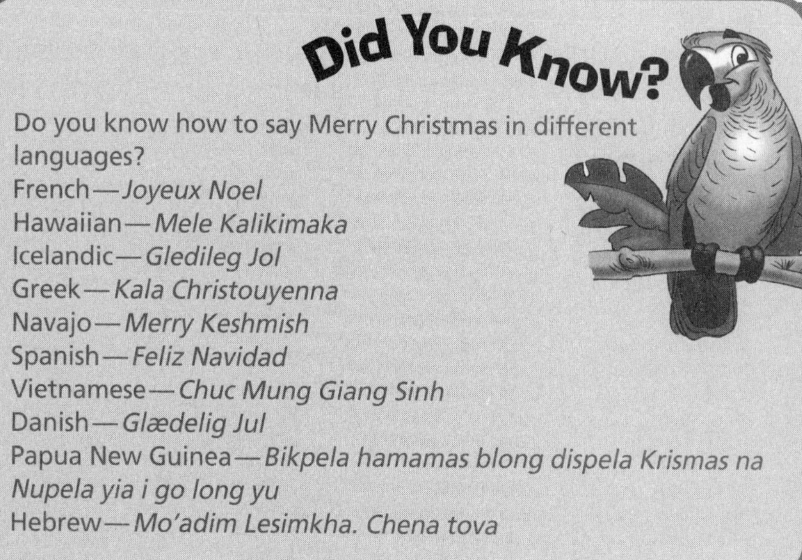

Did You Know?

Do you know how to say Merry Christmas in different languages?
French—*Joyeux Noel*
Hawaiian—*Mele Kalikimaka*
Icelandic—*Gledileg Jol*
Greek—*Kala Christouyenna*
Navajo—*Merry Keshmish*
Spanish—*Feliz Navidad*
Vietnamese—*Chuc Mung Giang Sinh*
Danish—*Glædelig Jul*
Papua New Guinea—*Bikpela hamamas blong dispela Krismas na Nupela yia i go long yu*
Hebrew—*Mo'adim Lesimkha. Chena tova*

December 16

Freedom

I am so happy to be here in church." Michael smiled and nodded a greeting to everybody around him.

Leonardo was actually a little bored. He had wanted to stay home to play video games. But Michael was their guest for three weeks, and he really wanted to go to church. And boy, did this guy get a charge out of going to church.

Words to Treasure

He ordered them to tie up Shadrach, Meshach and Abednego. Then he told his men to throw them into the blazing furnace.

Daniel 3:20

"In my country," explained Michael, "we are not allowed to go to church."

"Get out of here!" Leonardo didn't believe it. "Everybody can go to church."

Michael was very serious. "My government has outlawed Christian churches. But we meet in secret."

"What happens if you're caught?" Leonardo was shocked.

Michael shrugged. "You are beaten and arrested for a long time. It is not like here."

"Get out!" Leonardo was having a hard time with this. He looked around the church he took for granted.

Next time you're sitting in church, remember that many people in the world wish they had the same freedom to worship God anytime and any place they want. It's a gift you should never take for granted.

Live IT!

Daniel and his friends served King Nebuchadnezzar faithfully, but they would not worship his gods. The king decided to throw Daniel's three friends into a blazing hot furnace as punishment. But they had faith in God's protection. Would you have that same kind of faith?

December 17

Proof

What had happened? Kids were crying in the cold, dark bus. Pastor Jon searched around until he found a flashlight. He pointed it around the bus that was now tipped on its side. "Okay, everybody. We've been hit by a snow avalanche, and it looks like we're buried. First thing, I want to pray. Dear God, thank you for protecting us. Amen! Now, everybody who isn't hurt, raise your hand. You help the people who are hurt. Do what you can to make them comfortable. I'll help you. Sit close together for warmth. We're going to have to wait for rescue."

Words to Treasure

The king said, "Look! I see four men walking around in the fire. They aren't tied up. And the fire hasn't even harmed them. The fourth man looks like a son of the gods."

Daniel 3:25

Hours later, the television cameras focused on the hole where the rescuers were working. Then one young girl was helped out of the hole. Then another and another. They were quickly wrapped in blankets and taken to an ambulance. The last two out were the bus driver and Pastor Jon.

A rescuer put a blanket around Pastor Jon and said, "It's a miracle nobody was killed."

"God was with us." Pastor Jon gave a tired smile.

God is with us every day and in every situation.

People in Bible Times

King Nebuchadnezzar ordered Daniel's friends to be thrown into a raging furnace because Shadrach, Meshach, and Abednego were not willing to worship idols. The guys walked into the furnace sure God would protect them. And God did! Impressed, Nebuchadnezzar ordered that nobody in his kingdom could harm the Jews or talk badly about their God. (See Daniel 3.)

December 18

The Right Time

The two dogs growled and barked at the three little kids walking home from school. Monica saw what was happening and quietly walked from behind a car to stand beside them. "I want you to back up slowly, climb up onto the car, and sit on the roof." The kids did what she told them to do. Monica prayed as she opened up her music case with soft clicks of the latches. The dogs growled and showed their teeth. Their barks made her jump with fear. Sweat beaded on her forehead as she slowly pulled what she wanted out of the case.

Words to Treasure

Daniel! You serve the living God. You always serve him faithfully. So has he been able to save you from the lions?

Daniel 6:20

Then Monica blew on her trumpet as loudly as she could, and the dogs jumped back completely surprised. It was a blast that the entire neighborhood heard. The dogs were frightened and ran away. And people started coming out of their houses to see what was going on.

A man ran over. "Are you kids okay?" The three little kids burst into tears. Monica was trembling, but she had saved the day. Nobody got bitten.

Monica was the right kid for the right time with the right talents to save the day. Do you think God planned that?

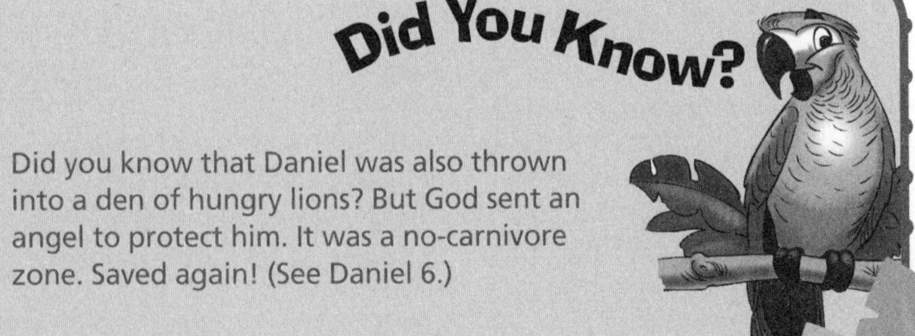

Did You Know?

Did you know that Daniel was also thrown into a den of hungry lions? But God sent an angel to protect him. It was a no-carnivore zone. Saved again! (See Daniel 6.)

One Brilliant Idea!

The police officer walked Monica over to the van so she could look in the window. The two dogs growled at her as they sat in cages inside. "Are those the dogs?"

Monica nodded and said, "Those are the dogs."

"Miss, you are very lucky." The police officer took off his cap and wiped his forehead. "They badly bit a man near here. Using your trumpet to scare them away was a smart thing to do. What made you think of that?"

Monica's mom put her hand on her daughter's shoulder. "I prayed and that's what came to my mind. It was the only thing I could think of," said Monica.

Words to Treasure

The king was filled with joy. He ordered his servants to lift Daniel out of the den. So they did. They didn't see any wounds on him. That's because he had trusted in his God.

Daniel 6:23

Daniel was saved from the lions. Not such good news for the wicked people who caused Daniel to be thrown to the lions. They were thrown to the lions as punishment for their wickedness, and they got eaten right away. It was proof that it wasn't about tame and gentle lions, it was about a protective God.

Thousands of years ago, lions were wild in Israel. Kings kept lions as a way of punishing people, the way it happened in the book of Daniel, by keeping them hungry in pits. Royalty would also hunt lions for sport. A male lion can weigh over 500 pounds. But there were also stories of the gentleness of these amazing creatures as in "Androcles and the Lion," the tale told by an ancient Greek named Aesop.

December 20

It Ain't Easy!

Ruth tried to get the graham cracker out of Milly's nose, but she wouldn't hold still. The twins had managed to get finger paint on everything in the house. A hamster was loose, and Ruth wasn't sure where the cat was. Apple juice had gotten into the fish tank, and Jackson had just wet his pants for the fourth time. And Ruth really wanted everybody to stop crying. Babysitting wasn't supposed to be like this.

Words to Treasure

He asked the Lord, "Why have you brought this trouble on me?"

Numbers 11:11

Ruth wanted the kids to sing songs with her, do puppet shows and talk about their favorite things. She wanted everything to be perfect, but nothing was turning out the way it was supposed to. Why was this happening? She was volunteering for the church!

That's the funny thing. Even when we're doing what God wants us to do, sometimes things still go wrong. And keep going wrong. Our job is to do our best even when everything's wrong.

People in Bible Times

Moses wondered why things kept going wrong after they left Egypt. His people were disobeying God and complaining *all* the time. And some wanted to go back to Egypt. His own leaders were giving him a big headache, and there was talk people wanted to stone him to death. And to top it off, other tribes were constantly attacking them. This wasn't what Moses thought it would be like! Maybe Moses should sing about his favorite things—God and getting to the Promised Land.

December 21

Baby Power

Henry looked at the little black and white photo. "So that's my baby brother inside you?" Henry asked, as he looked at his mother's round belly. "He must feel pretty squashed in there. What does he do in there all day?"

His mom smiled. "Grows, sleeps, moves around."

"Moves around. Really? Can he hear me?"

"He sure can," his mother replied.

Henry leaned close and shouted at his mom's belly. "Hi, Charlie! Charlie, you won't bite my finger, will you?"

Words to Treasure

"As soon as I heard the sound of your voice, the baby inside me jumped for joy."

Luke 1:44

Babies are people even before they are born. They hear the voices of their family and even get hiccups in there. The Bible tells the story of two babies who had a special relationship before they were even born: Jesus and his cousin John.

Even when baby John the Baptist was in his mother's womb, he was excited about his new unborn cousin Jesus coming to save the world. Babies know important stuff! Who knew? God did.

December 22

On the Map

Liz walked along the busy market in the city of Bethlehem. She couldn't believe she was here, and that it was a real place. Jesus was born here—cool! She stopped in front of a shop that sold little olive wood figures of Mary, Joseph, Jesus, the Wise Men, camels, sheep, donkeys, and shepherds. She picked out a little wood manger scene. It was the special thing she had been looking for to take home. Liz loved to travel. When she grew up, she wanted to go to far-off countries and explore everything.

Words to Treasure

Then Jesus went through the towns and villages, teaching the people. He was on his way to Jerusalem.

Luke 13:22

The places you read about in the Bible are real places. Some places like Jerusalem or Bethlehem are busy towns today. Other places in the Bible are harder to find because they've been lost in time. Some are little villages or cities people stopped living in thousands of years ago and are now buried in the ground. Archaeologists (people who study the past) are working hard to try to figure out where those lost places of the Bible are today.

Discovering Archaeology

Take the city of Ur. This two-letter city was mentioned in the Bible, but it wasn't until a guy named Sir Charles Leonard Woolley started digging around in Iraq in 1922 that Ur became more than just a name. It became a real city again when Sir Leo uncovered temples, 1,850 burial sites, and some royal tombs. Way to go, Sir Leo.

December 23

Knock, Knock

The basket was so heavy that Nicole and Marc could hardly carry it between them. The walkway was slippery, and Nicole was sure they were going to fall on their faces, sending the contents of the Christmas hamper into the front yard. Quietly they put the basket down on the front step. Then they knocked loudly on the door and ran. They quickly dove into the bushes and waited.

Words to Treasure

"When you give to needy people, don't let your left hand know what your right hand is doing. Then your giving will be done secretly."
Matthew 6: 3-4

Old Mr. and Mrs. Pickersgill opened the door and looked out. Their cat Leary walked between their legs, smelling the turkey inside the basket. They looked down, completely surprised. "What is this?" Mr. Pickersgill bent down and started to look through the basket. "Look, Leary, cat food for you too." Mrs. Pickersgill looked out into the dark searching for the mystery gift-givers. Together they lifted the big basket and went inside the house. Nicole and Marc crept out of their hiding place, careful not to let themselves be seen.

Doing good is not about looking good. Giving is never about what you get in return or how generous you appear. Remember, sometimes people are embarrassed about needing a helping hand, so be kind and don't put them on the spot. Giving is about love, kindness, and generosity. It's the best kind of secret to keep.

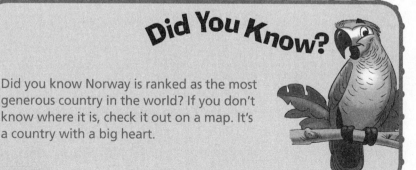

Did You Know?

Did you know Norway is ranked as the most generous country in the world? If you don't know where it is, check it out on a map. It's a country with a big heart.

December 24

Holy Is

The church smelled like pine needles and sweet candles. Red ribbons decorated the windows. Every space in the church was filled with people dressed in bright holiday clothes. Barb stood with the choir and sang the words to the Christmas carol. "Silent night, holy night, all is calm, all is bright." As she sang, Barb wondered how a night could be holy. What exactly did *holy* mean?

Words to Treasure

I want you to be my holy people.

Exodus 22:31

Holy means a few things.

God is holy, and that means he is perfect and without fault.

People, places, and things can also be holy, which means they belong to God because he has set them apart for his plans and purposes.

John the Baptist was considered a holy man. He worshiped and served God with all his heart.

The word *holy* is mentioned about 600 times in the Bible, and that makes it an important word to know. God wants his people to be holy. He wants you to be different from anybody else because you love him and dedicate your life to his plans.

Go through your Bible and see the different ways the word *holy* is used. Talk about it with your family.

December 25

The Gift

Gene took the present his grandfather offered him. It felt like a book, not exactly the most impressive thing on his Christmas list. He'd rather have a CD or DVD any day. He unwrapped a very, very old leather Bible. What gives or doesn't give? His grandfather had given him a used book? His grandfather explained, "That Bible has been in our family for a long time. My grandfather's father gave it to him. My father gave it to me. And now I'm giving it to you."

Words to Treasure

Everything written in the past was written to teach us. The Scriptures give us strength to go on. They encourage us and give us hope.

Romans 15:4

God's holy book and all the words and thoughts written in it are a gift to us. The Bible is a blueprint for how God wants us to live our lives. It tells us all the things God values; it tells us stories about amazing people of faith; and it also tells us about God's love. The Bible helps us understand more about God. But to learn more about God, we have to spend some time actually reading the Bible. Don't worry—it won't be boring. It's full of adventure and life-changing promises. It can answer some of your deepest questions. The Bible is the most important gift you can ever receive or read. So start now—read the book!

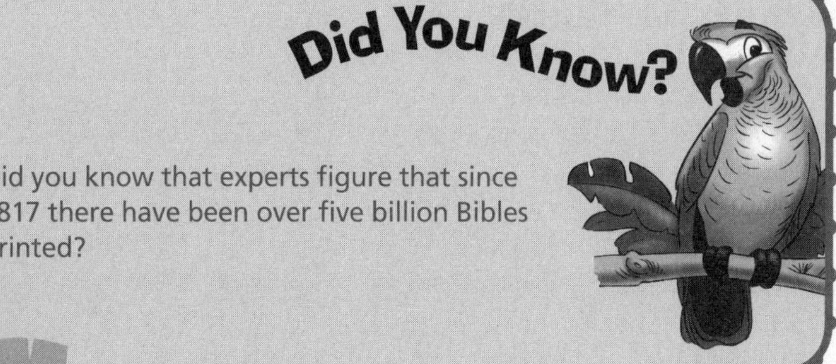

Did You Know?

Did you know that experts figure that since 1817 there have been over five billion Bibles printed?

December 26

Won't Last

Don't touch it!" Rudy flew across the room and wedged himself between his friends and his brand-new mountain bike. "You'll scratch it."

Words to Treasure

The king had all the words of the Book of the Covenant read to them.

2 Kings 23:2

"Dude." Lance shook his head. "It's a *mountain bike*. You're going to be riding down nasty mountain trails. Your bike's going to get scratched. It's going to get mangled."

Rudy polished the bike with his sleeve. "I'll be careful."

"The way you were with your old bike?" Lance couldn't help but laugh at his friend. "You rode it off a cliff into a river. It took your dad three days to get it out."

"I've changed." Rudy examined his bike for dents and scratches. It was perfect.

"It's important now." Lance touched the bike, just to annoy his best friend. "But later it won't be so important anymore. You'll see."

Funny how the things we're so proud of eventually get forgotten or less valued. The prophet Obadiah talked to the proud people of Edom. They had carved a very cool stone city into the cliff-side. It was surrounded by steep hills and canyons, and they felt like the coolest kids on the ancient block. But over time, the city was abandoned and forgotten. Sometimes what we're most proud of doesn't last very long.

People in Bible Times

When teenage king Josiah rebuilt the temple in Jerusalem, he discovered buried in the back the most precious thing in the world—God's holy book. It had been lost for years. He read God's words to all his people. Now that he knew God's laws, things were going to change for the better. Now that's a gift that lasts. Check out 2 Kings 22.

December 27

He Loves You More

Sarah stood by the door and called to her dog, Clancy. Her sister Vicky called for Clancy from against the opposite wall. This was a contest to settle once and for all—which one Clancy loved best. This was a contest Sarah was determined to win. Their dog did love her best, and now she'd have proof. Clancy wagged his tail and barked, but nothing Sarah said brought him closer to her. Finally he decided not to go to anybody; he jumped up on the couch and went to sleep.

Words to Treasure

His whole world filled me with joy. I took delight in all human beings.

Proverbs 8:31

Smart dog; he's not playing favorites. God doesn't play favorites either. He doesn't love one person more than another. God wants to be best friends with everybody.

He is your biggest fan, your closest friend. He cares about you every day, just like your family. God is proud of you and wants to spend time with you. But he also feels that way about other people too. And that's okay, because God's got enough love for everybody. That's what makes him such a very cool mystery.

Often in the Bible, we read about God finding favor with people. *Favor* means to like somebody. That doesn't mean God is playing favorites. It just means that he loves them and is doing things to help them. God also favors you, and that's something you can count on.

December 28

Tiny Church

Killian looked around the tiny island church and compared it to the church he went to back home. His church had thousands of members, and it was a huge complex. This church was one room with maybe a few hundred people sitting in the tiny space. "Mom, this church is so small," Killian whispered. "Where's the youth center for the kids? You know, like our church. Where's the pool table, the video games, and the couches to hang out in?"

Words to Treasure

People from many nations will go there. They will say. "Come, let us go up the Lord's mountain. Let's go to the house of Jacob's God. He will teach us how we should live."

Micah 4:2

An older man overheard Killian and leaned forward. "You are right. We are just a small island church, not like the kind you're used to. But God's word teaches a few people just as easily as it teaches thousands. Our youth center is out there." The old man pointed outside to the tropical beach and the blue water. "Our children seem to like it very much."

The completely amazing and incredible thing about God is that he loves every type of church. Big or small. City cathedrals or simple country chapels. God doesn't care and neither should we.

Did You Know?

Some prophets talked to kings and great rulers, while other prophets, like Micah, liked to live, work, and speak to simple ordinary everyday people who needed to hear God's voice too. Micah knew everybody needed God.

Keep Going!

Shane was so tired he couldn't even think straight. It took so much effort to put one foot before another, but he so wanted to finish the marathon. Each step got harder than the last. The finish line seemed a hundred miles away. When he started, he could only think about how fast he would finish. But now he wondered if he *could* finish.

He felt hands touch his back in encouragement. Suddenly family and friends were jogging beside him. "Come on, Shane. You can do it. You're almost there. We're proud of you, Shane."

Words to Treasure

The Lord also stirred up the rest of the people to help them. Then everyone began to work on the temple of the Lord who rules over all.

Haggai 1:14

From somewhere deep inside, Shane felt a new burst of energy, and he picked up the pace. He crossed the finish line and sank down in sweet victory.

Sometimes when we face tough challenges, we're tempted to stop. Just like the people of Jerusalem when they were rebuilding the city after returning from Babylon. It was a big job rebuilding an entire city. After awhile they just wanted to stop. But God's prophet Haggai was their cheering section! He kept telling them how beautiful the new temple would be and how great the city would be and how proud God was of them!

When you're facing tough challenges and you feel as if you just want to stop, pray and ask God for help. Then talk to that special someone who will encourage you to keep going. Sometimes you just need a little help, and God sent that person just for you.

December 30

Tell It Like It Is!

Braden," his new teacher called to him. "You wanted to talk to me?"

Braden sat down beside her desk. "Mrs. Cooper, I thought you should know . . . I'm smart, but over the last few years I've had a bad attitude about school."

Words to Treasure

The old is gone! The new is here!

2 Corinthians 5:17

"Really." Mrs. Cooper rested her chin on her hands.

"Last year I put snakes, crickets, and three slugs in Mr. Rodriguez's desk. I talked in class, didn't do my homework, and I broke the school record for the number of times being sent to the principal's office in one year."

Mrs. Cooper smiled. "Braden, why are you telling me this?"

"Well," he paused. "I thought I should, you know, be open about everything. I'm going to try to do better this year."

"Thank you. I'm glad you were honest with me. This is a good start to a new year, Braden." Mrs. Cooper smiled. "I love mice, crickets, slugs, and snakes."

"How about spiders?"

"Love spiders." She laughed as Braden left the room.

Even if your past behavior isn't the greatest, being honest about it and working toward a better future is exactly the type of person God's proud of.

Funny thing is, when you're honest about yourself, you never have to hide any secrets. People will always know exactly who you are and who you hope to be in the future. Honestly!

December 31

A New Adventure

Dean approached Liam as he was climbing on a snowmobile video game. "How come when I invited you to go up to our cabin to snowmobile you said no?" asked Dean.

Liam leaned into a turn. "Doing it for real can break bones. This way I can do jumps and tricks and still make it to the sixth grade. No danger, bro."

"Liam, at some point you're going to have to experience real life doing real things. This pretend stuff just isn't as good."

Liam's video machine took a jump off a cliff. "Yeah, but can you do that? That's a drop, baby."

Dean shook his head. "Hopeless."

Sure, doing anything in real life is harder, but isn't that the point? Life is not one long virtual tour. At some point you have to get out and explore the world for real. Try doing the real thing and see how that feels. It's good for your mind, body, and spirit. God made a real world for real people to have real adventures.

Words to Treasure

They saw him walking on the lake and were terrified.
Matthew 14:26

People in Bible Times

Peter and the other disciples were in a boat in the middle of a lake. When they woke up, they saw Jesus walking on top of the water toward them. They kind of freaked, but Peter decided to try this water-walking thing too. Sadly, Peter didn't quite have the faith to do it so he started sinking. But no worries—Jesus saved him. See, with God's real-life adventures, who needs computer-generated ones. (See Matthew 14:22–33.)

Topic Index

A

B

C

D

E

F

G

H

I

J

K

L

M

Q

R

S

T

U

V

W

Z

Scripture Index